The Legend of
LAKE SANGRE
Summer's Reign

By **J.C. Plaza**

Cover Illustration & Photography - Jerome J. Plaza V
Cover Design & Book Layout - DBree - StoneBear Design

ISBN: 979-8-9885214-0-2 Hardcover
ISBN: 979-8-9885214-1-9 Paperback
ISBN: 979-8-9885214-2-6 eBook
Library of Congress Control Number: 2023911146

StoneBear Publishing & Design
https://stonebearpublishing.com/

DEDICATION

To my late father, Robert Cruver,
who was my cheerleader right up until the end.
Two days before his passing, he told the entire
Cardiology team about me writing this book.
I know his spirit is with me today and
is still proud of my accomplishments.

ACKNOWLEDGMENTS

To my mom, Donna Cruver, my number one fan,
even after reading numerous versions, she still exhibits
undying love for this story.

To my husband, Jerry, who has listened to many read
aloud sessions and played the parts as needed. He created
the amazing cover art, developed my website, and is my
manager. He's tied for number one fan.

To my children Jerry and Tory, who stand beside me
in my writing career and for being brutally honest.
To my editor, RJ Patterson, for her wit,
determination, and loyalty.

And a big shout out to my writing group, Pencils NEPA,
who gave me their undying support. I thank you all.

SPECIAL THANK YOU

I want to thank Carol McManus, my friend and mentor. Your encouragement and belief in my work has given me the confidence to bring my stories to the world. Before meeting you, my writing was a passion. With your guidance, it became a career. Today, in addition to my own writing, I am ghostwriting for others. Thank you for pointing me in the right direction, keeping me moving forward, and taking a chance on me.

Also, I want to thank Dana Bree, founder of StoneBear Publishing. When we spoke over holiday brunch, you were passionate about the fantasy world I created in Lake Sangre. Your confidence in my writing has fostered the courage to let someone read the manuscript.

Now, we are going to print. Thank you for believing in me and taking me under your wing.

TABLE OF CONTENTS

PROLOGUE

"Three-Year-Old Girl Dead"
(*Mount Mort Times*, 2000)—*a victim of paternal rage.*

"Father Paroled After Two Years Behind Bars"
(*Lake Gazette*, 2003)

He'd brutalized a fourteen-year-old girl. Had she died, the punishment might have been worse. Had she died, my best friend wouldn't be here. I was a girl; I should have been next, or so I thought. Maybe then, my sullen face wouldn't have been plastered on the five o'clock news, beneath the breaking headline:

"Body of Eight-Year-Old Girl Found at Black River"
(Channel 6 News, 2007)

I was seventeen then. And the mother-fucking school was to blame, that damned teacher and her consorts of New York haute couture followers. Probably talking about their acrylic nails and Brazilian waxes that came with a free anal bleaching. Never minding the sixty kids on their field trip to Black River, or the wild horses that pranced through the violent October currents.

Mrs. Greene was in charge of that trip. A trip to a river to see what? Water erosion. Instead, every elementary aged kid came home with a lifetime of baggage. They learned what genuine fear felt like. They learned how to talk to the nice policemen in their freshly pressed uniforms and shiny metals. And how to go home without one of their own.

Reporters found ways to dig into those experiences and rubbed them raw, nice and bloody. They needled their telescopic lenses into private lives—my private life. Even the funeral was televised.

Then there were the social workers and nun-counselors who offered the family coping strategies they could stick up their self-righteous asses. They worked in symphony with the TV crews and investigators, all carrying their iPads and tablets.

See, that eight-year-old girl was my little sister. She was as blonde and blue-eyed as any Seelic offspring. She was my first best friend, my bud. She was the reason I had a secret. A secret I only shared with my stand-in mother, Gale. Though the townsfolk, I swear they knew. It haunted me daily, because—the guilt—it covets you. It drives you mad.

Yeah, thirteen years was a lot. But I hadn't forgotten, and neither had the townsfolk who fostered me, after my parents went missing. So, I've decided to go to the mount for the first time since . . . well, I'd talk to her. Make her see that I'm not a monster, maybe. Well, I'd tell her something.

CHAPTER 1

I meandered through the weed laden gravestones, careful not to step on any graves. My mother always said not to step on them out of respect for the dead. I read a few as I recalled Dani's comment, "Ever notice how small the graveyard is for such an old town?" She'd said that at Mrs. Greene's wake. I didn't go to the funeral.

I found my sister's plot and knelt beside the headstone. The decayed leaves burned my throat and nostrils. For thirteen years, I avoided her name. I couldn't say it. But there it was; I glanced at the etching.

"I don't know if you can hear this, sis, but it's me, Summer. I miss you." I sat on the leaf-littered ground and plucked a few blades of rye grass. "Mrs. Greene's dead now. Mom and Dad never came home." I sobbed and succumbed to hysterics. "I can't accept you're all gone. I should've been there. When the chief said you didn't make it..." I huddled into my arms and wept. A deep sorrow filled cry, the guttural sobs that rip every ounce of energy and life from within you.

"I shouldn't have waited thirteen years to come," I whispered back to the pink granite heart. "For that too, I'm sorry. Believe me, Sheena, I never meant for anyone to die."

But mid-way down the mount, smoke billowed, interrupting my thoughts. Its white columns penetrated the cerulean sky and caught my attention. After all these years, someone finally inhabited the lakeside manor. Perfect, I had a neighbor, sort of. It was a melancholy moment. I took refuge in my solitude, but that too was to be taken.

There hadn't been anyone in the stone mansion for as long as I could remember. It was for sale, though I heard it was a hard sell, being landlocked with no electricity. It just sat in the middle of the woods. Personally, I'd thought the Legend of Lake Sangre had a lot to do with it. Guess not.

I wiped the tears with the back of my sleeve, content that I finally made the journey, aware that I'd never be satisfied until I learned the truth. Because my sister was dead, Mrs. Greene killed herself, and wild horses don't kill people in upstate New York.

I kissed the stone and stripped the thorns off a white rose I'd kept tucked in my jacket, before laying it in the leaves beneath her name. The ivory petals were out of place in the solemnity. I slipped my dirk back in the sheath and tucked it in my velvet boot.

I read several eroded monuments that dappled the grounds on my way out—until I spotted Mrs. Greene's. The odor from the new grave's disturbed earth opened a pit of despair in my stomach. I shivered, ran to the chained iron gates, and slid through.

I climbed in my '95 powder blue Geo Tracker and sped down the dirt road plastered with multicolored leaves. The summer green faded to a mix of harvest yellows and browns. From the mountaintop, they looked like sponge painted splotches of color that descended to India green in the ravine. I liked the green, in spring, but it wasn't spring and I wasn't in the mood for bright and cheery. I knew autumn beckoned and with it came the cold and dark. I didn't like being cold, and I was afraid of the dark.

At the moment, I didn't like anything.

My Mary Kay concealer slid across the dash. It was great for hiding the faded henna-like tattoo that stretched around the back of my neck to just under each ear. Between my platinum hair that reached the middle of my back and the collar of my chef coat, I only had to conceal the spiraling vines below my lobes. I reached for the tube, got blinded by the damned September sun, and lost my grip on the wheel.

I skidded around the bend of that dusty mountain pass as a band of tourists stretched across the roadway. I slammed on the brake, nearly hit one, and veered toward the shoulder.

I peered out over the guardrail and thought about what I had to live for: work. Whoopi-fuckin'-do. Gale told me destiny guides us, work fulfills us. Fuck destiny; fuck work. I wasn't in the right mindset for work. I was even oblivious to the procession of people who coursed up the shoulder from Mount Mort as they passed me by. That is until the nearly victimized elder approached my window. I just blinked.

"They will find you, Summer. You're the last." She mumbled something else about being careful and her death, but I wasn't one to be bitched at. So, I gunned it, cut the wheel hard, and made a fishtailing right onto the oil and chipped secondary that led to Mount Mort and Tiny's Diner.

CHAPTER 2

There had to be twenty cars in the diner's parking lot. Busy nights weren't usual in our neck of the woods, but it made the time go quick. It was a good thing. But finding a spot to park was fruitless. I'd intended to be early, however daydreams in the cemetery thwarted my attempt. Not that I was ever on time, but late was an understatement. Cars filled the middle dirt patch of the lot, forcing others to create new rows along the evergreen forest line on three sides of the metallic silver building.

I drove along the border until I spotted a narrow slip of grass between the dumpster and my boss, Tiny's, black F-150. They named the diner after him when he took it over from the Finches years ago. I wedged the tracker in with the passenger side a mere three inches from the truck. I parked and soon found myself in the kitchen, making people happy with their strange requests.

"Summer?" Gale hollered from the front. "Customer wants to know what's in the quiche."

Gale was the waitress at Tiny's. She wouldn't tell anyone her real age, but I guessed she was in her sixties. She always said that it's rude to try and find out. But her thick white hair and large amber eyes made her a beautiful woman, regardless of her age. In a way, she reminded me of a plump Mother Goose, hooked nose and all.

"I'll be right there, Gale." Honestly, what the hell did they think was in the quiche? Eggs, cheese, milk, maybe a veggie or two. I was in no mood for people, let alone finicky people. Besides, she knew what was in the quiche. I pushed through the double doors harder than necessary, tucked my towel through my apron string, and followed the counter to where Gale waited.

See, Tiny's was a typical 1950s style diner with metal on the outside, red seats on the inside, and bug-eyed windows with booths along the wall adjacent to a counter facing the fountain station and dessert cases. She was at the end of the counter where the desserts ended, and the dining room started.

"Yeah, Gale?" I said. Then I froze, only for a moment, but I froze, nonetheless.

There stood a man dressed all in black with an Italian fedora. My attention was drawn to the silk dress shirt that melted into his slacks and ostrich skin boots, sunglasses, and silver bolo. An uncanny ensemble in these parts. I stared at him the way some women stare at chocolate. I didn't usually fall for looks, but my best friends Dawn and Dani were right—he was delightful.

He lowered his sunglasses and peered over the tops. "*Je suis Gérard D'Aquitaine, mademoiselle.*" His dark chocolate waves escaped their place. I reached to tuck them behind a flawless, sculpted ear, but caught myself.

Gale sidled between the customers' sagging girths perched on the *too small* stools and the few customers daring to pass us by. She gripped my shoulder harder than usual. "Perhaps you'd be so kind as to show our guest your kitchen."

I gaped at her. "Uh, yeah, but he'll need a hair net and gloves. I pride myself on the cleanliness of my kitchen." I pulled an extra set from my apron pocket and handed them to him with an exaggerated glance at my watch. "We close at ten."

"*Pas de problème,* Ms. Candella." He took the gloves and tapped at the fedora. "Is this not sufficient?" His words seemed to glide down my spine while his well-practiced fingers worked the length of his hair into a neat bun that he tucked under the hat.

Still, I didn't like him.

Gale kissed my cheek and whispered, "He knew your father, now git."

I sighed, confused yet obedient, wishing I were someone else. Someone clever enough to contemplate an escape. The liquid heat of humility coursed through my veins. I headed back to the kitchen and motioned for him to follow, but hoped he wouldn't.

Gérard's boots clicked on the tile floor, precise footfalls that sounded over the silenced dining guests. He followed me through the swinging double doors.

I backed against the stainless steel prepping counter, arms folded. "You're not here for the quiche, I presume."

"*Merci, mais non.*" He folded his gloved hands in front of him. People like him didn't eat at our diner. They went further into town to Chez Fenris. Everyone knew that. But he was new and needed to learn that ours was a mom-and-pop thing.

"If you want something exotic, I have black pudding pie." I twisted the corner of my apron. "I make a mutton burger that melts in your mouth. I grind the meat myself." It wasn't a lie. I learned from Robert, our butcher. I shrugged. "What are you in the mood for?"

"What I am in the mood for will not be ready before ten o'clock this evening."

"You know, there isn't much that'd take me two hours to prepare. If you require something special, I'd be more than happy to make it." I could be thick sometimes.

"You misunderstand. I wish to meet with you; when you get off work." He lowered the sunglasses and winked. "You close at ten."

"Oh!" The burning rose up my neck and spilled into my cheeks, but only because I realized I was an idiot. Dani and Dawn would have given their left pinkies to see me squirm. "No! I don't know. I guess, well—okay. Where shall we meet?"

"Ah, you are lovely. You will be here, *n'est pas?*"

That scorching heat pulsed, raw and relentless against my fair skin. Damn. "Right. Here. Okay. See you at ten then." I turned to the stainless steel counter and waited for him to leave.

The next thing I knew, the doors swung open and slammed into the walls. It was Gale. She attempted to give me a hug, but I wasn't in the mood. I gave her a one-arm-open squeeze and backed away. "I was afraid to turn around and see him still standing there." I flipped the apron over my face, hoping it would help. "I'm such a fool."

"For heaven's sake, girl, I wouldn't have set this up if I didn't think you could handle it. Besides, your services were requested." She lifted her chin and screeched. "Tiny. TINY!"

"What?" Tiny called back.

The bald Spanish man emerged from the back office. He was an even five-feet tall, and slender with bright green eyes. His face was sunken with a squared jaw, and his skin was a pinkish tan, as though he'd spent too much time in the sun. His head was shined; accented only by his thick black brows and pointed chin beard. I always wondered what kind of hair he had, because although he was from Spain, you'd never guess it. I dared not ask. He didn't want to be known in any respect and guarded his secrets well. My mom always said that Tiny looked up to the men in town, but only out of necessity. What he lacked in height, he made up for in attitude. And that attitude kept all his secrets safe and secure. Tiny melted for no one.

"Get over here," Gale insisted.

"What are you hollerin' about?" He nodded at me; eyebrows raised. "What's wrong with her?"

"Nothing." I dropped the apron.

"She's got a date with Gérard!"

"A date?" I gasped.

Gale gave me her pouty face and squeezed my lips together—sideways. "I thought we'd close early. She can't go out lookin' like she does."

"She does, does she?"

"Yup," Gale touted.

Tiny rubbed a handkerchief around his head and over his eyes. It was a habit that curdled my stomach. He cooked and used the same damn handkerchief every time, stuffing it in his T-shirt pocket, standing over the food. "Then what can I say? Wait 'til the double Ds hear this." He grabbed her hand and squeezed. "Good for him. I'll close up the front." He went to the dining room to turn off the *Open* sign.

We followed him, Gale first. I never liked to be near Tiny when he was pissy, and I was already on his shitlist for being late. Though he hadn't mentioned it yet, there was a ray of hope.

But pissiness or not, Gale's enlightening bite-sized bait was still dangling. "So, which father'd he know?"

The brother and sister duo exchanged glances. Odd, they didn't answer. Gale was far from the quiet type.

"Something wrong?" I asked.

"Hey, I've been meaning to talk to you about the *Chez* job for Cushing. Think you'll start prepping soon?" Tiny changed the subject. I wasn't stupid.

"Actually, yeah, I ordered the mutton and pork. Figured I'd dress 'em. No need to pay Robert for the knife wielding. Cushing wants a strudel, so I've got to get that done. It's cheap, and you can really stretch a strudel." I winked, knowing Tiny had a passion for pinching pennies. Albeit my spirits weren't into teasing. It didn't look like his were, either, but I wasn't letting him off the hook. "Back to the father thing."

"Thought Dawn told you," Tiny snapped.

"What's your problem?" I snapped back. "You don't go telling a girl that some guy knew her father when you know, damn well, he's dead."

"Tiny," Gale warned, her white brows furrowed.

"No, it's time. You've all coddled her and look at this mess." He kicked at the garbage can.

"Tiny, enough," Gale hissed through gritted teeth.

"Would someone please tell me what the hell he's talking about?" I interrupted. "What did I do?"

"You've lived here all your life, Sum. Yeah, you lost your family.

We all have." Tiny sneered and swiped his sleeve across his forehead. "You know the legend of Lake Sangre. Yet there you stand, oblivious. You don't know how good you have it. It's the 700th anniversary of our founding. Another hundred years for the mount," he sighed. "You know I want you happy, Summer. Tourists are here and more come." He motioned to the filled dining room.

I'd forgotten we had customers. I settled back against the dessert case. "It's hard to believe Mount Mort is that old."

Gale hugged me—tight. "Hon, like everything else in life, we use what we know to make sense of the things we can't control." She lifted my chin, so our eyes met. "What you need to do, is start asking the right questions. Knowledge is key, to get you through."

A mother rushed her child from their red booth and hurried her toward the exit ahead of the rest. "Damn," I whispered. "I hate being the center of attention, Tiny. You know that."

Gale thew a glance back at Tiny. "Summer, Hon, you're not."

"Yes, she is, damn it," Tiny yelled.

"Then tell me what we're really talking about," I yelled back, pulling away from Gale. "Just tell me. Obviously, you know what it is he's angry about." My eyes stung.

"Dani and Dawn told you about Gérard. Let's focus on him," Gale reminded.

"Eck," Tiny interrupted. "You think those two know the truth? Hell, anyone here? They don't know shit."

"And you do?" I asked.

"Of course," Tiny spat.

Gale peered over her shoulder at Tiny, and then back to me. "Sum, you already know the Legend of Lake Sangre."

"Yeah." I did. "Followers come to the mount every year." I'd heard stories of animal sacrifices and birthing ceremonies up at the old church. There was even a wedding at some point. Were Tiny and Gale followers? My heart thudded at the thought of them inducting me in some kind of ritual or something. Dani, Dawn, and I were going to have a long talk after tonight.

Tiny stepped closer and stared into my face. I looked away. He was intimidating as hell, not my Tiny. "Sí, Summer, the Legend of Lake Sangre." He gripped my shoulders and whispered, "But in reality, it was the Red Terror—the embodiment of evil. He fled Europe to wreak havoc here in the New World—a mountainous refuge from the regime. But the seer knew and sent a witch with immense power. He imprisoned that murderous beast with his dark essence, the blood from his own breast. The Álfar's daughters, dead, forever restless beneath the conjured waters, a prison born of blood and pestilence. It's how Lake Sangre earned its name, and why they come."

I stepped back. I didn't want Tiny touching me. "They, as in the followers?"

"Yes, the followers, the witnesses, and the hunters. Believe the legend, Sum," Tiny urged.

"Shit," I groaned and sat on one of the stools. The cool red leather added to my discomfort. The subject, the seat, hell, the whole damned day was wrong. I never should have gone up to that cemetery. "So why tell me?"

"Let's just say you interest them," Tiny taunted.

"But . . ."

"It's true, Summer," Gale said.

I took a moment to figure out how to talk to them without insulting the gawking customers. If there was anything my father taught me, it was to respect the beliefs of others. Not one culture was superior to the other, therefore their beliefs were as justifiable as my own. This only put a crick in the matter, but I composed myself, went into the kitchen, and let out a slow, discreet breath, before I spoke again.

"So, you're telling me I live next to a mass grave, for real?" I closed my eyes, a fruitless attempt to ignore the burning ache in my stomach. When I opened them, Gale was there. "Fuck!"

"Yeah, well. You're still not getting it," Tiny said.

"What then?" I threw my hands up in exasperation.

Tiny grabbed his short knife from the cutting board. "Summer, it is what it is. Be pissed, scared or whatever, but make sure you understand Mount Mort is one community—a sanctuary. There are more of us. This is only the anniversary for those who came here. Some are family, some are friends, and some were sent to kill you."

"What?" I sucked in a deep breath, my voice wheezed. "What the fuck did you just say?"

Gale fidgeted with the escaped hairs by my ears. "Forget that. Gérard's gonna be here. All you do is sit home with your nose in a book. You're young, too young to be alone."

"No, back up one. What the fuck does he mean?" I scowled.

"Oh, invite Gérard to the ball on Samhain. You won't have to go alone. It's a big event this year," she said.

"Really, Gale?" I pushed her hands away.

"The tourists, the hunters, even fellow practitioners will come for the septcentennial," Tiny reasoned, sliding the knife in the leather sheath on his belt. "It's only 'cause of you we've pretended we're something we're not,"

"Me?" I took a napkin from the dispenser and wiped my face. "How can you stand here, acting like this is real? I haven't been oblivious to what's been goin' on around me. I live on Lake Sangre for Christ's sake. No one's ever bothered me before." I pressed the napkin into my eyes. "I didn't even know anyone bought the mansion 'til today."

"It was never for sale, hon," Gale said.

"Damn it. I trusted you, all of you." I gestured to the dining room. "Everyone in this godforsaken town. And then you tell me this." I turned back around.

"You aren't wrong to call this place God forsaken," Tiny said.

"Nonsense," Gale hissed.

"You should be careful, but you're right. I always said keeping you blind of us wasn't necessary," Tiny said.

"It's only the beginning. The closer it gets, the more visitors will come," Gale added.

"So, what? Are they stupid? This just draws more attention. I assume, from what you're both saying, they don't want the attention."

"That's where you're wrong," she said.

"Know what?" I put my hands up and exhaled, heavy. "It's all good. I'm just gonna head home. Tell your friends I'm not joining whatever cult they're in. I'm not interested in graves, worshipping the dead or any other bullshit they come up with. It's a lot to take in for one day."

"Please don't be angry, Summer, but your parents never had a chance to tell you." She untied her apron and tucked it under the counter. "Now, you have a date. Gérard is different. Give him a chance, hon. Ask him."

"No."

"You're just shy."

"Shy? Maybe, but not stupid. Since when do I approach people I don't know, with an invitation to go anywhere?" I put my hands on my hips and smirked. "Maybe he's the one trying to kill me."

It was Gale's turn to groan. "It's called setting up another date, smarty-pants."

She pulled me with her to the ladies' room. It was an old-fashioned parlor with a sitting room and vanity mirrors before the inside stall.

Not surprising, the décor matched the dining room's red on red, except there were globe lights surrounding the Hollywood style mirrors. Of course, the stale potpourri didn't stink anymore, so we had Glade plug-ins, fresh linen. It was a background smell. Not something you noticed, but you'd miss it if it wasn't there. I was so nervous my stomach ached, but I sat in front of the mirror and let her take charge as she brushed my hair and pinched my cheeks.

I dabbed on a glittery strawberry lip-gloss and touched up my mascara. I had a perfume sample from a magazine she insisted I put on—honeysuckle musk, my favorite—after I changed into my regular clothes.

"Gale, you never answered my question. How did he know my father?"

"You'd better tuck those in." She smoothed over the faded black jeans that hugged my hips and made sure the legs were tucked inside my ankle boots. With two-inch heels, they offered some height. "Summer, we're giving our lives to you by letting you know. We didn't have to. And neither did they."

"Who? Tiny? Gérard?"

She fussed while I pulled little balls off the sweater and cuffed the sleeves to hide the tear stains. "The people at the diner, Dawn, Gérard, Tiny. All of us."

I stared in the mirror at my five-foot-four frame, blue aquamarine eyes, and lengthy, placid blonde hair. I'd changed back into my pink sweater with a V-neck that accented the gold rosebud necklace my parents had given to me. Normally, it reminded me of who I was and kept me grounded. I wanted them to be proud of who I'd become. But that notion was blown to hell.

"He's here, Summer," Tiny voiced through the door, a singsong tone I'd never heard him use before. I didn't like it.

"You'd better get out there," Gale urged.

"He's early," I grumbled.

"Don't you start, now. Hurry along."

"You didn't answer me, Gale."

She opened the door just enough for me to see a crowd of locals had returned, filling the booths and stools. They stared at the crevice. I was surprised, but at the same time I wasn't. I mean, you couldn't keep things quiet in our small town, that's for sure. Especially when it came to me.

Gale pulled the door wider and pushed me through.

I waded through the sea of smiling faces to where Gérard waited, propped against the cashier counter.

He bowed and held his hand out to me. I tried to hide my trembling and peered into his eyes—an even mix of sapphire and coal. His hair had spilled around his shoulders. He tucked it back on one side as he stood.

"Come on," I said, and pulled him by his sleeve through the exit to the bottom step. I stopped short to glance up at him. "So, hi."

He chuckled, touched my wrist to his lips, and breathed across the skin. He was warm and soft, almost as if his lips were made of feathers.

"Shall we?" He waved toward a limousine parked behind my car.

Fear spasmed in the pit of my stomach. "Brady's is great, but I'll meet you there." My voice wavered in time to the pounding of my heart and my heart pounded so hard I could feel it in my throat. I knew Gale handpicked him and all, but I trusted no one. Besides, who had a limo here? Nobody I knew, and I knew everyone. Then again, no, I didn't.

Of course, that's why my dad always said, "A girl has to be careful of the situations set before her. Take notice of changes in the norm, identify strange people; recognize possible dangers. Observant people rarely get targeted." It took everything I had to keep from running back inside. Knowing how many eyes were staring out the windows, and trying to keep from disappointing Gale, helped. The mere realization of my audience made the hair on my arms hurt, like fire ants crawling, stinging. I fought the urge to rub them and traipsed toward my car.

Gérard stuck his hands in his pockets and followed dutifully. My guess was that he was trying to figure out what to do with me. Funny, so was I.

CHAPTER 3

A quick glance in the rearview mirror confirmed the limo was still behind me. I eased off the accelerator as Brady's café emerged from the tree-lined knoll. A neon sign blinked *Welcome.* A yellow-green halo lingered after each pulse.

There wasn't a single car in the lot, which was highly unusual since it was the only bar in town, and the only place open after the witching hour. But I knew all the nosy patrons were still at the diner.

I turned into a parking spot and clicked off the engine. As I reached to open the door, I glimpsed Gérard standing there. I jumped and hit the horn. He didn't so much as flinch. Instead, he smiled. His slender fingers lifted the handle. The door creaked in protest.

"Boo," he said.

"Sorry," I said.

He put his hand out and waited for me to take it. "Come, Brady is waiting."

When our fingers touched, there was a tingling sensation. It was something I hadn't felt in years. Only my mother made me feel that way. I'd forgotten how she felt. Actually, I hadn't thought about it at all until right then.

He guided me out, which forced me to step closer. A waft of his cologne mingled with the autumn fog. I couldn't recognize it, but it was spicy, with undertones of vetiver, juniper, and jasmine with a strong leather and cinnamon presence. It was intoxicating. Maybe Dawn and Gale were right; it had been too long since I'd been on a date.

"What a coincidence." The voice came from a blond guy who strutted up behind us. He encircled us both, but his focus was on

Gérard. "My pleasure, Ms. Candella." He tipped his white Stetson before he continued to the bar. The tension was thick and electrifying against my skin when he passed. It was unpleasant, to say the least.

"Who was that?" I asked.

"*Guillaume*, an old—*euh*—acquaintance."

We watched him as he walked into the bar and tipped his hat at Brady. Where he came from, I had no idea.

Gérard pressed his hand lightly against the small of my back and escorted me to where Brady held the door open. The smell of stale beer and cigars stole my breath.

Brady, a gentleman of about fifty years, owned the café. His round dark face, framed with short white hair, was simply smooth and dark as pitch. He was in his usual black three-piece suit with white button up, and gold pocket watch. He smiled, patted Gérard on the back, and winked up at me with coal-black eyes. Gérard gave a slight bow of his head.

The tavern's dark walnut floors and walls had welcomed many customers over the centuries. Brady once said the bar itself was hand carved by a Nordic shipbuilder. There were dragons and long-haired goddesses that surrounded the shelving. It was a unit that took up the entire wall. In the middle was a mirror where liquor bottles sparkled from iron torches in the framework. Cranberry glass and wooden tankards adorned the shelves. The stools were made of the same wood, with scrolls carved into the backs. The tables and booths were the same dark wood, a smidge lighter than the floorboards. Only the seats had brown leather and brass nails. And in the back was a dark set of steps that led to the second level.

Brady led Gérard and I to a small candlelit table in the back corner. Our boots clacked against the floor. I expected the bar to be quiet with the lack of cars, but it was too quiet. I longed to hear the townsfolk's drunken banter upstairs.

Gérard pulled out a chair. "Please, have a seat."

"Thank you," I said.

Brady brought me a steaming mug of cocoa and nothing for Gérard. I hadn't even ordered.

"What about you? Aren't you having anything?" I asked.

"Mmm, perhaps later," Gérard said.

"Yes, later. Best to wait, eh, old man?" Guillaume called from the bar.

I had no idea how to react to that, so I continued to sip my cocoa, avoid eye contact, and hide my face all at the same time. Sure, Gérard was gorgeous but having a spectator made it that much worse. At thirty years old, I felt like a teenager faced with her high school crush, uncomfortable as all hell.

Gérard smiled. "Have you lived here long, Summer?"

He sat back; I sipped.

"All my life."

He removed the Italian Fedora and set the hat on the table. "Not all."

"Huh, I didn't know Gale talked about me that much." I rubbed my hands on my jeans and spoke to the hat. "Most, then."

I tilted my head just enough to see him watching me. There was no expression to read. A poker face, if you will. I wasn't sure what to make of his silence, which compelled me to continue.

"I consider this my home. I love Mount Mort, the people, the shops. It's small and I'm a small-town kind of girl." I sipped, wincing when the hot liquid scalded my lips. I was self-conscious drinking in front of him, but he was watching Guillaume. "I feel like we're hidden, a secret or something. A place time forgot, only us, lost in the wilderness, in the shadows of the Adirondack Mountains of New York." I stopped. Tiny was wrong. I wasn't oblivious. I spent years searching the forests and ravines for anything. I wanted my parents back. Today proved my heart hadn't let go. "Leaving's never crossed my mind," I whispered.

Gérard pulled the candle in the middle of the table toward him. The flame danced, reflecting in his sunglasses. "There is no shame,

Summer. Our souls are often tethered by bonds of which we know not. Do you come to *Monsieur Brady's* often?"

"I guess, well, not really. I like the café. Something about the underground room makes it feel safe. The subtle lighting is easy on the eyes, especially after working under the fluorescents all day. When we were kids, we used to hear the adults call Brady's the cave." It was the first time I'd truly thought about that, the cave. It was quite fitting. "There's a dance floor upstairs. When the people pour in, it can get pretty loud, but I like it. I mean, I live alone. Sometimes the quiet gets to me."

He raised his face and gestured to the floor above us. "This night is not so loud."

"Yeah," I sighed. "But it's different tonight. Too quiet. Usually when a new face comes to town, everyone knows. As you saw, they're not afraid to show it either."

I didn't understand why the bar wasn't crowded yet. It was clear they wanted to spy on me. They certainly had no qualms at the diner. I blew across the steaming mug and waited.

"Silence befalls you. *Pour quoi, chérie?*" He leaned closer.

"Nerves I guess." I let go of the mug and rubbed my palms over my thighs. It was a nervous habit. I sat on them. "Sorry, so your name is Gérard, and you have a limousine here in Mount Mort." I raised my eyebrow and peered up at him through my overgrown bangs. "Don't you think it's a little over the top to go out for coffee?"

"*Oui, mais,* I have, as you would say, come into an early retirement and enjoy my spoils. After all, I am French." He shifted lower to meet my eyes again. I kept my focus on the cocktail napkin under my mug.

"I don't think she's impressed," Guillaume disparaged from the bar.

Gérard didn't pay him any mind. "My turn again," he whispered. "You are catering for *Chez*, and you are the chef at the diner?"

"I wouldn't call myself a chef, more of a short-order cook. Anyway, I don't have any spoils. Just a house I rent on Lake Sangre," I shrugged.

"Really?" He drew the word out so that the French "R" was well enunciated, a guttural sound.

"You know of Lake Sangre?"

"*Ah, oui.* It is beautiful this time of year."

"It is. I have a large picture window that looks out on the lake." I glanced up at him, then back to the napkin. "It's only a small lake. There's a stone mansion on the far side. I heard from the real estate agent that it was a hard sell because it lacks all the modern amenities. But I guess it wasn't ever actually on the market."

Guillaume strolled toward our table, uninvited, of course. "Intriguing, isn't she?"

"Quite." Gérard said, removing his sunglasses. He folded the arms, retrieved a black silk kerchief from his shirt pocket, and wrapped them. He peered at the blonde before sliding them into their home. "We were discussing Lake Sangre, the source of the legend."

Guillaume pulled a chair out, turned it around, and straddled the seat. "Well, Summer, I thought of a better subject for the two of you."

"And that would be?" I asked.

"Your parents," he taunted.

"That's a sore subject I prefer not to discuss, thank you." Though, it sparked my curiosity because he shouldn't have known about them. Nobody talked about them, not even me. "How could you know my parents?"

"May I call you Summer?" he asked.

"I guess."

"Well, Summer, if it were up to me, I'd tell you. But it's not."

"Listen, I want closure. I'll listen to anything you have to say if it brings me that much closer to knowing the truth." A tear rolled down my cheek. He handed me a napkin. "Point me in the direction and I'll ask them myself."

He let out a whistling breath. "Well, you know the deserted church atop the mount?"

"Yeah."

He leaned in and whispered, "The church was not a church for the Christian God, but rather the forbidden practices."

"Yeah, okay. I think I'd know something like that."

"No, you wouldn't." He yanked my chair closer. "Augusto, your father, was the founder of one of those groups well before the structure was abandoned. You weren't a part because he wanted you innocent. They kept you—a secret."

"You know, come to think of it, when I was in school, kids used to talk about going to the cemetery, but my mother wouldn't let me go. Even now, Gale tends to frown on me going up there. My mother said it was a dark place, but she believed in demons and was crazy superstitious."

Guillaume hunched in. "She wasn't as crazy as you think. Truth is, the guardian of the mount left, leaving some of you girls endangered. Think on it. Practitioners, powerful people of great influence, made their way here. The people were left to fend for themselves." Gérard eyed the blond man as he listened. "If he'd been there, none of this would have happened. Now we all suffer. Your sister died because of them—him." He grabbed my hand. I let him.

"It was an accident. Chief Wimmers, Mrs. Greene...."

"That's what they wanted you to believe. But have you ever stopped to think how small the cemetery is for such an old town?"

I lied, "Not really."

"Well, you should. The church was not the first structure built. The graveyard holds the first and houses the few deaths you know. Do you remember the last funeral, Summer?"

"Mm-hmm. My sister's, no, Mrs. Greene, last week her house caught fire, and well, they found her hanging in the cellar." I pulled the mug toward me. The warmth calmed the rattling I felt inside. "I've been waiting on a memorial for my parents."

"Ah, yes, Greene's mother. But your parents, perhaps they are simply presumed dead. Maybe you need to find them."

"What?" I rose from the chair, but he grabbed my arm, pulling me back down.

Gérard put his hand on Guillaume's and hissed, "Enough."

The blond leaned over the chair back to fold his arms on the table. "Why deny her?" He smiled, an unpleasant parting of the lips. "Each group went their own way, some to different territories. For most of your life, you haven't known anyone as what they truly are, but to be what they appear. I assure you, Summer. The town, as a whole, has many secrets. That is why I am here. It's exciting. Yet for someone who does not know, it can be—deadly."

"So why tell me this, now? Why am I in danger all of a sudden? This doesn't make any sense." I fought the absurdity of his story. "Do you know what happened to them or not?"

"Patience, Summer." Guillaume leaned in and glanced at Gérard. "What's it been, old friend, 700 years since this town was settled and the church built?"

Gérard sat back, flicked at his fedora, and peered through that same chocolate untamed lock of bang at Guillaume and elaborated. "It was also around that time that a wealthy settler built the Lake Sangre mansion. Recently, it would seem, someone is occupying said mansion." His eyes shifted toward me. "Summer, noticed."

"Then you know it's occupied?" Guillaume's pitch rose with interest.

"Yes," I said.

"Well, there you have it. As you can see, there is an influx of tourists. They're coming because every century there is an anniversary for the settlement. This is such a year. They practice. We all practice." His voice softened to a breathy whisper. "Do you understand now? You live near the mansion. It is home to one of the oldest secrets and you're out there—alone."

"What do you mean, you all practice? What the hell are you saying? Why isn't anyone else worried about it, if this is so dangerous?"

"Because innocence is a virtue. You have no obligations, no

preconceptions. Your parents didn't listen. They learned the hard way." He flicked his hat and flipped it on. "It's a shame they left you as prey."

"What does that even mean?"

"*Guillaume*, I believe you have shared enough," Gérard said.

"No, let him talk. Besides, Tiny said you knew my father. I want to know how either of you could possibly know shit."

"Perhaps the old man is right. Later may be better."

"Damn it, you started this. Tell me."

"There are a lot of us who will bait you. Some may even try to use you for practice. Are you ready for that?" Guillaume stood and pushed the chair back in place. "You should distance yourself from him. He's not good for you." He pointed a finger at Gérard.

A chestnut haired gentleman came up behind Guillaume and put his hand on the blonde's shoulder.

"Ah, Mr. Cushing, how perfect." Guillaume reached over and rubbed the back of his hand over my cheek. "Be safe, Summer." He shoved away from the table, strolled to the exit, tipped his white cowboy hat, and left.

"Damn," I whispered. The heat rose up my face again as I caught Brady staring at me, before he turned to go upstairs. "Thanks," I said to the chestnut haired stranger.

"No worries, Love." He hurried off to follow Brady.

I turned to Gérard, my gut burning with angst. "What the hell is all this about?"

He said nothing.

He rubbed his hand over his chin, the way a man does when he's thinking too hard. I peeked just long enough to notice there was no five o'clock shadow of any kind. I fought the urge to reach over and feel what looked like baby smooth skin.

I laced my fingers around the mug. "I love this town, but I hate the constant reminder of the pain. I was barely eighteen when they were taken from me. Even now, as a grown woman, the pain never lessens." What I didn't tell him was that it was this town with its loving and ubiquitous residents that saw me through.

He simply sat there watching me. I was never one for the limelight, especially at the expense of my own humility. I looked him square in his nose and spoke as clearly as I could. It was hard to be bold when avoiding eye contact.

"I'm sorry, but I have to get up early. I'm on for breakfast." I pushed away from the table. "If you'll excuse me."

He stood, his chair scraping the floor until it hit the wall. "*Pardonnez-moi?* Have I done something to upset you?"

"Yeah, not talking."

"But—"

"I don't feel right."

"Please, stay," Gérard whispered.

"I should go. I had a trying day as is. It's not your fault, honestly. It was nice meeting you, though." I turned to walk away, but he grabbed my hand. The tingling sensation I felt earlier was more pronounced, it mollified and intrigued.

"Please stay," he repeated. There were stars in those dark blue eyes I hadn't seen before. He caught me looking. I glanced down at the table. I hated looking people in the eye. "I apologize if I have caused you to be ill at ease. Please, Summer. I knew your father from the mount. He was a kind man and loved you with all his heart."

Brady came over with another mug of steaming chocolate. "Your father would have wanted you to stay."

"Until I finish my cocoa then." I forced myself to sit.

"Wonderful, I will order now." He nodded to Brady, who was on his way back to the bar. "*Monsieur*, the house red."

Brady brought out a cranberry glass goblet, filled it to the brim, and left the bottle. Gérard sipped and blotted his lips elegantly with his napkin. His manners were impeccable. I liked that.

"So, for real, why are you here?"

"Because I would like to get to know you, with your permission, of course." He stroked the stem of his glass, careful not to tip it over. And for once, he didn't look at me.

"What are you asking?"

"I would be honored if you would accept courtship." Gérard brought his eyes up level with mine. "Your father is not here for me to ask."

"Let's see what tonight brings and take it from there." I could barely suppress the excitement that arose in my chest. My pulse thudded in my ears. "I'm not usually into the whole luxury thing. But change is good." I gave him a toothy grin. Stupid.

"Then I have your permission, *oui*?"

"Yeah. You know, most guys wouldn't ask." Finally, I was in control. My face cooled; my mind cleared. And then panic. "It means we're a couple now, right?"

"Yes, Summer." He sat back, crossed his ankle over his knee, and swirled the wine. I watched as it neared the rim, almost but never spilling. "I am certain you will find that I am not most men."

"I noticed." My full concentration was aimed at the peeling laminate on the table. "You realize we must look like a couple of fools, sitting here trying not to look at each other. Maybe it's a good thing it's dead tonight—no one to witness such piteous behavior."

He reached across the table and lifted my chin with his finger. "I was looking at you." He sat back, wine in hand. His thumb caressed the stem.

I turned away, distracted by what those hands would feel like on my body. The warm caress of his touch sliding under my sweater. His lips, soft against my neck. I changed the subject. "So, when was the last time you were on a date?" Clearly, it was too long for me.

Gérard hesitated, then sipped his wine. "Many years. And you?"

I closed my eyes, ashamed of my own disclosure. "Several years for anything serious. Jesse, my fiancé, left me without a word. It still stings." I drew in a cautious breath. When I opened my eyes, he was squatting before me.

"I understand broken hearts well." He hooked his finger around mine and pulled me up with him. "Would you care to dance?" His lips barely parted for a smile.

"I would." I smiled back.

"*Bon.*"

Gérard led the way upstairs where DJ Liam's bass dominated the dance floor. I liked Liam because he was cute, but more so because he had an old-world charm and didn't treat me like a shunned parishioner. And maybe I liked his flowing white hair with its split ends that extended beyond his knees. I envied him. My hair wouldn't flow no matter what I did to it. I hadn't been to the tavern in weeks and wanted to be courteous, but he was busy chatting it up with the Cushing guy. Besides, my date intrigued me.

We danced among a growing crowd. Apparently, they'd found us. Everyone had their hands in the air. We stepped here and there in time to the beat. The surrounding couples shook their hips, and other things. I wasn't about to dance like that with Gérard yet. Then Liam changed the lights to sapphire and put on a slow song.

Rather than ask, Gérard assumed I wanted to stay, put an arm around my waist and took my hand in his. The whole time our bodies touched, I wanted him a little closer, a little tighter. The other couples watched us. I didn't like it at all.

I got stiff. He nudged the top of my head with his chin. I understood. He wanted me to rest my head against him. But I couldn't. I messed up our rhythm, but he took the lead and put his hands on my waist, more swaying than dancing. I relaxed enough to close my eyes and rest my cheek between the chiseled pecks hidden beneath that black silk shirt. The cologne enveloped me—consumed me. I relented and let him lead, even when the song ended.

The curious Mr. Cushing had come over to whisper in his ear at some point. I opened my eyes to witness their inaudible conversation. The two of them were freaking, like Hollywood hot.

The self-loathing to which I'd become accustomed resurfaced. I pushed away and scurried toward the stairs. I should have let Gérard lead the way back to our table, but I left him to trail behind.

I knew I was on a date, and just agreed to courtship, but I felt like a fool. I swore I would never let a man take over my life. I swore I would never get consumed by some false sense of security a man exuded. I swore off men. Why did I let Gérard break that barrier down? It took years to build a barrier to keep myself safe. It took years to gain self-confidence and heal the scars, both mental and physical. God, damn it! He tore it down. He tore the whole damned shelter down with one freaking dance!

He wasn't going to get me. Not like that. Jesse did, and he's why I needed the barrier to begin with. I'd be damned if I would let Gérard or anyone else hurt me again. Fuck men; fuck him. Fuck me, I liked him.

Back at the table, I sipped my refilled cocoa and waited for him. He stopped at the bar with Cushing and Brady before returning to our table.

He sat down in one fluid motion. He didn't try to look at me, but instead, turned sort of sideways, crossed his legs and took long swallows and sips from the wineglass, to match the level with my mug. He was either perceptive or creepy. I prayed against the latter.

I looked in the mug; half-wishing I hadn't drunk so fast. "Well, it's late, and I've finished." The heat of dancing still lingered throughout my body. Or was it my inner temper-tantrum with myself for losing control?

"*Oui, c'est* ça. May I walk you to your car?" he asked, while pulling out my chair with me in it.

"That'd be nice, thank you."

"You are most welcome."

"Before I forget, I had a good time tonight," I said, before thinking it through. Was it really a good time? What was good about it?

"As did I. May I see you tomorrow?"

"I'd like that."

We walked to the car, as we had to the café, with his hand lightly applied to the middle of my back. I unlocked my door; he opened it for me. That's when the panic set in. *Oh no, what if he wanted to kiss me goodnight?*

As if on cue, he pressed me back against the inside of the door and studied my face—his eyes dark and inviting. "You have lovely eyes," he breathed. His thick European accent whispered around me.

"You too," I mumbled, and bit my lip.

He lifted my hands to his lips and placed a single kiss on each. I studied the ground.

"*Bonne nuit, ma chérie.* Until we meet next." His voice lingered, but he was gone, just gone.

I climbed in my car and locked the doors. My senses were on edge. The culmination of the evening was almost too much. I looked in the rearview mirror and backed onto the road, wondering what the hell I just got myself into.

CHAPTER 4

I arrived at the white weather-beaten cottage I rented, a few miles from town. The grayed wood showed through the crackled paint. Years of hard winters and hot summers took their toll. It was just above the ravine, about halfway between the church in question and the diner. Okay, so maybe more than a few miles. But out here it's not considered far. I suppose if you're from Brooklyn, Chicago, or even LA, it'd be quite far. Actually, I'd bet it would be just as far as Manhattan is long, twelve miles, give or take. There were two houses out here on the dirt road; mine at the end, and three quarters of a stone foundation left at the beginning and, of course, the mansion on the other side of the lake.

I glanced at the cloud-covered moon as I turned into my driveway. The harvest moon would be in a couple days, but this was the epitome of darkness. The crunch of stones and dirt seemed louder when the night was darker. I never did like the dark.

I hesitated before I took the keys from the ignition and placed them one by one between my fingers. In self-defense class, Chief Wimmers said not to do that. But it kept my mind at ease while I made the small trek from the car to the house faster than usual and unlocked the door. I opened it in record time and slammed it shut before I turned on the main light switch, glancing in the moonlit bedroom.

The landlady, Mrs. Finch, had the house remodeled a couple months back. The new bedroom window resembled a porthole and cast the hazy moonlight over the room. It replaced the normal 1940s style that was original to the house. I liked the new window. It was high up and made the room feel solid; safe. I slid the boots off, added them to the pile by the door, and secured the deadbolt.

I padded toward the kitchen with the new slate countertop and oak cabinets. The matching wood floors were cool under my stocking feet. I grabbed a bottle of drinkable yogurt from the fridge and took it to the living room, where I flopped back on the taupe microfiber sofa. I unbuckled the black leather ankle sheath and tossed the dirk in the rocker before melting into the cushions, content for the first time in years. Normally, I would have taken a shower, but I didn't want to wash away the only evidence of Gérard that I had—his scent. The spicy cinnamon clung to my clothes; I rubbed my cheek over the sweater, taking it in.

My cell phone rang. I fumbled to answer it, not expectant, but half-hoping Gérard would be on the other end. It dawned on me that I never gave him my number, nor did I bother to get his. Damn.

"Hello?"

It was one of my regulars at the diner, and sort-of-friend, Officer Stevie Tangelo. A transplant from Westchester, New York and one of the prettiest cops I ever met. Her parents were from Trinidad, so she had that long silken espresso hair, slender frame, mocha skin, and deep brown eyes with lashes to die for. The day she joined the force, Chief Wimmers brought her to the diner to introduce us and grab lunch. She ordered steak and eggs from that day on; always rare and over easy. But we didn't have the chit-chatty kind of friendship to talk on the phone.

"Hey, Summer."

"What's up?"

"Thought you should know, the Chief called, wanted your cell. He wants you under my watch."

"Worried I'll wind up missing or something?" Gee, he could join the growing troupe of naysayers.

"Ok, what's with the sarcasm?"

"Nothing, just oh, let's see—Tiny, Gale, and this guy Guillaume."

"Guillaume? Never heard you talk 'bout him before."

"He knows something about my parents. I think he knows a lot more than that, but he's playin' some kind of game. He knows too much, and he was at Brady's tonight." I switched hands and looked at the still full container of yogurt. "You don't think there's anything real to worry about, do you?"

"I'd say be watchful, but don't let it inhibit you." There was a moment of silence before she came back. "I have nothing on a Guillaume in my database. Tell you what; I'll have Officer Greene look into it. Get some rest, and I'll check in on you at the diner."

"God, I feel stupid, Stevie."

"What else? I know you, Summer. Something's got you spooked."

I thought maybe asking about Gérard would be good, but he wasn't the one bothering me. "Nah, busy time of year, that's all."

"Well, rest and stop worrying. It's tourist season, it's always crazy. Relax."

"Yup, thanks again, Stevie."

"Hey, I called you. If it makes you feel better, I'll have Officer Greene check on ya."

"That's all right. I guess there's no need yet, but thanks for the offer." Not fuckin' Greene, that's for sure.

"Try to have a good night, Summer."

"G'night, Stevie."

I clicked the phone off and tossed the yogurt in the trash.

Since the mood was spoiled, I opted for the shower and brought one of my white cotton granny gowns with me. They were my favorite because they were baggy and warm, similar to the ones from *Little House on the Prairie.*

I loved that show when I was a kid—the books, not so much. Quite depressing when you think about it—especially when they thought their dog died. Or when they had to up and leave their home and family. Why would anyone want to leave their family? It's all you've got. When the family is gone, you have friends that are like family, hopefully, but they don't have that kinship. Their children or real family will always come first. Even Gale, who took me under her wing, would choose her daughter, Dani, over me. And rightfully so. Why shouldn't she? Family. That one word sucked the life from me.

I turned on the shower and lathered up. As the water and peach scented soap converged in rivulets that cascaded over my skin, worries about Guillaume's words washed away with them, though Tiny's didn't.

Once I dried, I slipped into the gown and started the hair dryer. I hated going to sleep with wet hair. Damp, I could live with, so I did a half-assed job, ran a brush through it, and climbed in bed. The percale sheets were inviting. I nestled into them and the comfort of the down pillows, but I was too wound up.

The masquerade ball being held at Chez Fenris in honor of the Samhain was a month away. I was catering the affair, but it worried me. And really, what was it with people? Samhain. Call it what it is, a Halloween party. Everyone had to go all chic and call things Pagan names or have Wiccan this or Gothic that. Get a grip. At least be original.

Of course, I loved that stuff too. I, myself, was guilty of having a lot of medieval and Celtic emblems around. I was even saving up enough money to take a trip to Stonehenge. Probably wouldn't be soon, but it was a dream I wanted to fulfill before I died. Yup, long bucket list there. I'd be fine even if I died at Stonehenge, or if the plane crashed on the way back home. But knowing my luck, it would crash on the way there—just because.

Now, I had to spend money I didn't have, to buy a costume I didn't want. I hated dressing up, but I didn't want to chase Gérard away by being too stiff. I liked him. Admittedly, I was curious about Guillaume, too. And who was Mr. Cushing? Did he have anything to do with the Cushing businesses in town? And was it possible; I didn't kill my parents?

I slid out of bed and pulled a box of Halloween decorations from my closet. If I wasn't going to sleep, I'd decorate.

CHAPTER 5

Having slept through my alarm, I crawled out of bed just before noon. No reason to get up early. I was on for the dinner shift; besides, I hadn't gone to sleep until somewhere around three. But the cobwebs and dangling bats looked great.

The coffee maker was programmed to brew at 6 in the morning, so I nuked myself a cup. Hot chocolate or coffee with a pinch of cinnamon, and a splash of rice milk were my favorites. I grabbed the milk and a cinnamon stick for the mug.

There are healing properties in cinnamon, according to my old restaurant ops professor. Said he learned it from an herbalist in New York City–Chinatown. I always loved cinnamon, but learning it was healthy too was a plus. Of course, everyone knows that nowadays. And at present it reminded me of Gérard. I was definitely happy.

I sipped.

The coffee was okay, but I needed to add a little water to lessen the strength. It amazed me how it always got stronger when it sat. Some things get better as they sit, but not coffee. That just gets nasty. I knew I put too much thought into those things. I wondered if Gérard felt the same. I wondered if he drank coffee.

I whipped up an egg white, tuna, and spinach omelet with ketchup and ate it out of the frying pan with a piece of rye toast. It sounds awful, but I was used to it. The yoga video I usually watched was already up on my laptop, so I washed my dishes and went to open the living room curtains to exercise in the warm sunlight, but howling curbed my intentions.

Images of wolves silhouetted against the mountain backdrop in the noonday sun and brought with them peace and contentment. I watched from the window as they hunted. Signaling of their prey, the howls grew even louder. I smiled as one trotted beneath my window.

I was used to the wolves; I knew they'd keep me safe. My father once told me they hunted in packs and tended to follow animals, and people, who didn't belong. Their path went along Lake Sangre and through my backyard for years now. I even befriended the one waiting by the door. I ran to the fridge and grabbed a container of meat scraps I kept, just in case.

I worried about their safety after they were blamed for the tourist Guillaume had referred to. But realistically, no one ever found him. He could have drowned in any one of the lakes around. He could have fallen into a fissure or off a cliff. We got a lot of hikers and rock climbers, so, hey. It didn't have to be the wolves. Hell, we had bobcats, black bears, wolves, coyotes, vultures, and a number of carrion eaters. Or maybe he suffered the same fate as my parents.

Although my folks went missing like eight years after he did. Maybe the incidents weren't related. Still, it was worth exploring. Why I had never thought of it before.

I finished my coffee and completed my yoga routine. The stretching felt good; it released the tension Guillaume caused. I readied myself for work and wore the typical jeans and a sweater going in. Today would be black on black. I'd change into my white chef coat and checkered pants at work—my uniforms from cooking school—it was strictly an as needed basis.

Unfortunately, my wardrobe reflected my attitude. I'd been lonely for a long time. After Jesse walked out on me, I stopped caring. In retrospect, I'm not sure why. He was an abusive bastard. I guess it was my pride that he hurt the most. Perhaps I'd grab something to jazz up my outfits when I went shopping for my costume.

The doorbell interrupted my thoughts; I wasn't at all sad about it. I unlocked the door and pulled it open, taking no heed to Guillaume's warning.

"Good afternoon, sweetie." Mrs. Finch pushed past me. She pulled her little white gloves off her arthritic hands, one finger at a time. I glanced at the clock on my cell; half-past one, I was going to be late.

"I passed a rosebush on the way from the car; roses are not part of the landscape."

"I hadn't noticed." I laughed, trying to earn a smile. "They're a little too high maintenance for a not-so-green-thumb like me."

I knew she chose the plants on her properties carefully so they wouldn't require a lot of maintenance. Rosebushes didn't fall in that category, which meant either someone planted it there by mistake or I needed to give Mother Nature some credit for germination.

At the same time, I wondered how much hairspray she used to tease the white hair that stayed perfectly molded in a poof around her head. With drawn in eyebrows and dark purple lipstick, she must have taken a lot of time. I also wondered if she had plastic surgery because, though her hair and hands were aged, her face was like Brady's—simply smooth and black as pitch.

"I have the rent if you'd give me a minute to write the check." I grabbed my purse from the pile of shoes by the door.

"Take your time, dear."

She wandered around, most likely doing a quick inspection. I knew she owned several properties, and it wasn't like we were close friends or anything. I'd heard horror stories from people who had tenants. Not good.

"I thought you were staying in Florida. Is everything alright?"

"We haven't planted anything this year. Enjoy the roses. They may have been there all along." She paused a second and then offered an afterthought. "Sometimes, when conditions are right, nature will do funny things."

"Yes, Mrs. Finch."

She didn't hear well, and I felt sorry for her. She'd worked hard all her life, as a dishwasher at the diner, until Tiny bought it. I never knew the previous owner, but word on the street was that he'd given her the money he got from the sale. Good retirement present.

"So, how was your time in Florida?" I repeated a little louder and handed her the check.

"Oh, it was wonderful. The weather was absolutely gorgeous. I hope to get back before winter sets in."

"Well, I'm sure you will. Take care." And with that, I hurried her out the door. Perhaps Mrs. Finch was right. Plants and I had never gotten along. Maybe, because I ignored them, the roses felt compelled to grow?

I gathered my things and stepped outside, locking the door behind me. The cool autumn breeze carried the spicy perfume of the newly fallen leaves. That scent pulled me. I longed to walk amongst those leaves, making my way to the lake. Sometimes I thought I heard whispers dancing across the calm waters.

I loved autumn by the lake.

A small cloud of russet dust on the road was all that was left from Mrs. Finch's visit. I smiled in spite of myself and went to work.

I couldn't believe the amount of people standing in line, waiting for tables. There were a lot of townsfolk, but even more unknown faces. I spotted Dani and hurried toward her.

Dani was Gale's daughter. She always dressed in black leather and had body piercings everywhere publicly visible. I didn't want to think about any others. At twenty-four, she was old enough to do what she wanted. Besides, Goth just looks good on some people. She was one of them. Especially with her onyx hair, bulging green eyes outlined in black liner, and ivory complexion. Though she was so thin, when she turned sideways, she practically disappeared.

"Hey, Dani, where's Tiny?"

"He's in back. Mom says you and Gérard hooked up. Very cool."

"Thanks." I hurried back to the kitchen.

Food stains dappled Tiny's apron, black T-shirt, and blue jeans. And there was a hair net on his shiny bald head, which made him look cute in a cuddly sort of way. He filled me in as soon as I pushed through the double doors.

"I haven't touched these yet." I followed his pointed finger to a stack of orders neatly hung.

I flipped through them. I always laughed when I got an order for a burger with no onions, and a side of onion rings. One that I was famous for was a side order of one pancake.

Gale and I tended to laugh that stuff off, but Tiny and Dani let it get on their nerves. That would have been normal, but these were too numerous. Tiny and I exchanged a questioning look.

"I can't do all this alone. If this keeps up. I need help, Tiny."

"'Tis the season; it's not always like this."

"No, besides, I enjoy it. Why else would I have worked here for ten years with no real time off?" I gave him a wicked smile.

"You are my hero, sweetie." He batted his eyelashes, which caught me off guard.

I laughed and let out a loud snort that made the both of us laugh, and tears ran down my cheeks. "Thanks, I needed that." I grabbed a brown paper towel to catch the tears. "Has anyone come asking for me?"

"Yup." He looked at the toaster, almost willing it to pop.

"It wasn't Stevie, was it?" I asked. He turned to face me; eyebrows drawn. "Strange night, that's all."

"Well, it must have been something if you called the cops. Didn't you have a date?"

"She's a friend. Sometimes I need that, especially when it's late."

"I'll be back." He pushed through the double doors.

Tiny returned in time for the toaster to pop and I jumped.

He squinted his eyes at me. "Forget the orders. You have a visitor." He strode to his office, his face red; taut.

"Thanks," I called.

"Go see what he wants. Now!" The office door slammed shut.

I wondered what the hell that was all about and hustled out to the dining area, eager to see who it might be. I wasn't expecting the curious yet handsome face at the counter; decorated with straight dirty blond hair hung almost to his shoulders, icy blue eyes, and slight tan complexion.

"Guillaume," I acknowledged.

"Summer." He stood and tipped his hat.

Dani stopped on her way to take my spot in the kitchen and whispered in my ear, "White suit, cranberry silk shirt, white tie, and check out those snakeskin boots. Nice."

I gave her a look that said, "Go away." But, I agreed, he was nice to look at, cowboy hat and all. He even spoke with a slight, exotic drawl.

He offered me a stool next to him. "Remember me?"

"How could I not?" I took the seat on the other side of it. "So, what's up?"

"Not sure where to begin." He took a sip of the coffee sitting on the counter and pushed a cinnamon bun and mug toward me.

"It's alright," I smiled. "I won't bite." I bit the bun.

"No, you won't." He smiled back. "But I know who will."

"Interesting pickup line."

"Thanks. Breakin' the ice, I guess."

"Broken," I smiled again, and licked my fingers.

"Good, but I still don't know where to begin." He folded his lips and peered at me from the side.

"Just finish telling me what you know about my parents."

"I told you last night, but you didn't like it."

"I expected actual answers."

"Ah, such naiveté. They're not the norm. Trust me." He let out a long breath, waiting for me to stop him. I didn't. "The regime comes; find out who they are, and they'll hurt you."

"Then I guess I don't need to find out."

"What of the rumor about the mount?"

"It's public record."

"It was the guardian's doing, Ms. Candella."

"No, it was a lost tourist wandering in the woods. I know the stories. He probably got disoriented. Hate to be obvious, but we live in the sticks. It gets thick out here. Even my parents didn't make it back." And that's when I shut my lips, folded them in, and berated myself. *Dumbass, just tell this guy from nowhere that you're alone in the woods. Tell him your whole life story. Why not invite him over for tea? Gossip at the fence? Shit.* I'd missed some of what he was saying and came back from my scolding. I did live alone too long.

"But don't you agree that you should be scared in order to stay safe?" he asked. "Even if you think they're petty rumors?"

"Rumors are made to scare those who are foolish enough to believe." I fiddled with a thread on my arm-sleeve. "Who is it I should be afraid of anyway—the guardian?"

"Among others. Some belong to the guardian; some of them are my own—"

"Your own what? Am I to believe you're a guardian? What the hell is a guardian, anyway?" I'd lost my cool and whisper-yelled.

"Ah Summer, I assure you, that I am not. Though it was someone you knew. We'll save that for another time." He shifted his eyes toward the diner patrons.

"Why can't you tell me now?"

"Well now, that'd be easy. Besides, I like mystery and competition."

"Thanks for the warning."

"Good, then consider yourself warned." He laughed; uncomical, demeaning.

Tiny said I was naïve, now Guillaume. Dawn and Dani had ganged up on me over Labor Day weekend to tell me they were hooking me up with an influential European, Gérard. Boy, was that an understatement.

But Dani waited 'til we were alone and told me to keep my eyes open. Gérard was coming, and I was the reason. That Chief Wimmers had been called away until after Samhain, and because we took care of our own. And that maybe if I paid more attention, I'd realize people never left, rarely died, and fewer moved in. She was trying to help me.

Maybe the elder woman wasn't bitching. Maybe Tiny was right. But that would mean Guillaume was right, too. And why the hell was Gale pushing Gérard so hard? Who the fuck was he? And what kind of practitioners were they? Crap.

"Not for nothing; I can take care of myself. I still don't see why I wouldn't be safe. I'm not some stupid blonde. I'm educated. Since I was eighteen, I've been on my own. No one looked out for me then; I sure as hell don't need anyone to do that now."

"I can prove it."

"How?" I regretted asking. I knew better.

"Meet me outside—at closing."

"Uh, no."

"Listen, if I had mal intentions, I would have acted by now. Face it, I know where you live; work." He reached over and rubbed his finger along my thumb. "Even your hours."

I pulled my hand back. "Everyone knows each other like family here, no worries." I tucked my hair behind my ears and leaned on the counter. "I'll be fine."

"No, you won't," he insisted. "Humor me. Do you believe any of what I've said?"

I shrugged.

"What about the legend of Lake Sangre?"

"Yeah, no."

He leaned to my ear, voice low, "Well, you may have left your mother, Faoltiarna, for dead, but you didn't kill her. Augusto had to get her out. They knew you followed them. And they did nothing. She hated you. Because, when it boils down to it, you're the real reason this place even exists. You were purpose-bred. She didn't want you.

Now, Sheena, she was the daughter she loved. Ask Gale, Tiny, or better yet, yourself."

My face must have shown the disbelief burning my core.

He slid back to the other stool. "If you're so sure of yourself, Summer, consider the fact that you sat here. The question is why? To humor me, or because somewhere deep down, you believe at least some of what I've said." He twisted to face the room, nodding toward the mothers, fathers, couples, and kids. "Anyone normal would have left by now."

Shit, I thought.

"You aren't capable of murder. Sure, you followed them into the woods. Yeah, you heard him tell her they had to raise you. And yup, you saw her drop to her knees, and he followed. She fell, bloodied. You felt it. You saw, and you left them there." He glanced back at the dining area. "Murder? Nah, but you wanted them to hurt. They loved her more than you, and you hated that. You're selfish. Dark."

"I loved them," I whispered.

"True, but they still left. You had hope though, I give you credit. You hoped they'd come home. Even after what you heard—felt." He drew a deep breath and laughed. "I include my kind in this celebration, Summer."

I pursed my lips and nodded, purposely not looking at him. "It's not true."

He gave a casual shrug. I pushed away from the counter harder than I intended and almost fell off the stool. I'd wanted to swivel away from the counter and him.

I stood to smooth my hands over my clothes, hoping he would get the message and leave. It worked.

"Enough said, but remember, you can't run, and they won't let you hide. I wish you well." I'd no sooner heard him, and he was gone.

CHAPTER 6

Guillaume wasn't the only one who vanished. The customers were gone. I was left alone in the quiet, with the exception of Gale. She'd mopped the floor, turned off the open sign, and was hitting the dining room lights. Tiny and Dani were closing down the kitchen. I guessed the visitors either left during our conversation, or—or what time was it? The parking lot was clear, besides our cars.

"Gale?" I said, sitting back down.

She perched on the stool next to me. "Yes, hon?"

"Do you know Guillaume, the guy I was just talking to?"

"I may."

"No games. Do you know him or not?"

She nodded. "What'd he say?"

"I don't know. He gives me the creeps."

Dani followed Tiny from the kitchen. She took the empty stool beside me while Tiny ran a bleach rag over the counter in front of me.

He put the rag down, pulled a toothpick from his pocket. "Listen, go home—get some rest."

"But he's right," I lamented. "I'm out there alone. What do I do?"

"Nothing," Tiny said.

Gale glanced at Tiny; her lips pulled tight. "Our word, Sum. We'll never let any harm come to you."

I didn't believe her.

I wished, more than ever, that one of those personal ads I'd placed, or blind dates I'd suffered, would have come through. Mental barrier or not, I wanted someone to go home to. Someone to make it all better or be there while I cried or didn't. But most of all, someone to keep me safe. It sucked to admit, if only to myself.

"You okay, Hon?" Gale made little circles on my back. Oddly, it didn't feel good.

"Truthfully? No." I slid off the stool and walked to the window. "I thought he'd tell me something about what happened to them—at least to their remains. It's the not knowing part that makes it impossible to get over. You and I both know they didn't just walk off. I thought I'd murdered them. Stupid, I know. But...."

I turned in time to catch Gale dabbing the corners of her eyes with the edge of her apron. "I'm sorry. I can't give you the answers you want. But maybe I can give Gérard your phone number? He enjoyed your company." She peered over my shoulder at the parking lot. I thought nothing of it at the time.

"He can call me tonight if you see him." It struck me. My strange reaction to him may not have been my fault after all. "He's involved in this, too. I want to know how."

"He is what he is. Can't say for him. Why's it matter?" Her face showed nothing, which, of course, I found frustrating.

"Why's it matter," I repeated. "Because it does."

Dani pulled the terry tie from my hair and raked her finger through, loosening the strands. "Talk with him. Meet with him. Enjoy your time together. You made a cute couple the other night. The whole town's buzzin' 'bout it," she said.

Gale cut in. "Don't let this nonsense ruin everything. We're still the people you know and love, and who love you."

"Thanks, guys." I laughed to myself. "I take it he's some sort of practitioner, then?"

"He's a good man, Summer," Gale said. "Don't lead him on. He's been hurt before. Meeting you was hard for him."

"Especially when the date was known by everyone. Talk about limelight," Dani said.

"Fine," I said, sliding off the stool.

Dani escorted me to the entrance. "Forget about Guillaume. We've got this."

Gale handed me my purse and keys. "Now, you git. I'll give Gérard your number, first thing tonight." She pushed me out the front door.

I stepped outside and glanced back at Dani. She locked the door. They'd already hit the lights in the parking lot. I waited for my eyes to adjust to the dark and descended the steps.

"Set me up on blind dates. Turn off the lights before I get to the car. Some jackass calls on me and expects me to just jump at meeting with him after scaring me to death," I ranted to myself, bustling to the car with my keys between my fingers. "Fucking people need to stay the fuck away from me. My parents always told me not to talk to strangers. You want to know why? Because they're all fucked in the head. That's why."

"*Hmm,* it is wise not to be alone with a stranger." Gérard's voice came from behind me.

I screamed, twirled around, and slashed him with my keys which got tangled in his sweater. I pulled. The last key tore loose, and I fell on my ass in the dirt.

"What the hell are you doing here?"

"We have a date, do we not?"

"Oh, my goodness, I'm so sorry, I forgot."

"Preoccupations own your thoughts. No harm." He offered me his hand and pulled me to my feet. "And I am no longer a stranger."

"No, I guess you're not." I rubbed the building ache on my hip. That was going to bruise. "So, what's the plan?"

"Dinner. *Mais,* this night I wish to visit *Chez Fenris.*"

I gasped, knowing just how expensive that place was. It was as fancy as you could get, within fifty miles. My bank account was strained to begin with. "Why Chez?"

"Because I would like to be alone with you."

"Can't we do that here?"

"*Non*, not as I wish it to be." He reached for my hair and brushed it aside.

I pretended to study the stars, not that there were any. "Gérard?"

"*Oui, ma chérie.*"

"Do you know of the guardian, if you don't mind my asking?"

"Ah, *Guillaume*." He pushed away from the car; his spicy cologne emanated. A lone finger traced along my knuckles, sending chills through me. His jacket was covered in dust. "I thought you would want to know more about me."

"Fine. How old are you and how did you know my father?" I stepped away from him and crossed my arms. "And what about the guardian?"

He peered through his bangs. "I would be thirty-two."

"So, you have a birthday coming up?"

"*Peut-être,* perhaps."

"And?"

"In time, Summer."

"And there lies the reason I'm saying no. I know nothing about you!" His actions raised my curiosity, to say the least. I didn't trust him, and it killed the mood. And he didn't answer my questions.

We stood by the car with our hands in our coat pockets.

My angst won. "Awful convenient you offered *Chez*. So, how do you know Gale?" I asked.

"Gale is my, *euh*, aunt." His eyes drifted toward the road and then back to me.

"Aunt, huh? Then the two of you are close?"

"At one time, *oui*. But I have not seen her for many years."

"Funny, she never mentioned you."

Again, silence.

My conscience kicked me in the ass. I didn't want to screw up any more than I already had. I should have just gone to the damned restaurant. "Thank you for offering dinner."

"Of course." He smiled, more of a curl in his lip. Something struck his funny bone. I'd be damned if I knew what, because nothing was funny at the moment.

"I saw smoke again this morning. I'm certain someone's living there; in the mansion, that is."

I felt like one of the potential victims on those undercover detective shows. I scanned the wood line and kept the limo in my sight. The majority of the time, I felt a cold sensation at my back and listened for anything out of the ordinary. I tried to lighten the mood, but it was difficult when you were expecting the boogeyman to jump out from nowhere. I'd also kept an eye on Gérard and took note of his inactions. And by inactions, I mean he wasn't nearly as interested in me as the night before. No ploy for eye contact, no sexy teasing, just a pouting man who didn't get his way. Tough; damn.

"Sorry if I ruined your plans."

"Simply altered." He pulled out a pocket watch. "*Euh*, it would not be wise to keep you whilst you have far to drive. Your safety concerns me."

"Oh, I'll be fine. I've lived there for years." Too bad I didn't believe my own words.

"Perhaps, *mais*, we should part before it is too late."

"Too late for what?" I stared him in the eye this time. Enough was enough.

"The time, Summer. That is all."

"Huh. Just so you know, I asked Gale to give you my number tonight."

"I know."

"How? Dani."

"Knowing your father, I expected your wit to be sharp."

"What?"

He smirked and pulled me to him; I stumbled.

"Never mind. I'm too tired to think about it. Maybe next time you can enlighten me."

"Mmm, next time. But you are tired, and it is late."

Well, that was worrisome. Usually, you set up a time or day, or kick ideas around. That was not what I expected. That and I was pretty well certain he was pissed because I didn't trust him. But two dates was a miracle. None of my others made it to round two. Though it was I who no longer wanted them; damn it. Would I actually get to round three?

We walked to my door where he stopped short, cupped my face, and bent to look in my eyes. He kissed my hand, and I could have sworn time stood still. When he let go, I bit my lip and scurried the last few steps to the door. He watched me get in before he climbed into the waiting limo. I watched as it turned on the roadway opposite of my direction.

I backed out of my spot and eased onto the roadway after him, taking on the detective role. I followed from a distance, keeping an eye on the taillights. But once I rounded the ninety-degree bend ascending the mount, I lost him. I continued until I found a safe place to turn around and headed home.

I pulled in, but this time I ran to the door, getting my key ready. After snagging them in Gérard's sweater, I knew why I was told not to do that. Maybe in a fight with someone in a T-shirt. I figured it was like the lollipop trick. If you put a lollipop between your fingers with the stick facing out, you can take someone's eye out with it. Well, wouldn't a key work too? Or maybe rake it across an attacker's face to give me a chance to get away? Instead, I slid the dirk from the sheath and held it at my side. I needed knife fighting skills. Though I had taken Aikido for a few months, back in my early twenties, and learned that you've got to step into the attack, I lacked confidence. Pulling away gives them the edge. That was the last thing I wanted. I needed to sign up again.

With all the crap from the day weighing me down, I locked the door behind me and climbed into bed—clothes and all. And for the first time in years, I was afraid. I'd left the living room light on and wondered who was watching me. I didn't care why, but more about who. When Jesse left, I was afraid, but only to be alone. This time, I felt like I was being hunted. Damn, Guillaume.

CHAPTER 7

The aroma of cinnamon coffee tickled my nose. I slid from the bed and went to the kitchen. I poured a mug and added a splash of vanilla rice milk. Thank goodness for automatic drip.

After screwing up my date, I felt obligated to break the news to Dawn, my best friend since college and co-conspirator with Gale. She was a perfectly packaged five-foot three-inch redhead with an attitude to rival Hollywood's biggest diva. With her auburn hair and bulging brown eyes, she looked like one of those disproportionate stuffed animals in the greeting card section. But what set her apart most from petite beauty was the unapt baby-belly. And the one reigning personality trait: she was always right. Therefore, since she was married, she was convinced that was what I needed. Everyone should be so happy. Yeah right.

I went through my yoga routine and readied myself for shopping. The usual outfit was jeans and a sweater, but the plan was to get something to jazz up my options, for Gérard, of course.

I called Dawn on my cell, ready to appeal to her addiction to shop. I could count on her to join me on my little excursion. I knew she had off because she just so happened to be the bookkeeper at Tiny's. I started out heading north on county Route 11 before I called. To my amazement, she was expecting me.

"How'd you know I'd call?"

"Tiny snitched when you left last night. He said you'd be needin' someone to do 'girly' talk with and 'to be prepared'." She dropped her voice for a rather high-pitched masculine version of Tiny.

"Yup, that's Tiny. I'm going to the mall. Want to tag along?"

"Of course, and I want details. I'm so excited for you, Summer," she nearly giggled.

"Great, I'll be at your place in about ten minutes." I clicked off the blue tooth and drove to her house.

She lived down from the intersection of Routes 24 and 25, in a new modular complete with a yard and chain-link fence. Luckily, it wasn't too far from Fladdermus Mall.

I pulled into the driveway and found her waiting on the porch. The sun accented the sienna highlights in her hair like an accessory to the denim jumper and brown leather boots. It suited her, a natural beauty. I was glad her father let her live. I opened the tracker's door for her to hop in and buckle up. While we headed to the mall, I filled her in on my date with Gerard and the one that didn't come to fruition.

"Get Gale alone, Officer Stevie can't help." She turned in her seat to look at me. "Either that, or Gérard directly. If you have questions about him or your family, he's the best place to start."

"Can't you tell me? Didn't you help set this up?"

"Hey, don't go blaming me for your indecisive traits. You've both been alone too long and you've both had heartache. But he's got quirks."

"Yeah, quirks."

"No, I mean real quirks. I mean, we all do, even you. Hey, ask Gale about Gérard if you want, but I think confronting him is a better idea."

"Maybe, if I see him again."

"Please, it'll take more than that to get rid of him. Now, what are you wearin' to Chez? I know it's gotta be feasible, because you're catering. How about a French maid outfit?" She bit her lip, knowing my response. "Come on, Gérard'll love it, he's French."

"But it's a ball. I don't think they make a maid's dress; I don't want to give the wrong impression. Besides, it's cliché."

"Uh, huh."

"I mean it, Dawn. I don't like feeling out of control over a guy I just met."

"Will you stop? You're smitten. And why won't you satisfy your womanly urges with him?"

"I won't get hurt again."

"So what? You're gonna shrivel up and die?" She sighed and looked out of the window. "You're a grown woman. There is absolutely no harm in a little casual sex." She patted her belly. "As long as you take precautions."

"I'd rather wait until I know him better, thank you. Plenty of guys would jump in bed and never be heard from again. I wouldn't be able to deal with that if it happened with Gérard." I pushed back against the headrest. "I probably destroyed my chances anyway."

"He's not Jesse. There are fewer of them out there. Don't sell yourself short because you're afraid. He's a lot more understanding than most."

"Maybe. I do feel something just by being around him."

"Lust."

"Yeah, lust."

The parking lot was a vast ocean of metal, gleaming in the sun. I pulled into a parking space about midway, before helping Dawn out of the car. We strolled toward the main entrance to the mall, the closest to the costume store. I held the door as she waddled full speed ahead through the addictive sweet cinnamon aroma of Sticky Sins to the clearance rack in front of the store. I could have licked the frosting from every bun.

It irked me how some of the costumes looked lifelike, while others were like giant puppets. The realistic scars were situated next to an oversized teddy bear suit with a fan in the head. Like what were they thinking? Watch someone go to the ball with the slice-a teddy get up. I'd die. Though a little stuffing hanging out could sell it, but no. That was just wrong, no bloody teddies for me. I kept scouring the racks.

The first costume I pulled was a vampiress gown, complete with a pair of porcelain fangs. I was buying the fangs, but continued to look over the racks until I'd exhausted the inventory. In the end, we both pulled the same costume parts out at the same time to show each other.

"Hey, what about this?" We both laughed, pointing out a black leotard with fishnet stockings, a long black tail, black velvet ears, and a black sequined tutu.

"This is perfect, Summer."

"Yeah, but the fishnets are a bit much." I never wore stuff like that. I'd lost fifty pounds but questioned my ability to pull off anything that risqué. The prior year, I'd been a scarecrow at the orchard. I stuffed real hay into a pair of overalls and wore a straw hat. If it weren't for Gérard, it's what I'd be again.

"Come on, get it. It'll look great on you. With your figure, all you need's a pair of black patent leather boots that come to about here." She drew a line across my mid-thigh to show just where it should be.

"Uh, we'll see." I put my fangs on the counter to go help her. "What did you decide for you and Richard?"

Richard was Dawn's husband and an accountant at a firm down from the mall. Honestly, he was the walking cliché accountant. He was 5'10, with short red hair, a military cut that grew in two years ago, black plastic glasses, a mechanical pencil in his pocket at all times, and was starting to lose his manly figure. At times, it seemed like he was the one who was pregnant and not Dawn.

"I found two adorable costumes: An 1800s Regency black tux with tails and a matching gold gown for me. There are peacock masks to go with. Maybe I can get a Moses basket to put little Richard in, if he's here." Her eyes sparkled at the notion.

"Elegant, Dawn. Shall we get out of here?"

She glanced over her shoulder. "Not getting anything?"

"Yeah, fangs, why?"

Dawn shook her head. "Fine, you won't get a real costume. How about something for the bedroom?"

"I hadn't thought of it." I wasn't planning on it.

"Don't tell me you plan on surprising Gérard with flannel? You're cute, though I doubt even you can pull that off, but with fangs." She wriggled her eyebrows and laughed. "I gotta pee!"

"Funny, Dawn. Food court it is."

"What if he wants to whisk you away with him for a weekend or something?"

I smiled. "Then I guess I'll have to go shopping again."

"Ooo, grown-up shopping," she squealed as she pulled me with her in full waddle to the cashier. I think getting me to buy something sexy was her secret mission. Comfort was my thing; lingerie was just overpriced and scratchy.

We wound up sharing a pretzel on the way to Scarlet's, of all places. Dawn chose a purple lace slip teddy with a snap-away crotch and matching garter belt. Of course, the saleslady had to point out the black silk thigh highs and suggest I find a pair of purple-feathered pumps. Guess they didn't trust me with intimate apparel.

"I told you this guy was fresh meat. You have to be fresh, too." She peered at me out of the corner of her eye and whispered. "There's more than one way to be fresh."

"You don't think my flannel'd be fresher to him? Don't you have to pee? Besides, women probably drool all over him and shower him with pictures of themselves, nude. I don't want to spinster him away, but he's not getting me that easy."

I couldn't keep the sarcasm out of my voice as memories of Jesse flashed to mind: him coming home with other women. The screaming matches, the times I pretended to be asleep, so he'd leave me alone. The times I ran and hid in the woods so he couldn't hit me anymore. Yeah, it's why I knew the wolves would protect me. At least they did when I hid.

"Sex is overrated," I said.

"You think too much."

"I know." But she didn't know. Nobody knew how bad it was. I was good at hiding—lots of things, like why Mrs. Greene wasn't alive. There were reasons I had a sheath on my sock. Though, I may have jumped the gun. Dawn might know. Her father went to prison for taking her to the church on the mount. I was too young when it happened, and she never spoke about it. Still, I remembered Augusto saying her father planned to kill her—leave her on the altar. She was to be his offering. Whomever he served, he needed to prove himself. If it wasn't for the wolves and Augusto, he would have succeeded. That's what the newspapers failed to report. That's why my parents gave me the dirk, and why I was in no hurry to learn about Tiny and Gale's practice. I worshiped nothing, and I planned to keep it that way.

Dawn picked a few more garments for me before I left to get the car. She waited at the entrance while I brought the car up. I put our packages in the trunk, then my cell rang; I let it go to voicemail.

"Tiny?" she asked.

"Yeah," I sighed.

"Better see what he wants."

"I will."

I finished putting the bags in and dialed my voicemail.

"Hey, Summer. We need you at the diner as soon as possible. Your date was a business booster. Oh yeah, a friend of Gérard's here asking for you, name's Douglas. You're a popular little lady." I clicked the phone closed.

"Well?" Dawn asked.

"He needs me. I'll drop you off and head in." I tried to keep the disappointment out of my voice. It had been a long time since I spent a day just shopping and being a girl. But I was curious to whether Douglas was the chestnut guy at Brady's. A new outfit could wait.

"That's okay. But please try, Summer. Gérard's different. Promise me you'll keep an open mind." She squeezed my free hand. "He's not Jesse."

"Honestly Dawn, I want someone who'll make me as happy as Richard makes you. I don't know how you got over your father, but I can't let Jesse go. Gérard has manners, he's gorgeous, but . . ."

"But I helped set this up. Give it a chance."

We rode in silence for what seemed like hours, though only a few minutes, before Dawn yelled a wordless, frustrated sound.

"Summer, you've lost in love, yeah. Boo-fucking-hoo! We both know Jesse was a dick. But you need to dust off the cobwebs and fuck Gérard before he gets away. It would be a shame to lose a piece that fine. Besides, you want to. You don't have Mommy and Daddy telling you sex is the temptation of the devil. You're 30 years old. Get over yourself, enjoy life."

"What's got into you?"

"I'm tired of it. Seriously, people talk more about your celibacy than they would if you fucked every man from here to Watertown. Maybe your family's dead, but you're not. If you don't enjoy life, then it goes wasted. You can't live in the past. I love you. Shit, we all love you, but you're not normal, Summer."

"So sorry to be a burden. Don't worry, you won't have to listen to my fucked-up life anymore."

"The truth sucks, Sum. It's time to grow up."

"Yeah, well. You don't know what it's like. You live in your perfect little world. Oops! No, you don't. You fucked that cop 'cause Richard was shootin' blanks. Does he know he's not the daddy? Does he know you're still fucking Greene? I don't want your normal." Tears burned my eyes, but I blinked them away.

She turned to the window. "I'm not sorry 'cause someone had to say it."

But why today? I thought, concentrating on the road, and keeping the tears at bay.

I stopped a car's length from her drive and backed in. Richard was home, so the conversation was over. He took her packages from the trunk while she went inside. Once he closed the zipper, I spun the tires in the dirt drive and left a cloud of maize dust in my wake.

I left for the diner, the bitter taste of fear on the back of my tongue. The sick pangs that angst brings when you've said things you didn't ever want to say. When you've been told exactly what you never wanted to hear.

Gale and Dawn were hell bent on me hooking up with Gérard, but I'd never even met him 'til the other night. It shocked me. The whole damned community shocked me. What the hell was I thinking? And what was with Dawn? Not once in our friendship did we fight. She was the picture of mellow, the reasonable one. The kind of friend that took you by the hand, dragging you to the dance floor, or setting up dates because you don't believe you're worth the effort. I owed her an apology. I wanted to go home, salvage my friendship, and talk to Gérard. I wanted answers, and he was a good place to start. And who the hell was Douglas?

CHAPTER 8

Without realizing it, I pulled into my driveway. I didn't even remember driving home. A good night's sleep was in order. Screw Tiny, it was my night off.

I went into the house, determined to put the crap from my shopping trip with Dawn behind me. I didn't mean to be a burden. It was just that the holidays were coming up and every year I sat home alone. Gale and Dani had a religious retreat they went on. And Tiny, well, he wasn't someone I hung out with after work. He was kind of strange anyway. He didn't even like the decorations we put up in the diner. I at least had a small fiber optic tree and drank cocoa to Christmas music on Christmas morning. But Dawn and Richard always went to England to visit his family. I hated being lonely.

Being that it was nearly Halloween meant the downward spiral had begun. My memories of Halloween ended when Sheena was seven. She died before the next and my parents disappeared before there was a chance to get through the first one together. I'd spent that first Halloween lighting candles in small paper bags outside the house. I hoped they might find their way back. I was eighteen and still had hope.

Maybe I was selfish, which even now is hard to admit. I wanted my family back as a whole, but I needed my father over them all. He was my protector. I was riddled with guilt over the realization that if only one of them could come back; I wanted my dad. Though I wanted my mom to be at my wedding, or to be there when I had a baby. Guillaume was right—I still had that same hope.

It hurt too because their disappearance felt like a betrayal. In fact, had they not gone missing, I may never have been subjected to Jesse's wrath. I may not have gone to that specific college or agreed to date him. I may not have moved out, or maybe my dad would have kicked his ass. Maybe my mom would have held me one last time and told me it'd be okay. Maybes—all maybes.

I took off my clothes, careful to toss them in the hamper, attempting to shed away the day. Trying for a little normalcy, I'd started the shower when the phone rang. Running, almost tripping, I grabbed the phone.

"Summer? It is I, *Gérard*."

"Hi." I had to catch my breath, which gave my voice a seductive air. I didn't doubt fear of the unknown, and the excitement of hearing his voice played a part in it, too.

"Is this a bad time? Are you *euh*—busy?" It was nearly nine at night. What did he think I was doing?

"No, no. Not at all. I was just going to get in the shower." Oh, great. Now he knew I was naked. I was such an ass.

"Really?" he said, drawing out the "R" as he had done before. "Are you alone?"

"Uh, yeah." Maybe I shouldn't have said that.

"Should I call when you have had time to—*euh*—finish?"

"No, this is fine. I will turn off the water, though. Hold on." I ran to the bedroom and turned off the water, grabbed my towel and tied it around me so he couldn't see me through the phone. I repeat—I was an ass. "Okay."

"Please, it is nice, for you like to be clean."

"Yeah, have you been around many who don't?"

"*Excusez-moi?* I do not understand."

"Forget it."

"Why? Because you were going to shower?"

"No, because I was about to get in."

"Oh, *Mon Dieu. Vraiment?*"

"I'm sorry, Gérard, but I don't understand French all that well."

"Ah, *oui*. I understand. You are *euh*—without attire?"

"I have a towel now." I laughed nervously.

"Then I shall let you go. I will say good night."

"No, it's okay. I'm covered, now. Besides, you said you wanted to get to know me, and I gave my permission, remember?" Oh my god, I was flirting.

"Yes," he said, while drawing the "s" out almost snake like. It sent chills down my spine.

Shit. "So, let's start with why you called."

"Ah, I hoped to see you, *ce soir*." I just bet he would.

"Sure. How about I hop in the shower, and you meet me here? I'm assuming Gale's already filled you in on where I live."

"*Oui, et*—you do not have to change what you are wearing for me." A masculine chuckle made things low in my stomach flutter.

"Get to know my personality first. My body comes later."

"Really?" he said, with the "R" drawn out again.

"Ok, I'm gonna hang up now."

"*Bon.*"

I hung up.

Again, I was about to get in the shower, and the doorbell rang. I grabbed my robe from the bedroom closet and cautiously walked to the door.

"Who is it?"

"*C'est moi, ma chérie.*"

"Gérard?"

"*Oui.*"

"Uh, one second." What was I going to do? Okay, at thirty-years old I was not a virgin, and most certainly wasn't the first nude woman to be around him. I took a breath and opened the door.

As he seemed to glide in, he raised my hand and placed a feather light kiss on the back—breathy and warm. The sensation was intense; I felt things I shouldn't have. Especially while standing practically nude after barely two dates. I shivered.

"Why do you do that?"

"What do you mean?"

"You know what I mean. I am not dressed appropriately for this."

"Ah, but you are." He smiled that magnificent smile and had that look that a man gets when he's pleased with himself. "These are for you." He stepped back and handed me a bouquet of long white stem roses.

"Thank you. They're beautiful." I forced myself to casually walk to the kitchen and put the flowers in a glass of water. "I'd better change. Where are we going tonight?"

When I turned, I was shocked to find him right behind me.

"We do not have to go out if you would rather be—*euh*—comfortable." He let his eyes wander down my toweledness.

"Stay here?" I gasped. I wasn't prepared for that. Dawn was right. It was a third date, albeit they were a short two dates previously, but wasn't I obligated to some sort of physical play after the third date? And was it on or after the third date? Was there really some dating etiquette I had to follow? What if I didn't? What if I did? I didn't want to. Why did I invite him over? I should have met him somewhere.

"*Oui,* or we could go to my place."

"Just out of curiosity, where is your place?" If I went to his place, would he expect it more? How did I get out of riding this time?

"On the other side of Lake Sangre."

Oh. "You're the new owner—of the mansion." My heart skipped a beat; the words caught in my throat. No riding.

"*Oui.* But not new. I enjoy old homes. One never knows what stories they hold. Would you like a tour?"

"Um, okay. Mind if I shower first?"

"Not at all."

I did a quick wash with my peach scented soaps, brushed my teeth, and rinsed as quickly as possible. The whole time I could have doubled over, hyperventilating. We were neighbors! It was surreal. Perhaps, in comparison, it was like meeting a celebrity and having them talk to you. I could barely breathe. I grabbed my towel, wrapped it around my body, and rushed into the bedroom.

"Ahhh," I screamed, and backed into the edge of the door. He was propped on my bed. "You scared the hell out of me."

"I apologize. I did not intend to startle you. After all, I have your permission to get to know you, and you did say your body comes later." He smiled, dipping his head to the side, purposely to make his hair fall forward. His voice deepened. "It is later."

"Ha, funny." I squeaked. "I didn't mean that we would do anything. I won't do that casually. I do need to get dressed before we go. It wouldn't be fair for you to get a show and not me. Not that I mean I want one, or that I don't. Just, I don't think we should right now."

"Ah, you are lovely. If you want me to go, I will." His voice was low and soft; masculine and seductive.

"No, I mean—just wait out in the living room while I get ready." I couldn't talk fast enough. I really didn't want him to leave.

He turned his head to give me a once over before leaving. I gasped when I saw the blue had darkened but there was movement; something like stars glinted. I knew I saw something the other night. He closed the door behind him.

"I'll be out in a minute. What would be appropriate for a late night hike?" I called to him.

"Again, too lovely, *ma chérie*. We will not have to hike, unless you wish to do so," he called back.

"How will we get there? By boat? I've never been on a boat."

"If you prefer."

"How did you get here?"

"A hike will be fine."

At this, I came out of the bedroom with just a long black cotton turtleneck that reached mid-thigh and a pair of new black lace panties. I wasn't such a prude after all.

I raked a shower comb through my hair. "How did you get here?"

He perched himself on the arm of the couch. "You have learned a lot of information about our community. Have you not?" he asked.

"You could say that."

I tried to prepare myself for what he could possibly have to say, and felt ridiculous. My insides were in a whirlwind. It was like having the breath knocked out of me repeatedly, but I wouldn't give up. I guess I was still hoping for the truth after my disappointment with Guillaume.

"Not that I got any answers," I said.

"I am quite taken by you, Summer, but I envisage your reaction and it frightens me." He straightened to avoid talking to my face.

"I feel something for you too, but I want to know more. It's like you're too good to be true. If there's a skeleton in your closet, it might make me feel better." I bit my tongue. After what Guillaume had said, I might not want to know.

He knelt in front of me, looking up, but I wouldn't look him in his eyes. I was too nervous. "I assure you, Summer, I will not harm you. We will not harm you. You have my word."

"Gale and Tiny said they'd never let anyone hurt me." A tremor went through me; I fought to control it.

"You are frightened." He took my hand and brought me down to his level. "Why?" He lifted my chin with his finger.

"Do you want some tea or something? I don't have any wine." I scrambled to my feet, but he pulled me back down.

"Let us talk for now. Tell me."

"I think you're all batshit crazy. But who am I to judge? I've never been religious anyway. If you want to run naked through the woods, be my guest. Call yourself whatever you want: occultist, Satanist, Wiccan. I don't get the drama. A cult's a cult." He studied my face in silence.

There was no clock ticking—no leaky faucet. I needed to fill the void.

"Look, I'm not putting you down. But . . . Oh my God!" Epiphany! "I'm not some kind of sacrifice, am I?" A tear leaked from the corner of my eye. He caught it with the edge of his finger but still said nothing. "I'm so stupid. That's what Guillaume was talking about. The whole virtue thing. Jesus, I'm thirty, Gérard. I'm not a virgin; trust me. Maybe it's been a while, but nope, you've got the wrong girl here." Danger, what the hell was the danger? "Do you need blood? For real, people use goats you don't need to use me. I can get you one." I pulled away, but he held my wrists tighter. "Shit, you do know what happened to my parents, don't you?" He let go.

I scrambled across the room and yelled, "Speak, damn it! Tell me what you want from me."

"You really want to know?" His voice remained calm. Bastard!

"Yeah, I do."

"Then let us go. There is someone I want you to meet."

"Who? How?"

"Ah, again *ma chérie,* you are lovely. Enough of this. I would love to show you my mansion, and if I may be so bold, will you please accept my offer to be your *euh* . . . date at the costume party at *Chez Fenris?*"

"See? That's my point. You don't answer any of my questions. Was Guillaume right? Should I even go with you? Should we even be alone? The answer is no. No, no, and no again. I am cooking. I will be working. I am not going with a date of any sort. Not you, not Guillaume, not anyone else who decides that I can play the sacrificial lamb. I will not be alone with any of you."

"Forgive the obvious, but I am in your house. Alone. *Maintenant*, are you going out as you are, or would you prefer pants?"

"Oh, I forgot I wasn't wearing any. I'll be just a minute." Yup, ass for the evening, that was me. I couldn't believe I forgot I was standing there half-naked. It was humiliating. The blood coursed through my veins, pulsing in my neck and body. I could have died.

I did a quick pull down of the shirt and ran on tiptoe to the bedroom and slammed the door practically in his face. No man had seen me like that—well, Jesse, but that was years back. I was still self-conscious from his taunting during my heavier days. I was comfortable, fifty pounds lighter, but what about the stretch marks? Damn it.

How could I lose myself in him so easily? How could I be so comfortable? Lust was definitely a factor, but there was more. I wanted to believe him; I wanted him. I hated him. I was scared. I walked out of the bedroom having added blue jeans, a Ruger 9mm, and a pair of black flats.

CHAPTER 9

I'd left the lights on but locked the door when we left. I motioned for him to go first, ignoring his hand, as we embarked on the three-mile hike along Lake Sangre. The calm water, the moon on a clear night, and the generous smattering of stars all performed as nature's nightlight.

I stopped to watch the reflection, barely affected by an occasional ripple. Gérard had stopped too, though it took me a moment to notice. The dancing light was hypnotic. If we had taken a moment to sit by the shore, I would have been content. The lake always acted as a buffer to the rest of the world. At least that's how it made me feel. Like when some people listen to whale song, or watch fish, I loved spending time there. Sometimes I spoke to the lake like a friend who could keep my deepest, darkest secrets. Sometimes I simply sat and listened to the water life. But the one thing I'd never done was sit by the lake at night.

My mother warned me not to go near the water's edge from the time I could walk. She was always afraid I would drown. She told me stories of cousins who drowned in water only a few inches deep, and one who got their foot stuck in the mud and couldn't come up for air, in a pond somewhere near Walton. I mean, I never went near Lake Sangre as a child. It wasn't until I was engaged that I moved to the cottage, but her fear was for any body of water. It's a shame she didn't harp on it as much with my sister.

"I've never been close to the water at night before," I whispered.

Gérard appeared behind me. I was too awestruck to hear the leaves. He startled me and I toppled forward. He caught my arm before I hit the rocks.

"I told you; I will not harm you. In fact, I like you. A lot." He stepped to the shoreline and stared at the water. "I do not know how to answer your questions, Summer. That is the truth."

"Then just do it."

"*Alors*, you are not my sacrifice of any sort. I do not run the woods nude, and I do not worship Satan. I am no longer a religious man, though long ago it was so. Gale told me you are too shy to ask for me to accompany you to *Chez Fenris*; that is why I asked you to be my date." He let go and put his hand out for me again. I still didn't take it.

"And what about my family?"

"Sheena is at peace. Your father is deceased. Faoltiarna and Augusto live, *mais*—I am unable to say where. Not because I do not want to help, but because I am incapable. I know, it is not enough."

"Who are you? Why do you know these things?" I asked.

He didn't answer.

"Fine." I pushed past him to forge ahead until I heard the slightest rustle in the underbrush. It was well past midnight, and I had completely forgotten about the plethora of wildlife that graced the woods with their carnivorous presence. I stopped.

"Don't move," I whispered.

The dark figure stepped into the moonlight; its shabby gray hackles eased. I couldn't be sure, but I felt connected to it. He stepped closer and nuzzled my hand with his coal black nose. I slid my hand around the front of his neck and kneaded the scruff of fur that made up a kind of wolf's mane. And then his eyes hit me. The eyes—like amber orbs with an inner light. He licked my hand; a slow, firm swipe of tongue. Yup, he was mine. I knelt before him and kissed between his ears.

"It's okay, he's my stray," I confessed.

"Stray? What is this?"

"An animal with no home."

"But the forest is a home, *non*?"

"I guess, but he's so tame. I've been feeding him for years. He's like a pet." I patted the wolf's head and scratched behind his ears.

"He's been the only true friend I've had. He doesn't judge me, and he makes me feel safe."

"And I do not," Gérard sighed in dismay. "Perhaps in time you will find that I too am loyal and will indeed keep you from harm."

I peered up to see him smile at the wolf that was now licking my chin. The slow hard licks a dog gives when they want to take care of you. Gérard lifted his hand to show the pink grip of the Ruger I'd tucked in the back of my jeans.

"You do not need this. I will give it back once I deliver you home. For now, let us all be safe."

A lump filled my throat. I wasn't sure what to say. A whole hell of a lot of good it did when I had it to protect myself from him. Damn it.

The stray scampered off while we had our little stare down. For whatever reason, I felt empowered: the lake to my back, a wolf looking out for me, and a gun in the hands of my would-be attacker. Yup—justifiable empowerment. Nope.

"I look forward to our getting to know one another, Summer. You are a creature of great complexity. I shall enjoy every moment."

I couldn't help but smile. "I guess. But you're an annoying pain in the ass with the cloak and dagger shit."

He laughed and tucked the Ruger through his belt before he took the lead on the path. He hadn't offered his hand; I wouldn't have taken it anyway.

We trekked on in silence. I kept watching the water. The sleek glass-like surface developed a fine mist in the center. I hurried after him; mists creeped me out. Fog, too. I hated fog.

As I drew closer, he slowed his pace and stretched his hand behind him. I took it and felt a wash of relief.

We stepped from the trees onto a stone walkway. Strange, there were stone pavers that began at the end of the woods. At least I thought so. We followed the pavers through the clearing to the front of the mansion.

I never dreamed that I would be that close to it. The Lake Sangre Mansion was a mystery. No one went in; no one came out. Every morning, for years, I sipped my coffee and stared at the chimney tops across the lake. And there I was, about to go inside. I froze. The mere fact that it was inhabited hadn't even sunk in yet. I was never actually alone.

I ogled the front of the mansion, which was rough granite, and resembled a gothic castle. A large staircase led to a massive set of mahogany wooden doors that, while closed, formed an arch. Black iron hinges reached around either side of the doors to end in a beautiful wolf's head decoration. There were no windows, but on each was a wolf shaped doorknocker.

Ivy grew up the side of the house, around the windows, and extended to where grotesques were perched overlooking the entrance. More were positioned about every twelve feet along the patina covered copper roof, in between the spires, perhaps guarding those who resided within.

He pulled me after him to the main entrance.

I climbed up the stone steps toward the doors, which opened as if all on their own. I would have thought it mystical, but a young man of about twenty-five peered around one of the doors. Gérard acknowledged him with a small nod.

"*Merci*, Douglas." He kissed the gentleman on his cheek.

"Sir." Douglas nodded.

"*Mademoiselle* Candella will join us this evening."

"Certainly, a pleasure." His eyes, more amber than brown, met mine before he bent to kiss my free hand. "Please, call me Doug."

All I could manage was, "Hi." That certainly made things interesting.

"Please, *le chocolat,* in the library," Gérard said.

Doug bowed. "Of course, sir."

Before he left, he glanced back. I caught him and noticed his eyes held what looked like an orange spark. Doug was definitely a good-looking man. And when he left, he moved with that air a man has when he knows he looks good; shoulders back, a warm smile, and eye contact. I died inside, sucked in my breath, and stared at the stone floor under my feet.

At nearly six feet, with shoulder length chestnut hair, and a white silk shirt tucked into faded blue jeans that stretched over the muscles barely hidden beneath either garment to show no underwear lines—yeah, he looked good.

He disappeared where iron torches lit the vestibule, and shadows danced across the scabrous stone walls. I surveyed the rest of the entrance. There were actually three archways with the same burgundy drapes, one to the left, one to the right, and one directly in front of us where Doug had gone.

Gérard took my hand to lead the way through the archway on the left. "Welcome to my home. While we have much to learn from one another, there is much to learn here as well. Come, we will start your tour, *après le chocolat.*"

The mere size of the place was intimidating, but the inside made me ashamed of my little house. Truthfully, mine was a cottage, small and neat. This was larger than any home I'd visited. I felt insignificant to his grand stature. It's no wonder why Gale wanted me to meet him. But I wasn't turned on by money. Surprising to myself, it frightened me. It made me more self-conscious. I tried to hide my discomfort and inner turmoil.

"This reminds me of some of the castles I saw on a virtual tour of England. I imagine you must have thought so too, or you wouldn't have bought it."

"Come." He advanced through the hall into an entranceway of sorts, clasping his hands behind his back; the heels of his boots clicked evenly on the bare stone floor. The spicy cologne, his fluid yet carefully placed steps, and gentle clasp of hand on wrist, made me dizzy. The idea of being alone with someone like him, and the possibility of Doug's presence in the near future, was too much.

Perhaps it wasn't the money that caused my inner turmoil. It was men. Again, that damn wall was useless. That mental wall was crap. I was vulnerable. A couple nice smiles and mannerisms undid everything I strove to avoid. Guillaume was right; I needed to be careful. Trouble was—I was tired and scared. I didn't want to be alone anymore.

There were more draped archways lining the walls, with two hallways at angles in front of us. I couldn't imagine what he'd paid for it. Or how much it would cost to build, considering the cost of materials and labor these days.

"Are these all antiques?" I ran my hand over a jade dragon statue, of what dynasty I had no clue. There was nothing modern from what I could tell, though that's not sayin' much.

"Well, a tour of that sort would take longer than time allows. Much of what you see, I acquired over the last three centuries. Some date back as far as eight."

I laughed and caught myself. "You mean decades. Centuries are a hundred years."

He smiled shyly. "Ah, well, you caught me."

I followed him through another archway, which led to a set of descending stairs. Again, nothing but torchlight.

The bottom landing was in the middle of a triangular opening with more hallways, archways, and a set of arched double doors, which he pulled open and bowed. "Shall we?"

I stepped through on tiptoe. It was impossible not to look like a tourist. I mean, in the center of the room was a large two-sided fireplace with a small fire that set the room aglow. Shadows undulated over the walls, which were lined from floor to ceiling with books. The marble chimney and hearth were possibly white granite. A ghostly contrast.

The center of the ceiling opened to a glass dome that emulated an autumn night sky. A crystal and gold chandelier that hung from its center reflected the light from the fire and brought the room to life—almost like magic.

"Breathtaking, isn't it?" Doug spoke from behind me.

"Oh, my God!" I exclaimed louder than I would have liked and spun on my heel, a little dizzy from looking up. I bumped his arm and watched the cocoa slosh, but he maneuvered the tray so that the liquid didn't make it over the edge of the mug. I giggled goofily. "Ha, you startled me. Sorry."

"No worries. Where will you have it, Ms. Candella?"

"I wouldn't have anything in here. God forbid it got spilled."

He stepped closer and smiled, a warm pucker. "Have a seat by the fire; I'll set up there." He pointed to a small iron table with two matching chairs. I followed. "I whipped fresh cream and brought cinnamon, unsure of your preference." He set the tray down, dabbed at the pot of cream, licked it off the tip of his finger, and winked, before heading to the door.

"Douglas," Gérard called.

"Gérard?"

"Await my presence in the hall." He strode toward Doug and stopped. "I will be but a moment, *ma chérie.*"

"Ok, but I feel funny, without you joining me, I mean."

He raised an eyebrow. "As it was at the *café*?"

"Mhmm." I chewed the inside of my lip.

"Then I will join you, upon my return." He paused by the door, his face hidden by his hair. "Please excuse me. I have arranged for a few guests to make you more comfortable. I expect their arrival shortly." He followed Doug into the hall, the door slightly ajar.

I sipped the cocoa, which tasted more like melted chocolate, not powder. I drank half, turned around, and tried to take in all the room had to offer. I loved castles and antiques, but nothing could keep my curiosity at bay.

I set the mug on the tray and crept to the open door. I flattened against the closed one so I could peer out the small opening of the other. Detective Candella, yeah, a work in progress.

Doug stood with his back to me. His hands were going; his voice low. "Alas, your personage—tell her."

"Not now, *mon ami,*" Gérard whispered back.

"They leave us no choice, Gérard. They're coming and Guillaume won't wait."

"Then consider it done. But not about them. *Non,* not them, not yet."

"*Elle est près, monsieur.*" Of course, why wouldn't he speak French? And to think, I took Spanish in high school.

"*Je sais, mon ami, je sais.*" Gérard pulled Doug in for a hug and kissed him. His face ended up by the man's ear, which was my cue to slink away before they came back. I slithered along the outer wall and hurried to grab my cocoa.

Doug was insistent, but I didn't have long to contemplate why, because low and behold, Tiny and Gale walked in with Dani trailing behind. Guess I'd found out who the visitors were.

"Hey, Tiny," I said.

"You didn't come to work," he said back.

Dani pushed past him. "What am I chopped liver?"

"If you were, I wouldn't come near you." I laughed and felt better. Leave it to her.

"What d'ya think? Nice pad, right?" Dani said.

"Oh, yeah," I said. "So, why's he need you guys to make me comfy?"

Dani sat on the hearth and stoked the fire. Gale slid behind her and squeezed her shoulders.

They didn't answer.

"Why does everyone keep doing this?" I said to no one in particular.

"We're different," Dani said. "We don't want to scare you off."

"I never knew, so why be scared now?" It was true. Practice what you like. Just leave me out, was what I wanted to say. But I kept my comments to myself.

"But?" Dani asked.

"I'm not, it's okay, really." I went to her side and gave her a reassuring hug.

"I hate being one of them, all the hiding. It sucks."

"So." I shrugged. "I suppose hiding your beliefs is in your best interest, but intellect and logic must intervene."

Gale searched my face. "You truly believe that?"

I laughed, not a good sound. "Don't ask me that. What bothers me is that I'm not scared. Not really. I probably should be, but I'm pissed. You want to live the fantasy. I can handle that. But don't force it on me. Whether you believe in witchcraft or role-playing, I won't judge. But don't get angry with me for not following. I was never a performer and don't wish to be."

"Summer, you're not listening." Dani hugged into Gale. "We live life as it was dealt. We don't flaunt what we are."

"Like this isn't flaunting," I huffed and waved my hand to acknowledge the room; them included.

"No, it's not. Shit, I'm a shifter; Mom's a witch—it doesn't bother you?"

"Know what bothers me? That none of you will tell me who the fuck is trying to kill me." I knew there was a reason Gérard took my gun. I knew there was a reason I had it. "Answer me, damn it."

"You don't want to know," Tiny said.

"Yeah, I think I do."

Dani whispered, just enough for me to hear. "But we're not allowed to talk about it. Can't you see? We're not free, Sum, you just think you are. You just need to listen."

"Fuck no. I'm so done with this shit. The best I got was from Guillaume and I don't even know him. I want to go home; no, I need to go home." I stood, brushed myself off, and walked out of the library right into Gérard. I didn't look at him.

"Leaving so soon? Without saying good night?" He leaned against the wall, blocking my way.

"Yeah, well, you were preoccupied with Doug and let's just say I'm not up to visitors."

"I apologize for leaving. It was rude." He tucked my hair behind my ears, his touch barely noticeable. I wanted to notice it. I wanted him to do it again.

"It's okay, I figured you had business to tend to."

"Come." He walked into the library, his hands in his pockets, chin up, and no smile. I followed, hopeful for answers. "Thank you for keeping Summer entertained while I attended to business." He was formal, not what I expected. I mean, stiff when he addressed them, but winked at me.

"Of course, sir," Gale said.

He crossed to the iron table and motioned for me to sit. A waft of cinnamon followed him. Doug had brought some. I intended to put it in the chocolate.

"You never answered my question," I said.

"*Quoi?*"

"How you got to my house." I thought about what Gale and Dani had said. Tiny's attitude, too. I knew Gérard was one of them somehow. I sat in the chair opposite him.

He stroked the back of my hand with his finger, leaving a trail of tingling sensations. I pulled my hand back. There were onlookers—Gale, Tiny, and Dani—they needed to leave. I wanted to be alone with him. Strange twist of emotions there!

"As you wish, but not yet." He no sooner spoke, and they were waiting by the door.

Doug stepped inside and propped himself against the closed door. "It doesn't confirm their drivel, but still, that was cool, and you can't explain it."

"What?" I asked.

He looked from me to the fire and back to me again. "He flew," he whispered, eyes steady, and focused on me.

"Did you say he flew?" I pulled my hands off the table and pushed out my chair. "Like flying?"

"More of a gliding," Dani said.

"Great, so now I'm surrounded by a bunch of humanity challenged individuals." I pointed to Dani and Gérard. "So, the two of you are shifters and they're witches."

"Not exactly," Dani sighed.

"Mmm, talkative, were you? More than expected," Gérard said to her.

Tiny rubbed his arms.

"Yeah, well, with that being said, really, it doesn't bother me." I looked at Gérard. "I pegged you for something, the night I met you."

He put his hand up to interrupt. "Something? Is there more or am I to guess?"

"Well, right now, as it stands, I'm guessing human, but I think you want me to say otherwise."

"With either instance, you are disturbed," he stated.

"Disturbed?" I shrieked. "Yeah, I'm fuckin' disturbed. But what disturbs me is that someone wants to kill me. Is it you?" I stood and turned my back to him. I wasn't a sacrifice, he said. "You said you'd never harm me, but you didn't say you wouldn't kill me." Fear hit me like a ton of bricks. "Are you my Grimm reaper or something?" I plopped down on the floor. "You're it. That's what Guillaume warned about. It explains everything. The black clothes, no car, the talking in circles. It's you!"

"For the love of us all, stop!" Gale yelled. "If it wasn't for him, you'd be dead by now."

"She's tellin' the truth, Summer," Dani added. "Your father wanted him to keep you. He's the only one who can keep you safe."

"Please, leave us," Gérard requested, voice soft.

Dani hugged me while the other two scurried out. "We're still people, remember that, Summer." She clicked the door closed behind her. Doug stayed.

"You let me go on, knowing full well what you are." I was angry and spoke louder than I'd intended. "I made an ass out of myself in front of you. All of you. I'm tired of the lies. I want truth. No facades."

"No facades? *Bon*, I want you to be mine." He smiled, softening the lines around his eyes. "Now that makes you nervous."

"Of course, I'm nervous around you. I have been since I met you. You must have figured that out by now. Perhaps the reason has just changed, or not." I went back to the table, studied the bowl of whipped cream, and put a dollop in my half-empty mug. "I'm nervous, not because of this shit, mind you, but because I like you."

He cupped my cheek with his palm. "Summer, I have already told you how I feel. It is not one-sided."

"It's just hard for me. I've always been this way." I glanced up at him. "This scares me. Not this nonsense about the aforementioned afflictions. But the real you."

He lifted my chin with the side of his finger. "I know what you think, but none of us are living a belief. We are real, and we are here. And so are you," he said, and then his eyes changed. This time I saw them change. They went from dark blue to the slow swirl I saw the night before, then sapphire flames.

"Whoa. You're not playin'." I stood quicker than I'd intended and knocked the chair over. I wrung my hands and turned around. My heart pounded in my chest. I clutched my face in my own hands; tears welled. Each breath hurt. "I thought it was contacts."

He stepped up behind me, clasped his hands behind his back, and bent forward slightly. "It is fine of you to have considered us human." He circled to the front of me. "We live in secret. Most do not kill for the sake of killing. But still, we are not accepted." He spread his hands wide. "As you, yourself, have shown."

I fought the lump in my throat. It was shock. I recognized my own symptoms: clammy hands, shallow breathing, eyes darting around looking for normalcy to bring back consciousness with what was familiar. "I'm sorry people don't accept you. Perhaps if they understood you'd do them no harm. You said no harm, right? Perhaps there could be willing victims for you, so they wouldn't be afraid." I was afraid and so not willing. I sat on a little wooden stool by the farthest wall of books. I couldn't escape if I wanted to.

"Out of curiosity, would you be willing? Would you let me roll you, a willing victim? You might like it." He was teasing or flirting, I wasn't sure. He squatted in front of me, gave me a cautious smile, and dipped his head to see my eyes. "Why must an affliction or disease cause fear? If I had leprosy, it would be contagious, HIV, AIDS, even the common cold." He lifted my chin with his finger again. "But I must purposely bring someone to be vampire."

"I take it you're a vampire, then?" I asked indifferently and surprised myself. I thought, *Drama!* "I've read a lot of vampire novels, you know. Stake 'em, wear a cross, whole nine yards." I peered up at him. "Is that what I'm supposed to do to get rid of you?"

He smiled and I actually looked for fangs. Lest ye forget, I bought a pair myself earlier. But I was disappointed.

I wasn't sure I could take anymore, but he hadn't bitten me so far. At least I didn't think he had. I hopped up, felt around my neck, and immediately felt like a fool. "Do you plan on biting me? Am I supposed to be food? Is that why I'm here?" I plopped on the stool again. I absolutely could not look at him. Not one piece of his body. He was taboo.

He leaned in enough for his hair to brush against my cheek. "As for biting you—since you asked for honesty, perhaps."

"Am I your victim tonight? You are going to kill me," I lamented.

"Do you plan on turning me?" My lip trembled, so I bit it hoping to hide the sudden attack of nerves plaguing my body.

He whispered, his lips feathers on my cheek. "*Non.* I wish to keep you as you are. Changing you is not necessary."

"Oh." My heart dropped. I pulled away.

"Disappointed?" Doug chided.

I frowned harder than necessary. "No, I mean, still he'll let me live, like, he likes me, for real?" I hadn't entertained the idea of being a vampire, but—why'd he choose me?

I turned to Gérard. "You haven't hypnotized me, have you?"

"Summer, I really like you. I really want you; I really do not want to kill you."

For whatever reason, I believed he had no intention of eating me. That in itself was a relief. Odd but true. Besides, they said my father entrusted me to him. God, I hoped they were right.

"I'm sorry, guys. Right now, vampires or not, you're still humans, and I need to have that part of you."

The two men glanced at each other.

"What?" I was plagued with nerves again. "What?" My voice got higher.

"Shall we—*euh*—go to your place? It is late." Gérard raised his eyebrows and nodded toward the doors.

"I didn't realize. Is it a problem?" The thought of us alone in the woods brought forth an instant phobia of the dark. I thought I was afraid of the dark before. This was a new fear.

"Not for me, Summer. Let me take you."

"I don't want to trouble you; I'm a big girl."

"And I am a gentleman who will walk his lady to her door."

"Ok," I said. Then I turned to Doug. "I really appreciate what you did at Brady's the other night. I'm sorry I didn't acknowledge you sooner."

"No worries, love," he said. He smiled that warm half-smile from before, winked, and slipped out the door.

Gérard held my finger and led me through the corridors and stairwells until we reached the main entrance. He bent to my ear and whispered, "My word, this night you are safe."

It was still dark, but the fog had set in, making visibility low. I huddled into myself from the chill, but the way the white mist hovered over the darkened water of Lake Sangre intrigued me.

An owl hooted in the distance and a black critter scampered along a stone wall that led to the back of the mansion. I hurried along the stone path with Gérard at my heels. He walked beside me through the woods though, assisting me when needed, but pretty much, we didn't talk, and he didn't try anything.

We finally reached the wood line on my side of the lake. The porch light was on and made it easier to find my keys. He waited beside me with his hands in his pockets. I was surprised because I was sure he would've at least kissed me. He never made a move. My heart heaved because it wasn't normal. I thought after walking me home, he would kiss me goodnight. Instead, he bowed and vanished.

I slipped inside the door, locked it, and perched in the rocker to look out the window at the sunrise over Lake Sangre and Gérard's mansion.

CHAPTER 10

Needless to say, the sun had set by the time I awoke, still in the rocker. At first, I thought I hadn't slept that long; then I glanced at the cable box. It was seven o'clock.

I was a responsible employee; never missed a shift. I needed to get my shit together. I scrambled to get the phone and picked it up from the table. I had one voicemail and two missed calls. I clicked through them and saw they were from the diner.

Reluctantly, I listened to the voicemail, which was from Tiny—surprise, surprise.

"Summer, take the day. You need it. Don't bother calling in. It's a freebie. We've got you covered."

Gale was in the background. "We love you."

Well, that settled it. I wasn't going in. I poured a bowl of bran flakes with almond milk, sat in the recliner, and pushed back to put my feet up. The cushion felt good against my sore muscles. I was used to exercise, but stairs and six miles of hiking were way out of my realm of normal activity.

I looked around my living room. I'd spent a lot of time reading horror novels and watching monster movies escaping reality. But what was reality? And how did I know there wasn't something in the cocoa? None of the others drank anything. Hallucinogenics could be slipped into beverages without people knowing. Was I a victim? Did any of it matter?

I asked myself, "What really changed?" The answer was: nothing. If these people practiced their ways before I knew, then why did it matter after they told me? Bi, gay, lesbian, vampire—so?

I finished the cereal and closed the recliner. I laid out a purple velour lounge suit. I hit the shower, did a quick once over with the razor and dried in front of the mirror. I looked straight on; sideways. I liked the side look better.

I slathered some peach lotion with vitamin E on my stomach to help the stretch marks and scars, which I was happy to see were barely visible. It took a whole year to get them to that point. I also slathered it on because the sweet faux peach scent stayed with me all day. It was not just sweet, but dessert like. I swear you could smell the cream and sugar. I loved that stuff.

I put black eyeliner on my lash lines and black eye shadow on my lids. A little wine-colored lipstick, a pinch of my cheeks and I was done. I put on a comfy bra, with a pair of white briefs, before the leisure suit. I was set. It was soft and warm.

The more I fussed, the more I felt like a victim.

I grabbed the hamper and went to the kitchen to throw my cooking uniforms in the washer. After that, I was going to get back to writing a cookbook I'd started. I was about ninety recipes in. I needed another dessert, so I left the hamper by the washer and opened the fridge.

There wasn't a whole lot in there.

I chose an egg, some strawberries, a plain yogurt, and the carton of orange juice. I grabbed my pink zebra striped journal and pink feather pen so I could record each step. But I didn't know where I was going with it.

I wound up putting the egg back and eating the yogurt with the berries and drank a glass of juice. I was bored. That in itself was new.

I sat in the rocker and watched the smoke rise from the chimneys across the lake. I thought about my life and my sister's death after she'd drowned in Black River. It was something I never stopped thinking about. How could she have been saved? Why was she on that horse, alone? What made it go in the water? She was eight years old. I never went horseback riding before I was ten. Why did they let her go? Since then, horses have brought on panic attacks. It destroyed my family—my life. A year later, my parents went missing. They were never found and were presumed dead. Well, my adopted parents. But Guillaume and Gérard said—nah.

I knew the school had field trips, but I wasn't allowed to go to Black River. It's part of my guilt. She was their real daughter. I wasn't afforded such luxuries. Instead, I got to watch. There were times I'd missed being an only child, but it wasn't wanted. I loved her. She was my best friend—my little sister.

Don't ever take that for granted.

I remembered the school called and said there was an accident, she'd been taken to the hospital. The teachers didn't know which one since there were three within driving distance. So, I wound up driving to the two furthest while my parents went to the closest. She was at the one they went to. Come to think of it, maybe they didn't want me there. Maybe they knew.

I thought about my ex-fiancé, Jesse, my first love. I questioned whether I really was in love with him. I never felt like I did around Gérard with him. Even Gérard's servant invoked more of an allure than Jesse ever had. Guess it didn't matter because I awoke one morning and Jesse was gone—no note, no phone call.

And none of this had anything to do with the preternatural. Then why was I so afraid of Gérard? Did I care about being turned into a vampire? Actually, I didn't. It would take away all the fear of illness and death. I won't lie; death frightens me, but not if it could give me my life and take away the worry. But what did I know?

I wondered how he got my gun.

I'd forgotten about the Ruger. In NY they license the pistol with the owner. I needed to get it back. I contemplated hiking over there. The pistol was expensive and if these visitors were a threat; I needed to protect myself.

I never liked the gun. I always liked the little derringers, but I needed something I knew had more than one shot. I had a muzzle-loader with fiber optic sites in the closet, but it wouldn't do much good against an attacker. I knew from experience that muzzleloaders needed practice and skill to bring down big game. I was out of practice.

I grew up in a family that hunted and grew their own food. We target practiced until we could hit a dime taped to a branch. I was a good shot. Better than good. My dad made sure of that. His philosophy was that if you couldn't hit the broad side of a barn, then you would maim an animal and cause it to suffer. To cause anything to suffer was against my father's nature.

I missed him. After all these years, the sorrow returned over the last few days. I thought I'd put it behind me, but I guess it stays with you—always.

His name was Augusto Candella, a true nature lover—a huntsman and gardener in both trade and personal aspects of his life. He always said to thank your kill for their sacrifice and to offer the entrails to the Lord of the Hunt to ensure a good hunt next time. Also, he believed in rebirth. He believed that the circle of life was a transference of energy. That when the animal died, its spirit became a part of you and whatever lie around it; be it the trees, bushes, grass, or even the earth beneath your feet.

For the longest time, as a child, I felt guilty for killing insects I had unintentionally stepped on. I stopped believing his fantastic ways when my sister died. Granted, it was a freak accident, but nonetheless, I stopped thinking about death and engrossed myself in science fiction and things that made me busy.

I guess I felt guilty because, before they disappeared, my parents not only lost my sister; they lost me. I stopped hunting, hiking, and target practicing. I spent my time reading and cooking. I conjured up all kinds of recipes. Some were good, some weren't. I wasn't the Summer they needed. But they weren't the parents I knew and loved, either.

My father stopped hunting. My mother stopped cooking. They spent all their time in the woods, hiking, searching. Just like the night they disappeared. I saw my mother fall. I saw my father beside her. I knew where they were because I followed them. I wanted to know because I loved them.

Why, after Sheena died, did they stop loving me? What were they looking for? Why didn't I try to help them? I ran to Gale, but I couldn't tell her what really happened. There was darkness and pain, and then they were down. Was I really the reason Sheena died? I never did figure out what they were looking for.

A shadow over the lake drew me back to the present. I peeked out the side of the curtains and saw Gérard beneath the window—waiting.

I unlocked the door and poked my head out. "Wouldn't knocking be easier?"

"*Oui.*"

"You want to come in?"

"I have something of yours." He stepped on the top step and presented the Ruger to me. "Do you want me to stay?"

"Yeah, actually I do." Not only could he cure my boredom, which turned to a healthy dose of depression, but I felt better knowing he was there. Odd. Besides, I had questions.

I opened the door wider, took the gun, and slipped it inside the buffet drawer. He stepped through and stooped to take his boots off. They were black leather ankle boots with silver zippers. He had black socks and soft black pants and a white sweater. He looked warm. I realized—I was cold. I forgot to shut the door. He reached over and pushed it closed.

I always dreamed of having a vampire boyfriend, usually out of a book or movie, but the chance for a real one was standing in my living room with the bluest eyes. I thought maybe I shouldn't be looking at his eyes so much.

"I'm glad you came over tonight."

He stepped forward and lifted my hand. The tingling sensation he sent was softer, less noticeable. It wasn't as strong as the other times, but still nice. I folded my lips in and pinched them together. God forbid I should open my mouth; some ignorant comment was sure to fly out. *Oh my God! Should I be thinking of deities around him or using their names in vain?*

He smiled, showing those beautiful white teeth. This time, with the barest of fangs.

Fear flashed through my core, but dissipated as quickly as it came. "Tease," I chided. "If you won't finish what you've started, then I would suggest not doing anymore of whatever it is you are doing." I was flirting. I never flirted. Why not? He started it.

"Ah, with successful patience, there is reward. *Mais*, for now, enjoy yourself. I know I am."

I tossed my hair over my shoulder and flashed a sinister smile; he visibly shuddered. I wondered if he had to do it intentionally. Come to think of it, I hadn't seen him do a lot of human gestures. Damn, I reprimanded myself. *Christ. Oh, shit! There I go again. He's still human. And maybe I shouldn't be thinking about damning anything. Was he damned? I said Christ!*

I threw my hand over my mouth, even though I hadn't spoken aloud, and hastened to the kitchen and grabbed a glass of water. I didn't know whether to offer him a glass or my neck. What was appropriate etiquette for having a vampire for a house guest? I dumped the water down the drain, put the glass on the side, and slipped past him to the living room.

I didn't know where to sit. I glanced around and spotted a little vampire I'd taped to the mirror over the buffet. The couch put us too close. The rocker or recliner would be too evasive. I sat on the floor in front of the couch, which would put his back to the mirror. That worked. I made a mental note to get rid of the little vamp.

"Gérard?" I whispered.

He sighed, and ran his hand through his hair, drawing a lone curly lock forward. I looked away. "You let me into your mind, at Brady's, when you saw the power in my eyes."

"I didn't feel anything." I shifted my focus from his boots to the floor; I tried to figure out when he did it.

"You would not know unless I want you to. Then, *ma chérie*, you will know." The excitement raced through me and caught my breath. His foot appeared in front of me; I flinched. "Only a taste, Summer."

I bent my knees and locked them in place. "What do you mean?"

He knelt before me and clasped my hands in his; the tingling flowed through me. Sensations of being caressed turned inward. I shivered.

He let go.

I inspected my hands; no marks, though mine were clammy, his were dry. *Shouldn't he be cold?*

"You like it, *oui?*" He winked.

I turned my hands over and studied them. They looked normal. My insides leapt with a desire I hadn't felt since we'd danced. But an attack of nerves struck.

A smirk played at the corners of his mouth while he spoke. "Ah, you are lovely and assuredly unscathed. I would bring you much pleasure, but not tonight, for you have said that you still want to get to know me."

He slid off his heels and pulled his knees to his chest to mimic my own pose. He wrapped his arms around them, clasping his wrist in one hand. It wasn't threatening, but with the couch at my back and him in front of me, I felt cornered. I got sick in my stomach. A slow achy burn. I tucked my head in so I couldn't see him.

He stood and whispered, "Your silence suggests that perhaps I should leave."

I peered up at him; his eyes engulfed in sapphire flames. "I—I don't know what to say." I sat up, cross-legged, and ran a finger along the cuff of his pants. They were soft. "I don't want you to go, but I don't know how to act."

He clasped my finger and stood, pulling me with him.

"I'm scared, Gérard." I frowned at him. "I don't want to be."

"I know."

"It's more than you." I thought about that. It was true. "I'm afraid, in general. I mean, my world changed in the matter of a few hours. How do I make it normal? How do I make it feel right?" I searched his eyes, pleading for some wisdom I wasn't certain he could offer.

"*Apprenez-vous*." He smiled, no teeth. "Learn. Learn all you are able. Not in a book, but by talking. Ask anything you wish. My Douglas, Gale, we are all you need. Your world did not change, *mais*—your knowledge—*oui*."

"Gale said to ask the right questions. Guess she was sayin' the same thing in her own way."

"Come."

He put his boots on and opened the front door. I grabbed a pink poncho and slipped a pair of white sneakers on before stepping outside. He turned the lights off, had somehow gotten my keys, and locked the door.

"*Maintenant*, I would like to show you my home, without the guests this time."

"I'd like that. But no biting, right?" I laughed nervously.

"I would hope you would not bite. It is not in your nature." He winked again, offered a crooked smile, and scooped me into his arms. He was strong and solid. I held on with all I had and buried my head in his chest. He leapt, and we flew across the lake toward the mansion.

We landed at the main entrance, where cement grotesques guarded the enchanted, or damned, residents within. I forced the thought from my mind.

He opened the double doors and led me through the left archway. When I passed the Chinese vase, a thought occurred to me.

"So, how old are you? For real this time."

"Hmm, I will say that I remember the third crusade well. I find it easier to calculate my age with every century in *Mount Mort*.

Although at my turning, I was thirty-two. That was about a hundred years before I came to North America."

"No shit!"

He turned away, avoiding a hurtful reprise. It reminded me to think before I spoke. "Sorry, I didn't think anyone could be so— old."

"And why would you, Summer?"

He opened the doors to the library again. This time I sat on the hearth like Dani had done. There was a black hand-crafted mug with a pewter shield or crest. It had a tiny dragon, rose, and wolf embossed in the three sections. And nearing the brim was the creamy steaming cocoa and a silver pot of cinnamon on a matching tray by the fire.

"You gonna join me this time?"

He sat at the little table set. "*Non.*"

"Don't turn away. I find what you are and what you do to be interesting, if not fascinating. I haven't met any others, but you gave me your word—you won't hurt me." I picked up the mug. "Hell, you won't even finish my good time." I peered through the steam, catching his gaze. "This cocoa isn't cooling me, you know."

"Ah, *ma chérie*. You still know naught." He put his hands over his eyes, leaning his elbows on the table. "You are—beautiful."

"I don't feel it. I feel like a fry cook spinster. So, we both have self-esteem issues. Now what?" I fought the urge to touch him; unsure if he'd want me to.

"Perhaps we will do well for one another. You speak the truth." He straightened and rolled his sleeves. "I will join you with my Douglas."

My heart dropped. I wasn't prepared to see Doug. Why did I even care? He was hot, but like, really? I had to be insane to feel that way with a man like Gérard to call mine. Shit. And two vamps at once? I meant in the same room, not that way.

"Well, that'll do it." My mug shook as I took a sip. "I have to warn you, I don't take blood well. I mean, I don't faint, but sometimes I get—queasy."

"Ah, not so wonderful." He took the mug from my hand and set it on the table. He took a tiny spoon, sprinkled cinnamon atop, and handed it back to me.

"I don't care. I asked you to join me; I'm still willing."

He smirked, and a small swirl of stars captured my attention. "I wish for you to see what I am, and that is . . ."

"My master," Doug said. He appeared in the doorway and took his spot against the closed wooden door again. "He feeds from me, but you probably had that figured out." He winked.

No, the understanding was lost on me. "So, you're not a vamp, then?"

Doug smiled a full warm smile with a glimpse of teeth, and shook his head to say, "No."

I glanced back at Gérard. "I'll enjoy my cocoa while you enjoy Doug, then." What did I just say? My brain did not agree with my words.

"Our guest is merely curious." He circled behind the chair, patting the back. "*Reposez-vous.*"

"Yes, Sir. But . . ."

"*Mon ami*, do you not agree, she needs to see what I am?"

Doug wriggled his eyebrows at me. I think he liked the idea of being watched. "As you wish."

The earlier talk didn't hit home, the flying did, but this was as surreal as it could get. It was the final nail in the coffin, no pun intended. I couldn't deny it. What I was about to witness would surpass everything they said. Knowing the way I felt about Gérard, and the promises he made, raised a panic that caused my chest to tighten.

Doug lifted my hand, which he sniffed, and smiled at Gérard. "Not yet."

Gérard looped his arm through Doug's and glided to the door. It opened to reveal a tall, slender woman. All I could see was long black hair as she peeked through to get a look at me. Doug guided her back to the hallway.

Gérard closed the door and spread his hands wide. "You see, I am simply a man. Are you still afraid?"

I took a moment to mull that over. Was I? Maybe. But more because I thought about what it would be like to be in Doug's place; realizing I wanted it. "Yes." Truth be told, I felt like a child on Christmas Eve. You didn't know what you were going to get, but you knew it was something special. "I guess I feel better." I lied.

"*Magnifique, ma chérie.* I want to show you more of my home." He straightened and waited for me with his hand held out. I took it as he led me on a tour of the main floor. There were stained- glass windows, a ballroom, and a dining hall. Everything you'd expect in a castle. It scared me more. Money. Master. He had to have power, to have those things. I wasn't stupid. And he knew I wasn't. I leaned my forehead against the cool stone wall for clarity. The coolness kept the panic at bay.

"Perhaps a little air would serve you well."

"Nah, I'm good."

"I want to show you something. Since you find me interesting, then perhaps this will be of interest for you as well."

"What?"

"The mount."

The thought of going to a cemetery at night scared me more than anything else that evening. Maybe the old tourist rumor was just that, but I questioned it. The cemetery also reminded me of my parents. Until the other day, I hadn't been up there since my sister's funeral. I wasn't sure I was ready to do it again. Was I willing to face more fears? Or would he lay them to rest?

CHAPTER 11

I held onto Gérard as we strolled to a clearing in the forest next to his limo. It was a short drive to the secondary that led to the pinnacle of the mount. When we got there, dread set in.

"Summer?" He wound his arms around me and pulled me close on the seat.

Guillaume's words haunted my thoughts. *Distance yourself from him.* I fought to ignore them. "The church doesn't look like a church anymore. From below, it always looks like a church. I could have sworn it was. I can't remember." I shook my head, trying to make it right. "My father made this?"

He smoothed the prickled hairs on my arms as he lowered his face to my hair. "Do you wish to leave?"

"No," I lied.

Before I was ready, he opened the door and stepped out. He offered his hand. I took it.

"Allow me to introduce you to the part of your father you never knew." He kept a step ahead, his hand squeezed slightly.

We climbed up the small stairway to the church entrance; the weathered door creaked open. I stepped through. The building looked to be in good shape, solid and sturdy. Pews and an altar shone in the moonlight. A small fireplace in the front of the building had a number of strange symbols drawn on alternating stones. I was drawn to it but fought the urge and pulled him after me as I rushed out of the building. The large stones that made up the walls pulsed in throbbing shadows against the blackening sky.

"Are those runes?" I knew the cold of the night wasn't enough to cause the cold I felt deep in my bones.

"I am afraid my knowledge of witchcraft is limited. Perhaps that is a question for Gale." He smiled. The moonlight glinted on his fangs. The effect made the hair on my arms stand on end, painfully.

"There's a garden in the back." I'd just remembered that. "My father planted it with me. I was too young to remember exactly. But it was by the gates." I scrambled along the crumbling sidewalk intent on finding it. However, a large monument with foreign words stood in its stead. "But I remember; he knelt in the dirt—here." I pointed. "I'd had flowers."

"Let me show you something. It has great meaning to many of us here." He stepped in the pile of crumbled cement, reaching his hand out for me. "And you."

"Okay." I went back to him, but my thoughts were clouded. I'd seen my father on his knees with a spade. I was standing beside him in my little red sneakers. I was in the dirt. But the image faded. The red turned grey, and the memory was lost. I couldn't tell whether it was fear or the place. It had never happened to me before.

The driver came from the limo with a heavy black cloak. Gérard placed it over my shoulders. He held it in place by putting his arm around me while we walked through the path of gravestones. The ground was soft and squished under my feet.

"Do you feel better now, *ma chérie?*"

"No."

"Are you certain you do not wish to leave?" There was no emotion behind his question.

"No, but I want to see whatever it is."

"As you wish." He held me a little tighter, guiding me to a mausoleum overtaken by ivy and moss. "This was mine."

I clutched the collar of the cloak in my fist, ducking away from him. "You mean you died here?" What did I just ask? I knew I was scared, but stupidity had no excuses.

He pressed his hand to the dark stone façade. "At one time it was so."

"I just meant, how is this yours?"

"Ah, do not shy away from what I am." He looked down at me from the step, like he was reading my mind. "You know now what I am, Summer. It is here where I served my repose. At the time, I thought it necessary." He scanned the grounds and stones. "Shall we go? I do not believe you are ready for all of this tonight. We will come again when you are."

"I am cold." I shivered, but tried to hide it, but couldn't. "One day, I hope you'll trust me enough to share your regrets. I don't fault you for keeping those memories and reasons private. Lord knows I have a basket full of my own."

He pressed his nose to my cheek and led me away from the crypt, through the headstones. I purposely avoided my sister's and believed I'd seen enough, until I noticed a clearing between his mausoleum and the church.

I stopped in awe of the view. You could see for miles, the entire valley.

"*Oui*, it is all of Mount Mort, *ma chérie*. Beautiful, *non?*"

"I never knew." The lights twinkled in the distance, and it dawned on me. "The legend says he used his own blood with the dragon's to seal the unsettled souls, to protect the founders before they came." I stepped up on a stone that protruded from the leaves for a better view. "It's not much different from the legend of Mount Mort. Just that it got its nickname from the slaughter of the Norse people. I mean, obviously, since Sangre is for blood and Mort is for death. But the anniversary isn't for any of that." I turned around to face him full on. "Tiny called this a sanctuary. He wasn't kidding, was he?"

"In time, Summer."

I shivered and clasped the cloak tighter. A week ago, I'd have said I had no patience left, but that was before. My curiosity was satisfied with the promise of an answer. When didn't matter. With Gérard it seemed like time didn't matter. In an odd way, I liked that.

"Will you stay tonight? I will arrange to have night clothes ready for you." He gave a weak smile and bowed his head to meet my eyes. "I will behave. It has been too long since I have had someone to hold."

He looked out at the twinkling lights in the valley; his eyes flickered with illuminated shades of blue. The mountain breeze tousled the curls around his face. The mass was not unlike that of a wild horse's mane. As the locks blew across his face, I realized I wasn't in some fantastical scene. I didn't know what he could do; would do. I still knew nothing about him. And yet, I was drawn to him. I wanted him. He watched me from the corner of his eye. I think he was still waiting for me to run, screaming.

"Although a wonderful offer, I should go home." I didn't want to be too forward, although I wanted to go with him. "Would you be my escort home instead?"

"I would be honored. When you are ready, my offer stands." He bowed and caught me by surprise when he wrapped me in his arms. "Come. You need warmth." We hurried toward the limo.

It seemed like a much shorter ride to my house than it was to the mount. The limo driver opened the door for us and stepped aside. Gérard let me take the lead up the stairs until he noticed the door was ajar. He tucked me behind him and entered the house.

"Wait here."

"I don't like this. I don't like this at all." I followed him.

I crept toward the bedroom. A stale wetness burned my throat. I made my way into the bathroom; the odor was definitely in the bedroom. I hurried back out and caught a flicker of light outside the circular window. I screamed.

Gérard gripped my shoulders a heartbeat after. Even though I didn't know what a real vampire was, I was impressed by him. None of the townsfolk ever showed so much unnatural behavior.

He stood, breathless in the living room, one brow raised in my direction. "I thought you were to wait outside."

I stepped up to him, staring at his reflection in the window behind him. Guess that answered that. "Yeah, well, anyway, I hope it's not too forward, but I would like to take you up on your earlier offer. I mean, if it still stands." I was so damned nervous my lips quavered my words. I wasn't ready to trust a man. But that damned barrier had TNT jammed in all the little cracks he'd made at Brady's. The mental wall was coming down, whether I liked it or not. I accepted his offer because of fear. Fear caused dependency and dependency was not something I was willing to allow back in my life. He may have planted the dynamite, but I was determined to snip the line before it exploded into something I wasn't ready for. But for one night, I'd let the fuse smolder.

"You mean to stay the day?" The blank expression on his face was betrayed by the shock in his voice.

"Yes, if that's okay. I mean . . . Oh, no! It wasn't a real offer, was it?"

His shoulders softened; the human side returned. He rubbed his hands over my arms. "Ah, *ma chérie*, the offer was most real. Get what you need if you like; *quoique* I am certain I will be able to accommodate you in every way. I will even have cinnamon coffee for you in the morning."

"Thank you," I said, turning to go back to grab my things, but the mirror over the buffet reflected yellow eyes from the darkened room. I grabbed Gérard, tucked into his arm, and buried my face.

He pulled me to the stairs and leapt, his arms wrapped around me, my legs around him. His voice calmed me, even though the words should have made me more afraid. "I summoned my Douglas. He will secure your house and assign guards to the perimeter."

We landed outside the mansion doors, but this time, he didn't let me go.

"Gérard?"

"Mmmm?" He listened and studied the stairway to the main entrance; his was perfectly still and expressionless.

"Why the sudden interest in me? No one ever wanted me before. Why now? You, Guillaume, and whoever was in the house. Guillaume told me I would be baited." I took a deep breath and looked out at the forest behind us. "Are you doing that now?"

"I wish to keep you from harm. I will not make you mine if you do not wish it to be." He rubbed his cheek against my hair. "Do you like roses, Summer?"

"I do. Why do you ask?" It was an odd question for the moment.

"You will learn much as we court. Your own secrets will surface, as will your desires." He smiled, folding his bottom lip. "Roses are my favorite flower."

"Did you plant the rosebush by my house?"

"*Non, ma chérie.*" He searched my face. The lines across his forehead melted away, leaving behind the perfection to which I'd never be accustomed.

"It matters, *mais*, in time you will understand. Not all is cause for alarm."

"I believe you. I don't know why, but I do."

My stomach ached at the realization—someone was trying to sabotage the little life I had built and the happiness I finally found. But my father always said, "Beware of happiness, for happiness always comes with a cost."

I wrapped my arms around his neck a little tighter and breathed in the cool air as he whisked me up the stairs. I knew, somehow, that Doug would be waiting. That, for the evening, Gérard would keep me safe. And that Guillaume didn't lie—someone was after me, and my dad was right about everything.

CHAPTER 12

The white-haired DJ Liam stood at the entrance with the door open. Gérard didn't stop. Instead, he hoisted me over his shoulder and went through the left archway to an unlit stairwell that led down to what I thought was the basement.

"What the hell, Gérard!"

My stomach ached from the descent. Pressure from my weight pressing against his shoulder rendered me speechless.

We went down what seemed to be a hundred steps until he set me on my feet.

"Please, tell me why?" I screeched and latched onto him. The tears finally came.

"It is not as you believe." He unwrapped my hands from his neck, unlocked a solid wooden door, and glided with me to a small salon. He clasped my hands and lowered his eyes to mine, his voice soft, barely a whisper. "This is where you shall stay." He pressed his finger to his lips and gestured to his ear, then pointed up. He stepped closer and forced me further into the room. "Summer, if nothing else, please remember my intent has and always will be to keep you safe. It will always come first, though you may not understand what comes. I assure you this night, that it is my reigning conviction."

He closed the stairwell door before leading me through a set of wooden double doors that opened to a room aglow with candlelight.

The candlelit room was huge, to say the least. The walls were covered with long drapes alternating between royal blue and black velvet. There was a large chandelier with hanging silver and crystal pieces. The lights were tear drop shards of crystal alight with fire. Breathtaking didn't come close to the effect the piece gave.

To the far left was a petite ebony vanity with an oval silver trimmed mirror, and a royal blue velvet cushioned stool that matched the walls. To the far right was an ebony wardrobe with silver drawer pulls and cabinet handles shaped like roses. The theme was repeated as I looked over an enormous canopy bed.

The tops of the four posts had a silver rose that matched the headboard adorned with even more roses etched in silver. There were more pillows than I knew what to do with. They varied in being royal blue, black, and silver, and all velvet with silk cord. To top it off, there was a puffy comforter done in a checkerboard of royal blue, black, and silver accented by a matching blue canopy.

The fabric on the walls parted to reveal a single black door with silver hinges and a crystal doorknob. The black carpet was flecked with silver.

"What is this place? Please tell me I'm not a captive."

"It is a haven, Summer. You are not a prisoner. *Maintenant*, you will find night clothes in the wardrobe, and the bathroom is through the door." He kissed my forehead, as a mother would to a child. "I will leave you now. I may change as well." And like that, he was gone.

An ankle length burgundy gown that had a low V-neck and spaghetti straps was the most conservative of the choices in the wardrobe. Taking it with me, I stopped on the threshold inside the draped door and paused, breathless.

The pinnacle of the space was most definitely the bathroom. I followed the carpet, which continued to the edge of a black marble tub with a spout that was a silver rose that curved over the edge with another rose on each side. I assumed they were the knobs.

Two steps led to the carpeted landing that housed the tub and what seemed like a hundred candles. The flames danced in the mirrors that lined the walls and ceiling.

A smaller version of the bedroom's chandelier hung in the middle of the room. To the right was a large black marble counter with double sinks and silver faucet sets to match those on the bath. The same theme was carried through with the toilet and bidet.

A small basket waited on the counter with a note scented with exotic spices; like him.

Ma chérie,

I hope all is to your liking. Please find the necessary toiletries you may be missing from your home.

Je t'aime,

Gérard

My heart caught in my throat. Had he planned to keep me? I trusted him, Gale trusted him, hell, they all trusted him. I took a calming breath when a soft knock on the door brought me back to my senses.

"Ma chérie?"

"I'll be right out." I pulled on the gown and opened the door I didn't remember closing.

Gérard was stretched across the bed with his back to the main doors. He had turned the duvet down already. "Did you find all you required?"

"I did. Thank you." As I spoke, he slid off the bed and glided toward me. My heart pounded. I trembled and took a step back, stumbling over a chaise moderne I hadn't seen. Take a guess—the chaise was black velvet.

He stopped for a moment and then stalked toward me with one careful step in front of the other. His movements were fluid, like a trained dancer. "The fear is great; the beat of your heart—it races. Are you well?"

"I'm fine." My mouth went dry. I fought not to look at him.

"Ah," he hummed, with a soft chuckle. "Perhaps I know." He appeared instantly at my side.

He donned a pair of silver silk pajama pants. His skin had a pale golden hue, and his hair brushed the top of the pants. He swept it to one side and allowed his eyes to mix with the colors of the room.

The most terrific smile was outlined with strawberry pink lips that made things low inside of me ache. I wanted him with more than lust this time. I was falling for him.

He bent over to cup his hands under my chin and lifted my face so that our eyes met. Tears streamed down my face and my body quivered. He was so beautiful—I had to cry.

With his face lowered to mine, he brushed his lips along my own. He kissed me with small, soft passes, and then parted his lips, his tongue—soft and warm. I opened for him.

He lifted me effortlessly from the chaise, laid me on the sheets, and positioned himself on top. Kissing a little harder, he slid his hands up my bare arms until he reached my wrists and pinned them gently to the bed—his weight suspended over my body. I wanted, no, needed, him.

Before I knew what happened, he slid off to the side and propped himself up on one arm, looking at me with a sinister smile.

"I have not affected a woman like this in over a century. You are lovely, *ma chérie.*"

He rolled me over; spooned against me and traced down my body until he slid his arm in front of my hips. Snuggled into his warmth, I felt the familiar tingling of his power except this time—it wasn't pleasure I felt, but safety.

He pulled the comforter over us. His voice seemed to whisper inside me, "Sleep, *ma chérie.*"

"No," I fought. "I need answers."

The next time I opened my eyes, I was alone. The room was dark except for a soft white glow from a candle reflecting in the mirror on the vanity. There was also a white fox asleep on the chaise. I brushed back the covers and went into the bathroom.

After I'd brushed my teeth, I went back into the bedroom to find last night's clothes when the fox leapt off the chaise and turned into a woman. I sat on the floor, not bothering to move. Not knowing if I should.

"Sure, why not?" I said to myself.

She still had the creature's amethyst eyes, but her hair was long and onyx. The white fur of the fox was nowhere to be seen, though her skin was fair, and she was thin, delicate. The woman was a decent half a foot taller than me.

Needless to say, as a fox she wasn't wearing any clothes, and now standing as a human, she wasn't either. It should have been more awkward than it was, but nudity was nothing compared to the week I was having.

"Gérard said to stay with you." She went to the wardrobe and pulled on a red silk robe.

"Until he rises at dusk?"

She frowned. "It's already evening. He was waiting for you."

"I can't find my clothes." I stayed put. Should I be afraid? Why did I stay there? I knew better.

"What about the clothes in here?" She pointed to the wardrobe. "Wilma took yours to the washroom." She smiled. "Gérard wants you to meet some of his people tonight. They're important." She dropped her eyes and backed to the door. "I'm sorry. I should go."

"Wait." I wanted her to stay. "My name's Summer."

She laughed. "Of course, we all know you."

"No kidding."

"Call me Kitty."

I nodded.

"Before you ask, no, I am not a shifter. I am Kitsune, so naturally, everyone calls me Kitty."

Guess I wouldn't be the first to think before they speak. Talk about worries of discrimination or being politically incorrect, this added a whole new level. "It's a pretty name. Nice to meet you."

She squinted at me. "Thanks." I missed something.

I ventured to the wardrobe since she stood there holding the door open. There were no real clothes. I checked the drawers and didn't find any jeans or sweaters.

"Elegant, aren't they?" I swear she purred as she rubbed the silk robe.

"Yeah, but they're good clothes."

"And why wouldn't they be?"

I sighed.

She chose a pair of black velour slacks and an antique white camisole with a black cashmere sweater and handed them to me. Luckily, Gérard had the crew that staked out my house bring my bras. I was too endowed to wear the ones in the wardrobe.

After dressing, she showed me the dress Gérard chose for the evening. It was black velvet from the waist down, with a white satin beaded bodice, and long lace sleeves. The neckline dipped to a V-neck; the back was all eye hooks. Great for exaggerated cleavage. Damn.

There was a selection of footwear, from black lace ankle boots with three-inch heels to black patent leather flats. I chose the lace ankle boots to go with the sleeves. They would give me a little height since Gérard was about a foot taller than me.

"Why do I need to do this, anyway?" I asked.

"'Because Gérard wants you to."

"Well, I have to work."

"Oh, you won't be going in. Doug already called Tiny."

"What did he say? Tiny's expecting me. There's supposed to be another group coming." I shuddered, like a kid about to get in trouble. "Is he mad?"

"Trust me, Tiny's fine. He said he already got some help."

"Who? He said he'd talk to me about getting help, but this soon?" My mouth went dry. "Do you know who?"

"Samuel something." She bowed her head to me. "You need to stop or you'll make yourself sick. Gérard'll take care of it if he has to."

"I don't even know of a Samuel here."

She shrugged. "Well, he started this morning."

Kitty slid into a white knit dress, an over-sized cow neck sweater of sorts, when the woman I'd glimpsed in the library lolled into the bedroom. Her straight black hair fell past her waist and accentuated a tight red leather miniskirt that came to the bottom of her cheeks. To add to this charming skirt, she wore black fishnet stockings, a pair of thigh high lace up patent leather boots with a four-inch heel, and a black fishnet tank top—nothing underneath.

I was embarrassed just looking at her. It was like trying not to look made you want to look. I had to give her credit; she had guts to wear that in front of people. She floated, or glided, or whatever across the room to where I stood and smiled a healthy, warm smile. It didn't fit the ensemble.

Her face was well tanned, her eyes grey like slate. Her lips held the same strawberry pink I'd noticed on Gérard. I expected her to be super bitch or something.

I said, "I'm Summer. We almost met the other night, in the library."

She threw her head back and laughed like a maniacal child, delighted with torturing a new toy. "I know exactly who you are. I also know why you're here. I'm insulted." She spoke in a thick Romanian accent. A sudden coldness settled in the room as she turned and glanced over her shoulder at me. "But Gérard will choose whatever he wants. All women like the games at first."

"What the hell? I don't even know you."

"You want to see the monsters, but do you really want to play? I've made the bravest men piss where they stand. I'm proud of what I am. I don't want your pity."

"None offered." If I'd possessed any abilities, I would have given her a glare to turn her to stone. But I didn't. "I'm not afraid of you."

She laughed, demeaning. "I am not the one to fear, I promise.

But, Gérard, he likes playing the games. Now what do you suppose he wants with you?"

I should have stopped, but my big mouth had a mind of its own. "Are we jealous because Gérard chose a human over a shallow bitch like you?"

She stepped closer. I stood my ground. Anger and fear flowed up my neck, my hands trembled. I folded my arms.

The door opened, and Doug walked through—hair damp, towel dried and smelling like fresh cologne. I tried not to peek at the exposed morsel of chest beneath his red terry bathrobe. His chestnut locks were tied back in a small ponytail. His eyes were a warm amber. As he walked into the room, a rush of heat washed over me.

I wanted to turn away, but I couldn't move. I wanted to run. I wanted to hide. The bitch and Kitty felt it too because Kitty curled up in the chaise and the bitch was backed against the wardrobe holding herself. Doug took a seat on the edge of the bed. I got nauseous.

Gérard glided into the room and, without seeing him move from the doorway, was suddenly standing in front of the bitch; his eyes filled with blue fire. The flames danced; no words spoken. I ran to the bathroom but stopped when she screamed and collapsed on the floor. She put her hands up to her face. "Please, Master. I have not hurt her. Please stop this. I apologize."

"*Oui, mais*, Patricia, Summer is my guest and is thus our guest. She is to be kept safe. I will not accept otherwise. Do not forget." He spoke low, his voice scolded.

Patricia scrambled to her feet, sobbing. She ran from the bedroom without stumbling in those ridiculous boots. As soon as she was gone, Kitty slipped through the door, and Doug took a new position on the chaise after he closed the door.

"*Ah, ma chérie,* I apologize for Patricia's rude behavior. I have given you my word, you will be safe, and they assure it." The anger in Gérard's voice quieted, as did the fire in his eyes. I wasn't sure what I should do, so I stayed put. "She intended no harm."

"What will you do to her?" Did I really want to know how to punish his people? Why not?

"I will not suffer her to a cruel fate as you imagine. Much to your dismay," he smiled. "She will join us this evening."

"No silver? Then again, everything in this place has silver." Again, stating the obvious, but it made no sense.

"All you see is platinum," Doug informed. "The silver myth is fact; if it pierces our flesh, it is tough to heal, meaning vamps and lycans. But it won't kill us."

"But that's insane! Platinum is like-wait, lycan?"

"It is not an issue here, Summer," Doug explained. "We've been 'round a long time, and as you see," he pointed around the room, "we are not poor."

"Let us remain humble," Gérard interrupted.

"Agreed," Doug said.

I shook my head. "Ok, back to the witch."

"No, not a witch," Doug corrected.

"I didn't mean a witch witch, but rather a witch with a capital 'B'." They stared at me. "Forget it. Just tell me why she tried to scare me? Might I add, she was doing a great job of it when Doug came in."

"It was not all my Patricia." Gérard tucked his hair behind his ear. I figured it was a nervous habit. "I am unable to answer you at this time. Perhaps some was my power. I am vampire; you must understand what I am."

"Correction, sir—a master vampire." Doug raised an eyebrow as he looked at Gérard, and then at me. "It is quite different in comparison with Patricia."

"As interesting as all this is, I'm still not afraid of her. It's almost exciting." My head started to pound behind my left eye. I needed to eat—food. "I couldn't care less what you do to her. She hasn't earned my respect."

Gérard eyed me, the flames gone, and left behind a sea of blue. "You are most curious." His voice dropped to a whisper. "Which brings me to Douglas." He glanced toward the chaise and nodded at Doug before stretching across the bed.

Doug appeared before me. I hadn't seen him move. "Well, I'm Doug, obviously. We finally meet, formally." He lifted my hand to rub over his chin. The stubble was rough but nice. "I've awaited the right moment to do this."

"Tell her, *mon ami*. I must go." Gérard bowed before me and breathed over my wrist. "Until full dark."

Doug nodded. "Consider it done."

"She must know, as I am taken by her." After that, Gérard was gone.

Doug patted the chaise for me to sit.

I sat on the edge of the bed, reluctant to learn whatever he could possibly have to share.

"Summer, love, 'tis a great deal to take in with the last week." His English accent was thick and reminded me of my father.

"True, but after last night . . ."

"Uh, uh, you must listen. As I said, it 'as been a lot to learn, but time hastens." He stood in front of me and leaned against the bedpost, arms folded. "You eavesdropped in the hall."

I fought the urge to squirm. "Sorry about that. I . . ."

He cut me off, "No excuses. You hadn't known about Gérard, and you most certainly wouldn't have known about me. But, for future reference, try to remember that you can't sneak around us. We feel your presence, smell you, hear you; it's pointless."

"I won't." I tucked my feet under me. Having him standing there, arms folded, leaning against the thin post, was hot as hell. I tried not to look at him.

"I've been here a long time, Summer. Longer than you are old. But the reason I'm here is not to go over my history or even enlighten you with vamp etiquette, but rather, to do something that frightens me terribly."

I didn't like that. "Then don't."

"Gérard has left me no choice. He offered himself, and now I am offering you knowledge that you never sought—a secret of my own. But know that it was never my intent to do other than protect you."

"What do you mean?"

"It was before the anniversary. I had to keep the outsiders from the cemetery, as our master's repose was upon us."

He went to the door and brought back a tray with orange juice. After handing it to me, he continued. "I went to Watertown to ride the bus back to Mount Mort, in my human form, of course. I posed as a tourist. It was easy because it had been too long for the outsiders to remember me. I was virtually a stranger. Anyway, I am the lost tourist." He bowed.

I sipped the juice.

The entire time he spoke, each time we met, I tried to figure out where I knew him from. The newspaper wasn't it.

After a long hesitation, and an uneasy breath, he looked at me; his eyes flashed amber sparks. "I watched over someone, someone special. I guarded her with my life."

"Me?" I more sought affirmation than questioned.

"Drink. It will help your headache." He raised his hand to stop me before I said anymore. "I watched over you. This may be the last you speak with me. He looked away. "I'm sorry, Summer."

"For what? You didn't do anything."

He turned back to face me. "I saw your reaction to the others. I know how you felt."

"Yeah, but I'm sort of seasoned now."

He spread his arms and the robe fell open; a waft of cologne rich in pepper, citrus, ambergris, and cedar engulfed the bed space. The red accented the black slacks, and the scent distracted me for a heartbeat. He appeared on the bed behind me, tucked my hair behind my ear, and whispered, "I'm your stray."

I chugged the juice, set the glass on the bed, and physically pinched my lips shut. He breathed small, shallow breaths. Already faced with such absurdities, I felt responsible for his self-consciousness.

"My stray?" I mumbled.

He slid his hands down my arms. I looked at the floor. "I was comfortable around you." His chin brushed my shoulder. "I urged Gérard to awaken early, to introduce you."

I happened to think of the real estate agent. The house wasn't for sale. Doug was there all along. "So why go through the ruse with the house?"

"Through Gérard, you will learn the rest. However, please try to understand, at no time had any of us meant to mislead you. I know Gale spoke to Gérard because he was reluctant to meet with you. We've all played a part in your introduction, Summer. But the rest is up to you." He smiled wide, his teeth even and white.

"You make a cute couple." Kitty appeared in the doorway.

"What?" I choked.

"Doug, it would be best to show her the way upstairs, so she doesn't feel cooped up."

"Agreed," he said. Kitty left content. He turned his attention back to me. "Not going to say anything?"

"If you were my stray, then you know—a lot." I thought about how much. "Most likely more than I ever wanted anyone to know." I paused to choose my words, mainly because I needed to digest the complexity of the situation. "I don't know how to handle that right now. Looking at an animal is a lot different than facing a person who knows your secrets."

He slid around me and stopped a heartbeat away on the mattress. "I've wanted to do this for years." He pulled my legs to straddle him and enveloped me in his arms. I was reluctant at first, but it felt right. I breathed in the woodland scent mingled with citrus and relaxed into him. He gave a squeeze and slid back, my hands in his, our eyes even. "I don't ever want to see you cry as you have. You only need call, and I will come."

"Gérard knows?"

"Most."

"Oh, my God." Doug witnessed too many instances with Jesse. I never wanted anyone to know about them. "I just said God." I sobbed, dry and hiccup-like.

"I would apologize, but you needed me. As you said, you would never talk to anyone. Though you spoke to me. Had you kept it to yourself, you may have lost who you were meant to be. You have an inner strength yet to be recognized."

He hugged me to him and stroked the top of my hair; I laughed. "Isn't it I who's usually petting you?" He laughed with me.

He held me til my tears ran dry. No words. Just warmth and comfort from his scent and bare skin.

"I'm sorry, Doug. I'm so ashamed." I pushed away; heat flooded my neck and cheeks. "I've never done that before." I scurried off the bed and huddled on the chaise.

He slid off the bed and squatted before me. "Come on, love, let me show you around."

I followed him up the endless stairwell to the library, where he left me to gather my thoughts. I thumbed through numerous books, and even wandered back down to the bedroom, learning my way. He left the door ajar for the night.

I wasn't sure how to feel about Doug. He saw me through some tough times, but he also came to visit when things were going well. We ate together, walked together, and he licked me. How is a person supposed to process that? I was licked! I laughed at myself. Damn, I wanted Doug to come back just as much as I wanted Gérard. Shit.

I shuffled through the wardrobe, every so often smelling the note Gérard had left for me. The scent of exotic spices was nearly intoxicating. I would've liked to see his coffin, but that may have been the one thing to send me over the edge. It could wait. Then again, he was up.

I sat on the chaise and checked my voicemail. As I signed on, I scrolled through the recent calls on my cell. I'd missed a call from Chief Wimmers, but he wasn't due back to the mount for months.

CHAPTER 13

I lazed at the foot of the bed, debating whether to return the Chief's call, when Doug came in wearing a braided white wig, blue bow, and matching velvet knickers.

"Gérard," he announced.

He stepped aside to let Gérard through the door; I spotted two tiny drops of blood on the nape of Doug's neck. I wondered if Gérard was gentle when mealtime feedings came around. I hoped so. But then, what if it wasn't Gérard?

Gérard glided toward the bed and sat, taking my hands in his. "I will introduce a selection of my people this evening."

"Not regulars, love," Doug clarified.

"*Non.* I ordered this mansion built to overlook Lake Sangre; no human will ever discover its secrets." Gérard's smile faded. "But there was something I had not accounted for. I did not acquire the property that rested on the opposite shore. Although I own all the land surrounding this side of the lake, the land on which you live is the one lot I did not."

"You own all of it?" I asked. "Like, the mount?"

"*Oui.*" Gérard let out a shallow breath. "Unfortunately, yours is not for sale at this time."

"Did you talk to Mrs. Finch? She might sell." I closed my mouth. What if he wanted me to leave if he did buy it? I loved that house and the lake.

"No urgency, *ma chérie.* I like my neighbor." He smiled, showing a little fang.

My stomach growled; I changed the subject. "So, when's dinner? I, for one, am starved." *Crap,* I happened to think, *vampire—dinner.*

Was there actually going to be food? What if there wasn't, and I just said I was expecting to eat. "I mean, I'd like to eat something tonight, not that you have to feed me. I don't expect you to supply food for me. I mean. Oh, hell. I don't know how to say it."

It wasn't the idea of being around those people that bothered me; it was how I acted and my ignorance of what they do. Tears welled and my face had gone a humiliating shade of red. I just couldn't speak around him. What the hell was wrong with me? I couldn't talk about food without thinking it was a bad word.

Silence loomed for several minutes before I realized Doug was still propped by the door. He nodded at Gérard. "I'm hungry too," he said, and left us, clicking the door closed behind him.

"*Ma chérie*, I feel your confusion, but am unsure of the source." He posed gracefully on the chaise. He was so beautiful; I remembered last night and became bashfully uncomfortable. Red was to be my shade for the evening, without a doubt.

"Gérard?"

"*Oui*, Summer."

"You said I can ask you anything, did you mean that?"

"*Mais oui, ma chérie. Pour quoi?* Why?"

"I feel so stupid."

"You are too harsh."

"But it's true. It's how I feel. Like when you talk to me. I hear you."

"That is why we call it talking, *n'est pas*?"

"That's not what I mean. I know you do it, the mind thing." I sat on my knees, resting on my heels. "You actually talk to me. And what do you think of when I say food or that I'm hungry or . . .?" I sobbed and blurted out, "I'm starving. My head is pounding, and I didn't know how to leave so I could eat something. Damn it." I closed my eyes and threw my head back. "I said damn," and cried.

"Ah, *je sais*." His lips parted slightly, showing more fang. It was a sexy smile, and he didn't even need to try. I had the sudden urge to kiss him, so I did. A quick brush of lips.

"I'm sorry, I . . ." I looked up into his eyes, which had the stars again.

He lifted my face toward his so that he met my lips and brushed them with his own, at the same time bringing me off my knees. He urged me to his lap and drew my legs across his. I felt like a little girl sitting like that, but I was not a little girl and what I was doing was not what a little girl would do.

He pressed his lips harder. I wanted him to be mine. His beauty, his gentleness, his body—I wanted it all. I opened to his kiss, his voice an extrasensory transmission. *Ma chérie, do not be alarmed. This is how I speak with the others but have not with you, for fear of frightening you further. And now you may do so, with me.* I opened my eyes to see him watching me. I pushed away.

"I should have known you would not ask for food and would not take it upon yourself. It will not happen again. Your pain is gone, *oui*?"

"Uh, huh."

"*Bon*. Now, to answer your earlier hysterics, when I say I need to feed, I am thinking of blood. I know you need food. Though religion forewarns of our damnation, it remains to be seen. *S'il vous plaît*, talk with me. I was human, although long ago. It is why I adore you. Your questions humor me. They remind me of an innocence I have long lost."

He let out a purposeful breath. My body shivered with a low tingling. He pulled away; it was his turn to study me. His thumbs caressed my cheeks as his hands kneaded my hair. He peered at my henna tattoo that was faded to almost nothing.

"My guest of honor is hungry. What sort of host would I be if I were to deny her what she wants? I must ask that she dress for dinner. I will return to be her escort." He kissed the back of my hand with a feather kiss and was gone.

It wasn't fair. Our encounters were always short. I could stamp my foot like a child, but the sooner I was dressed, the sooner I would see him again.

I slipped off the pantsuit and bra. Since the dress was all eye hooks and Kitty was there to help me into it, I wouldn't need the standard version. She pulled a set of silicone stick'ems from the wardrobe drawer. I didn't know how to use them, so she positioned the hollow over my nipples, pulled the upper strip and secured it to the top of my breasts. It was strange having someone do that, but she didn't make a big deal out of it. She helped me step into the stockings, secured them to the garter, and held the skirt for me to step into. After that, I put on the boots. Last was the corset.

"Do these have to be so tight?" I asked, fighting for breath.

Kitty laughed. "Beauty hurts, it's all there is to it. Just suck it in, and I'll be done in a minute."

The dress was elegant, with a black top and white satin bottom. Admittedly, it made me feel pretty. "I'll see you at dinner, Summer." She left me to enjoy my new ensemble, and to get used to sitting with my back straight. She loosened it so I wouldn't faint.

I was twirling around, watching the skirt flare, when I heard the faintest knock on the door. I opened it eagerly since I couldn't wait to see Gérard's outfit. And there he was with his long dark curls pulled back with black silk ribbon. He was stunning, adorned with black knickers, white tights, black riding boots and vest, white—I guess you would call it blouse—and a black overcoat. The boots were leather, but the rest of the outfit was silk except for the velvet knickers and, of course, the silvery buttons and cords. He should have looked ridiculous, but he didn't. He was flawless.

I hoped I affected him in the slightest way.

He lifted my chin with his index finger curled, gave a small bow, and breathed across my hand.

"Do you do this to all women?" I asked.

He smiled playfully. "*Non*, only those whom I pursue."

"For the sake of curiosity, do I affect you at all?"

"*Mais oui, ma chérie.* I am intoxicated by your presence. The way your hair falls, the light of your face when you see me, the beat of your heart, the flow of your blood, the wonderful questions. Ah, you are lovely. I could go on and on, *ma chérie*."

"Oh," I was at a sudden loss for words, but managed to be an ass. "Please take me."

"*Pardonnez-moi?* From such a lady?" He kissed the top of my head. "I speak in jest, *chérie*."

"I meant to dinner."

"*D'accord,* of course. Shall we?" He extended his elbow. I looped my arm through his and followed him up the stairs, down the corridor, and into the large dining room.

We walked past the dining table and another room. It was the ballroom. All the décor was as if from a storybook. Gilded gold on the ceiling, and large carved wooden doors with white and black swirls. I'd only glimpsed it the night before.

He escorted me through yet another set of archways to a room I hadn't seen on our tour. The room was outlined in gold and reflected hues of yellow and white on everything, including the cold marble floor, flowered wallpaper, and thick golden drapes. There was a chamber orchestra playing renaissance music and wearing white wigs with black tuxes with long tails. The room echoed with laughter and chatter, but there were only a dozen and a half guests. When we entered, the room fell silent.

Gérard bowed. "Good evening, *mes amis*. I am pleased you all found your way, and am even more pleased to introduce *ma chérie*, Summer Candella." He slipped his hand into mine and brought me in front of him, earning a soft murmur.

"I ask everyone to introduce themselves to Summer as you pass to the dining hall."

The small crowd hurried into an organized line that advanced toward us. Gérard stood beside me, greeting guests, and passing them to me. Unexpectedly, there were quite a few townsfolk and beloved friends, but only one disturbed me.

Gérard introduced me to the angelic blonde with the greenest eyes I'd ever seen. Her hair lay flawless, straight, short, and flat. She had large black saucer eyes and a mezzosoprano voice, all a part of her five foot eight-ish big-boned frame, though not chunky.

Now there are people who fit their looks, and people who are like demonic super bitches in sheep's clothing. Well, her attitude rivaled Patricia's, and as soon as she spoke, my human hackles arose to fight the hairspray keeping the hairs smooth.

"This is the fuss?" she taunted.

"Regina, lovely to see you. It has been too long. Miss Candella was searching for Mr. *Perfectif,* and I happened to be here. Timing is everything, *non*?"

"It would seem she hasn't stripped your ego, so full of yourself these days. It makes one wonder why we've stayed away for so long." The woman circled around him with white stiletto boots clicking the floor. They worked wonderfully with the heavy blue satin hi-lo gown. "Though times change, Mr. President."

"President?" I whispered.

"Oh, you didn't know." She slid her eyes toward him, then back to me. "Gérard is President of the Preternatural Regime, the international unified government for all prets."

I swallowed to rid myself of a newly formed lump in my throat. "That's why you're rich," I whispered.

Regina laughed. "Gérard, darling. She is simply raw. Wherever did you keep her?"

"Enough, give my love to *Francois,* would you?" he warned.

"If I must." She wasn't pleased with him but satisfied enough, or disgusted, to leave the conversation.

After she passed, I followed. Servants stood behind each chair. Gérard sat at the head of the table. I was seated in the first chair on his left.

To my surprise, there were place settings for everyone, and water goblets with water in them. I didn't think vampires could drink water, so it must have been for show in their case.

The wait staff bustled about. They served plates filled with boeuf bourguignon, garlic mashed potatoes, garden salad with raspberry vinaigrette, and fresh potato rolls to all of the place settings, along with wine and blood. I didn't know it was blood until Gérard informed me of what it was and not to drink it. To my relief, he didn't do it aloud.

The food smelled delicious, and was superb, however the dinner conversation was normal. Every now and then I would hear him in my mind, but it was usually to clarify what the individual was who I was talking to. Andy the butcher was a vamp, his wife Lil was Sidhe, Tavin was wolf as was his wife, Regina was the daughter of Loreley. Of course, there were familiar faces like Doug on his right; Gale, Dani, Tiny, Dawn, and Richard. Unexpectedly, Mrs. Finch and Brady were there. I was full and happy.

After dessert, we all retreated to the gold room where everyone took to dancing. It was intimidating since I had no clue how to dance to such music. I'd seen it in the movies, where they pointed their toes, did a hop, traded hands and curtsied. It was elegant. I wasn't.

I tried to think how I felt into Gérard, but I wasn't telepathically inclined in the least.

After refusing to partner anyone who asked, including Doug, Gérard took my hand. "May I?" Though his voice posed the question, his raised eyebrows impressed the opposite.

I was scared to death. There were people watching. I couldn't move; his voice whispered through me.

Ah, ma chérie. Do not fear dancing when you do not fear me. I love to dance; please allow me to share this joy with you. I will not force you, but please trust me. He pressed his face to my hair. *Look at my eyes, Summer. I will give you all you need to know.*

"Okay." I whispered.

He cupped my face with his palms; our eyes met. Images of Gérard dancing with many beautiful women in a large ballroom, and then in several parlors, were imprinted. I had memories of dancing.

"Shall we, *ma chérie*?" He gave a small bow.

"Okay." I whispered again.

I was still nervous, but I knew what to do. It was strange but exciting because I had never done this sort of dancing before.

We walked to the middle of the room as the guests cleared to the walls. Gérard bowed; I made a small curtsy. We began standing side by side with my hand raised in his. I recalled his memory of the happiness he felt toward dancing and allowed it to mingle with my own.

Once we separated and turned, the guests returned to the floor. We danced and danced, until Gérard escorted me to the small stage where the chamber orchestra performed.

The room fell silent, all faces turned toward us. Gérard stepped forward and spoke. His voice echoed through the room.

"Please continue to dance, and drink, however, we will be leaving you for the rest of the evening."

The crowd formed two lines as we passed through the room. I clung to Gérard's arm and concentrated on the floor as he nodded to each guest. Doug and Patricia were the last in line. Her white rhinestone gown matched Doug's ensemble. I wondered if they were a thing, or if it was a coincidence. I hadn't thought about anyone but myself until then. Selfish, true, but how presumptuous to not even consider their lives, loves, and what not. I'd dare not admit it to Dawn, but her little rant replayed as we left, and Patricia and Doug joined the other guests on the ballroom floor. They all looked happy.

Gérard led me back to the bedroom, where my clothes were freshly laundered and folded on the bed. He sat beside them. Dawn and Gale were right, he was a chance I needed to take if I wanted to find the love and joy I saw in the others. I wanted to be happy, to have a life with love and trust. But who was I to demand trust.

"Will you stay the day again? We do not have to part this early before dawn; I want to be alone with you."

"Yes, please. I also want to be alone." I stammered, "with you."

He pulled me close with his arm around my waist, gentlemanly. "You gave me your trust. For that I am honored."

He brushed my lips with his thumb. I bit my lip. He chuckled and slid it slowly down the side, continuing along my neck. *You feel there must be something wrong because it is too soon.*

I pushed away. "You're reading me!" The blood raced to my cheeks as I thought about the asinine antics I'd displayed since I'd met him.

"It is not my intent to bring discomfort. Though your thoughts of yourself are low. You must afford yourself higher regards."

He danced across the room and disappeared into the bathroom. I heard him brushing his teeth. Unsure of what to do, I sat on the chaise and waited for him to come out. I also tried to think of thinking about nothing. It didn't work.

"*Chérie,* please come in."

"But you're in the bathroom."

"*Oui,* but I am not indecent."

I stepped into the massive bathroom.

"I will grant your privacy, Summer, but I cannot promise it will not be void if need be. Now, would you care for a bath before bed? I will return in an hour, for dawn is looming."

"But it seems rude. How about you draw the bath, and join me?" Did I just ask him to join me naked in a big tub? Why not?

"*Vraiment?*" he gasped.

"What?"

"I apologize, you caught me without guard. Are you certain?" He blushed.

Good, damn it. I hated that he affected me the way he did. I liked the fact that I could embarrass him. It was cute as hell.

"I never said you'd get any. Just join me in the tub. Besides, I've never seen a naked vampire, at least not to my knowledge."

"Eh, you will be nude as well?"

"Yeah, haven't you been with hundreds of women or something? I doubt I'm anything different." I thought about that. He was over 800. If he laid with one woman a year—the fun feelings melted away. My lungs betrayed me. My eyes burned, but why? I wasn't even an option for him then.

He looked away and then at the floor, playing the toe of his boot against the carpet. "Summer, I have been with but only four women, in love. The first was before I was brought over to this life. The second was my mistress, the woman who sired my lineage. And the third was Marie, one of the reasons the others have told was for my repose; I could not bear her loss. My grief weakened our community and made us vulnerable. I nearly failed in my position."

Sorrow thickened his voice; I wanted to go to him, hold him. He knew hurt. I hadn't thought he would be capable of feeling shy, but coupled with his sorrow, it was comforting. To me, it proved he was capable of caring, loving. These were qualities that meant more to me than he would ever know. But it also reminded me that they were human like me. I had to remember that.

"Maybe this isn't such a good idea," I whispered.

"*Non, mais*, I thought you should know."

"Only four?"

"In love. Female conquests were not a part of the code of chivalry. I was unwilling to sacrifice my honor."

"I shouldn't have thought that." I swallowed hard. "You didn't mention the fourth."

His sapphire and coal eyes were blanketed by the fall of bang that curtained his face. He tucked the hair behind his ear and peered up at me. "I believe you already know."

Did I? Was it me? I had to change the subject. "Did your repose help?"

"I have awakened; it is all that matters."

The grieving period for a regular mortal human must have been a fraction of the time it would take for someone who had an indefinite life expectancy. I assumed he had to grieve not only for Marie, but also for his mother, family, and other girlfriends. All the losses he endured over the last seven or eight centuries must have still weighed on him. I dared not ask, but I wondered how his memory was. If it was anything like the books, he'd have a photographic memory which would make their deaths haunt him for eternity—a true damnation.

"Did going to sleep prevent you from thinking about Marie?"

"*Non*, but I had no will to live this life. I longed for eternal death. Do you not see, Summer? I am forced to live. I dreamt, but I did not have to go on pretending to be alive."

"Were you in love with her for a long time?"

"In your years, yes. We were together for centuries." He started the water, added bubbles, and turned on the jets.

"Are you sure you don't want to be alone?"

"It is the last thing I want. I wish she had remained human. It was not my doing that caused her immortality, and for that, I am punished. I promise, as our relationship matures, so will your understanding. There are secrets we are both reluctant to share. Although I am afraid to love again, it has already begun."

He sat on the edge of the tub and glanced through a loose lock of black hair; blood-tinged tears stole down his cheeks. I went to him, wrapped my arms around his neck, and kissed the top of his head. I pressed his head to my chest and sat beside him on the edge of the tub. He wrapped his arms around me and sobbed. I didn't know what else to do, but he needed me.

"Gérard," I whispered, "Enjoy me, be happy. If nothing else, tonight we will bathe in each other's company and talk. I have questions, and you have things you need to share." I turned the water off and started to take off the boots when he lifted me from my feet and carried me to the bed.

He sat me on the edge and undid all the eye hooks on the dress—one by one. He removed the boots, hose, garter, and dress. I slid off the pink lace panties, took his hand, and led him back to the tub. "You don't have to get in. I just want to wash out this hairspray. Don't leave." I stepped in, but he pulled me back and patted the marble platform.

"You wanted to see me." He backed slowly and removed his overcoat, vest, and blouse, letting them fall to the floor. He continued with his boots, knickers, and stockings. Standing in the candlelight, he was a lively, warm but pale golden tan, and well-built with a six-pack and a nice package below. Minimal body hair and a small pair of fangs completed him. I no longer saw him as an accessory, a fascination. He was someone I agreed to date. And that made him mine.

"Did those people, the guests, know my real parents?"

"*Oui.* There are none on the mount who did not."

I slid into the water and reached my hand out to him, but he wouldn't get in the tub.

He tried to cover himself with his hands in a not so noticeable, to the point it was noticeable, sort of way. "I am afraid." He studied the floor as if something wonderful were woven into the carpet.

"Of what?"

"You, this—how I feel. I will not put my people at risk again." His voice soft, but regretful; I strained to hear him. "But it is already too late."

My body never experienced such a quick washing. The shampoo was in, and my skin soaped before I had time to think. I rinsed off under the water, stepped out, dried, and brushed my teeth.

The whole time he just stood there staring at the floor, repeating, "I am sorry." I glanced at him in the mirror; his shoulders shook. He wasn't just crying, he was sobbing.

I couldn't take seeing him that way, so I figured to hell with dressing, took his hand, led him to the bed, and motioned for him to get in. He climbed on. I followed, spooned against his back, tucking my arm under his neck, and pulled myself to him with the other clasping his chest. A sudden rush of heat pushed at my arm. I held him tighter.

He tried to cover his feelings with his power, but he wasn't dealing with just anyone, he was dealing with me. He needed this, and he was damn well going to let himself have a good cry and be held while doing it. It was a shame that he had to wait a hundred years, or whatever it was, to be able to do so.

Chief Wimmers's voicemail would have to wait.

CHAPTER 14

It had been two weeks since I'd started dating Gérard and listened to Chief Wimmers's voicemail. I had listened to it every day before I went back to work. The chief was a nice man, but not all cops were. And like any other force, we had one who was a total asshole. And for whatever reason, Wimmers called me to remind me of that fact.

"Summer, it's Leo. Stevie said she's seen people askin' for Augusto, and how they can find you. I don't like it. You keep your distance. You go to Gale's if you get antsy. Don't play tough. I don't know why, but I got this inkling. Call me if you need me. And carry that gun."

It didn't matter; Greene and I had no reason to cross paths. That message just made sure I kept it that way.

I'd finally met Sam and was relieved he hadn't changed my recipes. In fact, he followed them more closely than I usually did.

Tiny was more than pleased with having two cooks and was thinking of adding an addition to the side of the diner. I hated to burst his bubble, but after the Samhain, we'd probably go back to having our regulars and the occasional tourist.

It was a shame because Sam was fun to work with and left me notes since we worked different shifts. Sometimes he would come in to help me out. He really lifted the workload, and wasn't bad to look at either, with short black hair, dark brown eyes, and natural tan. He was close to six feet and built like a football player. Judging from his accent, I'd say he was from Spain, like Tiny.

So, yeah, Tiny was originally from Spain, but he'd told me he'd traveled the world when he was younger and settled in England awhile. After that, he journeyed to America and set up camp in good ole Mount Mort.

And Gale wasn't working a whole lot lately. She was uncomfortable around Sam; I think because he was new. I never saw Gale call off work like that. It was strange. I knew she and Tiny had grown close over the last several years, but to be jealous over a new employee was a bit much. It had to be something else. Maybe Sam was a practitioner, too.

Tiny and Sam started going over to Brady's after hours, and even ventured out for some male bonding with some of the other men in town. But Gale and Tiny never went anywhere after work. Her be jealous? Nah, she wouldn't be. It wasn't in her nature. But I missed a lot of somethings in my life. Especially in Mount Mort.

Either way, Gale and Dani were coming over to my house for dinner since we were all off for the night. Gérard said he'd stop at around ten or so. That way, we could eat without feeling like we were doing something taboo in front of him.

After I closed out the lunch specials, I set up the dinner stuff and left a short list of what needed to be done for Sam. I couldn't wait to see Gérard and hurried out to the parking lot. There was a winky-faced balloon sitting in the front seat of my car. When I opened the door, I saw it was attached to a small teddy bear in a chef's outfit. There was no note or anything. Gérard was full of surprises; at least, I hoped it was from Gérard. I plopped it in the back seat, backed out, and sped home.

It was nearly dark when I pulled into the driveway at my house. A large snowy owl sat on the tree limb above my door. It hooted softly; I crept out of the car. Snowy owls were the official bird for Quebec, and were seen in the northeast, and various provinces of Canada. I'd seen a few of them over the years, but not as early in the year as this. It was early fall, yet there it was. I knew it was a female because of the brown barring on the wings, but it took flight as soon as I closed the car door.

I loved all wildlife, but owls especially. Their calls; the all-knowing eyes. The soft knickers that lined their stubby legs. Not that they have stubby legs, they just sit on them, but still, they are cute and look stubby. The little ear-like tufts, the tongues, and the tiny beaks fascinated me. The soft, delicate snowy owl was a vicious predator. At some point, its tiny beak and thick talons would be blood deep in the bowels of some poor critter.

Owls—what not to love.

I opened the door and tossed my keys on the table as I clicked it shut. I hung my jacket in the closet and turned to the sound of the soft hooting outside my door. I tip-toed across the floor in fear of the bird hearing my approach and carefully pulled the door open.

The bird sat in front of me. It swiveled its head from side to side. After a quick sweeping glance, she would blink in my direction. I had never encountered a snowy owl within a touchable distance before in my life.

Well, that wasn't entirely true. I saw one once when I was on a snowmobile with my ex-boyfriend. The owl flew at him, knocking him off. I jumped, and the snowmobile crashed in a cluster of young pines. He was pissed. I was forced to walk home. We broke up the next day, so...

Anyway, this one perched right in front of me. She must have been half a meter high, and beautiful. All at once, the hooting turned to a voice. A familiar voice, but I could not, for the life of me, understand it. After a few seconds, I realized it was Gale's!

I squatted to peer into the glassy yellow eyes and put my hand out. I patted the bird on the head and stroked its back.

"Gale? Is that you?" I know it sounded stupid, but except for the bird, I was alone. The last two weeks taught me that as long as you're alone, being stupid isn't so bad.

"Yes, hon. It's one reason why I wanted to meet you here. I wanted to show myself to you." The bird transformed—it was Gale. She reached under the rosebush and grabbed a small brown paper bag.

"Are you in awe 'cause it's new or because it's me?"

"I'm not sure. A little of both, I guess."

She donned a white dress from the little bag.

"I thought you were a witch."

"I'm one of them too." She winked. "Dani mentioned it in the library."

Dani emerged from the shadows. "She must have missed that, Mama." Her black hair was tucked behind her ears; they were pointed. She stepped onto the stairs pale and nude except for the fine black fur covering her backward knees and claw-formed feet.

I straightened, reached for the door, and stopped.

Gale's plump Mother Goosed self, patted my arm and headed toward the kitchen. "Gonna be a fun night, Summer. Now, what are we eatin'? I'll help."

"I'll watch. I hate to cook." Dani added as she took my hands and led me inside.

The door closed on its own.

"What do you eat?" I whispered.

"Shrimp is nice. We like shrimp," Dani chimed.

"Well, since you're wearing white, how about shrimp scampi and rice pilaf?" I said.

"Ooh, that sounds great. I'll have to watch, too. I don't know how to cook that stuff."

I plucked a bag of shrimp from the freezer and dumped it in a baking dish. They stood at the end of the counter, staring at me. I grabbed a butter knife and pried the pre-peeled gray bodies apart.

Silence.

I picked a peeled garlic clove from the fridge and spotted an open container of cranberry juice. "Want some?" I offered the plastic bottle to them.

"No wine? I swear, girl, loosen up. I bet you didn't even bed Gérard yet. How can you resist? Isn't he just scrumptious?"

"Gale," I whined. "Of course not, but I'm having fun. Honestly, though, I think I might . . ."

"In love? My goodness girl, I told you he was a good man. You, see? You need to trust the instincts of an old woman. I know these things." She grabbed two mugs from the dishwasher.

"He feels the same about you," Dani added.

For whatever reason, that didn't make me as happy as I would have thought. I changed the subject. "Enough about me; how about you? First of all, an owl, what other talents do you possess that I may be graced with?" I squinted at Gale like a sly detective. Yeah right.

"Well, I'm a shifter, Sum." Gale reassured; her head cocked unnaturally to the side.

"Different from Doug, right?" I finished the scampi and pushed the dish into the oven.

"You're learnin'. Shifters transform into one or more things. A lycan has the senses and abilities of the animal they turn into, even in human form. We carry a strain of DNA from that animal which we can carry and pass to our children. For a lycan to pass lycanthropy, they have to infect someone. It's a disease."

"Which explains Dani?"

"Exactly. My father was too, though, a multi-shifter. He could turn into half a dozen animals," Dani explained.

"That is awesome. And you're witches too. I'm surprised you didn't make a love potion for me or something by now." I laughed and grabbed the sink with both hands. "Shit, I'm sorry. I don't know why, but this is hard to swallow. Witches I can deal with. Vampires, even. But—Dani." I waved at her still bare breasts and furred legs.

Dani straightened her legs. The knees popped and toes uncurled from beneath the clawed paws. The fur retracted and lily-white skin exposing a tattoo of a lazing cat entwined in a triquetra, or trinity knot.

"Aren't cats supposed to be evil? And that's a trinity knot. Christian, I believe." I was staring and hadn't meant to.

Gale huffed, "That's all nonsense. I practice the white craft. Dawn's into all that Wiccan stuff and Tiny, well he dabbled in the dark arts for centuries. Dani can tell her part, but I assure you she's certainly not evil." She gulped half the glass of juice. "Now, Richard. He's the interestin' one. He descends from a line of Druid witches, although he hasn't practiced since Wimmers closed the mount. A little stray cat can't harm anything." She kissed Dani's nose and handed her the crumpled brown bag. "Unless it's a mage."

"Dani?" I nodded at her.

Dani sidled up to me, her palm pressed against my cheek. "In medieval France, mages served as guards and go-betweens. They offered protection and were loyal, often until death. Because of my mother, those abilities were passed to me. I am the mage of Gérard's court."

"Gérard's court?" Had he mentioned he had a court? He was a knight. "Wait, how? I mean when?" Damn it. "Like how old are you?"

Dani pulled on a short red sundress. "How old is Gérard? No outsiders. Remember it, Summer. You want answers, think."

"Why didn't he use Tiny or Gale?" I asked. I thought he knew Gale longer and Tiny was older than her. "Wouldn't an older practitioner be stronger?"

"Because sometimes, practicing isn't as effective. A physical advantage serves a greater purpose."

Gale glanced at Dani and frowned. "Back to the witchcraft. Put all this other stuff aside."

Damn, I'd have to get Dani alone. "So, what's the difference between all of you and Dawn? What's so great about Richard?" Really, I didn't think Richard was worth a breath of thought.

Gale patted my hand. "How 'bout you cook, and I'll talk."

"Sounds like a plan." I grabbed the rice, eager for her to start.

She leaned against the counter, somewhat at home since she dropped by more than a few times over the years, while she pondered where to begin. And probably what to avoid.

"Mom's a witch from old," Dani finally said. "Her line does more with herbs. You know, for healing. It's a lot to do with nature."

"In fact, we worship Mother Earth. Back in the old days, we possessed dogs and cats, which tipped off the regulars. Eventually we were brought to trials and burned alive." Gale elaborated, sat at the table, and watched me mince the garlic.

"So, the Salem Witch Trials were for a good—" I bit my tongue.

"Hush your tongue. There've been witch-hunts all over Europe for centuries. None of them are taught to be the horrors they really are." The disgust was thick in her words. "Anyway, we were feared when the regulars, who didn't understand us, tried to blame their bad luck on sorcery. Of course, some were capable, but most of it was coincidence, or simple bad luck."

"So, the odds of catching an actual witch weren't very good, I assume."

"No. Many innocent people died at the hands of liars and so- called witch hunters," Dani implored. "People we loved."

"I'm so sorry, guys."

"For what? You weren't there, and we have the sanctuary now. Funny thing though, the witches got back at each other or convinced the townsfolk the one who'd found out about them were witches," Gale said.

"So, the ones doing the hunting weren't always on the up and up."

"Yup. Today's witches have it made. Like Dawn. They're Wiccan," Dani said. "They aren't feared and don't have to be born with the ability. You get what I mean?"

"They believe in using witchcraft as a religion to fit their lifestyle, right?" I asked.

Gale stroked my hair and tucked it behind my ear. "Don't you go dismissin' them now. They believe that when you do someone harm, no matter how, it'll come back on you three-fold. Wicca's the new form of witchcraft, but I don't think of 'em as witches." She grabbed a piece of tomato and popped it in her mouth. "Still, they hold it within them."

"Then what's the deal with Richard? I thought druids were the wise ones in the Celtic region. They don't exist anymore," I said.

"As I explained to Dani, don't be so sure. It often took twenty years for a student to become a Druid. They worshipped nature, especially the oak. Many of them were lawyers, judges, doctors, teachers, and magicians. It's said that they could control the weather and command nature. I never actually witnessed that, but who's to say?"

Richard didn't strike me as the kind of guy to venture into the forest. He seemed devoted to his career and spending time inside. I couldn't recall a single time he did anything in nature. "Are you sure we're talking about Dawn's Richard?"

Dani leaned against the refrigerator. "He visits the altar on the mount often and lights the candles for the things you can't or don't see."

I wiped my hands on the dish towel I had over my shoulder. They were free with information, but not the big three, as far as I was concerned. "So, what about Tiny?"

"Well, you know I'm his sister," Gale reminded.

"Of course."

"Well, we're a little different. See, the difference between a witch and a wizard is simply what they believe. A wizard has a way of twisting truth, where my kind of witch speaks truth as it is. Men choose their title pretty much. Witch, wizard, warlock, they're all practitioners of some sort."

"Then he's a shifter too." I put the scampi under the broiler; the smell of garlic and shrimp filled the kitchen.

"No, we had different mothers; mine was a shifter. I don't know who his was. But our father, now he was a wizard. He worked under several kings throughout Europe. Over the centuries, he developed a reputation that made the kings want him on their side, more as a seer. It was unfortunate for him, but a blessing for the world when the regime intervened. He wanted to call upon the spirits he had no right messing with, but enough about that."

"It must have been hard for you."

Gale went to the picture window and traced the fold in the burgundy curtain. "I never knew my father. My mother made sure of it. I learned from Elizabeth, my mother's friend. She was a healer but was burned at the stake when I was two hundred four years old." She smiled at me, the kind with tight lips to keep the emotions in check. "I don't remember my age now. I think I stopped counting after that. My mother was burned the year before, and then Elizabeth. I lost the only people I loved. I was alone for quite some time."

I wasn't sure what to say, but the timer saved me. "Dinner's ready." I'd set the table and waited for them to join me. "We even have orange sherbet parfaits for dessert." My efforts to redirect her thoughts were weak. She looked sad; true and genuine.

I was overwhelmed and heartbroken for her all the same. I knew how she felt being left alone. She kept watching toward Gérard's. "Gale, come eat while it's still hot. Besides, he's coming."

"You're a sweet girl, Summer. Know this, whatever happens in life, I will die to keep you from harm. I love you, hon. I swear, if it weren't for Dani, I'd have adopted you for my daughter. Lord knows she's more than enough to handle, though." She giggled at some thought. "I guess, in the 1300s, I was two hundred. I'm older than Gérard, I know that."

I choked on my salad. "Older? 'Cause you're a witch or a shifter?"

"Actually, witches don't have immortality," Dani offered.

Gale glared at her. "We get reincarnated, but I have immortality, so to speak, 'cause I'm a shifter." She picked the tomatoes from the salad, abstracted. "The way to kill any one of us truly is to cut off our head; some destroy the heart." She made a swooping motion with her fork. "I know Gérard likes to burn 'em, for good measure."

Did they kill people regularly? For good measure? I lost my appetite. I pushed the pink shrimp around the white porcelain plate; they resembled miniature pink roses. With specks of parsley, they reminded me of the rosebush. I never actually told anyone, but roses depressed me.

"So much for folklore," I sighed.

"Well, history and folklore go hand in hand. They influence one another," Gale said.

"I really should've studied anthropology, or at least history. Instead, I chose culinary arts. Doesn't make me very bright, huh?"

"Don't sell yourself short. Just living in this town, you'll learn more than you bargained for. It's your life, Summer. Not some book."

Was I in danger with her? If so, would she really tell me how to kill Gérard, or her for that matter?

The only danger I foresaw was Gérard. He made me feel like I couldn't think; like a babbling idiot most of the time. Tonight, he would sit across from me. No touching and I was not looking him in the eyes. I wanted answers before I let myself get any deeper. He killed people!

"You're thinking too hard," Dani said.

"Let's eat before Gérard gets here. It's almost time for him now." I wolfed down my food, so to speak. They did the same. I wondered if they felt as awkward as I did, eating in front of him.

"This is some of the best shrimp I've ever eaten. Tiny's isn't right for you. You should be in some fancy restaurant somewhere cookin' for the rich. Hell, Hon, you should open your own," Gale praised the food, but she ate my cooking all the time.

"Maybe, someday." I was just about to take a bite when a fly landed in my juice glass. "Holy shit." I jumped up from the table. Dani laughed and choked.

"Damn flies." Gale swatted toward me, but the fly was already gone.

"Yeah, first fly I've had since July, I think." My heart raced as I looked around for it. "Any idea where it went?"

Gale kept eating. "No, hon. Why so jumpy? Relax. A girl your age doesn't need to scare herself over a fly."

"Yeah, it's just that whenever I'm around Gérard, I get stupid. I swear he thinks I have no brains. You don't want to know what I've done. I've completely humiliated myself."

"I can imagine. I've been around you a long time." Dani laughed.

"I'm serious. Something comes over me when he's around, and lately when I know he's coming or I'm going to meet him, I become a complete ass."

"Sounds like a crush to me. You're already in love. Can't get much deeper." Gale pointed at me with her fork. "Well, it's 'bout time, girl. Now, finish your dinner." She stared at the parfait in front of her.

"There's so much I want to know, but there is one big thing weighing on my mind." That night that Guillaume showed up at Brady's, he said I was in danger—with Gérard.

It bothered me that I couldn't act like a sane human being when I was around Gérard, from the time I met him. Although all the books I read were fiction, they said vampires could use compulsion. What if Gérard was influencing me? What if he wasn't? Could someone be? Was I to ask Gérard outright? Did I ask Gale before he showed up? What to do, what to do. I was so confused. I bit my lip.

"Why so quiet?" Dani asked.

"Just thinking. I'm afraid to love him." Besides, I wasn't sure if it was trickery or true wooing. I guess I'd decide when he arrived.

My cell rang while we were eating our desserts. I didn't know who it could've been since the diner was closing in 10 minutes. But remembered Dawn could be in labor. I picked it up right before it went to voicemail.

"Hello?"

"*Ma chérie, c'est moi, Gérard.*"

"You're not coming."

"*Non.*"

He sounded strange, even for him. "Is everything okay?" Asking seemed foolish, since there wasn't anything I could do to help, anyway.

"*Oui*, is Gale with you?"

"Yeah, she's right here, want to talk to her?"

"*Non*, I did not want to leave you alone when you were expecting company. I will not detain you. *Je t'aime, ma chérie.*" He hung up.

I wondered if saying I love you in French held as strong of a meaning as it did in English. We'd only been together for two weeks, but was it possible he felt like I did? Then again, what did I truly feel? God, I hated this shit. It was so much easier when I was alone.

"Not comin'?" Dani asked.

"No, guess it's a girls' night." I tried to keep the disappointment out of my voice, not wanting to insult them, but I was looking forward to seeing him.

"He's a wise man. Don't bother yourself about him. He's fine." Dani smiled, which made me feel a little better.

"I guess. But I waited for him so I could ask questions."

"Maybe I have the answers," Gale said.

"Would you mind?"

"I'll do my best, but I don't know what you have questions about. Assuredly you are compelled to make him a god or devil, and his omniscience comes at a cost. One you will learn." She sipped her wine. "I'll do my best, Summer."

"Fine, but I want honesty. Don't try to spare my feelings or protect me. Look at the good it's done so far. I have to know the truth. I don't want to be lied to, because right now, I don't know what's true and what isn't." I sat back in the chair and crossed my ankles; my foot twitched from the adrenaline racing through me.

"Why don't you tell me what's on your mind? My guess is that you have one thing botherin' you and the rest is curiosity."

I wasn't certain, but it was a pretty good guess that Gale was a subordinate—ancillary. It didn't feel right, like she was watching me and more concerned with what I had to say than usual. Ever since I went on that date, the whole damn community had been a little off. Conspiracy theories were never my thing, but things were suspect.

CHAPTER 15

Dani had plans to meet her friends in Watertown. Before she left, she squeezed my hand and said, "People come together, then go away. But we don't, we stay." Her words echoed and dominated my thoughts.

I sat in the recliner. Gale sat on the sofa, worried. I hoped my paranoia wasn't going to hurt our relationship. It didn't help that I kept thinking about Guillaume. If Gérard wanted to hurt me, would he resort to deceit? Oh, hell.

Gale broke the silence. "Cat gotch'er tongue?"

"No," I sighed. "Remember when Guillaume said I was in danger because of the newcomers? That they'd bait me and use me in their practice because I'm innocent."

"I don't think that's what's really botherin' you but go on."

"I don't know if he's using his powers to make me think I have feelings for *him*?" I yanked my thumb toward the lake.

Her back went straight.

"Jesus! Doug said Gérard's master of Mount Mort; doesn't that make him your master? Does that mean that you could be using your witchcraft against me, to make me think I have feelings for him? Or is Tiny using any of his sorcery to make me feel this way? Am I really feeling anything or is all of this some sort of spell? Dani's his mage."

The tears brimmed. My head was a whirlwind with thoughts that turned into questions.

Gale stared at the closed curtains that kept the lake from view. I wondered what she was thinking. Before this night, I didn't think much of what Gale might have thought. She turned to face me.

"Summer, you dare question my intentions? You think I'd do harm to you? That I'd hurt you on purpose? Because someone told me too?"

Shit, ten minutes before, she'd been content, confident. But now everything was different. Now she was pissed because I told her the way it was. Gérard was her boss. My accusatory demeanor came from her reaction. At the moment, my alter ego had its arms crossed and saying, "Fuck you!"

How did I know I could trust her answers? How did I know anything? She was always there for me. I was so close to Gale; I couldn't imagine being crushed by her. "You just have to be real," I blurted.

"You have too much going on in that pretty mind of yours. Listen to me. I would never use you, and I would most definitely never let anyone else use you. I love you like you were one of my own."

"I'm sorry, Gale."

"Guillaume is a dark creature. I'm not sayin' he's a liar, but don't get worked up over something he said, unless he made a threat to you himself."

I tried to remember if he did. She went on. "Now, don't be gittin' no ideas about Gérard. He lost someone dear to his heart not long ago. Oh, how that man loved her. He wouldn't play with his own heart, which is just what he'd be doin' if he was playin' with yours. Be he a vampire or a man, I would bet my life on him not playin' with you."

I settled back in the chair and tucked my feet in. The movement must have made her feel better because she sat back and stretched her legs along the couch. "If you've been put under a spell, it's not by me."

"I don't know what to believe anymore."

She stared at the floor, hard. "If you'd like, I could put wards at the entrances of your house, but to be truly effective, they have to be built in. A wizard as strong as Tiny wouldn't be deterred from such wards. As I said, I practice good, white magic. I don't know enough black to stop it. If Dani was still here, she could've."

The town was turned upside down with all the people coming in.

The motels within a fifty-mile radius were booked, and the diner had a constant flow of customers. It wasn't just Gérard and Gale that had me worried, but these new people, too.

"What now?" she asked.

"I keep asking myself, why? Why would they want me? Gérard was supposed to come, and I miss him. And that scares the hell out of me."

"Hon, if you want my advice, talk to him. Sit down and talk. But don't be afraid to feel what your heart is tellin' you. If it's a spell, it can be broken, if it isn't, then you might be throwin' away your only chance at something special. What if Gérard is your Mr. Perfect?"

"Maybe." I rubbed my head on my sleeve. "How well do you know him? You're not French. You sound southern, but you're too old to be from America. Shit, you're older than our country. Where are you from? Where'd you meet? How did you know about Tiny? How did . . ."

"Slow down. I don't have to be anywhere in the mornin' and neither do you. We can talk all night. Do you have any tea? Let's get you a cup." She went to the kitchen and searched through the cabinets.

"It's over the toaster. Thanks Gale."

"Got it."

The microwave beeped, and she walked back in with a steaming hot cup of cocoa that she left in the microwave a little too long. "Drink it. The brown'll keep you grounded while you sort through this mess. Cocoa alone is homeopathic. It's good for you."

"Couldn't you just zap up a cup with magic?"

Laughing, almost hysterically, she gasped and squeaked out, "Oh, you are too, too sweet. Oh, Summer. This is no fairytale. I have spells, but they're metaphysical. I can't just zap up a cup of something. I have a lot to teach you. Right now, let's focus on you, and leave the spells for later." She wiped her eyes through small spurts of giggles.

"Fine."

"Where were we, ah." One more breath and she was settled. "Well,

I'm originally from England, though I've lived all over Europe. I lived in Georgia for over a hundred years, and happened to pick up their drawl since it tied in so well with my native English accent. I don't hear it myself, mind you. Besides, after living so long and in so many places, you're bound to pick up pieces and make them part of you."

"That's sensible."

She gave a final blot to her eyes. "As for Gérard, I met him a little before we came here. It was in Paris after a meeting of the witches to try and come up with a plan. Every year we tried to help the regulars by increasin' the harvest. But that night I was attacked by a young man." She smacked her knee. "He appeared from nowhere and flew at me."

"My God, did Gérard really do that?"

"Just listen." She was a good storyteller and took her time. But I was impatient and wanted answers. "Now, he pushed me up against a wall and tried to bite me. I caught him unaware 'cause I transformed. I tried to fly, but he held my wings and kept apologizing. He said he thought I was an old woman. He'd been so hungry he just needed a bit of blood. Well, I turned back to my human form, and offered him my wrist, but only to wet his whistle. He accepted gratefully and drank, as I said I'd help him find a full meal."

"Then you were Gérard's victim?" I asked impatiently.

"No, as I said, we have nowhere to be. Anyway, I found a nice young couple on the bank of the Seine. I instructed him to feed from them equally. This way, they'd both recover; no lives lost. He agreed, and upon his fill, asked me to meet his master."

"And that was Gérard?"

She blinked at me. "Honestly, Summer. You need to learn patience."

"Sorry."

She frowned. "Well, I agreed, and the young man took me to the Saint-Germaine-des-Prés, the oldest church in Paris. The young man dropped to his knee and a younger man emerged from the shadows.

His steps were slow, his demeanor was non-threatening. When he approached the young man, he offered his hand and urged him to his feet. I found myself walking toward them. I was drawn to him, so I went to him askin' if he needed anythin', but he stood and lifted my hand laying, the softest kiss upon it."

"Like his lips were made of feathers." I sighed, remembering the night we met.

"Exactly. Well, he looked me in the eye, and said I must be a good person 'cause only the pure can be a snowy owl. Well, I almost fainted; he couldn't have known what I was unless he held the ability to call on the shifters and lycans, which meant he was strong. Real power."

"Then who was the other guy? It couldn't be Doug, he's a lycan."

"The other young man stepped over and introduced me to his master. That's when Gérard gave a small bow, told me his name, and thanked me for assisting his blood-son, and teaching him how not to kill."

"I didn't think about that. Gérard didn't have Doug back then, did he? How did he feed?" After I asked, I wasn't sure I really wanted to know.

"Patience, Hon. Gérard offered to walk me home, I accepted. We told each other our stories, and found I was a little older than he was. We grew to be great friends. I fussed over him like a mother hen for a couple centuries; still do. If you want details, ye need to talk to him."

"Were you always just friends?"

"Imagine a hot young thing like you getting' all jealous over a coot like me," she jeered, "I had my eye on a handsome multi-shifter for a while; but he met his death when Dani was a baby." Her face betrayed her thoughts as she tried to hide the hurtful memory. "Now, when he said he was going to North America, I asked if I could join him. I've moved around, but he's stayed here. It's his home."

"I still want to know how my parents fit into all this." I tried to stifle a yawn. "The mount was closed, because of my parents."

"Uh-huh."

"Does Wimmers know about the preternatural stuff?"

"Call it pret or your tongue'll get worn out if you don't. We've a concentrated community here." She gulped the rest of her juice. "He can't, Sum."

"Why not?"

"You need to get some sleep."

As fascinated as I was, I couldn't stifle a string of yawns that kept breaking my concentration. My eyes burned with the need for sleep. "You want to spend the night? It's late; I wouldn't want you going out there alone."

"I'm an owl, hon. I'll be fine but thank you. I think I'll go sit in the tree above Doug's rosebush. It's beautiful, and this house is peaceful. Besides, it's a lovely night to fly." Before I could protest, she opened the door, and turned into an owl; perched in the same tree as when I pulled in earlier. Her dress pooled on the step.

I had a lot of answers, but not to my questions. It frustrated me to no end. The cycle didn't look like it would ever end—a round robin of sorts.

I listened to the soft hooting outside, intent on learning what she avoided telling me. She was a sweet old lady; a woman I loved, but one of them. And what did she mean Doug's rosebush?

CHAPTER 16

"Gale! Gale, oh no, God, no."

It was around three-thirty in the morning when I heard squawks from a bird in distress.

I slipped from the bed, ran to the front of the house, and pulled the door open. Black dog-like creatures surrounded Gale's smaller form.

"Gale," I screamed.

This time, one of the creatures turned its squared face and drooling jaws to look at me. Its ebony fur lackluster in the clouded moonlight, one iridescent eye focused on me. It stalked toward the door. I slammed it shut. All I thought about was her white figure on the ground; she had to be hurt.

I went to the buffet drawer, grabbed the gun, and pushed the magazine in. I pulled back the slide and went to the door, hesitating to open it when a body hit the brass kick-plate. I pulled it open and pointed the barrel toward the black dog creature. It leapt toward me, and I fired.

I hit it. Once, twice, three times.

It didn't stop. I'd just made it angry. It shook its head, buying me enough time. I slammed the door shut and bolted it. I grabbed the sword from the wall, and my cell off the table, but the only person I could think of to help me was Gérard. I dialed—Doug picked up.

"Doug, Gale's in trouble." I crouched to the floor, afraid that at any moment, one of those dogs would come crashing in.

"Give me a minute," he said.

A breath later I heard his voice, *"Ma chérie,* Doug summoned."

"Help me, something's out there." I'd no sooner spoken, and

glass breaking in the bedroom sent me scrambling under the kitchen counter, in the double cabinet. I dropped the phone.

I'd never not felt safe until that damned anniversary. The false sense of security I'd imagined around me had come crashing down along with that damned mental wall. Reality was biting my ass and honestly, I couldn't handle being afraid. And believe me, I was afraid. Up until that point, the reality of the monsters hadn't proved real. What the hell was I supposed to do? I didn't know what took Gale. I didn't know what was trying to kill me.

The faint smell of garlic and shrimp that made my mouth water only moments ago, sickened me. My mouth went dry, tears stung my eyes. I gripped the sword two-handed. My teeth chattered; I tried to keep my mouth clenched shut so as not to make any noise. I also tried not to breathe.

Ma chérie, I am here. It took a second to realize Gérard was in my mind as he'd done before.

Heavy sniffing ran down the perimeter of the doors. The beast whimpered. I tucked my head in my knees just as a black claw dug into the cabinet. I screamed as it ripped the door off its hinges and grabbed my arm with its putrid mouth. I struggled, but it dragged me from the box. Pain shot through my arm like nothing I'd ever felt before. The creature pulled me through the broken pieces, cutting my free arm on the splintered wood. Blood ran down my arm in a steady stream.

I swung the sword one-armed and struck the black beast right across the hind quarters before Gérard appeared in the kitchen and knocked into it from the side. I went with it as the jaws clenched tighter. I dropped the sword. Gérard picked up the weapon and hurled it at the beast and me.

"No!" I screamed and scrambled backward in time to see the creature lying in a growing pool of blood; decapitated.

Gérard was nowhere to be seen, but I could hear him. *You are safe, ma chérie. I will be with you in a moment.*

My heart refused to settle back in my chest. I cried and laughed, not in a good way. A shard of wood stuck in my arm through my pajama sleeve; pain radiated up and down in electric shocks. I wrapped my good arm around my knees and rocked. I rocked and cried until that damned fly landed on my hand. It kept coming back even after I swatted at it. Call me crazy, but the stupid thing brought me out of hysteria. It made me angry. To be honest, I'd rather be angry than hysterical any day.

I blew at the fly and wiped my tears on my shoulder. Doug, and about eight others of Gérard's people, came in to check on me and to remove the body. Doug carried me to the couch, while the others cleaned up the broken glass in the bedroom and the blood in the kitchen. The bite burned; I wondered if the saliva was acidic. I had never seen such a beast. The pain forced tears to run in streams. I dreaded going to the hospital.

"I don't want to go to the hospital," I groaned.

Doug sat on the edge of the couch and lifted my arm. "Hold tight, love."

I expected him to pull up a car or get the limo, but he grabbed the protruding wood with his teeth and tore it from my arm. I gasped. Nausea and disbelief turned my silent scream to a deep groan.

Doug licked at the open wound. It hurt, but the shock kept it manageable, so I didn't say anything. Besides, what would I say?

"You'll be okay. I can smell your fear, but there's nothing left to be afraid of, trust me. The danger's gone." He spoke between licks. "Your fear increases, love. Talk to me."

"Nothing—everything." I said quickly. "What was that, in there?"

Actually, I was afraid because I wasn't so sure I wanted a werewolf licking my blood. I mean, were they like dogs, you give them a taste of your blood and they want it forever? And, *okay okay*, I was kind of hoping the only person to ever get to taste my blood would be Gérard. Sick? Stupid? But I felt ruined for him; somehow less virtuous. It was strange.

Ma chérie, although I am flattered, you are not ruined. My Douglas is healing your wound, not taking from you, for he is not vampire. I am most certain you have shed blood before our meeting and will do so when I am not near.

I'd forgotten he could hear my thoughts. Did he always hear them? Could he hear this? Oh, no. Damn it, that's not right. My mind was my own; he shouldn't have been in there. All I could think was *stop it.*

I didn't get a response, but Doug looked at me. His eyes had a citrine flame similar to Gérard's blue. His expression scared me.

"Doug?" My voice and body shivered. "What's going on?"

"You're afraid of me. I could tell you were lying. I can sense that, we all can. Gérard apologizes, you are angry with him," he whispered, as he looked at the floor. "Why be afraid of me now, Summer?"

"I . . . I don't . . ."

"Please, spare the lies." Doug whispered, "Tell me."

I tried not to compare at the bloody mouth print and Doug's bloodless lips. He'd torn the sleeve to lap at the gash, and removed the shard, but the creature's bite burned, and Doug hadn't touched it yet. Was that how his bite felt?

"Summer?"

No point in sugar coating, especially since Gérard already knew. "If you tasted my blood, would you want it more? Really, I didn't know a shifter could heal wounds. I'm ashamed of my own thoughts. I like you, Doug. Please, don't hurt me."

Doug frowned at me. Anger or hurt caused his eyes to smolder, a mix of amber and citrine. "I am not a shifter, nor am I a dog. Perhaps you claimed me as your stray, but clearly, I am not good enough as a man."

"Gérard said you wouldn't hurt me, and besides you said you've been around me for years, and I never knew. If you wanted to, I'd think you'd have been smarter to do it before I started dating your master, right?" I tried to put the semblance of a smile on.

"Master?" He laughed. "I'm grateful. You told the truth. I guess not knowing us, meaning lycanthropes," he put the emphasis on lycanthropes. "Or our ways it would seem frightful. But to answer your concern, I get plenty of raw meat."

"When the moon is full?"

He laughed again. "No, I don't hunt in the woods for animals. For the record, the moon has nothing to do with it." And then his face drained of emotion. I leaned back to distance myself from him. His eyes illuminated, with that same amber glow. "As for hurting you, well . . ." He grabbed the burning arm and sucked.

I gasped. The pain tore through me. His tongue explored the holes the creature had left and eased each painful throb with his circular licks.

"Although I enjoy blood, I am not vampire, nor do I crave blood. But I'll take any that comes along." He smiled. "I have not acquired a taste for you in particular; in fact, look at yourself. You're healing." I rubbed over a scab that formed around the edges. "Besides, aren't I allowed a small treat for fixing you up? It isn't fair that Gérard gets you all to himself." He was joking now. It made me feel better.

"I guess."

"Gérard wants to know if he may enter."

"Of course. Why would he ask?"

Gérard appeared in the opened door. *"Oui, ma chérie*, I listened to your thoughts; it angered you. I honored your request." He lowered his head, a sort of bow, his eyes focused on mine. "Will you forgive me?"

Damn. I couldn't keep an angry face around him. "Sometimes it's okay."

"You mean when you need help. Otherwise, stay out of your private thoughts." His words stung. I didn't like it.

"No, I mean, when I need help, or if I let you know you can, or if you want to speak to me privately." I realized he was right. Fuck, dependency reared again. "I'm sorry."

"Ah, you are lovely. The shades you turn are wonderful. I love them all." He chuckled, gave a full bow, and offered his hand to help me up. "And what lovely night clothes you have."

I took his hand and stood exposing my naked feet, stubbly legs from the ankles down, and my hair all matted from sleep. A literal bloody mess. "Ha," I laughed at my own pun. Pathetic.

"I may never know what it is to awaken in the morning next to you, but this helps. I shall dream of you all day." He whisked me into his arms and out the broken door.

"Where are we going?" I held onto his neck for dear life. I certainly didn't expect to be outside, especially so fast. It amazed me at how he kept awing me with those small displays of his abilities. And what happened to my door?

"My place, *ma chérie*. Where else?"

"Oh." I managed to squeak out before we were flying over the lake to his doorstep.

I will never get on an airplane. The thought scares me to death, and to fly in Gérard's arms was no exception to my fear.

I'd like to say that I felt safe wrapped in his arms, especially when we flew high enough that if he dropped me, I'd perish. But it would be a lie. Besides, those weren't the thoughts to be having while doing it. I'd have to inquire further about vampire flying accidents and their statistical ratings.

Gérard landed in his courtyard and set me beneath a vine tangled trellis. When he turned, I realized he was wearing the long black cloak from the cemetery. It flowed around his body as he strode toward the doors to the dining hall. "Come."

I followed dutifully as I hopped from paver to paver, to avoid stepping on something unpleasant in my bare feet. I was cold, but still found the courtyard inviting. I'd never been in it before and liked the way I felt, almost like my whole being was at peace.

Gérard watched me make my way. "Kitty has prepared the library."

He took my elbow with more force than I expected and pulled me with him.

Kitty sat on the hearth ledge of the fireplace in the library's central fireplace. I sat on a daybed and glanced around the room. I wanted to explore, but I was cold and tired.

"The fire will warm you." He frowned.

"Do you think Gale's okay? I want to cry thinking of those horrible sounds."

"*Je ne sais pas*, we have not found her." He raised a pale finger and pressed it to his lips. "Ah, before you speculate, you must know more. Those were not dogs, as you thought. They are legendary—the crocotta."

"Never heard of them."

"And there is no reason why you should have. It is rare for them to be here, in North America. Originally, they were a dog-wolf hybrid. They learned to speak as humans and used that skill to lure victims into the forests."

"And that's what wanted to kill me?"

"Eh, Summer, there is too much, you are an innocent."

"Because I'm ignorant in this life."

He sat on the hearth and stoked the fire. "In the medieval era, say the 1200s, several crocottas were captured. An organization of tyrannical lords, led by the Turkish vampire Aldatmak, forced imprisoned shifters to mate with the creatures. This went on for several hundred years until the crocotta hybrid procreated without human interference, thus creating the creatures you saw this evening."

"Those poor people. I'm surprised the crocottas didn't kill the shifters."

Kitty came over to sit by me. "They are highly intelligent and evolved to become accepted members of society. Most of our kind are unable to detect them."

"You're saying they're people, they just shift into this monster?" I confirmed.

Gérard slid a brown leatherbound book from the shelf and thumbed through. Satisfied with the page, he turned it around to show me. "They become the crocotta through transition, the same as lycanthropes. And just like them, they have all the strength and cunning, but the crocotta are born like shifters."

"They're worse than werewolves?"

"Ooo, *ma chérie*, your words sting. Is this how you feel about my Douglas?"

"No, I was just saying. I mean, I forgot about him and any others." He had a good point. "I meant, before I knew it was how I thought."

"It is that reaction which has prohibited our safety and forced our secrecy throughout history. These individuals are not from my territory and do not yet answer to me. They will when I acquire them, but for now, they answer to the servant of *Michel*, the Master of Toronto. I believe you know his servant as Samuel."

"Sam?" I gasped. "Gérard, Gale told me she was concerned with the relationship between Tiny and Sam. Could Sam have something against Gale and Tiny?"

"*Oui*, I do not want you to go to work. Stay here. At least until the passing of the Samhain."

"I can't. I'm catering the big party at *Chez*. I do it every year."

"Not this year."

"It's for the best," Kitty said, "Consider for now, that the gates to Mount Mort are open. With what you know now, think of what it means." She squeezed my hand before leaving the library.

"Are there gates?" I asked.

Gérard motioned for me to come to him with a quick nod of his head. "Metaphysical, Summer. As I said before, no one is a prisoner. You are free to go, but not all are permitted entry."

"It wouldn't be a sanctuary if they were, would it?"

He held his hand out to me. I took it and followed him through the corridors and stairwell, into the bedroom in silence.

He kissed my hair and whispered, "I will change; do not move." He was gone. I did not feel him go.

I climbed in the bed, and waited, wondering what Gale was going through; wondering why those creatures were at my house. I was lost in thought when he came back and stood beside the bed in a pair of black silk boxers with red, glittery lips. And, just like all the men I know, he still had his socks on.

"Do the socks have a purpose?" I had room to talk; I was still in my bloody granny gown.

"I forgot them." He bowed his head and took them off before he slid beneath the covers with me. He slipped his arm under my pillow, his eyes even with mine. "Samuel is the Toronto clan's leader. I need you to do as I ask."

I avoided that. I wasn't sure what I wanted to do yet. "What's an Aldatmak?"

"Not a what, but a who. He's ruthless and older than I."

"Shit, poor Gale."

"Make no mistake, *ma chérie*. I will find her. Now rest, you need your courage. No matter what has happened, I am with you now and you are safe." He kissed the end of my nose as he whispered, "Sleep."

CHAPTER 17

I never thought life would take the turn it had. In all my three decades, I never would have predicted the events of late. The crocottas, the conversation with Gale—falling asleep in a nightgown soaked in my own blood. The stiffness of dried blood on the fabric made sleeping uncomfortable. My arms ached, which roused me from the restless sleep. I rolled over to the right, toward the chaise and bathroom door. The deeper part with the vanity had dark recesses. I preferred to have the expanse before me, and the curtained wall behind. Being with Gérard hadn't changed my hatred of the dark.

I slid a leg out from under the covers, but stopped when I glimpsed a figure standing in the bedroom doorway. It was Guillaume.

"Good afternoon," he said.

I stuck my leg back in, clutching the duvet. "I didn't think you were friends with Gérard."

"He and I share a common interest." He stared down at me, eyes soft and wanting.

It was nice, but not a look I wanted from him. I could think of a few faces I'd rather see standing there. Of course, Gérard would obviously have been acceptable, but the mysterious and elusive Douglas would have been my choice for the day. Kitty, Dani, Dawn—maybe. Guillaume hadn't even been a thought.

"I hope you like the breakfast I chose for you." He walked over to the vanity and picked up a small coffee cup next to a brown bag. "Do you take sugar?"

"Sometimes."

He dumped two packets in and stirred. "Kitty called Tiny to say you wouldn't be in today. Creamer?"

"Please."

"I stopped in to see you and found out you weren't working. I thought it best to bring breakfast. After all, you're staying in a vampire's lair." I couldn't tell if it was sarcasm or an attempt at mild humor.

A rush of heat flushed through my chest. "It's not a lair."

"Isn't it though?" He handed me the coffee. "A safe harbor for aggressive creatures."

I put my hand up to refuse the coffee. "Though a nice gesture, you could have called. If you don't mind, I need to get dressed." I nodded toward the door while fighting the urge to tell him to get the hell out. Really, I was asleep with him in there!

He picked up the paper bag and strode to the door. "I'll wait out here. I do look forward to your company."

"Thanks." I didn't mean it.

He closed the door behind him, and I scurried to the wardrobe. I pulled a navy-blue velvet jumpsuit with matching undergarments from the drawers and slipped into the bathroom. There was no shower, so I ran a quick bath to scrub the crusted blood from my arms and legs, before getting dressed.

It would seem someone had been a sneaky little vampire because the bra was my true size. Hmmm. Oh, I liked the sound of that. I guess the strangeness of my life was finally catching up to me. I folded my pajamas and put them in the bathroom receptacle. I wasn't going to keep them while they were tattered and stained. The last thing I wanted was another reminder of everything.

Which led me to think, I was dating a dangerous man and staying in a house full of people or beings that were all capable of killing. Everyone I knew had the ability. Whether they practiced, or not, it didn't matter.

I dabbed on some lip gloss from the vanity tray and swiped a quick line of black liner before opening the door to the den.

Guillaume was sitting in a wingback chair facing the fireplace with the bag on his lap. "All freshened up?" he asked without looking at me. He was staring at the fireplace, which had no fire.

"Yup. Shall we eat?" I was uncomfortable, like dating behind your significant other's back—guilt riddled, but innocent.

"Sure," he said. Our answers were short. The feeling seemed to be mutual, or he picked up on mine, which turned a good deed awkward.

"By the way, how'd you get in there without waking me?"

"I told Kitty that Tiny sent me, and I brought you breakfast. I insisted she let me check on you myself, see how you were doing," he said.

"Thanks, but it wasn't necessary. I mean, I appreciate your coming all the way out here, but I'm fine. Really." I didn't want to be rude, but I wasn't flattered. I'd speak with Gérard or Kitty later.

He handed me a napkin with a cinnamon bun and a coffee. He made a cup for himself and took a bun after setting the bag on the hearth. We ate in silence, just staring at the cold fireplace. After we finished, he stood and grabbed the bag.

"I'll take your cup." He put his hand out and waited while I finished the last bit. "You going to work in that?"

"Why?"

"It's too nice for kitchen duty."

"I'm thinking I should hang around for Gérard to get up, spend time with him. I don't really feel like doing much today. Besides, I'm worried about Gale, and am anxious to . . . never mind."

He reached over and stroked my forearm. "No, tell me. I want to help."

Guillaume made me nervous. I wanted Gérard so bad it hurt, and where the hell was Doug?

"You still have several hours before Gérard wakes. It's hardly two in the afternoon. Why don't we at least head to the diner? Let everyone see you're still alive? You know Tiny's concerned. He's upset."

"I guess. My uniform's there if I change my mind."

"Good. I'll drive since we're both going the same way." He looked at the floor before he spoke again. "Unless, of course, you don't trust me."

"Funny you should say that 'cause no, I don't. Besides, wasn't it you who told me not to trust anyone? Don't you think your being here is even the slightest bit—"

"Strange?" He smiled and shook his head. "Guess you could say that. Truthfully, I'm disquieted, as I have been all along. I've been up front with you, Summer. You can't deny that."

"No, I can't. I'm sorry, Guillaume." I fought my nerves and stepped in front of him to study his eyes. There was no flicker, no light. I gave him a slight squeeze of a hug.

"You think it's an unbelievable coincidence having me pop up out of the blue, but you don't think that about Gérard or his followers?"

"Actually, I do. Guillaume, I've come up with questions I never thought would need asking."

He smirked, "You believe, inside your gut, this being you just met has good intentions?"

"Of course."

"Has he taken blood yet? Honestly, I don't bite or need blood." He put his finger up. "Just think about it."

"For your information, no, he hasn't. I'm not used to this, but I'm happy right now. I don't want to change that."

"I understand. Perhaps a little put off that he beat me to you." He winked and smiled. "Shall we get going?"

"You know, I think I'll take the limo and meet you over there. I kind of want to hang around here a little longer. I feel safe here."

"Summer." His voice wrapped around the room; his power ruffled the hairs on the back of my neck. "Won't you at least permit me to show you something? If you come with me, I'll buy you lunch. I supposed to stop by Tiny's house on the way anyway."

I didn't answer. I pulled the wooden door open and walked up the stairs, not looking back, even though I could tell he was behind me.

"Please, wait." He reached for my hand, but I trotted up the stairs a little faster. "Please," he pleaded.

"I don't feel comfortable with you. I think it'd be better if we met at Tiny's." I hastened through the open door at the top of the stairs and headed toward the library. As I was about to go through, Guillaume grabbed my arm and pulled me to him.

"I cannot hold off much longer. I want you, Summer," he said, his voice caught between pleading and groveling.

"You don't know me," I gasped.

"I know enough. Enough that I am desperate enough to come here to one of the most dangerous places I could put myself."

"But why? That's what I don't get."

"Because you're beautiful and kind, and I want a fair chance. Isn't that enough?"

"I think I'm going to stay here and wait for Gérard. If Tiny wants to see me, he's more than welcome to come. I can't do this, not with Gale missing and all. Try to understand, I don't see anything between us." I placed my hand on his chest, then mine.

"Fair enough, I tried and lost. May I escort you to wherever it is you are going?"

"That I'll say yes to."

"Splendid." He took out a tube of Chap Stick and rubbed it over his lips. "It's getting chilly outside." He smiled.

"Really, Guillaume, I'm sorry. Maybe you'll find someone at the festival." I patted his shoulder as reassurance and truly felt bad. But you can't help who you have feelings for, and who you don't.

"I hope you're right. It gets lonely in our world."

I smiled and turned toward the library. "Mine too."

"Summer, wait."

"What, Guillaume?"

"Never mind."

"Damn it, Guillaume. Spit it out." I'd lost my patience. He obviously had something he wanted to say. I don't think he'd ever gotten it out. Not in any of the times we'd spoken. That shit gets old, real quick. "Tell me what it is you keep stalking me for. Seriously, you're like tryin' to tell me something, but every time you do, you don't say anything. Honestly, your information, so far, isn't worth a shit!"

"Gee, thanks." He took his hat off and pulled his bolo loose. "I'm trying. I'm not the bad guy here. Trust me."

"Try harder," I said.

"Your sister wasn't supposed to die. It was . . ."

That was the last thing I heard. Everything went white— bright white, cold, and silent. I didn't think I'd passed out. But my pulse was in my throat, my body covered in a cold, clammy sweat. I had asked, but what for? I hadn't expected that. How did he know that? Why did he say that? I stood there, dizzy and confused. "What do you mean?" I beat his lapels with my fists. "What the fuck did you mean?"

I swear on my life if I was more than human, he'd be crying.

I wanted to peel the flesh from his muscles, layer by layer. I wanted him to cry and feel the agony he caused. I knew he knew more than he let on. I knew he knew more about my parents and knew too much about me. But I didn't know he knew about her.

I grabbed his arm and yelled, "Then who?"

He slid his thumb over my cheek. "You."

"What?"

He strolled to the chessboard and peered at me through blonde and gold strands that had escaped a neat ponytail with a thin brown streak. His eyes shone like glass as the sunlight from the windows played on them. He was wearing a white suit with a black silk shirt and white tie. His boots looked like white snakeskin. Altogether, he was a nice spectacle. A spectacle I wanted to beat the shit out of.

"How long have you been following me?" I asked, unsure of what he was doing there to begin with, or myself for that matter. I pushed a stack of books from the end table by the door and stormed him.

He caught my wrists.

"What the fuck kind of psycho are you?" I fought to think clearly. It was one of those moments when you knew you had to do something, but it was surreal. All my thoughts seemed blurred and in slow motion. I wanted to run but didn't know where to go. I wanted to kill him but didn't know how. I wanted Gérard but didn't because nothing assured me more than that moment that he knew, too.

What was I supposed to do? I just—l didn't know. I couldn't think of anything. In fact, a wave of calm came over me and I fought it. It wasn't like everything was just plain peachy. It wasn't, and I had to figure out if he was there to kill me or save me. If so, then why or from whom? Shit.

CHAPTER 18

Guillaume stood by the double doors of the library. He'd donned his hat and waited. "Now, might I suggest we go see Tiny?"

"Fine," I huffed.

He took my hand, walked to the front door, and led me through the woods toward my house. I wished I had my gun.

His car was there, next to the edge of the path. "I'll go ahead and warm her up."

"Okay."

I watched him jog off and sat by the lake. It was cold, but the water always calmed my nerves. A beaver scurried along the opposite shore, and I let out a long sigh. One day, when life was normal again, I swore to spend an afternoon lolling by the lake.

"All set," Guillaume called out.

Sadly, I strolled toward the car, not caring if he waited or not—secretly wishing I were rich, so I didn't have to work. Which reminded me, what the hell did they all do for a living?

Guillaume drove to the diner; he held my hand the whole time. I let him. It was strange being sought after, first Gérard, and then Guillaume. Then there was Doug, on my part. I hoped *he* didn't want to kill me.

The drive took longer than usual because we had to stop at Tiny's house. Guillaume ran inside, coming out empty-handed. He eased onto Main Avenue back toward the diner.

Once we arrived and he parked, I headed to the building and called back. "You got what you needed from Tiny's?" I figured Guillaume had whatever it was in his pocket unless he shoved it somewhere. I would have liked to shove something somewhere. I wasn't that naïve. Why would he need to go to Tiny's, be it good or bad, when it involved me?

I pulled the door with more vigor than necessary.

"Hey, Summer." Tiny hurried over and gave me a big hug. "I was worried about you. How ya' holdin' up?"

"I'm fine." That was so far from the truth it shamed me. "We stopped by your house. Guillaume's got whatever it is. How are things? I feel like I'm hardly here anymore." I always rambled when I got nervous.

Guillaume popped a butter mint from by the register in his mouth. "Sam here?"

Tiny nodded to acknowledge him but kept his attention on me. "There's been so much crazy shit going on with you. I can't believe you came in."

"Me either." I stepped away from both men. "So, how's Dani taking it?" I asked.

Tiny blotted the beading sweat on his forehead with a rag he pulled from his back pocket. "Don't know, I can't reach her either."

"She must be beside herself. I can't imagine what she's going through. On second thought, I can." I was almost shoulder-to-shoulder with Guillaume, my eyes focused on his; my curiosity was eating me from the inside out.

Guillaume slid into a booth. "You got to let it go. It'll eat you alive."

"Yeah, well. Apparently, some people know better than others."

"I feel like it's my fault," Tiny said.

"My parents and I always went off on trips together, albeit locally. They were fascinated by the beauty of the mountains and notorious for hikes that lasted days," I said. "That had nothing to do with you. I'm the one to blame."

"How?" Tiny asked.

"How? Because I was a typical teenager. I grew out of wanting to spend all my time with them and chose to stay behind. I was selfish."

I slid on the bench across from Guillaume. "That was the first time I didn't go. I didn't get a second chance."

"I know, the anniversary of their disappearance is coming up," he said.

"Yup. It'll be twelve years. They planned for a week and wanted me to come. We were supposed to chart rare birds. It was the last trip before the temperatures dropped. I didn't enjoy the cold weather outings, which is why it was our last for the year."

"You were a kid, Summer," Tiny said.

"I was seventeen, hardly a child. I'll never forget how I felt when they didn't come back. After the police search ended, I kept going. I put fliers around and left my information with everyone, hoping someone knew something." I forced the tears back with a deep breath and heard a welcoming voice.

"We haven't been able to . . ." Dawn walked in from the kitchen. "Summer! God, it seems like forever since I've seen you." She waddled over and hugged my neck and head. "Sorry, we ended on a bad note."

"Let's forget it happened." I squeezed her hand. "Little Richard's getting big." Her stomach dropped. She was due November first.

"He's a kicker, too. And the heartburn is unreal." She put my hand on the side of her belly. "Feel."

"The little guy kicked against my hand!"

She smiled. "Wish I could stay, but Richard's on his way.

"You do what you need. Is Sam here?"

"Yeah, he's in the kitchen making stocks," Tiny said. "He's been quiet—shook up about Gale. They didn't get along all that well, but he still feels bad. I think we're all being too pessimistic. She's probably fine. I'm sure she'll turn up soon."

His looks betrayed him because he was a mess. He was unshaved, and it looked like he slept in the clothes. Tiny never went anywhere without having been showered, shaved, and clothed in clean clothes. There was even stubble growing on his head.

The whole situation was so damned depressingly suspicious; I couldn't take it. His sister was attacked and missing, then he couldn't get a hold of his niece. There were no customers in the diner, and Sam was brooding in the kitchen. Why the hell wasn't the diner closed? What did I really know about him?

"I wish there were some miracle to help, but I know from experience, that time heals all wounds. They may scar, but they heal." I scooted from the bench. "I'm goin' in the back."

Guillaume stayed in the booth, and Dawn slid in where I'd been. "Maybe make some fliers, Tiny. You never know," I called over my shoulder.

Sam didn't lift his eyes from the chopping block when I walked into the kitchen.

"If I was you, I'd start preppin' for *Chez*. You're here anyway," he said.

"I could start the apple strudel, so all I'd have to do is throw it in the oven."

"I can stuff the quails and wrap the pineapple chunks in bacon. With the party a week away, it's got to be done." He wiped his hair back with his wrist. "If you don't mind my help."

"Be my guest. I'm not in the mood to do all this." I picked at a dried piece of lettuce on the chopping block.

"Good, I'll set the mis-en-place. You go wash."

Sam grabbed a bunch of dishes from the cart and set them out on the counter. I washed my hands and set to work.

"Damn." I started to cry while dicing the apples.

Sam stared at me. "Aw come now, sweetheart." He wandered over, put his overly muscular arm around my shoulder and squeezed. "You don't know nothin' yet. Keep your chin up."

Guillaume walked in and took over the hug. "Sam, you can finish up here for a bit, can't you?"

"No problema. Take all the time you need. I wasn't expecting an extra pair of hands today."

Guillaume pulled me after him toward the seating area. "Summer?" he whispered. "Want to go?"

"Yeah." That was the truth, but not with him.

He led me to his car and opened the door for me.

Guillaume pressed the back of my hand to his lips. "Why so upset? You don't know if anything happened to her. You shouldn't get upset over things you don't know."

His lips were cold. "It's like having a death in the family. I feel sick." Sick over the fact that I still didn't know what the hell he was. Sick of the fucking games. "She's not coming back."

"Now you're jumping to conclusions," he sighed. "You don't even know what happened."

"Déjà vu."

"Not necessarily." He left the parking lot in the opposite direction of my house.

"Where are we going?"

"I told you. I want to show you something."

"Fine." I wasn't in the mood for surprises. It annoyed me.

Having all the male attention had me unsettled. I wasn't exclusive with Gérard, but it didn't feel proper being with another man. Hell, I hardly knew either of them. Guillaume was no Gérard, but he was alluring. Handsome as hell, but no fuzzy feelings stirred within me like they did with Gérard and Doug. I didn't feel anything around Guillaume, anything good, that is. But I did like the long stubble on his chin, and the way his icy blue eyes stood out from his blondish features.

"What're ya thinkin' 'bout?" He laid on a thick drawl.

"I'm numb. I don't like feeling nothing. I should feel something. It's like I'm crying but not feeling sad."

"A part of your life is missing. It makes sense."

He turned into a long dirt driveway. I'd passed it before. There was a fieldstone house on one of the smaller lakes. It wasn't big enough for a boat with a motor, more rowboat sized. The remnants of cattails and pussy willows grew along the farther banks. Surprisingly, there were several white horses. No fencing, just horses grazing around the water.

"Is this your house?"

"No, afraid not. I've rented it until the beginning of November. Then I go back to Wales."

A wave of relief washed over me. I'd be dead before the festivities at *Chez*, or he wanted a fling. To date two men was not my style. I don't believe in being hypocritical. If I dated both, then they could date others. With all the weird shit going on, I'd be a fool to put myself at risk. Besides, I wouldn't be able to handle it, mentally I mean. I'd had enough with Jesse. Death was a fix.

"You don't look so good," he said. We'd stopped; the car was off. "My father was from Wales. My mother was Scottish if you want to know." He didn't sound like my dad, and he was Welsh. "I wouldn't have pegged you for Welsh, maybe Texan."

"I'm not, but I live there now. Come on, there's a bench over here. We can watch the horses." He opened the glove compartment and took out a box of sugar cubes. He popped one in his mouth. "Want one?"

"No, thanks." That was new.

We got out of the car; he waited with his hands in his pants pockets. I walked around the back of the car to meet him. He lifted my hand and gave me a sugar cube.

"Once we sit, they'll come up to you," he whispered.

I followed him to a bench on the edge of the water. There was a large white stallion standing in the lake up to its withers. He raised his head and bobbed it at us. I wasn't used to being around horses. I was ashamed to say it frightened me a little. More than a little, a lot. I was just glad they weren't black. I scanned the yard for a black stallion—that's what my sister had mounted before he charged off into the river. She'd drowned as a result. Maybe it wasn't so freak after all. Maybe I should have stopped for my gun, not that it did any good. Maybe Guillaume was my white knight.

The stallion made his way toward us while the others watched. A few snorts and nods between them and another stepped closer. That was a male, too. He stomped the ground and pawed with his front hoof. I scooted closer to Guillaume.

Guillaume muffled a laugh. "They won't hurt you. They're only horses, Summer."

"I know." I waited until one of them came over. "Can I give this to him?" I held the sugar cube up.

I didn't have to wait for Guillaume to answer because the horse sniffed my hand and took the cube with his lips. The other one came up next to him; he sniffed for one.

"Take all you want." Guillaume sprinkled a few more in my hands.

"I've never done this before. The last time I was around a horse, I jumped off when it moved. I don't like heights and it scared me."

He glanced at me from the side with a soft smile. "They're sure-footed, graceful—handsome. What's not to love?"

He reached out to the one who came from the water. The stallion went to Guillaume and nuzzled him. His whiskers must have tickled because Guillaume crinkled his face and kissed the horse's muzzle. Guillaume was actually cute. It was refreshing, having all the drama taken away for the day. I relaxed and fed all my cubes to the horses that came over.

"They like you," Guillaume said.

"No, they like sugar."

"I think they like you, too," he winked.

"Thanks." I turned away from him.

"Come on, let's go for a ride," he called.

I turned around to see him on a horse, bareback. "I can't. Seriously, I hate horseback riding."

"That's because you probably went to one of those pay by the hour places. These are seasoned professionals." He patted the neck of his companion. "You can ride with me."

"Uh-uh."

"Try it, Summer," he implored.

"No, I can't." I clasped my hands and sat on the edge of my seat, stiff as could be.

"Why not?"

"I told you; I don't like heights."

"But you flew with Gérard."

"But . . ." He had me there.

"No buts; come on." He patted the horse's neck and maneuvered the creature in front of me.

"I don't want to ruin my outfit."

He hopped down. "At least I'm still human. Those vampires are a nasty sort. They're wicked, conniving, and dark. There's no good to come from being with a vamp. I'd bet he has plans to turn you into one." He spread his arms. "You can never do this with him, Summer. It's warm, the sun is shining, and you love it. How is your life going to be if you stay with him?"

"You don't know him."

"Neither do you."

I knew he was right, but I didn't have to like it. I got up and faced the car.

"Summer, I can't offer you a mansion, but I can offer you a life unlike any you ever had. Think about it."

The sound of hooves hitting the ground forced me to look back. He took off across the field and disappeared through the wood line.

I knew there was no such thing as Mr. Perfect. But why did men have to be that way? Pigheaded; competitive. That was why some women stayed single or found companionship in other women. Why couldn't we simply have an intellectual, platonic relationship? Why did it always have to be more?

CHAPTER 19

There were no cars in sight, as Guillaume's house disappeared behind me. The heels of my shoes clicked against the road and syncopated with the pounding of my heart. I was a nervous wreck walking alone, dusk or not, but I had to get over those fears.

In retrospect, I could have tried summoning Gérard, but I needed to depend on myself. I needed to be self-sufficient. Independence was more important to me than romance. Besides, I could trust myself.

I had no idea how far I was from the diner, but I knew I lived a good twelve miles in the opposite direction from which we came. I took off my shoes and walked in my stocking feet.

It was dark, and I hadn't reached the diner yet. My feet were sore because we mainly had oil and chip. No nice smooth roads in the sticks.

"Argh," I groaned. "Why did he have to be so nice? I should have told him no." Guilt took over. I wasn't playing fair. Maybe if he had known, he wouldn't have pushed. *It wouldn't work anyway, I thought, he likes horses too much.*

I finally reached the diner, which was empty except for Tiny and Sam. I went in the back door, grabbed my uniform from my locker in Tiny's office, and set out to put on my uniform. After I'd emerged from the ladies' room, I sat down at the counter and sipped the coffee that Tiny had waiting for me. He was rolling silverware in large paper napkins.

I wouldn't have thought it peculiar that the diner had no customers. I mean, ordinarily, people would pay their respects. Especially since gossip is like the gospel. But Tiny and Sam wouldn't win any popularity contests. I hoped Gale was okay, but I had no hope. Once you disappeared, there was no coming back. Not in Mount Mort.

I pushed through the double doors. Bleach fumes burned my eyes and added to my angst. I was still pissed at Guillaume. I nodded at Sam as he cleaned and hurried past him. It wasn't his fault, but at that moment, he was the recipient in-wait.

Now, I was pissed because I knew I shouldn't have gone with Guillaume. He was more of a dark cloud, cold and damp. I could feel it deep inside, like an ache. It was a conscious feeling rather than a true emotion. I was also plagued with guilt. Guillaume was right, Gérard couldn't be there by day. It was the classic vampiric dilemma.

I grabbed a wedge of Gruyere from the refrigerator and slammed it on the stainless steel counter.

Tiny pushed through the double doors.

"What?" I asked.

"Talk, now." He came over, slid his hands down my arms, grabbed one of my wrists, and led me out of the kitchen. His free hand pulled out a stool at the counter.

"Summer, I know you feel responsible, but don't. It's not your fault." He ran both his hands over his head, smoothing back hair he didn't have. He'd shaved. That was fast. "Sam says you and Gérard are getting comfortable. But Guillaume—something's afoot there as well."

He'd gone where I didn't want to go. Why couldn't it be simple? Doug. Why was I pining for him? That would have been easy. I already loved him, though as a stray. He knew me. Granted, I didn't know him that well, but—ah, it would be easier than choosing. And now I was seeing his master. "Fuck me," I said, as I pressed my forehead to the edge of the cold counter.

How much was I willing to give? How much would I pay in the end—if I continued with Gérard? The truth sucked. Vampirism sucked. Men, no matter the species, sucked.

"Tiny, don't," I said.

He took a seat on the stool next to me. "I've known you a long time. We're close, damn it, Summer." He pounded his fist on the counter. "I'm closer than that—that damned vamp. I know Gale set you up, but I don't like it."

"Wait, Tiny." I put my hand up to stop him. "I can't let you do this. You're his friend. Now, I'm sorry; I love you, as a friend. I don't want to ruin that, but Gérard has become a big part of my life; I won't ruin that."

"Fuck, you think I want you?" he laughed, not a good sound. "I've done things, people died, Summer. And like it or not, it's necessary. But no matter the intent, there're times when plans fail. Take the Álfar, for instance. They were in the way. Even the French and English discovered that. When something stands in your way, what's the first thing you do?" He leaned in my face. "You eliminate it. But there are consequences. Like you, for instance. You were left alone, but it stands to be corrected. And sometimes the reasons stand before us in full glory; and we refuse to accept them. Gérard, Guillaume, doesn't matter. Believe it or not, their intent is the same. It's cowardly at best. Now, as for me, honestly, I'm more interested in what side is going to get you. But me, personally? Na, I don't want you."

I turned away so I wouldn't have to look him in the face. Perhaps it was cowardly, but my inflating ego took a hit. "I'm going to prep the burgers for *Chez*."

"Attempting to change the subject." He smiled and slid behind the counter. "So, which one is the liar? They're both on the P.R., how do you like politics, Summer?"

I glanced at him sideways. "I'll be in the kitchen."

I hurried through the doors. Sam had taken the garbage out and used it as a smoke break. It was my chance to be alone for at least a few minutes.

I went back to the fridge and grabbed the mutton legs I'd ordered. I'd ordered four; there were six. Goody.

I unhooked the cover on the grinder, plugged it in, and unwrapped the first leg. It was amazing how much pent-up emotion was released in the deboning process. I was a knife wielding wonder. Three legs down, three to go. I turned on the grinder and pressed the meat through intermittently with the Gruyere. The vulgar sound of wet flesh masticated by the machine, relieved only by the need for more knife wielding, resounded against the tiled walls. It was satisfying.

The back door opened. Sam came through, went in the office, and went back outside with a manila folder. I didn't like Sam or this new Tiny.

I paused by Sam's station, entranced by the white dragonesque vapor hovering over the stockpot. It reminded me of home. I yearned to go home, sit by Lake Sangre surrounded by small furry critters searching through the crisp leaf litter, or to cuddle up with a blanket and mug of soup. That desire drew me back to reality. I needed to get done and go. It was dark. I had no car. And I'd be damned if I asked Tiny or Sam for a ride.

I cut the rest of the meat from the leg bones, taking care to remove sinew and tendons. Two of the last three legs were lean and tough, probably not mutton or meant for *Chez*, but I used them anyway. I threw all the meat in the grinder and went to the freezer for a pork loin to thaw for an upcoming daily special. I figured I could put it in the fridge and grab the thawed one for the burgers. Pork would make the burgers tender.

I opened the freezer. With the new shipment, there were a lot of sides hanging, but they were up front. I pushed them toward the back to ensure we kept with the first in, first out policy. And to make my way to the back shelves.

There was a fresh side hanging in the middle. I decided to switch it to the front by the drain because it was dripping blood all over the freezer floor. So, I grabbed it, to slide around, and felt the warmth. My stomach cramped; nausea bore down. That sixth sense kicked in, along with the realization that it did not belong there. I had to look.

I hesitated; my fingers pulsed against the bag's zipper. My fears were about to be confirmed. By the way the bag bulged at the bottom, I knew there was liquid. The likelihood that it was anything but human blood was nil. I knew I'd found Gale.

I pulled the zipper in one quick motion; my arms went limp. A human buttock rested in the center of the pooled blood. The torso had been trimmed of its limbs. My body shook, blood covered my hands, and uniform. I tried to close the bag, but the dismembered corpse pressed against the material. I couldn't close the bag. The nude body with missing parts took its toll.

I staggered back and tried my best to keep from passing out. The smell of fresh flesh, blood, and gases had me running from the kitchen to the ladies' room. I couldn't keep from throwing up. I grabbed hold of the toilet seat. There was red where my fingers were. The mutton burger was in the kitchen. Or—was it mutton?

Tiny and Sam still hadn't come back. "Those bastards!" I butted my head against the stall. Tiny and Sam had to know. I ran to the counter and dialed 9-1-1.

"I found a body—it's warm." I gagged and drew in a dry sob. "There's blood everywhere," I whispered. I explained that I was a cook at the diner. I told them that I wasn't alone and hung up. I ran back to the ladies' room and locked the door.

It didn't take long, though it seemed an eternity, before there were two police cars, an ambulance, a firetruck, and a partridge in a pear tree. I unlocked the door to peek and saw Officer Tangelo come in first, followed by three other officers and the EMTs. Tiny and Sam came back from wherever they were just as Greene pulled into the parking lot.

CHAPTER 20

Officer Tangelo was questioning Sam and Tiny at the side of the dining area, after she directed the EMTs and the coroner to the kitchen.

One of the other officers came to interview me. He was tall, about six feet something, and lean with little muscle, black hair, military style. He motioned for me to have a seat at the counter; poised with pad and pen. It was Greene.

"So, tell me everything that happened, Ms. Candella." His eyes locked on mine. Looking at him up close, I realized he resembled his mother. Shit, he'd only lost her a mere month ago. He looked like hell. Thin fingers rolled the pen back and forth. His face gaunt, dark hues filled the hollows beneath his eyes. Death was a bitch.

"Just like I told the 9-1-1 operator. I went into the freezer to get the meat. To start preparing for *Chez Fenris's* party, you know?"

"And then what happened?"

"Well, I noticed there'd been a shipment because there was so much meat. And when I walked to the back, I noticed one of the sides was too warm. I decided to move it to the front so I could check the internal temperature, because it was—" I took a deep breath and let it out sort of controlled. "It was warm when I touched it. I knew it wasn't right. With Gale missin' and all, I had to know. I opened the bag and saw the body. I ran to the ladies' room. After puking my brains out, I called you guys."

I blotted my eyes with the napkin he'd handed me. I still had blood under my nails. Damn, I wanted someone I trusted to hold me; to tell me it would be okay. But I knew better. There was no one to trust, and it was not going to get better. I watched a forensics detective take a clear plastic bag, with my burger mix, out to the police van.

"Oh, Gale," I lamented.

"Coincides with the report earlier. How about the truth now?" The officer never looked up. He just kept writing in his little notepad. God, I hated him. I wished Wimmers was there.

"I told you the truth. Also, I don't appreciate your tone." A bolt of fear shot through me. "Wait, am I a suspect?"

He straightened his shirt buttons so that they went in a straight line with the button on his pants. "You all are."

"Oh my God! I'm a suspect? I came here to work. I didn't do anything. I told you the truth. Why am I a suspect?" Hysterics bore down hard. "Why is this happening? I told you everything." I was screaming and hadn't meant to.

"Help me out. I'm here to help you. I can't help, if you don't tell the truth. Come now. Were you jealous over Dani's relationship with Sam? Maybe found the two of them having a hot and heavy time of it in the kitchen. You chase him out of the diner—confront her?"

"What?" I gasped.

He spoke louder. "The argument got out of hand. A crime of passion. It's better if you fess up to me now." Then he leaned in, to whisper. "I might let you live. I'm watching you, because when they get you, you'll rue the day you were born. You'll be wishing you were Dani." He sat back, voice normal. "What do ya' say you help us out and stop wasting our time, Miss Candella? Sam's already told us what happened."

"Stevie, he's a fucking liar!" I called to Tangelo. I scanned Greene's face.

He nodded. "Come now, whoring around like a newbie."

"Excuse me?" I closed my eyes and counted to ten. It didn't help. "Where's Officer Tangelo?"

"You don't need anyone but me." He gritted his teeth. The pen snapped just above the pad.

"Yeah, try again," I hissed.

"Stand up, you're under arrest."

"On what charges?"

"You are under arrest for the murder of Dani Larson. You have the right to remain silent." He grabbed my arm, yanked me from my stool, and shoved me face first into the counter.

"Get away from me, Greene!" I yelled.

". . . anything you say will be . . ."

I screamed. "Officer Tangelo—Stevie!" I kept repeating myself until finally she came over. The whole time, Greene shoved me into the counter, harder, with each Miranda line. Wimmers knew something.

"What's goin' on over here? Damn it, Greene. What the hell are you doing? Step away from her. Now, damn it." She was damn near growling at him, her hand on her sidearm.

He sneered through still gritted teeth. "She'll either talk now, or down at the station."

"Uncuff her, now!" He didn't move but instead scowled at her. "That's an order, Officer."

"Fine." He uncuffed me and threw the cuffs on the counter, along with a cold glance back at Tangelo before he stormed outside. What did Dawn see in him?

"What happened, Summer? I mean, with Greene?" Officer Tangelo asked.

"I told him exactly what happened, and then he gave me his version. I swear, I did tell the truth." I had to sit down on something stable, which Stevie helped me do. We slid into a booth by the front window, still stinking of cleaning ammonia. I swallowed to clear the smell. It didn't work. "He said I found out about Dani and Sam. Sam's a fucking liar. Why Dani?" I stared her right in the eyes.

It was her turn to look away. "Summer, the body in there is Dani's. I don't know how she was killed, but parts are missin'. We're waiting on the coroner now. I know you were close with her and even closer with Gale. Both Tiny and Sam back up your story of just getting here, so I'm not going to put you through anymore. But I do have to bring them down to the station. After all, they are the main suspects at current. By the way, where is Dawn?" She asked the last as if she just realized the diner had almost no employees or customers.

"I don't know. She went home with Richard." I slouched down in the booth. "Dani? Really?"

"If I were you, I'd lie low. Take precautions; stay around other people. Keep new acquaintances to a minimum and lock your doors. Until we have some leads, I want you to take it easy. I know you're catering, but they'll have to make do with what you've got. Until we get an idea, I'll talk to Mayor Krotte about canceling. The diner's off limits for the next few days. Even after that, I still want you to lie low."

"Will do." I wasn't sure what I should or shouldn't say, so I kept it short. "Gale's still missing." I didn't let her know about the shapeshifters because I wasn't sure she'd believe me unless she was part of the secret community herself. I didn't think so.

"I know. I'll talk with missing persons, but for now, this homicide takes priority. It's a small department and with the chief away, we make do."

One of the other Officers came over. "Mount Mort used to be a quiet little town. The more outsiders come, it seems, the more calls we get." He shook his head and gave a small baggie to Tangelo.

"Anyway, I'm sorry about Greene, he likes to play bad cop even when it isn't necessary," said Tangelo.

"I guess; just give me a ring if there's anything I can do. I hope you find who did this because this is just wrong. I can't believe it. Dani didn't do anything to anybody. She was a good person, Stevie. No one deserves this, but especially a twenty-four-year-old woman."

"That's why you need to take it easy. No big outings and stay with crowds. I've got to get these guys down to the station and meet with the coroner." She motioned to the other officers to take Tiny and Sam outside. "I mean it, Summer. Lie low. Have a good night if you can." She patted my hand and left for the kitchen.

I couldn't help but hope that it didn't mean Gale had been murdered too.

I wondered if Guillaume would have any insight. Then again, fuck that bastard. I left the false sense of security of the diner parking lot, well aware it was after nine at night, and headed home in my work shoes and uniform. I had blood all over me, vomit in my hair, and fear eating me alive. And why exactly did the time matter? Day, night, it didn't make a damn bit of difference.

I'd walked to the diner from Guillaume's and wasn't looking forward to the trek home. It was uphill most of the way and surrounded by forest. I wasn't talking to Guillaume. If he gave a damn, he would have come after me rather than letting me walk. Now, I was fodder for whatever being wanted an easy meal. I hated the dark more than ever.

There were no lights, just the owls hooting, and the sound of coyotes off in the distance. I had to admit that the last several weeks changed me. It made me stronger, but not how I would have liked.

I walked for a while, trying not to think about the blood on my clothes and the fact that I'd just ground up one of my best friends with cheese. I threw up where I stood. It was going to be a long seven miles of mountain roads to roam before I could find any semblance of shelter. That's a lot of throwing up to do.

It was against my better judgment, but I thought to Gérard. *Any chance you could send your limo?* I laughed at myself. Maybe he'd hear it, maybe not.

I walked a little further and saw what used to be a welcome sight—my stray. But I couldn't call him that anymore. I resisted the urge to pet him.

I was deceived by the others, but not with Gérard since I had to give him credit for being upfront, and I wasn't upset with Doug. Even though he hid what he was, and came back to me time and time again, knowing full well that I thought he was a wolf, I forgave him. Of course, I hadn't spoken any of this, but in my heart, I forgave him because I don't think I would have accepted the truth from him—them. I know I wouldn't have.

"Hey, Doug."

He leapt into the woods. I waited for a few minutes since I heard rustling and figured he was doing something. I was right. He stepped out on the road dressed in a pair of black parachute pants and white tank top. I thought the 80s were over. He was cute, though.

"Hey, love. Quite the night?"

"You could say that." I looked away. Right then, all I wanted was for him to wrap me in his arms and kiss me like we were lovers in a black and white movie. I wanted the warmth and comfort with real romance. No ulterior motives, no guilt, and no mal intentions. "Shit!" I whispered. I forgot Gérard could hear thoughts. What if he had? How was I going to face him when I got back?

"What?" he asked.

"Nothing, just trying to make sense of everything."

"Mmm, not true. Maybe you're not ready to feel what you're feeling. We'll talk more when you've had a chance to settle down."

He took my hand and walked by my side. I replayed the day, as the hours and miles ticked by. I wasn't used to walking so much and slowed on the ascent. But I wasn't in a hurry. I liked walking with Doug. We made it to my dirt road in silence. The soft waves slapping against the shore with the increased wind on Lake Sangre let me know we were there.

Without realizing it, we were in my drive, and I'd walked to the shore. "I never noticed before. The lake has a reddish hue, doesn't it?" I'd stopped walking. "Is the legend true, Doug?"

"Ay. But ne'er mind about that. I'll keep you safe tonight. No worries." He sniffed my hand and disappeared into the wood line.

I hurried inside, slammed the door, and walked straight to the bathroom. I didn't bother to look around. But instead dropped my clothes on the floor by the door and went to shower. I found comfort in the scent of my own peach soaps and then wrapped in my own towels. Once out, I decided to hell with everyone. I climbed in bed, buck naked, and wept.

CHAPTER 21

The answering machine clicked on as the incessant ringing came to an end. I ran to the kitchen to grab the phone and click off the machine. Cell service was sketchy in the mountains, so of course we all had the old standby.

"Hello?" I checked the clock on the microwave. It was three in the morning. What now? Couldn't anyone let me have one night's rest? Perhaps I should've considered changing my schedule so I could sleep all day. Everyone seemed to leave me alone during the day. Then again, that wasn't entirely true either. Besides, I had to work to pay the bills.

"*Ma chérie*, I woke you." It was Gérard. I guessed that was a decent hour for him.

Whatever. "You woke me," I stated, half-aware of what he just said. Forgive a girl. I was just sleeping, and now having a phone conversation at three fucking am. Excuse me if I was a little thick. "Why'd you do that?" Duh!

"May I come see you? Please."

"Yeah, see you in a few." I hung up and waited by the door.

"*Ma chérie*, it is I." I peeked out of the little peephole, just to be sure, and saw it was him. He looked beautiful wearing black silk pants and violet blouse. His hair was tied back in a ponytail with a black silk ribbon that would've made most men look feminine.

I unlocked the deadbolt and let him in.

He rushed past me, sweeping the area with his uncanny abilities. I hadn't even locked the deadbolt by the time he was back at my side, staring in bewilderment. It was then that I realized—well; I was still naked.

I knew people wore pajamas for a reason, even though they lived alone. The heat crept up my neck and spilled into my cheeks; I stood frozen in disbelief. How could I be so stupid?

I reminded myself that he'd already seen me naked in his bathtub, but it wasn't doing any good. I contemplated running to the bedroom to put something on or trying to shrug it off and stay that way. I decided to hell with the latter; I wasn't staying that way.

"If you'll excuse me," I avoided looking at any part of him and attempted to stay cool at the same time. It wasn't working.

"I shall remain here," he said.

With the blood scalding my veins, I went first to the kitchen to put a mug of water in the microwave, still trying to act nonchalant, and then to the bedroom. I figured I could slip into the pink pajamas I'd purchased at the mall. He'd seen enough for one night.

God, I felt foggy. I put the satin pajamas on and did a quick brushing of my hair and teeth. I wandered to the kitchen, purposely avoiding him, my head down. He'd already put a cocoa envelope on the counter and a spoon.

"Is there anything you want to tell me?" he asked as I finished up my hair with a satin pink bow to match my pajamas.

"No, not really. Why do you ask?" I took the mug from the microwave and stayed at the counter.

"Nothing at all? Danielle is dead, my Douglas walked you home for miles, and nothing happened?" His accent was thicker and much more difficult to understand. He sounded pissed.

"I figured you already knew." I sipped cautiously to avoid burning myself and keep from talking about it. I forgot to add the powder.

"This charade that nothing is wrong does not coincide with your state. Would you deny it?" he demanded.

"No, I wouldn't, but I'm still shaken by everything, especially *you*. There I said it. Happy?" He made me nervous, but not in a good way. I deposited the mug on the counter harder than I intended and spilled water all over my hand. It hurt like hell, but I went calmly to the faucet and rinsed it under the cold water.

"You are one of my people, Summer. Do you know what it means when I say, 'my people'? I ask one last time, what happened?" The last two words thundered through the little house, rattling the windows.

Yup, I was afraid. I didn't understand it at all. But instead of tears, it brought on a stillness, a foreign state I'd only now feigned. I grabbed a dishtowel and dried my hands, still staring at the sink. "I don't know what you want. I don't even know why you're here." I put my face in the towel; guilt bore down. "I awoke in your bed. Guillaume was there; he took me to see his horses." Guilt choked my words. "We had a disagreement and I left. I walked back to the diner."

I huddled in on myself; despair poured from within me. I hated death and wound up screaming. "I touched a piece of Dani. I was grinding meat and it was there. Do you understand what that's like? I found her body. She's dead, do you understand? Gale's gone and I'm here by myself. I can't do this again. I can't." I sobbed into my hands. "I won't."

"I'm scared," I whispered.

Doug came up beside me. I hadn't even known he was there. He scooped me off my feet and sat me in his lap on the sofa. Gérard sat next to us.

Doug nuzzled my head with his chin. "You are not alone, love."

Gérard reached over and lifted my face with the curve of his finger. "You will never be alone, *ma chérie*. That is what it means to be mine."

"Not everyone has both of us," Doug whispered.

"What?" I gasped.

Gérard knelt at Doug's feet, cupped my face, and spoke, voice controlled. "Tell me of your time with *Guillaume*, what happened?"

"Nothing, I swear. Don't be mad." Doug handed me a handkerchief. I blotted my eyes and dabbed my nose. I contemplated that because it was the old conundrum. Did I really return a hanky after that? Could

I slip it into my pajama pocket without them noticing so that I could wash it first? I should have gotten a tissue.

Gérard's voice softened, "Do you trust me, *ma chérie?*"

And there it was: the blain, raw, implacable moment of truth. I stared at Doug's knee. What could I say? The truth was, I didn't. I didn't trust anybody, and I couldn't lie. He probably knew anyway.

"I know you do not."

"What are you going to do? I feel like a hostage. Is Doug in on it? Is he going to restrain me in some vampire torture session to get the information you need? Am I the sacrificial pawn?"

"Again, with the sacrifice." He sighed and shook his head. It was too practiced, unnatural. "Please, let me enter. I do not wish to do so against your will."

"Against my will?" I tried to pull my chin from his hands. He held firm. I contemplated struggling, my eyes wide—frantic.

I accidentally glanced into his eyes, already a swirling mass of stars among the sapphire that was normally there and was caught. He rolled through me, peering into the most recent memories first. Then, it stopped. There was a wall between us.

He peered up at Doug. "Douglas, I cannot." And then his attention was back on me. "Tell me of *Guillaume.* How was he? What did he do?"

I was angry; I scurried from Doug's lap.

Gérard's eyes had turned a blue that was damn near black, and a low growl sounded from Doug. His growl stopped almost as soon as it started, but I still heard it.

"He dares betray me?" Gérard thundered through the house, although he didn't speak visibly. A current of air spread through the living room when he whispered, "Speak, Summer. Answer me." He paced in front of the door.

"Are you going to kill me over this?" I squeaked through my tears. I'd managed to scramble across the floor and put my back to the recliner.

"*Michel* dares a challenge?" He spoke normally, but stalked toward me, for real.

I tried to back up. "Who is Michel to Guillaume?" Just saying Guillaume's name made my chest tighten.

"*Qu'est que c'est?*" Gérard knelt in front of me.

"I know it'll sound crazy, but I think you've all gone mad. Jesus, Tiny and Guillaume are angry because I chose you over him. And who is this, Michel? Honestly, no man has ever wanted me. What aren't you telling me?" I couldn't look at him. "The only one who doesn't is Doug." It physically hurt to say that out loud. Shit.

He glanced down at me, his face expressionless. "Stay away from *Guillaume*. I will not lose you like this. I must go." He stood instantly and vanished. The door slammed shut.

Doug leaned back against the cushion. "Should I stay?" he asked.

"I don't know."

"Wow, didn't expect that." He drew his hands through his hair, stopping at the back. "If I had stayed wolf, would it be different?"

I frowned at him. "I don't know."

"None of this is easy, Summer, and we'll always be here for you. That doesn't mean you'll always agree with our ways. But accepting someone into your life means accepting them for who they and what they are." He went to the door, opened it, and looked back over his shoulder. "Maybe I'm not a stray, but I'm loyal. Remember that." He dashed from the door faster than I could see. I hadn't known he could move like that. Hell, I didn't know anything.

"Doug," I called, even though he was gone. I closed the door until it clicked, slid the dead bolt into place, and peeked out the living room window. I whispered, "Please stay."

Maybe Gérard thought Guillaume did something. Maybe Guillaume thought he was saving me from the dark side. I laughed at myself. Maybe I needed to consult a psychic.

I didn't know. I just didn't know. Perhaps Gérard was being challenged. Maybe, with a hope and a prayer, there would be a psychic with that traveller band I'd seen. It was worth a shot. And when did they replace my door?

CHAPTER 22

I'd gone back to bed and stared at the alarm clock until the sun shined on the wall next to the bathroom door.

I got up, dressed, and called Andy, who owned the print shop slash hardware store in town. I'd learned he was a vamp at Gérard's dinner party. I never knew. His wife picked up. She usually worked the day shift and he the night, which made it easier to ask the asinine question.

Tiny was right. I was oblivious.

"It's Summer, Lil. I was wondering if you got any new customers for, like, business cards or something."

"What are you looking for?" she asked, her voice dry and crackly. Perhaps I shouldn't have called so early. I hadn't thought about the time. They didn't even open until ten.

"This is going to sound ridiculous, but a psychic or mentalist," I cringed when I said it. I should have called the psychic hotline and kept the stupidity to myself.

"Oh, um, Madame Molly put an ad on a placemat for the diner last week." I heard papers rustling in the background. "Yup, here it is." She rattled the number off.

I scribbled it down.

"Thanks, Lil."

"No prob. Talk to you later." She hung up.

I had to admit, for a six-foot plus, stringy bleached blonde who came across half-baked most of the time, she knew her stuff.

She always walked around as if dazed and happy. If I hadn't known Andy, I would swear she was burnt out, but he said she'd always been that way. Said he liked it. Can't figure for the life of me why. He seemed like an intelligent, quick-witted guy.

I dialed the number and listened to the prerecorded message: "If you wish to speak with me directly, you will find me at *Chez Fenris* in suite 9 until Samhain. No need to leave a message." The recording ended and hung up on me. Interesting.

You know, you have to be leery. You always see frauds on the news where they show how they figure things out. I wasn't about to be led on. If she couldn't come up with something real on her own, then I wasn't going to waste my time hearing a bunch of crap.

I hurried to my car and drove to *Chez*.

I pulled in the paved parking lot and thought about Gérard. I'd forgotten about the night he wanted me to go to the woods with him. What the hell for? I'd have to ask him later. In the meantime, my newest venture was standing at the door waiting for me.

I slid out of the tracker, locked the door, and made my way to stand in front of her. A few people were standing in line, waiting to be seated. It was a bigger brunch crowd than I was used to at Tiny's. Guess the impending festivities were growing more than Tiny's wallet. Then again, the diner was closed indefinitely for investigation.

"I could feel your presence," she called. "I know about you. Don't you come in here."

"We've never met." I called back. "Do you even know who I am?" At this point, I was in disbelief with myself for resorting to such tactics.

"Your name is not important. But there is something—something there." She pointed her crooked finger toward my head. "Your past has not been true, nor your life. She looked at me with great suspicion. "Why have you come?"

"Shouldn't you know that?" I was trying to absorb how she could possibly know anything.

"Why do you think you have come?" she asked.

"To find out who's trying to ki—to see if anyone has cast any spells on me or any other hoopla." I was disappointed in myself.

"I'm sorry; I cannot help you any further. Beware, young lady. You have been led down a long, false path. Beware." She turned and closed the door behind her.

All of a sudden, the door popped back open. "Ahahaa, brilliant performance, eh? Positively brilliant. Come on in, Summer. Let's get us some vitals."

Well, I'd be damned if I knew what was going on. Was I expected to leave money for that? What I wouldn't have given for one straight answer. I smiled and she jounced over, took my hand, and pulled me with her through the line of waiting patrons.

She led me to the same booth Mrs. Krotte had wrapped napkins in the one time I'd been there. The lighting was up, which made for an ample opportunity to take in the ambience and the oddity seated before me.

And what an oddity. She was five-four like me, short, but beautiful flowing hair in a natural white with bluish gray highlights. When I was less aware, I would have pegged her for a gracefully aging hippie with salt and pepper hair, the kind that has the leathery skin from years of sun dancing. My newly acquired knowledge told me she was more than elderly. In fact, I'd peg her for damn near ancient. But I'd leave it for her to confirm by her own doing. Her eyes were a pale periwinkle blue, so I couldn't peg them either. Her fair-skinned skeletal fingers entwined, thumbs twiddling.

The rest of her was slender, damn near emaciated. Her dress looked more like a champagne pink silk slip. Her legs were as slender as her fingers and disappeared into a pair of fuzzy white slippers.

She smiled at me with a slight up curl at the corners of her mouth. A fang slipped over the bottom lip; I cringed. What kind of psychic had fangs?

I sat as far back as the bench allowed and glanced over the menu. Mrs. Krotte came over to take our order and wouldn't you know, Molly ordered for me. Yeah, I figured she was a vamp. But Gérard was at rest for the day. Maybe she was older.

Mrs. Krotte came back with a plate of champignons, pear tartan, and goat cheese salad. I wouldn't have ordered any of it. Well, maybe the tartan, but I wasn't crazy about pears—lemon, but not pears.

"It is a wonderful time. I come each year and now to be among so many friends," Molly continued, "I love it here. You have come for answers, but all answers are the ones born from choices you must make. The future has not yet been written, nor will it be. Prophecies are hogwash. Profits make me sick."

"Then why the ad?" I asked.

"Why not?" She bit a sausage hidden under the goat cheese. "I need to speak with Robert about this," she spit the chewed meat into her napkin. Robert was the town butcher and sausage maker. Apparently, his talents were sub-par to Molly's fine-tuned taste.

"You're eating!" I exclaimed.

"Isn't that why we ordered lunch?" she smirked at me and shook her head. She took a sip of tea and straightened herself in the seat. "Summer, your folks were special."

I put down my fork. "I know."

"No, you do not." She wiped her mouth with the napkin and the façade was over. "Your mother was Sidhe from the underworld, outcast by the Celtic fey to the Iceland territories."

"My mother was an outcast?"

She nodded. "The Álfar-Sidhe children were keepers. The church on the mount witnessed the asylum of the last."

Well, that sucked, because Guillaume had mentioned the practices at the church. I hadn't believed him. I didn't want to believe him. And that meant he was telling the truth. Damn. How could I not heed his warning? It wasn't like it was written in code. I mean, he told me time and time again.

"Ah, but your father, he is why you're here, and why they want you—"

The mirror behind the bottles at the bar shattered. People screamed; another pop sounded, and Molly was slumped down. A clean shot to the head. Brain matter spattered the booth, our food—me. I had blood on my face and hands. I started screaming, just screaming.

Molly's blood pooled from her head onto the table and ran like a small river into my lap. I couldn't get out of the booth. I was trapped. People were tripping over each other as more shots were fired through the open window frame. I recognized another face from the diner as its eyes glazed over. A shot to the heart had struck Andy's wife, Lil.

Officer Greene pulled into the parking lot lights on, siren blaring, and all hell broke loose. The bartender tried to climb over Lil and fell. A couple of women stepped on him in their attempt to flee, and another shot took the two out. I tried to get up, but Lil's body lay at my feet and when I moved, the table tipped, and more blood got on me from Molly. I tried to hold it in, but I threw up on Lil. The bartender stared up at me with eyes like black saucers.

"Help me!" I yelled.

Two officers in SWAT gear burst through the door. There must have been others 'cause voices came from their radios calling, "Clear". Two more officers burst from the kitchen and finally Greene stepped into the mess. He picked up the bartender by the arm and shoved him toward the bevy of other officers filing through the door.

"Well, well, Candella, we meet again." He took off his hat and fanned his face.

"Please get me out here, please." I sobbed, dry and tired.

"Not until we get pictures. Don't move, that's an order." He left the building.

From where the window had been, I glimpsed Gérard's limo parked across the street at Andy's. A sinking feeling plagued my gut. It was more than a coincidence that Doug was in the woods after I found Dani, and now the limo was across the street from this. Maybe Gérard wasn't the one I needed to be afraid of. Maybe Doug was behind everything. He was the one in the hall who told Gérard what he had to do. Why was he always around? I looked around for him but didn't see any sign. It was still daylight; no vamps could be responsible.

"Come on, Summer. Slide on out." An investigator had taken pictures of me and the table. They snapped away at Lil, the varying angles, and set up little numbered signs where they saw fit. It was finally time for me to get out of there. I took his hand and stepped as wide as I could, trying not to step on Lil. The least they could have done was cover the bodies.

I wound up stepping in the no longer growing pool of blood beside her body and slipped. My knee landed in the pool before the investigator's hand yanked me forward, away from the corpse. I must have looked horrified because he motioned for the EMTs to come take me.

They had a stretcher waiting outside, along with a group of onlookers. My clothes were drenched in blood with dried matter on my face and hands, which cracked with my every move.

A reporter shouted at me, "Did you know the shooter personally? Who were the victims? Would you like to give a statement for the record?"

I gave him the finger and stepped inside the ambulance.

"Jesus, Summer. What happened?" Tavin asked. He was one of my Tuesday-nighters and an EMT, but not someone I conversed with.

"Not sure. I'm okay, Tavin. Really."

"No, you're not. Let me take you in. Get checked out."

"No, I'm fine."

"Stubborn as usual. Don't suppose you have extra clothes with you." He twisted his lips and peeked out the back window.

"In a backpack, in the backseat."

"I'll be right back."

He hopped out and brought back my bag. "I'll wait outside." He tossed it on the front seat and closed the door to face the crowd.

I slipped off the bloodied clothes, donned my cooking uniform, and realized; I didn't want to be a cook anymore. I didn't want any part of any of whatever I'd stepped into. But damn it, I had to go through the motions. It was a life I'd chosen.

I escaped out of the back of the ambulance, got in my car, and drove to Guillaume's, grateful for Tavin's distraction. He'd started telling them about shotguns and that Cushing, the owner, had been contacted. I was out of there.

Guillaume sat on the bench until I was in sight. His white hat matched a pair of jeans and white sweatshirt. He strolled toward me, tucking the blonde fallen locks of hair behind his ears. I parked and met him half-way. I told him everything about Gale, Dani, and what just happened at Chez Fenris.

"There may be a connection between Gale's abduction and Dani's death," I said.

"Yeah, you."

Oh. "Then the fact that they're mother and daughter doesn't necessarily mean anything?"

"Dani had many acquaintances and was apparently murdered in true human fashion. Heinous, but human. Gale, on the other hand, fell victim to a shifter altercation. Neither incident is related."

"Even though Sam's crocottas attacked Gale? She didn't get along with him. I wonder if Tiny knows." It bothered me that Tiny was arrested. Sam didn't mean anything to me, so they could keep him for all I cared. But Tiny, arrested and having his diner closed because of his niece's death all after his sister gets abducted. I hoped he'd pull through okay. How much was he expected to handle? I knew I was at my wit's end.

"And you know what pisses me off? Greene accused me of being jealous over an affair between Dani and Sam!" I raised my voice unintentionally and the horses looked. "Aren't you going to say anything? Why am I even here?"

Guillaume didn't react to any of what I was telling him, though the part of Sam having an affair with Dani seemed to humor him. I didn't like that. I mean, she was just fucking murdered, and he found humor with the situation? That was just sick—sick and wrong.

He grabbed my arms and rubbed his thumbs over the backs, just on the side of pain. "You should go down to the station tomorrow, pick up Sam and Tiny. I'll go break the news to Dawn. Tonight, I'll talk to Richard and let him know, then if he wants to be there for Dawn, he can."

"Why can't Richard tell her himself?"

He leaned in and kissed my lower lip, sucking gently. My breath left me, and all my questions felt like too much baggage. It was easier to accept and relax. Maybe I did like him, a little. Besides, he was right; I was the common factor.

"Fine, I'll call the department and find out when."

"What? You like his kisses better?" He smiled.

"Stop, okay? Just stop."

"I told you to pick me over Gérard. Why does that piss you off?"

"Don't turn this day into something about you. I'm not in the mood for it, and quite frankly, I don't even know why I feel the way I do. I can't think of one reason why I came here. I went to that psychic to try and find out, but now she's dead."

"You went to Molly to find out why you have feelings for me?" As if this was the only thing that could shock him.

"Don't flatter yourself."

"The fact that you can't have him anytime you want him never occurred to you?"

I took off the neckerchief I wore with my uniform, spit on the corner, and wiped at the dried blood that powdered where his thumbs had been. "God, I hate this."

"You have the same feelings for me as Gérard then?"

"Haven't you been listening?" I was tired. My feelings for Guillaume were cautious. He didn't need to know all the details.

He kissed me on the cheek because I wouldn't let him kiss my lips again. I wasn't in the mood for romance, and I was annoyed with him.

"I'll talk to you later," I said.

I drove off, unexpectedly lighter. It was like a great weight lifted from my chest. I went home and poured a glass of pink lemonade. A fly landed on my arm, and I jumped. Lemonade spilled all over the place.

"Son-of-a-bitch! I don't know where you came from, but you need to go back. My patience is wearing thin." I spoke through clenched teeth at the creature. "That's it!"

After I cleaned up the lemonade, I went to the bedroom intent on a shower. Then paranoia struck. I didn't want to be alone. Since it was still an hour or two early for Gérard, I decided to call the mansion and ask Doug to come over for the interim. It'd be humbling after the wee-morning episode. But eating crow can lead to good growth. At least that's what Gale used to say. Plus, he was at *Chez*.

CHAPTER 23

It only took about ten minutes when I heard a knock on the door. I crept over and was about to look through the peephole when Doug's voice broke the silence.

"You can't sneak up on a lycan, Summer. It's me."

I still peered through the peephole before I let him in. "Thanks so much. I just can't be alone right now. There wasn't anyone else, and—I really appreciate this."

"Oh stop. You want me and you know it." A teasing smile danced across his face.

I laughed. "Yeah, that would make things so much more complicated. I don't need that. I wanted a shower; could you make sure everything's okay, while I'm in there?"

"No worries. When you come out, will you tell what's got you all upset?" He sat on the couch, leaned on his elbow, and tapped a finger across his nose. "Smells like you've been terrified. You also smell like blood, not yours. I need to know what happened." He was no longer teasing.

"Okay."

I scrubbed until my skin was wrinkled and raw; the blood didn't want to come off. I was afraid to touch my hair with hard dried bits embedded. Pink-tinged water circled the drain; my stomach churned.

"Summer, want some help?" Doug's voice—soft and endearing through the cracked door. My fragile state must have shown more than I realized.

"Yeah." There was no room for modesty. Besides, he'd seen me in bad shape before.

He pulled the curtain back enough to grab the shampoo and lathered my hair. He rinsed it through and did it again. I leaned back so the bits didn't get on me. After the second time, he pulled the curtain closed and left the room. I stepped out shortly after.

I didn't bother to dry my hair. I just wrapped it and put on some eyeliner and lip-gloss. I needed to feel pretty, or something.

I slipped on a pair of black sweats and fuchsia camisole with a white bra. I could see the straps, but I didn't care. I grabbed a pair of white tennis socks and went into the living room.

Doug had set up a TV tray next to my chair. He'd made me a cup of tea, and a bagel with cream cheese and strawberry jam. He was a very good friend.

"Gérard is a lucky man. Even in sweats you look like a dream," he said, putting that teasing smile back on. One thing had changed since I went to shower, though. The flames burned topaz; his eyes were alive.

"What's going on—your eyes?"

"Come sit, fill me in." He patted the chair cushion.

Taking the invitation, I curled up in my chair and sipped the tea. I offered him a piece of my bagel, but he declined. He stared at me intently, so I recapped the whole story.

I told him all about the diner and the conversation with Tiny, the murders at *Chez*, Greene, the warning Tangelo had given me, and the part about Guillaume pissing me off. I left out that I saw the limo. I also left out Wimmers.

"I know Guillaume pissed me off, but before that, even. I don't want him."

"Is that how you feel about Gérard as well?"

"No, I wanted Gérard now, but it's still too early for him."

"Summer, you should consider staying with us for a while. I have no doubt that Gérard would extend the same invitation. It will give you the peace of mind you can't have here."

"Alright." I glanced out the window. The tangerine and gold leaves eased the tension. "I love autumn, you know. I liked walking with you the other night."

"Mmm." he smiled and nodded. "Gérard will be here shortly."

I was relieved and disappointed all at once. I liked Doug, he made me feel normal-ish. "Can I ask you something personal?"

"Sure. Fire away."

"Doesn't it bother you that he knows your thoughts?"

"Ah. I see. Summer, he's quite a gentleman. He can hear the thoughts of those who've taken his blood. Once they're near him, be it Mount Mort or not; pret or not. He chooses to ignore most of it. He won't listen because it would ruin your relationship, unless he needs to. It is he who has tuned you out."

"Except, well, if someone challenged him?"

"Not quite, love."

"Great." I didn't mean it.

"Something else?" he asked.

"Yeah, but can you follow me into the bedroom?"

"Dare I ask why?"

"Please."

"After you." He stood and motioned for me to go first.

I walked into the bedroom and shut the door after he was through. I checked around and looked under the bed before I spoke.

"How do you know if a creature is just that?"

"What do you mean?" He raised an eyebrow and sat on the bed. "Why are you looking to see if there's someone under the bed?"

I climbed next to him and whispered in his ear, "Sort of. See, there's this fly. I've seen it a bunch of times now. I think it might be someone spying on me."

He smiled. "No worries, not everything is bad. I mean, as you learn more about our world, you will become more aware of nature and your surroundings. I don't believe the fly is anything to worry about."

"Because they don't exist?"

"Because I would know." He patted my thigh. "Nor do I smell anyone other than Guillaume and ourselves."

"Guillaume? He's never been here." Oh, the kiss. The heat burned my neck.

"Interesting." He strode to the door and opened it, but I already knew who it was. It was Gérard. He nodded at Doug, then glided toward me.

"Summer, I extend the invitation my Douglas has offered. I would be honored if you would stay with us."

I was speechless, not because of the invitation, but rather his choice of clothing for the night. I mean, red fishnet with black velvet pants?

"Can you read me right now?" I asked.

"I cannot."

"Sometimes, that's a good thing."

"Pack what you need, unless you like what I have chosen."

"I'll grab a few things, but as long as it's okay, I like your clothes better than mine."

"They are your clothes." He emphasized the "are" while drawing it out with that thick French accent. It was awesome but didn't cause that tingly feeling that his drawn out "Rs" usually did. Come to think of it, I hadn't felt it that morning either. I wondered if he stopped using it or if that too was blocked. Hmm.

"Thanks, both of you. I mean it."

I still didn't know how to act with them together, so I scurried to the kitchen, grabbed a plastic shopping bag, scuttled to the bedroom. They went to wait by the door, so I threw the lace teddy in the bag with my toothbrush, make-up, and feathered shoes. I grabbed the stuffed chef bear from my nightstand and stopped in the doorway.

"Was this from one of you?"

Doug winked.

I fought a smile and tossed it on the bed.

"Let us go." Gérard opened the door. He didn't offer to take my hand, instead he stepped outside and waited for me to say goodnight to Doug.

My emotions shocked me. It was like when I'd come home in high school, after Sheena died. The house quiet, my mother in bed—always in bed. Maybe it was the valium, maybe it was packing your child's belongings, knowing they would never be played with again. Maybe it was because with her, life ended. Would it have been better if it were me? Did I add to it in some way?

But there was one thing that made it go away. I had a boyfriend whom I left with on Friday, and didn't come back with until Sunday, every weekend. Then there were endless hours on the phone. I was dependent—dependent on him to take me away from my real life. And what made that any different from what I was doing with Gérard and Doug? I'd just called Doug and now I was leaving with Gérard. It had to stop.

I stepped outside, said goodnight to Gérard, thanked him for coming over, and slipped back inside, but before I closed the door, he caught my waist in his arm.

CHAPTER 24

Gérard sat on the chaise with his legs crossed, his hands locked over his knee. His hair had fallen over his eyes. He shook it back, causing it to fall randomly over the black cape; luckily it hid the red fishnet. His pants blended with the chaise and boots, so what wasn't so good in the light was much better in the dark.

His eyes had turned black, his body stilled. He wasn't breathing.

"Frightened?" he asked rather dryly.

"Can you still tell if I'm lying?"

He cocked an eyebrow.

"Then, no." Of course, I lied.

"Then, *oui*." He patted the space next to him on the chaise.

I sat.

He cupped my face in his palms. I gasped. I had a burning sensation that was almost spicy. His power—a heavy heat. It was different from any of the previous times I'd felt him. I didn't like it.

His grip tightened. My heart thudded, slow and daunting, I thought it would stop. I clawed at him, catching the rim of his shirt, and ripped.

He let go of my face and was across the room before I could tell he was off the chaise.

"Molly was an eccentric woman, but wise." He turned a little and peered over his shoulder. "She was Sidhe."

"As in fey?"

"You went to *Guillaume*." He turned back to the wall.

"You read me. It's good, right?" I tried for optimism; it didn't work. I thought a new approach might be nice. At least, if nothing else, I'd get to show him what I bought. "Listen Gérard, I bought something after that night on the mount." I whispered the last, disbelieving my own words. "I'd like to put it on for you in case I never get another chance after we have our discussion."

He smiled with a hint of fang. "Really? That early? Well please. Give me something to enjoy."

"Don't get the wrong idea; you still have to wait."

"Please, I will be all aflutter whilst I wait." He stretched across the foot of the enormous bed, facing the chaise.

I took my shopping bag into the bathroom with me and put on the purple lace slip teddy with thong back and lace up front. I arranged my hair, and slipped the open-toed feathered heels on, sans stockings. It was a good thing I'd shaved because the last time he saw me, my legs were covered in stubble. I checked myself in the mirror and rinsed with mouthwash. I have to say; I looked damn good. Dawn was right.

Once I was done, I clenched the doorknob and panicked. I felt like an idiot. Why did I even want to dress up?

"Summer?" he called.

I swallowed and pulled the door, my heart in my throat. My cheeks reddened instantly.

"*Zut alors, ma chérie.*" His reaction made it worse. "*C'est magnifique.*"

I wanted to run and jump under the covers, but I didn't. Instead, I closed my eyes, took a deep breath before opening them again, and bit my lip.

He stood from the bed in one liquid motion and stalked toward me as slowly as a cat about to pounce on a spring chick. He was sexy. Hell, he was sex just the way he moved. He dropped the cape and tore his shirt clean off.

It seemed like an eternity by the time he reached me. He wrapped his fingers softly around my waist and gave one of his feather kisses between my breasts. It was damn near orgasmic.

I ducked down and scurried on the bed to sit against several oversized pillows before he crawled up the bed catlike and sprang up to land over top of me. I thought for sure he was going to bite me, but instead, he placed my hands on his chest and pressed his body onto mine.

"Mmm, I think it would be wise to wait until this—celebration has passed." He sat back on his knees, his eyes studying the dark purple silk and black lace. "I want to fill you with all I have when we do finish this painfully awaited event."

Wait? All he has? He couldn't. I thought.

But wasn't that what the bad boys in school believed when they tried to get a good girl to screw them? Well, at least that thought took some of the heat away—until I looked at him again—a soft tan that accented his nipples and well-chiseled abs. His arms, muscular without being pumped, and his face, well, his face was perfect. The strawberry pink lips that allowed a glimpse of fang when he smiled, accented by a squared chin, and flowing chocolate locks.

"You can't," I breathed.

He chuckled with a triumphant look on his face. "I can and I shall. You dared wear this, expecting to talk? Oh, you must, as you say, have a taste of your own medicine, *ma chérie.*" He smiled, showing full fangs.

It was erotic yet frightening all at once. I couldn't imagine letting him sink those things into me, especially during sex. Yikes! He said it wouldn't hurt; guess I'd find out—someday.

There was a knock on the door. Gérard was there, reaching for the handle. He stood in the small opening, blocking me from view. I was grateful beyond words.

He brought a tray with a bowl of truffles and a goblet of blood to the bed. Yummy!

He excused himself for a moment and went into the bathroom. He came out wearing a black silk thong with little silver fangs dangling in the front.

He stretched across the bed and took the goblet from the tray. "Shall we start with why you ran to *Guillaume*?"

Shit, I had to own up. I couldn't have hidden anything from him anyway. "I swear, I don't want him, in any way, shape, or form." I closed my eyes, my lashes moist with guilt. "I asked Doug to come to the house because it was too early for you, but it was you who I wanted." I opened my eyes and humbly recapped the entire *Chez* situation, including the conversation with Guillaume. I also told him about the meeting with Molly, and why. When I'd finished, he was still. I wasn't even sure he saw me. I figured I may as well continue and started to discuss the incident between Doug and myself.

He put his hand up and slid the tray next to me. "I know Officer Greene; he is one of *Michel's* people. *Michel* is Master of Toronto; his followers are seeping into my territory."

"Then Greene is what—a witch?"

"*Non*, he is human. You must believe, as Chief Wimmers warned. Be careful."

He knew about Wimmers? What else did he know? "I'm to pick up Tiny at the station tomorrow. After that, I'd like to stop by the house and pick up a few more things. You know, half-and-half, milk, eggs, perishables. I'd rather bring them here and have them be used. Do you think this Michel is like infiltrating your territory or something?"

"*Oui*, I do."

"I'm scared, Gérard."

"Enough of this." His eyes changed to a slow swirl of stars. "I want to discuss intimate matters."

I almost choked on a truffle. "I can't," I whispered; he had exquisite hearing anyway. I couldn't look at him. I lost my appetite.

"I do not like this, not knowing what is in your mind, but it does make things more—*euh*, interesting." He rolled over to his back and had one knee bent. The goblet rested on his abs caught between two fingers; the other hand tucked behind his head. His hair was fanned out on the comforter before he turned to look at me and caught me staring. Everything he did made him look like a sex god; I swear.

I gasped and glanced away, which caused him to chuckle.

"You know that feeling I've gotten ever since I met you?" I pulled my knees into myself, sort of hunching in, as I spoke. "I don't feel it anymore. I guess I was wondering if you stopped doing it or if it just isn't getting through?"

He smiled and turned his whole body to face me. "Ah, the effect is gone, you say?" He reached out, caught my ankle as I attempted to turn into a ball, and pulled so fast and with such force, I flopped to my back. It didn't hurt, but it was unexpected. "Lovely. I could look at you all night." He lifted my leg and placed soft kisses on my thigh. He took his time to make his way down to my knee, French kissed behind it, and headed to my toes. He came back up to my ankle and asked, "May I?"

"May you what?" I managed to say, though my voice was mousy.

"Close your eyes."

I did as he slipped off my slipper, and licked ever so softly up my leg, back over my ankle and toes. He came back to my ankle and nicked me with his fangs. His tongue massaged the wound. Around and around, flicking, sucking, he worked it. It felt good, better than good. I started to get a feeling like the one earlier, but it was stronger. The more he worked my ankle, the more I felt his power. The power flowed and built, concentrating in the most private of my erogenous zones. The burn turned to tingling. I moaned, and found myself stifling a climax I hadn't expected, clutching my hands over my mouth.

He placed feather kisses up my body until he reached my hands and pulled them aside to kiss my lips—his eyes a starry mass. I squirmed beneath him.

"Better?"

"Uh, yeah. Better than any sex I ever had." I giggled.

"I know." He walked to the door before the knock came.

"What?" I asked rather, shocked by his reply.

"That was foreplay."

"How'd you do it? If I have something keeping you out of my mind, I mean."

"*Le sang, ma chérie*, there is little that can keep a master's power—euh, I believe you would say, at bay. *Mais,* I am a little different." He winked.

"So, we shared blood. What happens now?"

He came back with another tray. This one had dark chocolate truffles. There was also a small bowl with something, a red liquid, and pieces of what looked like sponge. Eeeewww!

"Have some nourishment." He said it as if sweets were nutritious. Empty calories, oh boy. But I loved truffles, so I decided to go for one. Of course, he grabbed my hand, took one of the sponge pieces, and dipped it in the red liquid.

He rubbed it on my lips; I was completely nauseated. I didn't want to insult him, so I opened my mouth. When it hit my tongue, I felt like an idiot.

"Surprise, warm raspberry sauce." He chuckled. "You are lovely, to think that it was blood, and would have taken it because you did not want to offend me. What did you believe this to be?" He held up a piece of cake.

"Nothing." I tried not to meet his eyes. He caught my face in his hands and brought my chin up with the side of his finger. I had no choice; I had to look at him. Damn it. "You've been full of surprises tonight."

"Would you have preferred it any other way?" He went in the bathroom and called me in, only for me to find him brushing his teeth. "You would not want to taste your own blood, would you?"

"Not really."

"You are tired, *ma chérie*. Would you like to draw a bath before bed?"

"Will you be joining me this time?"

"If that is your wish."

"Do you want to?"

"If you want me to."

"Stop. Do you want to get in the damn tub with me or not? A simple yes or no is all I want."

"*Oui.*" He smiled, slyly.

"You're something else, just exactly what, I don't know, but something." I squinted at him.

He went out, brought in the tray of goodies, and got in before me. I got undressed, which was a relief because they don't think of comfort when they make lingerie; I got in.

He whispered in my mind, while we kissed more passionately than Jesse ever kissed me. *Et, ma chérie, I tasted you, but did not drink nor feed. Nor did I share my blood with you. Still, you are mine.*

CHAPTER 25

With Gérard down for the next few hours, I got up and dressed. I was trying to mentally prepare myself to see Guillaume. He wouldn't like that I was staying with Gérard, but I wasn't going to hide my actions from him.

I hurried up the stairs and met Kitty. "Summer, just the person I was looking for. Gérard arranged for his driver to take you where you need. He doesn't want you hiking through the woods until everything calms down."

"I won't argue."

If it had been a month ago, and I thought the way I did then—you know, no such thing as monsters, then I would have ripped him a new one. Just because I'm a woman doesn't mean I can't handle a simple hike. But this was different. There were monsters, and they were threatening us, me, the regular human population of Mount Mort. Attentive caution had to take precedence.

"And, Summer, Dani's heart was missing. Spoke to the coroner. There'll be a 24-hour wake tomorrow, and a memorial on the Samhain."

"She would have liked that." I glanced at the floor more because it's awkward when people talk to you about the deceased, but I had been a part. How do you accept that?

"Well, Raul's waiting. I won't keep you." She scampered off down the corridor and disappeared.

I went out to the limo and jumped in. On the way to my house, I noticed a small barn owl perched on a limb overlooking the newly chipped road Gérard must have ordered. I was instantly saddened because it reminded me of Gale. If she was still alive, did she know Dani was murdered? And not by just anyone.

Gale had said taking the heart of a shapeshifter was one of the only ways to kill them. This meant the person who did it knew what Dani was. It had to be someone who was acquainted with us. No one else would or could know she was a shifter. I mean, it wasn't like she turned every chance she had. She never turned from what I knew.

When the limo pulled in, I hurried to my tracker. I didn't want to go into the house with no one around. I wasn't sure what would be waiting for me, if anything.

I drove to the police station and saw Greene. He sneered at me when he walked past my car. I waited until he was out of reach, and earshot, before I opened my door.

I hurried inside and up to the counter. Officer Tangelo came around the corner. She waved. "Hey, Summer. Come on back." I followed her to her desk. She started out by reviewing a file marked with an orange circle sticker. "You weren't home last night."

"No," I said.

She looked up from the file. "Summer, I need to know where you were. I need details."

"But I don't have any."

"Look. I'll be honest with you. Greene is pushing your involvement. There is only so much I can do. I'm trying to help you."

"I didn't do anything."

"I know that. You know that. The whole damn town knows that, but it still doesn't look good on paper. As Greene sees it, you were the last person to see your parents, and they were never found. The incident at Chez with you, Gale's alleged disappearance from your house, and you found Dani. Do you see my problem?"

"I didn't do anything wrong. None of those things were my fault."

Guilt panged my gut. I did feel like my parents were my fault. I was angry. I thought my anger killed them. They went down, and I ran away.

"But you understand, right?"

"I guess." I slumped in the chair.

"Then tell me where you were. And anything else you can think of."

"I haven't thought of anything else, but I'm not staying at my house until everything calms down. I'm staying at the Lake Sangre mansion with friends. I feel safer than when I'm at home; alone."

"Yes, Gérard's back."

I nodded. She knew Gérard.

"Good, 'cause we still don't have any leads. Sam left earlier, but Tiny's been held for further questioning. I'll see if he's ready for release if you don't mind waiting a few minutes." She started for the door. "There's fresh coffee brewing in the doorway to your left. Help yourself. You could probably use a cup." She turned and was gone.

I decided to take her up on the coffee and went in to fix a cup. Someone entered the room behind me. The hair on the back of my neck stood up. I turned around, subtly. To my surprise, it was Guillaume.

"Hi," I said. Time to face the music.

"Hello." His voice was gruff. "And where were you last night? Let me guess."

"At least he cared enough to stay with me."

"Wasn't it you who said you wanted to be alone?"

"I guess so."

"So? Did you fuck him? Did you like getting a nice stiff one?" He slammed his mug down, spilling coffee on the paper-toweled table.

"Fuck you," I whispered hard. "If you're so great, where were you? With a murder that just happened, and knowing what I've been dealing with, you suck at caring. If you cared, you wouldn't have let me go."

"Figures you'd turn out to be a whore."

"What? For your information, I don't have to fuck anyone to have a relationship."

"Yeah, like I'd believe he of all people would let you stay there for free. What's he doin' takin' your blood?" I went pale. "That clever bastard! He is, isn't he?"

"That's none of your damned business."

"Well, honey, you set the price."

"He's not that way. I know he's not."

"Isn't he?"

"No, this is what you want; to ruin my relationship with him. I bet you did whatever it was you did to me."

"Careful now, talk like that'll get you locked up in the nuthouse."

"You're a son-of-bitch, you know that?" I raised my voice; the secretary looked up.

"Is that a fact? Well, when Tiny gets out, drop him off. I'll be at your house," he whispered inaudibly.

"Fine." I turned my back to him. "You know, it would be easier if you would just die already."

"Who're you talking to?" Tangelo was behind me with her mug.

"Oh, sorry. Remember that weird phone call?"

"Yeah," she said.

"Well, he was just here. He complicates things and I'm trying to uncomplicate them."

"Let me give you some advice. Don't tell someone you want them to die in a police station, especially when you're a murder suspect." She smirked and poured her coffee.

"Guess that wasn't smart."

"No, not really. But anyway, here's my card. Call me whenever you feel like talking or if you think of anything to help with these cases."

"I will," I promised.

"Now, Tiny's out in the lobby. Stay safe, Summer." She walked into the chief's office, leaving me to find my way.

Tiny was waiting for me. He was calm for someone who'd spent the night in jail. I went to hug him, but he turned away and strode to the door.

I jogged to catch up. "Hey!"

"Let's go. The mattress wasn't exactly comfortable, and the food, well, I'm starving," he said, hurrying to the car.

"Would you like me to make you something when we get to your house?"

"You could spot me twenty bucks so I could pick up a pizza."

"Sure," I said.

We left the police station on Route 11 and headed toward Monty's Pizzeria. I gave Tiny the money and watched him amble into the front of the restaurant. It wasn't more than twenty minutes when he came back with his dinner.

"Are you sure you should be alone?" I asked.

He settled back in his seat, shifting toward the window. "I'm fine."

"Some company might cheer you up." Even though I knew what was waiting for me at my house. And Gérard would be rising because it was after five. Still, I figured I would offer.

"I said I'm fine, Summer."

"Okay."

We rode in silence to his house, and when we got there, he climbed out and called back, "I'll give you the money, next time I see you."

I wasn't sure when that would be, since the police had the diner closed for investigation. I wasn't going to worry about it. There were too many other issues that took precedence. I backed out of his driveway and headed home.

CHAPTER 26

I pulled into my driveway, relieved because there were no signs of anyone there. I got out of the car, and went into the house, taking notice that the rosebush had company. There was another on the other side of the steps; they were in full bloom. I was no gardener but come on. Late October depicted a mental image of dead plants and trees, not blooming rosebushes. Doug.

I threw my keys on the buffet. Guillaume was sitting on my sofa. I wasn't surprised.

"About time you got here," he said.

"It took longer than I thought," I said.

"You said you'd come home after dropping Tiny off. Where'd you go?" he demanded.

"Forget it, leave."

"Tell me what you were doing."

"It's none of your God damned business."

"The hell it isn't. I won't ask again." His eyes flared dark crimson. Blood dripped on my blouse. I went down on all fours in shock.

"You bastard. Don't even try to use your evil magic on me. I had one asshole a long time ago. I'll be damned if I'll have another." My eyes stung, but I'd be damned if I'd cry.

"I'm sorry, Summer. Really. I didn't mean it. Please. I'm so sorry." He rushed toward me. "You make me so angry. You don't listen. It's done; you're mine. Nothing you do will change that."

"Yours? I don't fuckin' think so."

"I can control my temper better than this." He tried to grab me; I backed away.

"No. Go sit down so I can think. Don't touch me ... with anything." I stood; brushed my hands over my knees. "Don't move."

I went to the bedroom and sat on my bed, trying to clear my head. I was certain Doug or Gérard, if not both, would have come. Well, I could take care of myself.

"Please come out, Summer. I said I was sorry," Guillaume pleaded.

"In a minute."

I glanced in the mirror before opening the door. Blood glistened from my nose. I grabbed a tissue and stood in the doorway. He was still on the sofa, so I sat in my rocking chair. I stared at him; he stared back. I rocked and stared; he sat and stared. I didn't know what I was going to do. It's not like I had a plan. I figured as long as we were silent, life was good.

Ma chérie, my Douglas and I are outside. I tried not to look like I was talking in my head. Well, it wasn't like I was talking, but listening. Whatever.

As far as I knew, Guillaume had no clue. He was still staring at me, and I at him when they knocked on the door. I hesitated to answer, but Gérard didn't wait. The door opened; he glided through.

"Calling the dead now, huh?" Guillaume snapped.

"*Drôle, très drôle mon ami.*"

"Please, don't fight," I said.

"Fighting? Nonsense. I simply told my friend that he is—*euh,* funny."

"Yeah, friend," Guillaume sneered.

"Why waste such energy, *Guillaume*? Regina met her. As mandated, the others will come. Your reigns are claimed, no matter your desire." Gérard rebuffed.

"Like you fucking know,"

"I do know."

"How?" Guillaume slid back on the sofa.

"Ask Bernard."

"You kid," Guillaume spat.

"Ah, *mon ami.* I assure you, I do not. Although *Michel* caught me by surprise."

"He thought it would buy more time."

"He underestimated me. Now, *monsieur,* what brings you here this night? You already caused harm." Gérard motioned to my face.

"I have orders, as do you."

"Not anymore."

"Really? Well, I know what you did. But does she know? Did you tell her?"

"She is fine. What I did will bring her no harm. Unlike you, who hurt her both physically and emotionally. I believe you had accused her of being a naughty girl." Gérard crossed his arms and leaned against the bedroom doorway.

Guillaume kept eye contact with Gérard. "As I said, I have orders. You're not the only one who wants her."

"For what reason?" I interrupted.

"The same reason we all do."

"*Non, mon ami.* Not for the same reason. Tell me, where is your master now?"

"You can't keep her from him. He will not allow this," Guillaume scorned.

Gérard sat in the recliner between us, his hands neatly folded in his lap; a smart grin toyed with his adversary. The power in the room pulsed to life. I recognized it. I couldn't remember from where. I was a kid. I rubbed my arms, a nervous habit.

"*Ma chérie,* do not fear this beast."

"Why not?" Guillaume snarled.

"Because you are nothing—an endangered breed. You truly wish a challenge?"

"Who said I wanted the challenge?" Guillaume cocked his brow.

Gérard smiled. "Your seduction on my beloved."

"Covetous, are we?"

"Please, such childish accusations."

I pushed to my feet. What they were doing was wrong. I wouldn't be victimized. Seduction. Guillaume wouldn't know seduction if it bit him on the ass. I didn't even want him. What the hell was wrong with people—me? I was dating Gérard. One man, not two.

"I don't want sloppy seconds after a dead man. I don't do dead," Guillaume snapped.

"Charming, *gros cheval.*" Gérard bowed slightly, giving me the floor, so to speak.

"Sorry, Guillaume, but seduction doesn't work on me," I snapped.

"You think he hasn't seduced you?"

"I don't think he's used deceit and trickery to entrap me. If I'm understanding this, you have. I don't like that."

"You actually believe him?"

No, I didn't. I questioned Gérard's actions back at dinner with Gale. Dani was dead, and I was a murder suspect. I hadn't forgotten someone wanted me dead. And they thought romantic intentions prevailed.

I had to find the murderer. Not for nothing, I was darned sure it would put me on track to who was after me. Which meant they were probably responsible for my family's shit. However, I had a small problem. I was afraid of getting arrested and becoming a real murderer. How would I kill my hunter anyway? Guess I'd cross that path when it arose. I never thought about the consequences before. Only the sweet gratification of revenge. Shit.

"Oh, how the truth hurts," Guillaume sneered, as Doug appeared in the doorway. "What's the matter? Can't fight your own battles anymore, old man?"

"My people never leave me. They will always be faithful, and *Michel*? Where are his people?"

"It's too late, anyway. She's mine." Guillaume smirked.

"Not anymore."

"Well, Michel challenges you, Gérard. You, not your people."

"I accept." Gérard pulled on black gloves and glided to the door. "Really, *mon ami*. You weaken him." Gérard hung on to the word *Really* before completing his statement. Blood streamed from Guillaume's eyes and nostrils. Guillaume gurgled and sprayed blood over the carpet. He collapsed to his knees, his white slacks, stained candy apple red. "I suggest you use what is left to run tail to *Michel*."

"Fuck off," Guillaume hissed.

Gérard walked out of the house, calling back, "It would suit us all to call a truce. I, for one, do not find amusement in grandstanding, nor do I enjoy tormenting, *l'innocent*."

Guillaume staggered toward me. "I'll leave, but you're fair game now, Summer." And he was gone.

I was left standing alone in my living room—mentally exhausted. I needed sleep, but I was afraid. I pondered whether to go to bed or stand watch in case something happened.

I decided to sit by the bedroom door, listening, waiting. From there, I could see the living room and kitchen. The main door and window were out of view. But there was no sound, though the quiet offered little comfort, as I imagined Guillaume's people drawing in around the house. I closed my eyes and heard Gérard.

Ma chérie, the war has begun. We shall meet again on the morrow, but at my place. Again, I apologize for all that has happened and for my imperious behavior.

I'm afraid, I thought back.

As you should be. Until tomorrow, Summer.

Another meeting tomorrow? With or without Guillaume? And how did I know Guillaume would wait? He hadn't mentioned taking any kind of oath of honor. I wasn't sure I could handle it. Again, who the hell was Michel? Why did these people want me? Who was Bernard?

I closed the door.

CHAPTER 27

"Suuummer," Guillaume taunted from the living room.

I scuttled under the bed; my eyes burned with tears that would not come. I lay, stomach pressed to the floor, each breath shallower than the next. The dust ruffle blocked my view, inhibiting my senses. I had that metallic taste on the back of my tongue that only fear can bring.

"Suuummer."

The knob on the bedroom door clicked.

The door creaked.

There was movement in the room. I squeezed my eyes shut to concentrate on calling for Gérard. He didn't answer. I guess tomorrow had come in a matter of hours.

"Boss," Officer Greene called.

I lifted the ruffle enough to see Guillaume's boots. I flattened and waited for him to step back out. Greene and a crocotta stalked passed.

Guillaume held the doorknob, and audibly hissed at Greene. But he drew the door enough to switch hands. "Speak," he growled.

My closet was out of sight from the living room. I wriggled from the bed and made it inside before Guillaume stepped back in. I hid amongst the shoes and hangers, cloaked in sweaters and flannels. I couldn't click the door closed. I gasped in shallow breaths as I watched through the small opening.

Guillaume's fury flashed across his face as he flung the mattress and box spring aside.

He knew I was there.

I pressed my lips to suppress the watery sounds saliva makes as it washes over teeth and soft tissues. But he was more than a wizard,

I realized then. No, he was more because he'd heard it, that damned water noise.

I leaned deeper in the clothes, breathless.

A single eye peered in the door crack.

Eye to eye, he saw me.

He traced the opening with his tongue, slid two fingers in, and whispered, "The legend comes by seer's sight, by way of they both black and white."

I slunk down against the unrelenting clothes.

"The keeper's chosen, right or left, reveals voices no more bereft." He eased the doors apart, a slow, hesitant move. His voice mimicked the action. "Two sides lie, two sides fight. The battle begins, a sorrowful night."

He thrust the doors open, his eyes masked in a blond curtain, piercing. He lowered his head and slid his arm around my neck.

I whimpered.

He stepped beside me and pulled me into his chest—his voice warm against my ear. "Of Álfar blood, she shall reign. Hence the dragon flies again."

I collapsed in his arms. He pulled me from the closet and laid me on the floor. My back burned between my shoulder blades. I shifted uncomfortably as his weight pressed me into the nylon plush.

"Be mine. Forget this mess, forget him." A lone finger traced my bangs, then a fist clenched my hair. I pulled. "You deserve your freedom. Choose me and you shall have it." He licked from my chin to my ear. "I'm here. Where's he?"

"You're here, but I haven't figured why. If you were the last piece of shit, I wouldn't choose you." I squirmed to break free. My skin protested. "What did you do to me?"

"Why, Summer? Why do you not see? I am the right choice."

"Right, my ass. None of this is right. Let me go." I fought to lift my arms.

He pressed harder and cupped my face. "The right choice for a fugitive. You place yourself within reach, but the temptation is too strong. And for that, I must kill you." He eased off as Greene stepped in the doorway.

"Green, watch the bloodsucker's whore." Greene handed him his hat. "You disgust me, Summer," he spat on the carpet next to me. "After all I've done for you."

Greene reached down and tore me from the floor. I thrashed about and slashed his face; a screaming pain emanated from my neck where the bastard's fingers dug in. A black crocotta stalked to the doorway and redirected my focus.

The bastard threw me against the slatted closet door, hard enough to knock it off its tracks. "You want to play?" Greene asked.

"You're a cop, for Christ's sake. Let me go."

"I said, do you want to play?"

I spit in his face.

He glared at Guillaume. "This is your fuckin' mess."

"You're walking a thin line, Greene."

"Number one rule, don't get emotionally involved, Guillaume."

"Explain Dawn."

"She ain't no job," Greene hissed.

Guillaume threw the tissue box at me. "Wipe your face."

He stormed out with calculated white snake-skin booted steps. Greene trailed behind. The crocotta loomed over me, staring at me like a piece of meat.

I wondered if Doug was out there, and if so, would Gérard be there too? He had a lot of people with him earlier. I'd never met them, but I bet there were more than just Doug as protectors. Which ones were good? Should I only fear the crocottas? I feared the one standing over me.

"I know what you are," I said.

The creature growled in my face. Its teeth, a harsh white against the black of its face, grazed my chin.

Greene came back to check on me, then sneered as he turned to go back out to the living room. Something crashed through where my picture window had been. Glass bits bounced into the bedroom next to me.

Greene yelled at someone. "Cover that door. Guillaume'll be pissed if anything happens to her."

Screams and howls sounded from the mount. The crocotta in charge of me responded with a throaty whimper, then leapt over the broken bedroom door.

He was gone.

I backed toward the corner, by the closet. I held my breath to listen, avoiding the urge to call out. There were wolves out there who needed to know I was still in the house. But I needed to hear what I couldn't see. Growls, hisses, Guillaume's angry voice, commands—it was all too much, too fast. I huddled in tighter.

The glass on the carpet didn't stop the fighting. They were back. Someone slammed against the wall; a yip followed. There was light, a clash of metal, and the lot of them left. The scuffling sounds dissipated, and someone whimpered. I strained to hear if there were more out there.

Nothing.

Silence overtook the evening; the serenity deafened me.

I stayed in the corner until the red-gold hue of sunrise poured in from the living room. I hadn't slept.

I scrambled to my feet and crept to the doorway. Broken glass and blood stains glistened in crimson hues on the oaken floor and torn carpet.

I donned my slippers and tiptoed to where the front door hung from a single hinge. There were no signs of a fight outside. I darted back into the cottage, determined to get out as quickly as possible, hopping through the obstacle course that was my living room.

I threw on a pair of jeans, a hoodie, and a pair of tennis shoes before I glimpsed the Ruger's pink grip laying beneath the demolished buffet. I checked the safety, tucked it in the back of my pants, grabbed a handful of bullets and shoved them in my pocket before I walked out the front door, not even locking it behind me. What would be the point?

The path from my house to the mansion wound around the lake, so that was what I started to do. I studied the ground, stepping lightly as my father had taught me. I didn't want to draw attention from pernicious stragglers.

Then, it dawned on me that whoever wanted me could lie in wait at Gérard's, as he'd be down for the day. Although shaken and weary, my mind was clear.

I sat on a half-submerged log, hollowed from the lapping lake water. It had landed next to a granite outcropping on the shore. The longer I sat, the better I felt. Drawing in a deep breath of crisp autumn air filled me with the energy my body craved as the wind whispered across the lake. I could have sworn it called my name. I decided to abandon my path, intent on reaching the mount cemetery before midday. I figured no one would think to look for me there.

The hike was long but invigorating. The earthy scents of decaying leaves and trees bore down on my spirits. I meandered up the mountain, reflecting on the carefree days of summer. Chipmunks and squirrels chattered around me, along with a handful of birds, but for the first time, I was alone and welcomed it.

I neared the edge of the cemetery and promised myself I wouldn't leave, no matter how nervous I felt. It was safer there than anywhere.

I stepped through the rusted iron gates. The first gravestone I saw had all the etching weathered away. Deeper in among the overgrowth was a mausoleum. It was Gérard's. I went to it cautiously, not knowing if anything awaited me there, but I felt obligated.

It stood out from the other two, which were small-ish, and granite. That and Gérard's mausoleum was set back from the cliff, barely visible from the parking area, or observers from below.

The gable drew my attention first. I knew it was his, the moment I saw it. *GDA* was carved in the stone. I hadn't even thought about him having a last name. Gargoyles perched on the corners where spires soared in the trees on stone towers. The archivolt added drama and warned of tragedy and death. A sign of something ominous. Gérard hadn't denied Guillaume's accusations that first night.

Even the jambs had carved stone roses resemblant to high gothic architecture, with the tracery on each rose window. I climbed the staircase, stunned by the magnificence in the setting light.

Since the church frightened me when I was with Gérard, I decided to stay in his mausoleum. Night was upon me, and I wasn't about to be caught in the woods alone.

I pulled on the wooden door. It wasn't locked.

I stepped inside and faced a single altar. There were no other surfaces where other coffins might lay. I was glad there wasn't one in there. Besides, Gérard probably took his to the mansion. I also don't know that I could have stayed in there with a bunch of real dead bodies. The thought made me shudder. I took the sheet that was on the floor and sat with it wrapped around me.

It was peaceful, but cold.

The silence forced me to relax. I was hungry but didn't care. Instead, I settled into a far corner, loaded the gun, and fell asleep. There were no dreams. No Gérard.

CHAPTER 28

The cemetery was quiet in the morning light. There was a relentless breeze, but the warmth of the sun felt good on my skin. The mausoleum had been cold during the night and left me chilled to the bone.

The wind licked my exposed skin. Sleet blew in sideways sheets. It was a quick event, the kind that created a misery that reminded us that we were nothing. All that happened made no difference. Life and nature proved it waited for no one. We live and die, but the wind goes on, the weather beats against the young and old alike. My mom told me that.

I made my way to the church and hesitated at the steps. The fear I'd had a few weeks back bore down. It was overpowering, but I forced myself to go in anyway. My windburned cheeks stung with the cold. The idea of getting into a building, either heated or not, forced the fear back.

The iron clad door creaked when I opened it. The smell of damp stones and mildew filled the air. In the front was an altar where I assumed the Christians would have communion. I didn't want to think about what the other practices would do.

The old fireplace was solid. It must have felt warm, on cool autumn days, which gave me the idea to find wood.

I went back outside to gather kindling and some manageable branches to bring to the fireplace. I searched along the edge of the cemetery, being careful not to wander too far. After all, if there was something lurking about, well, I didn't want to chance anything. I stuffed my pockets with dead leaves, grabbed a few sticks, and headed back to the church.

There was a candle burning on the altar by a small table supplied with a pile of nuts and dried fruit. My stomach ached with hunger; it would be the second night I hadn't eaten. It seemed like someone knew I was there, after all.

I placed the leaves and sticks in the fireplace, grabbed the candle from the table, and lit the leaves, but they went out. I ventured back outside to get more and tried again. It took several attempts, but it finally caught the sticks on fire.

I sat on the floor in front of the fireplace and admired the flames' dance. The orange glow reminded me of Doug. I missed him and Gérard and considered going to the mansion. I wouldn't make it before full dark. An ambush wasn't out of the question either. That and I still wasn't sure about Gérard.

My stomach growled and could no longer be ignored. I'd forgotten about the nuts on the table. I reached for my gun, held it in front of me, and crept over. If Guillaume and his entourage were to burst in, they'd be in for a surprise, though it proved useless against the crocotta. Still, it could make them all bleed.

Lying next to the pile was a beaver pelt. I nibbled on the fruit and used the butt of the gun to break the nuts open. They were more trouble than they were worth.

I contemplated going back to the mausoleum for the night, but decided to ride it out in the church. It was warmer. I threw on another piece of wood and sat on the floor in front of the fire. The crackling of the flames brought me back from deep thoughts of what the last several weeks had proven.

All I wanted was a companion. I was tired of being alone. But I missed my old life—simply going to work, having a good time with my friends, and coming home to the quiet. My peach soaps, my books, and just a normal cup of Swiss Miss.

Did I regret saying yes to Gérard that first night? No. Could any of this have been avoided? Probably not. I blamed it on our town and my parents for raising me here. Was it too much to ask that I have a normal life? A husband, two point four kids, and a dog?

Growing up, I lived on the edge of town. We had a small cottage on Druid Lane. Oh, come to think of it, I guess the knowledge was under my nose the whole time.

I got up and studied the runes on the fireplace.

I graduated from M&M high school. Went to Alexandria University, and later to culinary school. I still managed to work at the diner on weekends, and Tiny was nice enough to let me experiment with recipes I learned in school. Herbs and spices tickled my fancy and Tiny let me use however many I wanted, so long as the end product was edible and saleable.

My thoughts returned to Dani, the only Goth in town; until I'd met Gérard. That first night we met, I thought that was what he was. Never had I thought any of this was possible, but there I stood, hiding in a church filled with runes. Why? Because they were all real.

My guess was we, meaning society as a whole, have always regarded things as fables and legends, even when history throws it in our faces: The Dark Ages, gargoyles on the Notre Dame Cathedral, people hanging garlic and fishing nets over their doors in Eastern Europe; burying their dead with poppies; witch hunts, and people locked up in mental wards for believing in werewolves on the night of a full moon.

Yup, society is an egotistical bitch.

I opened the door a crack. Smoky clouds smothered the moonlight, leaving little illumination besides the glowing embers. The wind carried the howl of wolves in the distance. I wondered if Doug was one of them, maybe even coming to find me. I drew myself together, closed the door, and slid the iron latch in place. The lock was hefty and stood the test of time.

I nodded off in spurts; seated by the fire. Something told me I was being watched. When I blinked my eyes awake, five little people with platinum hair, pointed ears, and silver slanted eyes, donned in beaver pelts, blinked back at me. I thought about screaming, but it seemed pointless.

"Guess you're not here to kill me," I said.

One of the skins fell to the ground, revealing a silver naked female. I didn't want to frighten her, so I sat still. She stepped forward and touched my hand. Her skin was cool, yet soft.

"We did not feed you to kill you," she said.

"We are here to guide you," said another.

"It is for you, why we are here. You are special, Summer," said the first, her accent thick, Old Gaelic, maybe.

"How do you know my name?" I asked.

Another one dropped its beaver skin to look at me. It jounced over and examined my bruises. "The doer of evil seeks you still. Find safety you must. Here is not so. Follow me." It looked kind of male-ish with a tiny loin cloth. He took my hand into his impossibly small fingers, brought me to the door of the church, and pointed to the mausoleum. "You go."

I went without another word and found the mausoleum adorned with hay and animal pelts to sleep upon. There was a glass bottle with water and a plate with dried meat by a small candlelit table. I locked the door behind me and grabbed the glass bottle. I saved the food for morning.

One of the beaver pelts was spread on the floor. I tiptoed to the altar. The pelt moved and the brave creature peered out. Although only about a foot tall, I believe she could have made herself any size she wanted.

Her voice was small but mature. "Summer, tomorrow you learn. The Samhain comes."

"Hush!" one of the female beings screamed in a harsh whisper.

The male disappeared.

"How do you know my name?" I asked again.

"We are piskies," said the male, who reappeared in a shadowy corner.

"I didn't know there were piskies here. Hell, what am I saying?" Amazing how a few witches and vampires just made everything else seem hunky-dory.

"You are special," whispered the brave female.

"I've come to that conclusion myself," I said.

"You are the last of your kind, a keeper. You belong here."

"What do you mean, my kind?"

The male flitted in front of me, grasping my face in his hands. "A *Máistreás Dragan*, Álfar-Sidhe of the Norse. No more human than I."

I pulled away. "You have it wrong! I'm human. My parents would have told me." My heart skipped a beat.

"Eck!" The brave one pulled the beaver pelt over her. "Your father was *loach mór*, before Sidhe claimed him. Together they brought you here."

"To Lake Sangre," the male attested.

"You were a secret," whispered a fragile female from the doorway. She seemed older, thinner. "They were lost to protect you."

"Who was lost?"

"Rest. Tomorrow you learn," the male whispered. They slid beneath the pelts and didn't show again until morning.

CHAPTER 29

I hadn't slept. The pelts remained still for the evening. I caved and ate a piece of dried meat, one nibble at a time to stay awake. As of late, waking up was not something I enjoyed.

The pelts stirred when the little beings crept from beneath them.

The brave one took my hand. "Come now. No more talk."

"No," I said.

"Go now!" the male shrieked.

"Go? Where?"

"Safety," said the brave one.

She approached the door as it opened before her. I followed.

We ended up back at the church but descended into a trapdoor beneath the altar. The wide walnut planks hid a stone stairwell. At the bottom was a room lit by a single oil lamp. I sat on a heavy wooden table next to a black metal kettle. The looks of which were familiar. I ran my fingers over the twisted metal handle. I'd held that kettle before.

A bookshelf against the wall had scrolls tied with ribbons, leather, or sealing wax. A quill and parchment lay in wait at a small desk in the far corner. A candle in a brass holder sat beside them. The male piskie blew, igniting the wick. A cot with a straw mattress covered in fur had a leather-bound book. I picked it up, holding the cover near the desk's candle. The image of a winged dragon was embossed on the cover. Inside were symbols I couldn't read, though I knew them.

"What is this place?" I asked, clutching the book to my chest.

The male piskie was the only one left. He sat on the cot, pulling the fur over his lap. "It is here you were saved. Sleep, now. Tonight, the master calls you home." His little silver body reflected the flickering flames as he ascended the stairs. I laid on the cot beneath the fur and slept in a dreamless sleep.

We traveled quietly through the evening woods, down the mountainside. The moonlight illuminated Lake Sangre's waters, causing a hazy reflection. A path led to the mansion, but the piskies didn't take it. Instead, we made haste to the lake's shore. The frail silver female stopped, donned the beaver pelt, and lay on the ground.

"Get down," she hissed.

I did what I was told and saw a man lower down on the mount. Not just any man—it was Greene. He was looking for someone and wasn't happy about it either. A hundred dollars says it was me.

I put my head to the ground and lay flat. The piskie touched my hand when he headed our way. He walked past us; he never gave a second look.

"Go, quick." She pulled me toward the lake. "Evil nears."

She stopped again. This time, she peered from under the pelt. The piskie's voice was shrill in the quiet of the forest. "The guardian waits." She pointed her slender finger toward the mansion, Gérard's mansion.

"The guardian?" I repeated her words. It would explain a lot.

Before I could ask any questions, she vanished. No beaver pelt, no anything. She just plain disappeared. I was getting tired of that. I tried to hurry to the stone wall, but intuition dictated otherwise. I dropped every time I heard a noise. That was quite a lot if you've ever been in the woods. I rounded a rock mound and spotted another pelt. A smaller piskie pointed the way.

But I hid behind a stump and waited instead; I'd heard a familiar voice up ahead.

"Where the hell is she? I'll kill you, ya little bastard." I knew that voice.

"I don't know. She was there and then she left. She hasn't come back. You've been to Gérard's; you've got Greene going to the cemetery. What more can we do?"

"Pray we find her, Tiny, or your sister dies. Need I remind you of Dani?"

"Shh, you fool. Aldatmak wants me in position. I have held this community for seven centuries. She'll kill us all if she finds out. Do not think for a moment she would hesitate to end your existence. You're lucky it wasn't done after the mistake you made."

"Then it's confirmed when they come, he will die. You'll hold his position, but Michel promised. I get her. It's the only way to defeat the Council. Don't think they won't avenge Gér . . ."

"Shut up, you fool."

I tucked myself in, the same as I'd done with the piskie. I concentrated on being one with the earth and felt a calm come over me, a lightness. Guillaume was a stone's throw from the stump. I went numb. What were they talking about? Shit.

The male piskie leapt into view. His pelt created an illusion that fooled Guillaume, who kicked at him. The male attacked with a bite, drawing blood from Guillaume's ankle.

"God damned rodent. Shoot that fucking thing," he told Tiny.

"Shoot what? There's nothing here," Tiny said.

"Where'd it go? Find it. Forget it. I'll find it. You find her." Guillaume took off toward the lake, away from where I was hiding.

"Summer, if you're here, you tell no one, or I'll kill Gale myself. Don't believe me? Ask Greene about Brody. Go away. Don't come back," Tiny whispered. He turned and walked away from me, deliberately.

I crept along the stone wall until I hit the mansion yards and ran to the entrance as fast as I could. Dusk was upon us and a candle light flickered in the entrance window. I sprinted up the stairs, to the door, and smacked right into Doug in the doorway. He grabbed me, threw me over his shoulder, and took me straight down to the bedchamber.

"It took you long enough."

"Nice to see you too!" I said, in a sarcastic but meaningful way.

He set me on my feet. "Yeah, you too." He squeezed me breathless and licked my cheek. I licked him back.

Two hands grabbed my waist, pulling me in for a backward hug.

"Gérard!" I yipped in unexpected excitement. "Gérard, I was so worried, I was scared I didn't know if you were okay or what. You never came." I couldn't catch my breath.

I wanted to squeeze him until I could squeeze no more. I wanted him close but instead I backed against the bedpost. "I never heard you, in my head," I whispered.

Doug shrugged. "He couldn't."

"Douglas," Gérard said. "I must talk with our Summer. Go rest."

The amber in Doug's eyes burned with fire before he bowed to leave us alone.

"Somebody struck a nerve," I noted.

"Summer, I told you the cemetery was a special place. I meant that," Gérard said. His eyes had gone a dark, midnight blue, no stars.

I tossed the Ruger on the bed, crossing my arms after. "Gérard, I expect respect and honesty. Do you understand?"

"I do, but you must trust me when I am unable to do so." He'd wandered to the far corner and stood in the shadows.

"What's the matter?" I asked, notably nervous.

"I expect you to extend the courtesy," he said. Then he let out a thunderous yell.

I jumped.

"I am not angry at you. I am angry at myself for bringing you into this. I am angry at myself for scaring you. I am angry that I could not come to you when you needed me."

"You didn't do this to me. It just happened. Now, as for scaring me—well—don't ever do it again!" I yelled at him. I'd had enough of angry men. "I need a shower, or bath, or whatever, and food. A real meal. Have a cup of blood or bite Doug, but I want to sink my teeth into a piece of meat."

He blinked and let out a tumultuous laugh. It sent that tingling sensation through me in such a rush. I staggered back.

"The temper I have not seen. It is refreshing from the Summer who is afraid to hurt everyone and please them all at the same time. Magnifique! What do you want? Beefsteak? Potatoes? Perhaps *le chocolat*?"

Normally, I was a modest person, though not one of my newfound friends would have agreed. I was certain they'd all think I was some self-centered blonde who thought she was all high and mighty. The truth was far from that. Or so I assumed. You know what they say about assuming, though, right? Never assume anything because it'll just make an 'ass' out of 'u' and 'me'.

I snickered to myself at the thought. Remembering my seventh-grade math class where the teacher went on a long tangent about assuming and told us that catchy little phrase. It stuck with me all those years. Odd it would come up then, but who can control their own lunacy.

"Summer?" he whispered from the chaise.

"I don't care. My body's sore and I'm tired." He'd advanced to the chaise while I was reminiscing. "To tell the truth, I could bite you, I'm so hungry." I turned away from him.

"Really? Then you shall have it all." He was suddenly at my back, whispering along my neck. "I am not opposed to you biting me, Summer." He appeared before me, smiled wide and showed full fangs.

It was a moment where terror overpowered reasoning. I snatched the Ruger from the bed and cocked the hammer, pointing it at his chest.

He laughed. "Come, touch them."

He held his hand out to me, but I didn't go. Touch his fangs? I have to say that isn't anything I ever expected to do to anyone. "That's okay. I'd better wash up before anything, anyway." I removed the clip and emptied the chamber before putting the gun in the vanity drawer. Useless.

I aimed for the bathroom, intent on avoiding him, but he grabbed my hand as I walked by and pulled me into his lap. He kissed the tip of my nose and nodded toward the doorway. I followed him into the bathroom where he drew the bath, complete with bubbles.

"You may disrobe, I will leave."

"But—I," I faltered. "What do you want? Do you ever get what you want?"

"I will get what I want, in time. If I stay or go, it is your choice. Not mine. What I want does not matter."

"So, you do want something?" I squinted at him and slipped the muddied shoes off by the sink. I unbuttoned my jeans and slid my hands up behind me to undo my bra. "Do you want to stay?"

His smile faded and the unassured man I witnessed from weeks before seeped through the rigid exterior. "What do you want me to say, Summer? That I want to watch you, have you turn slow so that I may savor every move?"

I didn't know why, but I did what he said. Before a minute had passed, I had a pile of soiled clothes at my feet. My legs and armpits were stubbly. There was dirt under my nails and my hair was matted against my head.

Before I knew, he was cupping my breasts. His power surged through me; my nipples went hard.

He laughed and smacked my ass. "*Adorable.* Do you think 800 years ago women were as they are today? Non, they were buxom, beautiful, and smelled like women. You are divine, chérie. Get in the tub. I know you like the modern ways." He handed me a basket of toiletries from the sink and sat on the black velvet bench behind the door.

"Are you going to watch me do everything?"

"Oui, you are a curious creature. I want to learn more." He settled back, crossing his leg over his knee, raising his brow.

I sighed. "Have it your way, then."

"I will."

I slipped into the water, taking in the dried potpourri floating around, as I tried to rid my mind of the events that had plagued me this past week. The warm water alone wasn't enough.

I washed my hair twice and conditioned it. I took the sponge and rubbed down my body with the peaches and cream soap and finally grabbed the razor. It was an all-in-one job, so you didn't need shaving cream—my favorite. I put my leg up out of the water and started to shave. Not the sexiest thing I know, but he seemed to like it.

He came over and sat on the platform, licking his lips with each stroke of the razor. Then it hit me.

"Oh my God! Really?"

"*Quoi?*"

"You're waiting for me to cut myself."

"You already have."

I opened my mouth and closed it.

"*Problème?*" He peered through his curtained locks and blew me a kiss.

I put my back to him and finished, quick.

He reached over to let the water out and held a towel open and ready. I let him wrap it around me when I stepped out—it was warm.

We went into the bedroom, where I stood dripping on the floor. He went back to the bathroom and brought out a brush. To my surprise, he started brushing my hair. He did it better than I did. No pulling and no ouches.

When he finished, he put the brush on the chaise, tilted my head to the side, and kissed along my neck. I protested as he flicked his tongue over my beating pulse, but he raised his hand to my lips and lightly pinched them shut.

His breath tickled my skin as he breathed over my shoulders— down my spine. His hands wandered unknowingly along the contours of my body. He paused at my hips and urged me on the bed, stomach down. I was reluctant until he placed a velvet kiss on each of my lower cheeks.

I whimpered when he parted my legs, just a little, and licked over my thighs until he found the smallest of shaving wounds. His tongue danced, sending with it, hints of sensual inclination.

I wanted to roll over and grab him. I wanted to bring him to me, but he'd placed his hand on my back, to keep me the way I was. I was forced to lie there, squirming.

"Gérard," I squeaked.

"*Oui, ma chérie?*"

"Please stop."

"Why?" he asked, obviously amused.

"I want more."

"I know." He kissed the small of my back and tossed a turquoise nightie with glow in the dark stars on the chaise.

He brought back a dinner tray, placed it on the bed, and came to where I stood, peeking. "Are you going to come out, or will I have to come get you?"

I opened the door.

He ushered me toward the bed and held a spoonful of mousse in front of my mouth. "I used to like dessert first. I still do," he whispered, sexy.

I took the spoon and watched him stare at the plate. "You seem different."

"How? I do not feel changed." He glanced up with a raised eyebrow, while he cut a small piece of steak and put it in my mouth.

"It's like you're more in-charge, dominant—no—confident." In my head, I thought *arrogant*, and quickly tried to think about something else so he wouldn't hear it.

"And this bothers you?"

"A little. What happened?"

"It is what I am." He put the tray in my lap.

"The guardian," I confirmed.

He strolled toward the door and leaned against the frame; arms folded, eyes closed.

I thought, *okay*.

"*Guillaume* confounds me. He serves on the regime, of which I preside. *Michel* desires a challenge—for property. *Mais*, to his dismay; I have triumphed."

I swirled the potato around the plate, listening but not understanding. I'd finished the mousse.

He turned the doorknob; Doug walked through with a steaming mug, and handed it to Gérard, then padded toward me. "I hope you'll understand. We were there . . ."

"But I gave him strict orders not to interrupt." Gérard glared at him.

"Gérard knew what needed to be done, love. Please do not be cross." Doug stooped to kiss the top of my head and paused at the door to glare back at him before leaving.

After the door clicked closed, Gérard continued, "His sentries ensured you escaped—unscathed."

"You bastard!" I sprang off the bed, toppling the tray. "You purposely let me be there, alone? I was terrified. I ran to the cemetery because I didn't even feel safe coming here. And now you're pretty well standin' there telling me I was right? You're the fucking guardian Guillaume warned me about. Fuck."

"Finished?"

I nodded and whispered, "What do you want from me?"

He placed his finger under my chin. "What I want now," he gazed into my eyes, "is dinner."

"Then why didn't you keep Doug?" I could be thick sometimes.

"I want you." He flashed that gorgeous smile. He said it again and made it linger over my body.

"You said you didn't want me for food." I looked around the vast empty-ish room and my fear rekindled. It was a perfect trap. Where would I go? He had me.

He walked to the wardrobe, taking out a pair of red silk boxers. "I have not fed and would like to have a little of you—for dessert."

I gasped. "You want sex or blood? I mean, we call sex dessert. But you haven't eaten. Shit."

He took the tray to the door, where Kitty met him. She handed him a green bottle. He raised it to me. "Dinner." Then asked, "Will you be dessert?"

"You just did, though."

"Would you accept a lick of mousse and feel content?"

"No."

"Then?"

Then I remembered his fangs. "Please don't hurt me."

He climbed on the bed and sat with his legs crossed. I crossed to the middle of the room.

"There is more than one way to be a virgin," he averred.

"Aha!" I had my moment, or so I thought. "That's what Guillaume was talking about. I've never been bitten. That makes me a virgin, which is why you want me. If you bite me first, Michel will leave me alone."

He cupped his own cheek and shook his head.

I hadn't seen him move, but he'd made it to where I was, and drew his hand through his hair, bringing some of it forward. I put my hand on his chest, pushing enough to keep him away. "If your theory were correct, I would have taken you without a date." He tipped his head toward the door. "I live next door. I do not need your permission."

He glided to the vanity and came back to hand me the cocoa. "Let me finish, Summer. Do not assume. It was as if upon this hundredth year I am destined to damnation at the expense of the salvation of those whom I serve."

"Still not going to kill me then?"

"*Non, Mount Mort* is a preternatural sanctuary, Summer. I am not going to kill you. I am trying to save you."

I didn't know what to say.

"At last, you are speechless!" He let out a lurid laugh.

He pressed his lips to mine and kissed them softly, sliding his tongue along the parting in my lips. It was enough for a tender French kiss.

Tempt your fear. Touch me. Feel me. Taste me. He flicked his tongue over my lips with each whispered thought.

"How?" I felt like the proverbial virgin. I didn't know what the hell he wanted me to do.

He caught my hand and pressed it to his lips. He parted them; his fangs exposed. I explored them with my fingertips and found them to be warm, hard, and sharp!

"Ouch." I pierced my finger on the point.

He slid his tongue over the tiny drop of blood and kissed my finger. "Careful now, I do not want you to get hurt." He smiled, sinister, cavalier. It sent heat through my veins but resulted in goose bumps on every inch of me.

I ran my hands over his face, confirming it was baby smooth skin. I drew my hands away, but he guided them over his chest and stopped at the waist of his pants.

"I cannot, *ma chérie.*"

I kept going anyway. He was soft through the silk, and it lessened my fear somehow. I kissed his face and melted into his lips. He smelled of exotic spices and tasted–I drew back.

"*Quoi?*" It was his turn to be alarmed.

"You taste like cinnamon. You know I love cinnamon. How'd you do it?"

"I did not do it, Summer. In fact, I am suppressing my influence."

"Well, I like it. You know, you don't need power to get me. It's just a coincidence, I guess."

He smiled, no fangs.

"Promise to use your wiles?"

"Of course, *chérie,* I will." He sat me on the bed; pulled me to the edge.

He kissed my breasts through my nightie and slid his hands up. His tongue, soft and warm, licked down toward my most private parts and stopped.

"Ready?" He asked, but before I could answer, his power rose within me.

He nestled his face between my thighs, forcing them apart as he licked just below the groin. His power flowed, determined—it strengthened until—I screamed.

"Summer?"

"I can't, I can't! Please don't, I'm not ready."

He smiled at me and winked. "Then I shall have my dinner."

He sat back and gulped the contents of the bottle, then left to brush his teeth. I brooded over my lack of bravery as he stood by the bed. I'd turned away from him.

"Summer?"

"Mmm?"

"I would never take blood from you, without my influence. I promised. I will never hurt you."

He slid between the sheets and propped the pillows, his arm bent behind his head. He slipped his other arm beneath me, curling me to face his chest, tears and all. It was the first time I noticed; he didn't have a heartbeat.

CHAPTER 30

The smell of hot chocolate tantalized my senses. I plucked my head from the pillows, still foggy from sleep. Gérard was nowhere to be seen, but I knew he'd be down until dusk. A platinum tray with a double sized mug and two croissants sat on the chaise. A mauve silk pantsuit lay next to the tray.

The door creaked and Doug's head popped in. "Good afternoon, Summer," his voice lilting.

I sat up and stretched, soaking in my surroundings. "You can come in. I'm half-way decent."

"I thought it a good time to chat." With little effort, he caught the edge of the door with his toe and closed it behind him. He was fluid enough that his ponytail didn't sway over the silk dress shirt. Most men couldn't pull off royal purple. But coupled with that chestnut hair and deep sienna eyes, he was damn near irresistible. But I shouldn't have had such thoughts, not then. He sauntered toward me; his black trousers and socks absorbed by the room's décor.

I couldn't help but scoff at the thought of talking. After all, I hadn't enjoyed a conversation with anyone, as of late. And last night made me question Gérard. Granted, he stopped, but what he was going to do scared the hell out of me. And what did he mean, save me?

"Must we?" I lamented, scooting back toward the headboard, and pulling the duvet higher.

"Aw, come on. It's not that bad. My only intent is to get acquainted with the woman who'll be a part of my life for a *very* long time." He stressed the 'very' and smiled that smile again, confident arrogance.

"What—wait—what?"

He chuckled in a voice too old for him. "You truly are a love. I think we need to start over." He walked to the foot of the bed. "May I sit?"

"Ok," I said.

He stretched across the foot of the bed and rolled on his side, propping himself up on one elbow. His eyes met mine. I looked away.

"Summer," he sighed. "Gérard has—well, you must feel something or the piskies would not have sent you here. Ay?"

"Yeah."

"Good, but here's where it gets complicated."

"Now it gets complicated. Do you not know what's been going on?"

"Well, this is kind of a part of that. It is who we are."

"We who?"

"Right now, I mean Gérard and myself."

"And?"

He fidgeted with a loose thread on the comforter and peered up through his eyelashes. "Ok, the basics?"

"Please." I forced a smile and sat back against the pillows.

"I'm over 500. I'm not a child, Summer."

"Really?"

He shifted his eyes up. "Yes, well, Gérard means a lot to me. True, I am his, but he is mine as well. If anything happens to him, it affects me. If anything happens to me, well, it affects him. We're bound."

"500? Are you serious?" I was stuck on that.

"540 give or take a few years. Stay with me now, love."

"Sorry, go on."

"I love Gérard."

"Oh."

"In a brotherly or familial way. I will not let him get hurt again. I will not allow it."

"Brotherly," I stated more than asked.

"Ay, perhaps more, but 'tis hard to explain."

"Okay. Let's pretend I understand, since we both know I don't. Why tell me?"

"I want us to become friends; maybe closer. If you choose to be with Gérard, you can be with him for, as I said, a very long time."

"And that means?"

"It means we are a package deal." He smiled playfully as he rolled to his stomach and bent his knees to raise his feet over his buttocks. "Have some breakfast, love."

"I'm not sure I want to eat." I pulled the comforter up to my chin. Did Gérard want to share me with Doug? Was Doug going behind Gérard's back trying to get at me? Was this a test? Shit, did they know how I felt about him?

"Hmmm, I tell you what. I'll go out and sit by the fire. You get dressed and say my name. I'll know when you call." He slid off the foot of the bed, accentuating his fluid physique with every move, and strode out the door, closing it behind him.

I took a sip from the mug, which held a hint of coffee and cinnamon. Surprise—cinnamon mocha latte. Fancy. I ate a croissant which was filled with raspberry chocolate filling, and voila! My spirits were back up.

I wanted Doug. I didn't want to screw up with Gérard, but Jesus, I wanted them both. Shit. I put it from my mind and concentrated on finding out where this conversation was going.

I went to the wardrobe and pulled out a pair of ivory lace thongs with a matching bra. I never could have pulled that off. It's why I never bought stuff like that, but I liked it. I put on the mauve outfit and felt oddly promiscuous.

I sat on the bed with one leg dangling and the other tucked under me, attempting a sexy pose.

"Doug, you can come in now," I called.

He strode through the door and bowed. "You don't want another croissant?" He sat on the chaise.

"No, thanks. Nerves, I guess. Besides, a girl's got to watch her figure."

"Let someone else take care of that for you." He winked and my stomach flipped. I folded my lips. "Lighten up, love. I want to talk. It takes two people at least to have a decent conversation. Sometimes we forget; the little things have become unimportant. We must be reminded, as you are so young."

"Yeah, well, I'm talking to you right now."

He cut me off. "Us, love. Gérard is always with me. I give him his daytime life back by doing things he used to enjoy and by enjoying things I like to do. One thing he enjoys, and I, is you."

"Oh!" I said, the heat building in my core.

He smiled a sinister smile that reminded me of Gérard's. I could have melted. He crawled onto the bed next to me. "You keep mentioning that I haven't tried for you." He put his finger to my lips, shushing me. "Now, before you jump to conclusions, I have no intention of doing so, because I don't have to."

"I'm not sure what you're getting at, but I won't cheat on Gérard." Damn morals.

"Aw, love, I didn't ask you to. Use me to ease your mind—or not. I won't lie to you, and I won't hurt you. I mean, it's hard enough to accept one of our kind." He stared off for a moment and stood from the bed. "Gérard is a good man. Base your decisions on him, not me."

I stared at the floor as if there was something worth looking at. "Want the last croissant?"

"Thanks, but I can't have chocolate. Wolf, dog, chocolate." He wrinkled his nose as he said each word. "Come, let's take a walk." He took my hand, and we walked upstairs to the main floor. But it was different. The fun had left me. I followed him out of necessity with a new angst. Gérard won my heart. But at what cost?

We wound up in front of a stained-glass mural depicting a dragon asleep beneath a starlit sky. I studied it, the deep reds in the foreground in contrast with the indigo background. I reached out to trace the lead lines, but the window gave to my touch; it was a door.

Stunned, I stepped out onto a cobblestone walk, surrounded by white rosebushes, evergreens, and red dogwood planted in a repeated pattern on both sides which formed islands among the moss and stone pavers. There was a fountain in the middle with a woman, arms outstretched, reaching toward the sky. Water pooled around a rock beneath her feet and poured over the small mountaintop on which she stood.

It fit perfectly with the way the sun shone brightly over the garden and reflected on all of the walls and doors leading to the mansion. There were stained-glass murals everywhere I looked. The colors were deep and breathtaking, and there she stood, as if commanding it all. I could have stayed there all day. *Shit, day!*

"Do you like it?" Doug broke the silence.

"Mhmm."

We strolled, still holding hands. It was natural. Actually, I hadn't realized we were holding hands until he caressed the back of my hand with his thumb, gentle but firm.

I pulled away and sat on a carved stone bench just beyond the fountain. He straddled the seat to look at me.

"Please don't hurt us, Summer. And by us, I mean all of us."

"I'll try not to. I don't want to be hurt, either. You know Jesse betrayed me, but he hurt me in more ways than you could imagine."

"Mmm, I can," Doug murmured.

I glanced at him sideways and then back down to the pavers. "One time he brought a girl home. Her name was Arianna, and young, go figure." I trembled with the plethora of emotions that transformed to anger. "He made out with her; told me to either join them or get out. I went to Gale's." I didn't cry; it didn't hurt anymore. It felt good to be angry.

"Stop. I know of his ill practices. You need not remember." He rested his cheek on my head. "Summer, you can't judge all men by the way the one treated you."

"Explain Guillaume," I said.

I glanced at his eyes and wanted to stay there, looking, but I couldn't. It was as if staring into those large amber eyes would let him see my darkest secrets. That he would delve deep into my world and wouldn't like what he saw. My insides twisted like I was going to give something away, or get in trouble if I looked too long, a child in trouble. But his eyes were safe. He wasn't Gérard. But he already knew.

"One day, I will. For now, Gérard awaits." He grabbed my hand and pulled me inside one of the doors.

It was dark inside. I hadn't noticed before. There were wall sconces through the hallways. And they were all lit with real candles.

He took me to a stairwell hidden behind a heavy drape and slid behind me. "Here lies the secret of *La Maison D'Aquitaine.*"

I stepped down and followed him in silence. I thought there was a ridiculous number of stairs to the bedroom. I was wrong. This stairwell seemed endless. I felt my way along the wall until he stopped at a vast marble landing opposite our walkway; there was a circular opening surrounding the landing.

"Hold on, love," Doug said.

He leapt across and landed before a large wooden door with a platinum rose knocker mounted below a peephole. He knocked, and we waited.

The door opened to the most captivating, yet spine-chilling parlor I'd seen yet. There were wall panels just as upstairs. The biggest difference was that there was a black lacquer coffin, centered on which was a platinum rose, all on a black marble altar. The handles and hinges matched, bringing the theme full circle. My thoughts struck me as funny, since the room was circular. An oubliette, I guessed.

A baby grand, with a platinum candelabrum, was tucked against the far wall. An ebony door stood ajar, offering a small bathroom with a contrasting white marble theme.

"He feels the same as you. It's why I'm here. Think of me as your link to him as he sleeps."

"So you say."

"Gee, don't sound so thrilled." He mocked my pout.

I couldn't help but smile. "I didn't mean anything by it."

"I know; I jest. You're cute when you're red."

"You're going to kill me." I kidded back.

I turned to face the piano where Gérard was playing *Mariage d'Amour*, by Chopin. I happened to read the title when I saw the piano. Someone raised in a simple home like me didn't listen to that kind of music. I grew up with my father singing Irish ballads, and my mother humming the Welsh "Suo Gan", but not Chopin. I liked it, but it made the situation more obscene, more real, if that were at all possible. I ambled toward a pile of oversized burgundy cushions, sat, and patted a pillow next to me for Doug, but he left.

"*Bonsoir*, Summer." The playing stopped. I dropped my eyes; nervous tremors kept me seated. It was foolish, but the coffin in the room sucked the romance away and added to my fears, especially since there was no escape.

"Hi," I whispered.

"*Ma chérie, c'est le secret de la Maison D'Amour*. My name is *Gérard D'Amour*." He gave a low bow with one hand in front, and the other in back. "It was my name before I turned vampire, as I was a knight in *Queen Eleanor of Aquitaine's* court. I lived by the Code of Chivalry. It is a skill not easily mastered. After all, my queen created the code and held us to her highest standard, as we were a part of the *Courte D'Amour*."

"Well, you most certainly live up to it." I turned away, hoping the trembling in my voice went unnoticed. There was no way out for a puny human like myself. Damn oubliette!

"Please come see what fears you most." He took my hand and pulled forth. A flurry of emotions washed through me. The white silk lining, the small pillow, everything reminded me of my sister's funeral: the lace on the pillow, the smell of funeral flowers that burst from my memory but weren't really there.

The memories replayed, ingrained in my conscience. I remembered touching her small hand. It didn't feel like her; I didn't believe it was her. She was warm and soft; not hard and cold. I looked at her, the make-up that covered her facial discolorations. The soft pink lipstick that was a little too pink to be natural.

I sank back on the pillows and bowed my head. "I can't take the memories. Ever since I met you, all I do is reminisce about the horrible things in my life."

"It frightens you." He remained statuesque, unbreathing. "Tell me why."

"Fine. Because death is so final. I forget you're—well, I don't know what you are."

"I am dead. I am the living dead. I am Mr. Death." He did a quick tap dance. "It is hard for you to believe because I am here, now, talking with you. Tell me, if you were to come in the day, would you be afraid of seeing me? Or would you be afraid because I was dead?"

"I don't know." It was honest.

"It is something you must accept if we are to be together."

"Okay." What else could I say? I mean, I couldn't argue.

"Could it be you truly do not know?" His smile disappeared. He appeared, squatting before me. "Ah, I believe you do."

"What are you getting at?"

His eyes went serious, cold, and black. "Say it."

"Say what?"

"What you are truly afraid of."

"I don't know."

"Yes, you do." He whispered, and it went through me. "Say it."

"What? That I'm afraid to die? That someday I will, and that scares the hell out of me. I think about my sister and how she did it. It mustn't be that bad. Everyone does it, but it scares the hell out of me. It makes me sick to think of touching you warm and alive only to have your cold hard body next to me. I know what she felt like; it will never leave me. I don't ever want to feel anyone like that again."

Still unbreathing, he waited.

"You being dead and coming back to life is inconceivable because I can't do that, and neither can my family. I wish I were an immortal, like you. But sometimes I wish I'd died with them. I can't go to Dani's wake!"

My eyes swelled with the tears I fought back. I never admitted my fears, and it frightened me to say them aloud.

I tried to look away, but his hands flew up to my face and kept me still. I rolled my eyes to look at anything but his.

"It wasn't what you wanted to hear, was it? But you probably already knew somehow. It's what you do. You use your power for everything. Do you even remember what it was like to be mortal? Were you afraid to die?"

"You have much to learn." He took out a handkerchief and blotted my face, offered it to me, and stood erect. "If I were younger your words would sting, but time has proven there are few surprises left for someone as old as I."

"What the hell is that supposed to mean?"

"It means that you have many fears to face. I am not *un jouet*, a mere toy. There is more to me. It is not easy, Summer. I have lost all whom I loved. I lost my life and any life I could hope for. Was I afraid to die? *Oui*, every day. I still am. I am not immortal, Summer."

"How could you not be immortal?"

"Because I may still be killed." He closed the coffin. "You are young. Life is a cruel teacher. Come, let us ascend. I am famished. Shall we eat?" He glided toward the door. "You do realize that it is not human, do you not?"

I kept quiet. Had we covered that? He smiled wide, exposing his marvelous white fangs. The more I looked at them, the less they frightened me. They fit him perfectly. Without them, I think he would have looked weird. Go figure.

"Gérard, I . . ."

"Summer, please. Save me the humiliation of your sad attempt at salvation. I know how you felt. It was you who was afraid of the acknowledgement. Though it stung to hear, it has been on your mind since you discovered what I am."

"I'd deny it, but . . ."

"Do yourself a favor and stop talking. I already knew; it was you who needed to hear from yourself."

"I don't like hurting people."

"*C'est la vie.*" He shrugged.

We stepped through the door, and I swooned from the height, or lack of bottom, in the oubliette. He had his arms around me and crossed the abyss in a blink. He let me go and started the ascension one stair at a time—human speed.

I didn't like what he said, but he was right. I was an adult and had to accept it. Like it or not, the truth sucks.

"Doug and I had a nice time today."

"*Je sais.*"

"Do you really not care if I—I don't want to say date him, but spend time with him?"

"Is it not the same? A courtship with the promise of eternal companionship?"

"I think I missed something."

"*Non, ma chérie.* It is what you refuse to see."

Once we reached the top, he placed his hand in the middle of my back and led me to the dining hall. There was a long table with white candles lit by each setting. On one end was a meal under a silvery dome that I wasn't sure I wanted. On the other was a small ottoman alongside the dining chair. I walked to the end with food. He pushed me in and went to his chair.

Doug came in, taking a seat on the ottoman. It was awkward knowing he was the food. I almost wished he had the goblet instead.

I took the dome off of my plate and tried not to look, but I couldn't help watching the two of them. They had been talking and laughing. Then, Gérard stared at me and bit down.

The next thing I knew, he was behind me.

"*Ma chérie*, you have not eaten."

I was embarrassed to admit it but, hey. "I was a little preoccupied. I'm still getting used to this, you know. It isn't like I grew up in a house where we sat down to dinner and Dad said, 'Hold on, I have to bite someone before we finish the spaghetti.'"

"Interesting, you always resort to sarcasm or humor when you get nervous. It is a bad attempt at both. Truth, *ma chérie*, tell me you don't want me to feed with you. I would understand."

"Because it's not what I want. I find what you do fascinating. Gérard, this is all like a fairytale to someone like me."

"*Euh*, as a vampire I had never been the object of anyone's desire. Nightmares, *oui*. Dreams? *Non*. It is how you say—a change in times."

Doug came by with Gérard's cloak and draped it over me. He fastened the clasp below my chin and sniffed my cheek before he took a seat where Gérard had been.

He nodded and pulled out my chair. "Shall we, *ma chérie*?" he asked.

"I'd like to see the courtyard by moonlight; it was pretty in the sun." I clasped my hand over my mouth. "I'm sorry."

I drank whatever was in the goblet, clueless as to what it was—milky and sweet, but not milk. Odd, but it kept me from opening my mouth again.

"Although it is a pleasure I miss, it is not a forbidden word. Of course, you would enjoy the sun. I would be more surprised if you did not." He glided to the windows and opened the stained- glass doors. The torches in the courtyard cast shadows so that the beauty of the day's walk rivaled its comparison. "But we do not have long."

I took his hand and led him to the bench where Doug and I had been earlier. I cupped my hands under his chin and lifted his face enough to glimpse his eyes; I closed mine. *Kiss me*, I thought.

He put his hands on my buttocks and pulled me onto him. One hand slid up my back and guided me to the side as he bent in. The moment his lips met mine, I peeked and was surprised because he had his eyes closed. Somehow it made him more real, human—no mortal. He looked vulnerable. As if his eyes held all the power; with them closed, I was safe.

He withdrew and raised his face to the moonlight. The dark of his hair held a bluish hue, and I wondered if it was his power, or genetics. His antique white lace blouse was open to the third button. Unable to resist, I leaned in and kissed his neck.

He pulled me to my feet and guided me back inside. I knew it was time. *I'm ready*, I thought.

It was then that I felt the familiar tingling of his power trickle through me. He'd reclaimed the night.

CHAPTER 31

We met Doug in the limo with Kitty and Patricia, all of us dressed in black. Gérard had his sunglasses on; I finally came to the conclusion it was to keep the general public from questioning his eyes. I mean, they were constantly changing.

I sat in between Doug and Gérard and felt calm, even though I was sick over having to go to Cushing's Funeral Home. I hated them. Not the people, but the place in general. The smell of preserved flowers, the soft music, the eerie little lamps, and the altar. It haunted me. God, I didn't want to go through with it.

"You, alright?" Kitty asked.

"Uh-huh." I bit off the corners of my nails and was working on the little skin bits.

"Summer, it is an honor to pay your respects. It is the highest regard one may pay to the deceased." Gérard put his hand over mine and drew it away from my mouth. "I should know."

"You aren't dead, not really. It's an analogy. This is death, and I don't like it. I hate it. The finality, the goodbye." A tear dripped down my cheek. "I know you guys feel it, too. But does it get easier, with time?"

"Never," Patricia sighed. I wasn't sure how old she was, but I'd take her word for it.

Raul pulled up to the front of the Victorian house. They all climbed out, but I stayed put. I couldn't force myself to get out of the damned car. The tears came in regular streams, as if I wept for all the dead in Mount Mort. I hated Michel, and I didn't even know him. I hated Guillaume too. But most of all, I hated Tiny. I hated him because of the pain he caused Gale. And because his involvement in whatever it was that he was doing cost Dani her life. And the only life worth losing is that of those who are purely evil. Dani was far from that. I sobbed and Gérard slid back inside, shutting the door behind him.

"Summer," he whispered and slid next to me.

"Yes?"

"Do you remember dancing?" He seemed to be searching for the right words. "How I helped you?"

"Mmhmm."

He lifted my chin with the tips of his fingers and urged my eyes even with his. "I can do that now if you give me permission."

"What do you mean?"

"I can lessen your pain. Make it easier for you."

"But I owe Dani the tears. I should have been at the diner. I never should have gotten so deeply involved with all of this. If I had gone to work, she might still be here."

"If you had gone to work, you would undoubtedly be in there beside her." He kissed my forehead. "Please, let me do this for you."

"If I say okay, then what?"

"Then you step out of the car and pay your respects."

"No funny business?"

He smiled, a soft up-tilt of the corners of his mouth, no teeth. "My word."

"Okay." And like that, my mind cleared. My thoughts were coherent and focused. I was sad, but I was no longer compelled to cry. "How?" I hadn't looked him in the eye. Had I? I couldn't remember.

"Come, my Danielle awaits."

He opened the door and stepped out before me. The rest of our party had gone inside. He offered his hand to help me out. I took it but didn't need it. I felt better than I had in a month.

The mortician stood at the door talking with Doug. Gérard stepped over the threshold; I let go. I couldn't do it. He looked at me. I refused to look at him. I couldn't go in. I stood between Doug and the man in black. My insides twisted. I could almost see my emotions, dark and choking inside me. I gasped and glanced to Gérard—frantic.

His eyes caught me, and the feeling subsided. It scared me. I'd never felt that before.

Doug took my hand, bowed at the man staring at me, and brought me to the casket where Dani lay within. It was closed, which helped, but I knew all too well what happened. I knew that inside that box, there were pieces missing.

Guilt took over. I let out a bawling sob. "I found her. I prepared her. How the hell could I do that?" I was sick.

There wasn't anyone else but our little party, so Doug let go of me and left. I caught a glimpse of him taking the others from the room, Gérard included. He drew the double doors closed and left me alone with her.

"I'm so sorry, Dani. I never meant for this to happen," I breathed across the evergreen casket. "You were too young to die." I buried my face in my hands. "She was too young to die. I was afraid for months that I would die too. Every time her birthday comes or the anniversary of her death, I hope she's happy wherever she is. I don't believe in a heaven or a hell. Maybe that makes it worse, but I try not to think about her at any other time. I feel so guilty. You don't understand. The guilt, it stays with you. She was my sister, damn it!" I was screaming. "We had arguments; I said things I didn't mean. If I could take them back, I would, but I can't. I can never take anything back. I can never tell her I love her again. I can never tell you, I'm sorry."

I wished I had realized then; what Dani was trying to tell me. "Ever notice how small the graveyard is?" she'd asked, out of the blue one day. "No, you don't even realize; you've only been to one funeral in your life. And you never questioned why you were adopted, or why you keep coming back." I didn't get it. "Just know they're watchin', always knowing—ubiquitous. This isn't cookie-cutter America, Summer." But she never had a chance to tell me what it was she wanted to say, because Tiny burst in and started yelling about orders waiting, and her not pulling her weight. After that, he cut her hours and now her words would go to the grave.

I hugged the casket and spoke to the upper partition where her head should have been. "I swear I'll find who did this. I swear it. I'll find your momma too." I sobbed deeper. "Rest in peace, Dani. I love you."

I dropped to my knees and prayed. "Please, whoever is up there or in charge, please make this stop. I can't take it anymore. I don't want good people to die. Please take care of Dani and my family. Please watch over Gale if she isn't with you. I want her back. I don't know these people I've entrusted my life to. I don't know the people I grew up with. I don't know anything anymore. Please make it right. Help me make the right choices. I don't know what to do. I miss them. All of them. They say God never gives you anything you can't handle; well I'm telling you I can't handle anymore. And if this is some kind of test, then I don't want to take it," I pled from whatever was deeper than my soul.

I cried into my sleeves. The tears weren't just for Dani. They were for the last few weeks, months, hell, years. Dani was the catalyst to the release of all I'd kept hidden. I held her casket, reluctant to leave. It was like that with Sheena, too. I didn't want her to be alone.

I felt a hand on my shoulder and froze. I hadn't realized anyone else was there.

"Summer, it is time. We will return for Danielle's funeral," Gérard said, his voice wrapped around me like a blanket of safety. "Douglas has taken the others back."

I stood, straightened my dress, kissed the casket, and turned into Gérard's arms. He held me and I wept. I cried into him and wasn't sure I should have. It was too new. I wanted familiar comfort. The feeling you get from the arms you know; kisses from lips that no longer excite but tell you everything will be all right. Eyes that lied, saying it's okay. Voices that shushed even when you were alone. But I realized those days were gone. There wasn't anyone left to do those things. Those things I so badly wanted.

Gérard stroked my hair, and I felt a little better. The crying subsided, and I pushed away enough to wipe my face and gather myself.

We left the parlor and ran into Andy in the foyer. I'd forgotten he had a loss, too. I pulled away from Gérard and wrapped my arms around Andy. He hugged me with unexpected force. He wept softly on my shoulder. I had forgotten he was a vampire. He got pink tears all over my dress—I didn't care. I grabbed a tissue from the side table and blotted his eyes. He stooped to kiss my cheek, bowed at Gérard, and silently walked into the parlor from where we had come.

I glanced up at Gérard to see a single pink tear steal from the outer corner of his eye leaving a trail that disappeared into his black suit. I turned to look at him full on, and studied his face but avoided his eyes. It must have hurt him because of Marie. I hugged him and pulled him from the funeral home.

There was no limo. Instead, he took the lead as we walked toward the outside of town. I held his hand but didn't feel as though he held mine back. I didn't understand.

I let go and walked at his side in silence until we reached Brady's.

CHAPTER 32

érard escorted me through the entrance, but then glided past me to take a seat in the furthest corner booth. Brady brought a bottle out with a cranberry glass and a hot cocoa for me.

"You, okay?" I asked.

"*Non*, I have failed. I have lost those I swore to protect. Danielle trusted me—for five centuries. Gale has lost a daughter because I was weak. Andrew's loss was a result of my decisions. It is never easy to make choices. One day you will understand, there is always a price." He opened the bottle and filled his glass. "I have a duty, Summer." Pink tears streamed onto the table. He used a napkin to blot his eyes, but it was no use. "Excuse me," he whispered, and strode to the men's room.

Patricia and Kitty slid into Gérard's side of the booth. I hadn't known they were there. Patricia leaned against the wood rail. Kitty offered a pity smile to us both. The kind that isn't a smile but more of a puckered frown. It didn't reach her emerald cat-like eyes. They were both still in black.

"Hey," I said.

Patricia picked her head up. "Spare us all, Summer. This sucks. You don't have to pretend otherwise. Dani and Gale were here before I was born. I've never known a life without them."

"I didn't know that."

Kitty glanced at me through her bangs. "Not yet." She motioned to Brady. "It is not how anyone had planned, Summer, but we must talk. Your decisions impact more than yourself." Brady came back with a cranberry goblet and a tea.

Patricia took the bottle and filled the goblet. "It is where the complications occur. Marie would not accept Douglas, or the monstrosity she perceived Gérard to be." She sipped and stared at me full on. "I know how you feel about Doug."

Oh, shit. My heart skipped. "I don't—"

Kitty put her hand up. "Have we given you a reason to lie?"

"No."

She sipped her tea. "Then why attempt?"

I cradled the cocoa. "I won't hurt anyone. How I feel is confused. I know it's lame, but I like Gérard more. Neither of you understand. But either way, I agreed to go out with him. Besides, Doug is complicated."

"But you want him, *oui*?" Gérard came back and slid into the booth next to me.

I glanced around, panicked. "I'm sorry. But I assure you, I won't act on it. I'm not my ex."

Doug came in to join us and straddled a chair he'd pulled up to the table. He'd taken his hair out of the ponytail and shook it over his shoulders.

I studied the mug. My face burned. I wanted to die. Tears welled but didn't flow, my heart threatened to beat from my chest. Breathing became tight. I gripped the mug harder. In high school, I was confronted by two crushes. One humiliated me, the other pitied me. It was happening all over again.

"Summer," Doug said.

"Mmm?"

"Look at me, love."

"No." I bit my lip and a tear fell.

"Summer, there are times I share with Douglas and times I do not," Gérard mumbled.

"He shares enough," Doug added. "There are few secrets between us."

"Then, there are secrets between you?" I whispered.

"Of course," Doug declared. "I am not his slave."

"None of us are," Patricia added.

"But with me, you both know what I do with the other?" I hunched in on myself and glanced at them.

"Why Summer, do you have plans to do something with me?" Doug chided and wiggled his eyebrows.

Gérard laughed a deep laugh, the kind when you get caught off guard. Natural, real.

"Kill me now," I said.

"I waited to have this discussion because I questioned whether my decision was founded. My heart is not in this alone." Gérard spoke soft and low.

"I already told him, I'm yours if you'll have me," Doug whispered, lower still.

Kitty grasped my hand. "Will you try?"

"You're letting me go?" I asked Gérard, specifically. I choked on my words and gulped the cocoa. Hot or not, I couldn't feel it. My insides clenched; any breath or feeling I had was unrecognizable.

"No, Summer."

"Then what, be with both of you?" I pressed my forehead onto the table. "I don't know if I can do that."

"We're only talking, love," Doug assured.

"I know," I said.

"I do not question how you feel. But I do question whether or not you intend to include Douglas."

"Is it what you want?"

No answer.

Kitty broke the silence. "Normal doesn't exist, Summer. Stop trying to fit a mold that you created in your head. You live in a sanctuary and haven't thought to ask why. Either you're avoiding the truth, or you really are oblivious."

"The truth. The piskies told me about my real father, and Molly said my mother was Sidhe. I have no idea what it means. Dani kept telling me to think. But I don't know what it is I'm supposed to be thinking about."

Brady came over, his eyes reflected yellow in the dim light, illuminated by his coal black skin. He was barely as tall as Doug in his chair. He whispered, voice deep,

The legend comes by seer's sight, by way of they, both black and white.

The keeper's chosen, right or left, reveals voices no more bereft.

Two sides lie, two sides fight. The battle begins a sorrowful night.

Of Álfar blood she shall reign. Hence the dragon flies again.

My stomach dropped. I knew those words; Guillaume had said them. "Why did you say that—that thing?" I rubbed my arms and huddled into the corner. I glanced at Gérard, Patricia, and then Kitty. I didn't trust them. Not with fear, I turned to the only one I did trust. "Doug, what's going on?"

"You know the legend, Summer. All children in Mount Mort learn the legend," Brady offered. "Remember it, say it. Sleep on it." He waddled away and disappeared.

"Doug?"

Doug nodded at Patricia and Kitty. They slid from the booth.

Kitty smiled at me. "We'll see you tomorrow, Summer. Goodnight, Masters Gérard and Doug." She and Patricia left.

Doug slid into the booth where they had been. Gérard slid out from our side. "I will be out with Raul. Take all the time you need." He seemed to direct the latter to Doug.

Doug waited for the door to close before getting comfortable in his narrow space. He leaned his back against the wall, stretched his legs across the bench, and fiddled with a cardboard coaster under Patricia's goblet. "Summer, why did you ask me? You could have asked anyone here." He peered at me through a draped lock of hair that curtained his face.

"I'm scared, Doug."

"Rightly so, but why me?" He brushed his hair back to have a clearer view.

"I thought you knew everything from Gérard."

"What would be the point of living if all you have to do is listen to what people are thinking? It's not polite, and impractical. Now, why did you ask me and no one else?" He pulled a knee up and rested his head back. "You think I had something to do with it. Dani or Gale, maybe your parents or even Sheena."

"No!" I sat up and grabbed my mug. "No, Doug. The thought never occurred to me." Should I have trusted him? Who else did I have? "Confidentially?"

He nodded.

"I don't know them. I'm not exactly friends with Patricia, and I know nothing about Kitty. I don't even know where she is from."

"And why not Gérard?"

"Because I don't know him either." I sat back against the wall and put my feet up on the bench. "You're the only one I know. Yeah, I'd feel better if you were furry, but . . . God, I can't believe I just said that." I tucked my head to my knees. "I trust you to keep me safe. And Brady recited the same words Guillaume did at the house. I hate the rhyme. I hate the story it tells. It scares the hell out of me, and I just want the feelings I used to get when you came to me all through the years. I trust you, Doug."

He straightened in the booth and clasped my hand, his eyes level with mine, as I turned to face him. His eyes, like amber fire, made my pulse quicken. "Thank you, Summer."

"Why?"

"Because that means the world to me. You are special." He drew my hands to his nose and nuzzled them. He was warm, and his stubble reminded me of his fur.

"So I'm learning." I stroked his chin with my pinkie. "I've always accepted you. And that's the problem."

"How about we get out of here? I'll meet you in the den. The three of us can relax and talk." He breathed across my hands.

"Then take me home. I can't do this here," I stated.

He slid from the booth and waited for me. I followed him outside where Raul and Gérard waited with the limo. I climbed in after them, and Raul shut the door.

"I can't share either of you. I won't," I said, halfway to my house.

"It will not be a problem. But do you truly accept this?" Gérard asked.

"Don't ask me that right now. Please."

I stared out the window and watched the trees go by a little quicker than I'd liked. I couldn't go home. My house was still under remodel. I wondered if Mrs. Finch knew. It was Gérard's people who were working on it.

The limo drove past my pull-off and I knew I wouldn't have to worry about it, but I wondered if they thought I was too presumptuous to call the mansion my home. I knew it wasn't.

Raul pulled into the clearing and let Gérard out first. He came around to my side and let me out, but Gérard was gone.

"The master requests your presence in your chamber, Miss," he said.

Okay. "Thanks, Raul."

Doug emerged behind me. "I'll be along shortly."

"Okay." I ran to the main entrance and clamored up the stairs, surprisingly eager to be with them.

The draped archways were all closed except for the one I needed to go through. It led to the stairwell to the den. I skipped down a few stairs and slowed, trying to regain my breath. I did that on and off until I came to the thick wooden door. It was closed, so I knocked.

"Come in, love," Doug called.

I leaned on my knees to gain my bearings, and my breath, before I turned the knob. I had to hold my head high, since I was pretty sure they both knew, and I was hiding from no one. I pulled the door open and walked through.

"How'd you get here so fast?" I asked.

"Talent," Doug said with a raised brow.

They were by the fireplace just outside the bedroom. Doug was sprawled on the ivory shag rug in a pair of white silk boxers. His hair spilled over the floor as he lay resting, his hands clasped on his well-chiseled abs, knee raised. The thickness of his thighs pulled the material tight.

I studied the fire.

Gérard had settled in a wing-back chair and crossed his legs over the arm. His hair pulled around his shoulder as he watched me. I closed the door, sat in the other chair, and tried to mirror him but wound up flashing them, which was a complete accident.

"*Mon Dieu, ma chérie.*" He smiled and tilted his head to enact a peek. Doug crawled over on all fours.

I jumped up, turning all shades of red, smoothed my hands down my dress, and scurried around Doug to get to the bedroom. "I hope you enjoyed the show. It won't happen again."

"Aw, such a tease," Doug said. His words brought the heat rising up my neck with such force I couldn't believe embarrassment could hurt. I had no smart come back, only a quick retreat.

"I'm going to change."

"I can hardly wait," Gérard said, a tease of his power pulsed in the room. I wondered if Doug felt it, too.

I slipped into the bedroom and pulled a pink pajama set from the wardrobe. I put it on quickly and hurried back out, again eager to be with both of them, and startled to find I enjoyed it.

I tiptoed between them and sat back in the chair, pretzel style.

Gérard began, "*Ma chérie*, when you take me and accept me as a vampire, Douglas must be a part. It is likened to a parent with child.

They meet someone who has no children. The parent and child are one. The new person cannot take one without the other."

Doug knelt before me to peer into my eyes. "As for the analogy of the parent and child, I want to make it clear that I am not a child. I have needs. If you are not willing to meet them, over time, then I will find them elsewhere. As far as a relationship goes, I would be honored to court you. I would agree to be your daytime suitor; however, I will not be your lover."

"We will not share you lightly. If you want a kiss at noon, you cannot waken me. Douglas will be there. If you want full intimacy, then we must wait. All of us," Gérard elaborated.

"I agree. I've had my recreations, though none at present. I would not accept it until you take the fourth," Doug said.

"Then . . ." I walked to the door by the stairs to keep from looking at them. It was awkward and hardly a moment I was ready for, after a wake. "This is hard for me. Now, you've both humiliated me, and I can't go through this again. I'm going to be bold, no." I had to think about the right words. "Well, I don't know what to call it, but if you're mine, I won't share." I turned to Doug. "Doug, you'll have to be patient for now, but you are mine, too. No women, for either of you. I can't share, I won't. Ever."

Gérard smiled a genial smile. "You frightened me, *ma chérie*. I did not expect you to say this. I am happy to be yours. I want to be yours."

"As do I," Doug added.

"Listen, I'm not into dating more than one guy at once, let alone spending my life with both of them. Not that I'm saying you asked me to or expect to. I just meant; you know—I can't make any promises, but I'll try. I mean it. But no women for either of you. As I said, I won't share. It's out of the question." I sat in my chair and waited.

"Is that all?" Doug asked.

"It's a lot. I mean it. I don't know how you two can do it, but I can't. I'm selfish and have a huge problem with sharing."

"Makes me feel better," Doug said.

"Which of course offers a great reassurance for myself as well," Gérard confirmed.

"Really. You think we can pull this off?"

"I do not see why not, *ma chérie*."

"Jealousy," I said.

"Not with us, love."

"Why not?"

"Because we are bound." Gérard said it like it made sense, silly vampire.

"I don't get how you think this'll turn out good." I let out a breath I didn't know I was holding and went to the fireplace. "Now, I need to think about this more when I'm not humiliated or around either of you. Nonetheless, this was a huge accomplishment for me."

Little did they know how hard it truly was after Jesse. I hated other women turning him on. I hated that he needed them, and I wasn't enough.

"Well, I'm heading off to bed, alone," Doug said, jutting his lower lip out to pout as he did a push up from the floor to show all his muscles. He stood, tossed his hair over his shoulder, and strode up the stairs. "Good night, love, good night, Gérard."

Gérard appeared beside me and pushed me back into the bedroom door. He turned the knob and chased me into the room until I found the safety of the bed. He chuckled at this cat-and-mouse game, all the while both of us knowing he was perfectly capable of catching me anytime he wanted.

I laughed and flopped on the pillows to catch my breath, wondering if my feelings for Doug were going to fuck things up. He crawled up to me from the foot of the bed, attempting eye contact. The stardust swirled. He placed his knees on both sides of my hips, his hands on each side of my face, and looked down into my eyes—waiting.

I turned my head to the side and exposed my neck, unsure of what he would do. He lowered to lick along the line of my jugular and hovered there to take in the scent. He sat back on his knees and proceeded to unbutton my pajama top, and whispered, "I like this." He bent lower and bit the middle of my bra. The sharpness of his fangs cut through the fabric; my breasts spilled out.

"Gérard," I breathed.

"*Ma chérie*, we must not give in to such intimate desires until the Samhain has passed and *Michel* has been stopped."

"Yeah," I sighed. "After that."

"I do not want you to, *euh*, hate me in the morning."

"I'd hate myself, not you."

He seemed to be looking for some emotion that wasn't there.

I didn't tell him, but I didn't think it was fair to Doug. And I wasn't ready to be there half-naked in front of Doug. Ah, that was a lie. I was so ready to be with Doug. Uh, no I wasn't. That was the problem. I wanted him, but was a bundle of nerves with him.

Oui, and with me also. But I am going to enjoy tonight since it will be the last until we have passed this mess, he thought to me as he slid down.

I bit my lip.

He placed velvet kisses up my leg until he met my inner thigh. He lingered there, sniffing softly, flicking his tongue randomly. "Over, *s'il vous plait*."

I rolled over on my stomach. He rose to his knees and gave a low, manly laugh. I tried to look at him.

Tse, tse, he breathed.

He fanned my hair over my shoulders; kissed along my neck, my back, each cheek, and each thigh. The softness of his lips, and warmth of his breath, mixed with the slightest hint of his power and had me clenching the covers, squealing into the pillows. It tickled.

"Ah, *ma chérie*, I love the way you look, I love the way you feel, I love the way you taste, and I love the way you smell." He kissed his way back up to my neck between each phrase. "I feel your desire—your need. I do not want to give in to them and I do not want to take advantage of your–situation." He pressed his body to mine.

"But?" I said rather hastily.

"It has been a month that we have been together, *euh*—I feel it is more than you or I expected. But I have needs."

I rolled beneath him; he let me. "Like what?"

"Lust."

"I kinda figured that." Didn't that explain the current situation?

"*Non, ma chérie*. I feed from my Douglas, but I want you. I want you to be mine." He leaned his face near mine. "I tasted you."

"Oh," I took a few shallow uneven breaths. "I thought you said you didn't want me for food?" I tried to wriggle away. He pressed down.

"You asked if I planned on biting you; I told you only if you consent."

"I can't."

"I want to mark you. I will not do it unless you feel the same as I. I want you to be in my life, forever." That one word shivered down my spine and brought a need from deep within.

"You mean, you want me to be like Doug?"

"Summer, a mark is a special promise. We make a promise to one another, and you would truly be mine."

"What is the promise you give to me?" I thought about that. "Would you be mine?"

"Almost." He looked serious.

"Can it be removed?" I thought about Guillaume calling me a whore.

"*Oui, mais,* I ask your acceptance of the first; there are four."

"Four what?"

"Marks."

"I still don't see why I need to do this."

"I see. Then let us not discuss this again." He slid off the bed, serpent like.

"I didn't say no. But you'd better make a real promise. Forever is a long time." I sat on my knees. "I don't want to get hurt, and I mean both physically and mentally. I don't want you to vamp out on me and devour me in the night and I don't want you screwing around with other women or men or whatevers. I mean, as long as we are—"

"Vamp out!" He laughed. "I like this. You are lovely. I make a promise. He climbed back on the bed. "A vampire's promise. I will not vamp out on you. I will not have relations with anyone but you, so long as you live." He sat on his knees. "You are still mortal."

I took a big breath and let it out slow. "Okay." I was thinking, *if I could have this every day for the rest of my life or more, would it make me happy? But . . .*

"But what?"

"Oh." I fumbled with the edge of the comforter. He raised an eyebrow and waited.

I recalled the day with Guillaume. He'd said he could be there whenever I wanted; Gérard couldn't. And all of a sudden, Doug wants to be my daytime sweetie? The coincidences as of late were piling up. Guillaume said I would be baited, but which bite should I take? Which side was the right side? Granted, Guillaume turned out to be a dick, but I didn't know this Michel. I didn't know Gérard either. Doug a little, but—it was complicated.

"You avoided my question; how will you benefit?"

"Whilst you are mine, no one else can have you. It is a benefit for us both."

"What about Doug?"

"What about my Douglas?" He raised an eyebrow.

"If I am yours, how does Doug fit in?"

"Ah, Douglas. You offered to try; it is all we can hope. Think of it as two parts of a whole. Together, he and I make one." He made sense.

"I don't have to drink your blood, though, right?"

"*Ah, mon Dieu, non.*" He tossed his hair over his face.

"Enough talk, just do it." I tucked my hair behind my ears, as brave as I was capable of being.

"*Non*, this is our time. I want to enjoy it. I want you to enjoy it." He pushed me back on the pillows and lay atop me.

"Gérard?"

"*Oui.*"

"I won't be a vampire, will I?"

"*Mais non, ma chérie.* It is not necessary." He kissed me deep, sensuous. He'd apparently talked enough.

When he drew back, I grabbed his head and pulled him in to kiss me again. I wrapped my arms around his neck and shoulders, smoothing them over his tight arms. I traced over his back, earning a moan.

He did a push-up and looked down at me while I ran my hands over his pecks, down to his belly button. I played with the peach fuzz around his navel and traced my hand back up to his chest, sliding my hand along the outline of his muscles. I enjoyed the beauty of his body.

He lowered himself, this time nestling into my neck, hovering over my pulse again—grazing and licking. His thoughts came to me, *You do understand I mean to feed on occasion, ma chérie?*

"Uh, huh," I moaned.

He kissed down between my breasts before going to my belly button, gently flicking with his tongue. He kissed across my waist and licked his way back up. The warmth of arousal flowed through my veins like a fire building inside of me.

"Close your eyes, *ma chérie.* Do as I say. Give yourself to me. Want me. Love me."

"Okay," I managed.

He continued kissing my face, neck, and breasts. He licked up my nape and breathed, "Open your eyes." I did as told. His eyes burned, a mixture of cerulean and sapphire, then flames. His voice whispered through my head, "*Now.*"

I felt myself slip. The sensation was not unlike a dream where you fall and there is no end. There was pleasure, but not the same as uncontrollable wanting for sex, but rather a warmth that filled my being. His tongue danced over my neck before the sensation of his fangs slid in.

There was no pain. It was intimate, more intimate than sex. I was his. He could kill me if he wanted. He suckled at the blood as it streamed in time with my heart. My body arched involuntarily as my need grew. Relentlessly, his tongue pulled the flesh in, sucking the blood in the same rhythm, never faltering. The warm sensation turned to arousal and swelled within me. I tangled my fingers in his hair and brought the scent of him closer. The cinnamon intoxicated me as he flicked and sucked. I screamed, a guttural sound, when he brought that pleasure to its apex.

He pulled back with a hint of crimson on his lower lip. He licked it off slow, and smiled down at me. "How do you feel, *ma chérie?*"

I lay twitching in the afterglow, probably with a stupid look on my face. Regardless of the movies, after a real orgasm, nobody looks that great. It takes a lot out of a person. I gave him a thumbs up.

"Ah. You are delicious, so sweet. I feel strong and alive. I must be careful to only nibble. I would not want to intoxicate myself. Remember, you are far from human."

I sat up quicker than I should have and flopped back, dizzy and nauseous. "What?"

"I fed from Douglas already."

I couldn't believe how he looked. His eyes were bright, and his hair shined in the candlelight. His skin was tan and taught. The man was a spectacle to behold.

"I mean the human thing." I curled on my side, hugging a pillow to make the world stand still.

He sat up suddenly. "You have accepted the first mark; shall we celebrate?"

"How?"

"We shall have a ball. A masquerade ball."

"Sounds a bit much," I said.

"Should we not share our commitment? Besides, Douglas's at Chez Fenris was cancelled by Chief Wimmers and Mayor Krotte." He rolled off to the side. "I will be back." He glided to the door. I watched him leave before I pulled the pillows over my head.

Mere Human, no. But what was I?

CHAPTER 33

I awoke in the bed, the room cool and dark. There was no tray for breakfast this morning—no coffee, no intruders. A shiver sent a stabbing pain in my neck. I reached up to check for bite marks and found them all too real.

I got up and did the morning ritual of hair, toilet, hands, and teeth, then ran to the wardrobe; it was freezing. I looked for something warm—nothing. I wondered if he would oppose having more light colors in his life than the dark colors that were everywhere. I put on the undergarments and found a pair of black slacks and a black sequined camisole with a coordinated waist jacket. It was cold.

There was a pair of black flats with black sequins that I assumed were made for the outfit as well. Quite an ensemble—I could have worn it to a New Year's Eve party or even a wedding—or Dani's funeral.

As I opened the door, I peered around the den. Since there wasn't anyone there, I relaxed and moseyed upstairs to the dining room. I didn't know where the kitchen was.

The table was adorned with red roses and a large pitcher of orange juice. I spotted a glorious carafe with coffee, creamer, sugar, a little glass pot filled with cinnamon, and a plate complete with a cheese omelet and toast with grape jelly.

Doug sat in Gérard's place and had apparently been waiting for me. "Good morning, love. Did you sleep well?"

"Yes, thank you." I felt shy. Kind of like when you first lose your virginity, and you think everyone else knows too. Maybe coy would have been a better word.

"Have some juice. It helps. Eat something too, you need protein."

"You mean—" And my hand went up to the marks on my neck. I winced when I touched them, not meaning to.

He appeared behind me and brushed my hair aside. "Ah, you bruise easy. We'll fix that up after breakfast."

"Okay."

"I thought today would be a good day to spend in the library since it's raining." He motioned to the stained-glass windows that led to the courtyard. "Or if you'd rather, I can show you around a little more."

"That'd be nice."

"Alright, I give up. What's the problem? Did you consent?"

"Yes."

"Did Gérard roll you before he marked you?"

"Yes," I whispered.

"Did you like it?" he asked.

"Yeah," I whispered even more.

"Then what's wrong, love?"

I shrugged; tears trickled down my cheeks.

"I bet I do." He lifted my chin with his fingertips and wiped my tears away with his thumbs. "You feel like a one-night stand. You had an unbelievable night and now he's gone."

"No, Guillaume said I was Gérard's whore. And now it's true." I took a deep breath and let it out a little too fast, which resulted in my lower lip pouting.

"Don't think about Guillaume." He wrapped his arms around my head. "I've waited long enough. That bloody bastard is a cheval mallet. He was sent here by the regime, one of Gérard's—bastard!"

Doug's words thickened with his native accent. There were times when he didn't have one, and times when it was subtle. But this time it came on thick, curt, and filled with anger. I could have sworn his eyes sparked.

"What's a cheval mallet?"

"A demonic creature from the French territories. He feeds on children and travelers he lures to his waters. Ah, love, you're his assignment. You were the target when he killed your sister at Black River. He got the wrong girl."

"Guillaume?" I screeched and blacked out.

"Summer? Summer, you with me?" Doug knelt on one knee; my head propped in his elbow. "I'm sorry."

I blinked at him. "That fucking son-of-a-bitch!" I fought to stand straight. "He's a fucking hit man for me? Oh, I'll be damned if he thinks he's gonna win. He caused this hell? Finish your story," my lungs hurt, my breath was caught in my chest, and this dark feeling that overtook me. "How, Doug? How?"

"He's a shifter, one of the best. He appears as a man to you now, hoping to seduce you. Once you become his lover, he'll kill you."

"He doesn't stand a flying fuck of a chance of that. But he didn't seduce an eight-year-old, Doug."

"No. With children they appear in their natural form. They appear as a white or black—"

"Horse, standing by a river or lake. Oh my God!"

He clasped my face. "What?"

"There are like, ten of them where he's staying. He's brought an entourage." I sat back in the chair. "It was a school trip to Black River. The chaperone said she saw her with a black horse that got caught in the current. They found her body down river."

"I'm aware, love."

"No, I remember. She wore her new white fur coat that day. She had on my old jeans and—"

"And smelled like you. Black River is outside the sanctuary. It's why you weren't allowed to go anywhere."

"I want him dead, Doug. You need to help me. I can't let him get away. That son-of-a-bitch tried to get me on one of his stallions. He kept luring me in with him being available all day, while Gérard is only here at night."

"And what am I?"

I blushed instantly. "Well, now, you're here."

"And?"

I couldn't call him a boyfriend—should I?

Doug was comfortable when I wasn't looking at him. But I wasn't usually nervous with him like I was with Gérard. I already knew I wanted him, all the time. But I resented that in a way. I avoided the question.

"But will you help me find him?"

"It isn't Guillaume I'm worried about."

"Michel," I confirmed. My words came out soft, but not in that naïve, sweet Summer way. Doug didn't know it, but he changed me. I depended on too many people. Dawn was right, boo-fucking-hoo. Well, fuck them all. The tides had changed, and it was Summer's turn to shine. And shine is what I vowed to do.

I took a deep breath and caught myself on the table. "I don't need your help."

"I want to."

"Fine, let's go."

"Let us eat first. I'm starving." He went back to his food.

He was right. I could use him as a gateway to Gérard or I could take him as part of the package. I guess after last night, I'd accepted the package.

His eyes held a citrine light that warned and beckoned all at once.

"What are you doing?"

"Eating, as should you."

"No, you're talking to someone."

He put his silverware down and sat back, wiping his lips with the napkin. "I'm over five hundred, Summer. This is not new for me. I know you mean to put yourself in harm's way. I won't allow it. I protected you, all your life. And I mean all. Gérard rested whilst I maintained his stead. I'm not the young lycan you believe me to be. Gérard is our master, yes, but he is the protector of all. And right now, his biggest problem is sitting right here, listening to me. I will be damned myself if I let anything happen to you. Do not question my reasons, or what I do, but accept that I do what I must to keep you safe. Aye?"

I shook my head and ran from the dining room. A pain in my gut stole my breath; the bite on my neck throbbed. I sat down in the middle of the hall—defeated, tender.

Doug squatted next to me. "Come on. Let me have a look." He reached over and brushed my hair aside. I caught a glimpse of his eyes; there was a hint of orange dancing in them. "May I?" he asked, and before I could answer, he leaned in to work over the bite marks with his tongue.

I gave a surprised yelp. He licked softer and drew away. "Sorry, love. Feel better?" He shifted his eyes to my neck.

I touched where the marks were, but they were gone. "How?"

"I'm special." He smirked.

"Promise me you'll always be there when he does this. I don't like pain."

"Listen, Gérard tucked you in. He knew you would need me this morning; he felt bad for frightening you the other night too."

"He did?" He took my hand and led me toward the bedroom.

"Like I've said before, he's been around a long time. He knew he went too far when he watched you curl up. It tormented him because he was careless. I told him I would take care of it, and that is what I do. But—"

"Oh, no."

"Hey," he chided.

"You're right, I'm sorry. It's just, whenever there's a 'but' things turn for the worse," I groaned.

"Would you rather I not discuss my concerns?"

"Of course not; it was selfish."

"No worries. I was going to say, I don't just act as errand boy. I have a close relationship with Gérard. We have a long history together, and we love each other. We share our joys and our sorrows."

"Be honest with me Doug, now mind you, you said this last night too. Are you in love with him?"

"In a way, perhaps. But I like the ladies." He smiled and slid his eyes to glance out the corners. If I were to guess, he was a ladies' man, not even shy.

"I'm sorry. I didn't mean to pry."

"Nonsense. You have to do a lot more than that to insult an old guy like me. I have way too many years on you. Admit it, I look good for my age." We both laughed. "Now, down to business."

"Okay," I said.

He smiled cunningly. "Summer, Gérard asked you to let him mark you. You accepted him, but there are other people involved, and before you go further, you need to be sure of what you're doing. He's brought you into my circle, if you will. I told you yesterday, we're a package. If you make a commitment to Gérard, you make it to me. Our lives depend on it."

I opened my mouth to interrupt, but he leaned forward and put his finger over my lips. "Let me finish, love. Gérard presumes you will commit to me. You realize, every step closer to sealing that commitment means you accept me too. Your acceptance means that you plan to willingly work toward strengthening a relationship between us. He has hope, I don't."

Fuck, what'd he mean by that?

We arrived at the den, and he reached for the doorknob but didn't turn it. "Tell me why you won't look at me." His voice softened. Caution hung over his words.

I turned away. I figured he'd mistake it for rudeness, but I couldn't look at him, let alone say it. I thought it though. *Because looking at you embarrasses me. It's hard for someone like me to have one of you, let alone two. I mean, I could have died right back there when you licked me.* I was glad he couldn't hear it. But aloud I said, "You know things, I considered you mine—for years."

"You don't resent me for all those years as therapy dog?"

"I'd be a fool if I did." I shrugged. "You're better looking this way." I giggled. Stupid.

"Eventually, I hope you loosen up. I might have to use my wiles if you don't."

I made myself laugh, and this time thought well enough to take the conversation elsewhere. "I think I need Gérard." I glanced at him quickly. "Not like that."

He wrapped his arms around my shoulders and pulled me into him. I put my hands on his chest, unsure how to hug him. I dreaded having to kiss him. Not because I didn't want to, God knows that wasn't it, but because first kisses are always awkward, and I was still suffering a case of the firsts' with Gérard.

"I agree. Until he rises."

And with that, I was left to myself for the next few hours. He'd had my food sent down, and a basket of chocolate croissants. I decided to sit by the fire and wait. If I was to accept them both, I had to do it on my terms and at my pace. And that meant Doug couldn't know how I felt until I was sure he even wanted me. They'd made it clear that I was Gérard's choice, but not once had they said Doug chose me. Perhaps in a few hours I'd have an answer.

CHAPTER 34

Gérard met us in the den.

"No holds barred, everything on the table. I don't care if you feel shy, or think I'll get mad 'cause this is to clear the air. No miscommunications—sex, blood, food, murder—no matter. Tell me what you want, what you expect, and what you know about my past. Only then will I tell you if I have a problem with any of it. As it stands, I have no problems other than with Guillaume." I flopped in one of the den's wingback chairs, but they tarried by the door. I didn't like it.

They each cocked an eyebrow and leaned against the walls.

"Alright, take a moment. I like sitting here by the fire. Besides, it's not like I'm planning your murders."

I settled in the corner of the chair, my legs over the arm. I crossed them, but because I was wearing the black sequined set, I had no worries of sending mixed signals or flashing anyone. Life was good. And they were quiet. Yay, for me.

They stared at the floor as if concentrating hard. Suddenly, the silence broke.

"Murder, *ma chérie?*"

"Hey, we aren't having sex, I'm not getting any younger, and quite honestly, I want to kill Guillaume. So, roll me, take my blood, do it to Doug too if you want. But hurry up, I've been stalled enough."

They blinked at me.

"Give me the second, then."

"No," they spoke in unison.

"Damn it." I ran through the bedroom door and climbed on the bed.

It must have been a half-hour before they both came in wearing matching royal blue silk pajamas. Gérard climbed on the bed first; Doug climbed on his other side.

Gérard stuck his hands in his robe pockets and dipped his head to the side to look in my eyes. His eyes, always mysterious, showed no power. His face held no emotion. I couldn't understand.

"I'd think you'd want to jump on this, unless there's something you're not telling me." Most guys don't have to be told a second time. You give 'em an inch, they run a mile.

"I believe Gérard is worried." Doug looked at me tight-lipped. His hair had fallen to one side, exposing the side of his neck. There were no puncture marks, Gérard hadn't fed while they were out. It was confirmed—there was something they definitely weren't telling me.

"You guys better not lie to me."

"*Mon ami,* please leave us for a moment." Doug immediately slid off of the bed and strolled to the bathroom. He paused a moment at the door and glanced at me over his shoulder. I figured Gérard did this for my benefit since Doug could hear everything anyway.

Once he closed the door, Gérard lay on his side watching me. He patted the sheet, motioning for me to come to him. I didn't.

"*Ma chérie*, I believe it wise to put this off for this evening."

"What's the big deal? You said you weren't going to make me a vampire. I'll still be human-ish, right?"

"You are too eager, *ma chérie*. I am the President and a guardian. I cannot knowingly allow you to commit murder."

"Then don't."

"You are not a killer, Summer."

"Yeah, explain my real parents."

Doug came out of the bathroom, looking pissed—at Gérard.

Then it hit me. "I was too bold, right? You guys aren't used to an aggressive woman 'cause you're both really old. I mean, I'm not used to being the aggressor, so it kind of worked out. I probably would have regretted it at some point. Besides, I don't like blood." Crap.

"T'is not it at all, love. It isn't the right time; let's get through Samhain. You still need time to get to know yourself. Remember what I told you. We do not need to move quickly. We're not going anywhere."

"Yeah, but I am. I don't have a life expectancy of a thousand years like you guys. Besides, I'm not as dumb as you think. Eventually, if we get close, we can do it. Sex, I mean. Don't tell me it's not what you guys have been pussyfootin' around for. Give me a little credit." I looked away; it was too hard. My moral high ground got in the way. "But I won't promise because I can't." I pulled the pillow over my face.

"Well, that was unexpected," Doug said.

"That it was." Gérard leaned back on the bed pillows and clasped his hands over his stomach.

"Quite frankly, I'm hurt by it. I never wanted to be a sex object. But that's all you guys keep talking about."

"There's a grave misunderstanding, Gérard." Doug's voice cracked. I thought he might be angry, so I glanced at him. His eyes told a different story. They reminded me of the eyes you see on humane society posters. Not the look I expected.

Gérard slid from the bed, glided toward the door, bowed, and left.

"Summer, you intrigue us. You make us come alive; there is such a way about you." Doug stretched alongside me, propped up on his elbow, his voice soft, sincere. "I find it refreshing that you aren't freely giving into those carnal pleasures; you never did."

"Sorry if I read into things wrong. It's hard to believe either of you, let alone both of you, want me. Even Gale and Tiny confirmed it—I don't belong."

"You're destined to Lake Sangre. Life is more than sex and living in the past. You love the legend. You're intrigued by it. You've read about each one of us in lore, but you have yet to put it together. I've always thought you were a beautiful person, Summer. But you have secrets, too."

What the hell was that? Was it an insult, or a compliment? Damn it. "Any idea where Gérard ran off to?"

"Soon. Meanwhile, are you excited for the ball? T'is in two days."

"I guess, but you're stalling. Why?"

"You understand, you owe me no obligation until the fourth?"

"Yeah."

He frowned. Double damn.

"Listen, I know what it's like not to have a companion. I don't like it. I'm a daygirl. I can't sleep until night and be satisfied. I'm happy you're willing to be that person. Besides, we already have a unique relationship. I'd love to have you to watch the sunrise with or try new recipes on. I need a guinea pig and Gérard can't do that."

It wasn't a subject I was comfortable with. My nerves were uneasy; shyness befell me. I think it was because we were alone on the bed together and I'd never had a platonic relationship that allowed me to be like that. But it was temporarily platonic, maybe.

"What do you mean, guinea pig?" he asked.

I smiled, and he dipped his head, laughing.

He sat up and pulled me to him. Even in the candlelight, he probably saw me blush. "Love, the first time Gérard fed from me, I thought the mere sight of it would scare you off."

I debated as to whether to tell him how I really felt. I went for simple. "It was interesting."

He raised an eyebrow. "Interesting, huh?" He kissed my hand. It was neat because he didn't give that tingling sensation that Gérard had, but it was nice.

A faint knock on the door sent me scurrying from his arms. He got up to answer it.

Kitty waltzed through. "Hope I'm not interrupting." Her eyes went back and forth between us.

"Not at all." I hoped she didn't speculate. My pride was my greatest undoing.

She eyed Doug a little too long. "I passed Gérard upstairs; he told me to come down. I thought he'd be here by now."

There was another knock, so I got up to open it and hesitated. I wasn't sure I should be opening the door. I did it anyway but should have left it to Doug or Kitty.

"Still want to play?" Patricia strode through and pushed me out of her way. "Ah, Kitty, Douglas, how indignant we are to play slave with this subservient wench." She glanced over her red silk robed shoulder, her toe pointed and poised in a matching silk slipper with half-inch heel. She was missing something, maybe some black hose. Whatever. I think she was itching for me to fight with her, but I knew I couldn't win, so why bother. If I'd had a wooden stake and an ax, maybe then.

"Patricia, how nice to see you again. I'd almost forgotten about you." I gave my nastiest smirk. "You know, Doug and I had the most wonderful time in the courtyard the other day. Oh, that's right, it would kill you. Pity." I climbed over to Doug, backed myself into him, and pulled his arms around my waist.

"You think that little wolf can save you? I would kill you and take him, too. Watch your back. You won't always have someone to protect you." She'd stalked toward us when the door eased open.

"Tse, tse, tse. Patricia, *ma chérie* is welcome in our home and is the reason I have gathered all of you here. I have much to discuss and will not tolerate such debauchery. Douglas's honor should never be challenged." She hadn't turned but rather froze in her last step. A malevolent smile spread across her face.

"Ah, Gérard. You are the fool. This woman plays. She will have the hunt here before spring and you—you stand there playing the part. You believe she wants you? Ask her." With her black hair draped over her shoulders, she fit the dictionary definition for wicked.

"Ask me what? Don't talk about me like I'm not here." I was pissed and wasn't sure if I should still be in Doug's embrace or go to Gérard's side. I guessed this relationship was going to be tricky.

"Do you want him? Do you want the old man?" She emphasized old man like it was a dirty word.

"I don't need to answer to you. I especially don't need to acknowledge your insults."

"Not an answer. Do you *not* want to play with the monsters?" She turned and stared right into his eyes. "Or do you want to be a monster, little nonhuman?" She practically spat in his face. If I could have laid her out, I would have. What a bitch. "No, because you are afraid." She licked her ruby lips, her tongue serpentine. "I can taste it."

"Do not assume that which you do not know, bitch." I couldn't help it. My anger rose, my breathing tightened; my hands trembled. My head swam with something on the verge of rage when her eyes widened. She looked at Gérard, her mouth open—soundless.

Gérard's eyes had gone black. The look on his face demonized his effeminate beauty. The Mediterranean complexion that abolished my idealic vampire. A stark contrast to the Welsh wolf who served him, and by literary comparison, should hold the gold complexion as belonged in ancient Rome. And yet, I wearied of Patricia and everyone who wanted me dead.

I slumped in Doug's arms.

Kitty crawled across the bed. "They won't hurt you." Her voice purred over my skin. As soon as she touched my face, a tear trickled down my cheek. Doug pulled me closer and sniffed my hair. His hold—tight—unintentionally fueling my anxiety. I tried not to panic, but my blood was wild, an entity within me—a beast that wanted to rule on its own. Then Doug's eyes became citrine embers.

"The monsters have you, Summer. Are you having fun now?" Patricia had stood without me noticing, and faced Gérard, but not for long. She contorted to look at me; blood trickled from her nose. "The seed is sewn. It's too late." She maneuvered around him. He grabbed her arm; sapphire flames flickered in his eyes. I sat motionless.

This is her game. This is what she wants. You must show no fear.

He warned in my head. I tried to do as he said. "Take a slow, deep breath and calm down. Your fear is thick. We can smell it." He took a step toward me. "Taste it."

Patricia collapsed. Blood from her nose had formed a coagulating mass over her mouth and chin. She looked like she'd been sucker punched, though no one ever touched her.

She hadn't lied; Gérard did scare me. Was I prepared to play with the monsters? I kept trying to remember what the piskies said. They had sent me to the guardian. What had I gotten myself into?

She glided to the chaise and sat there bleeding all over herself and made no attempt to stop it. She sat there like nothing was wrong and kept that wicked smile plastered in place. I wondered if her face would stay that way when she died at dawn.

I decided *to hell with it.*

"Hey Patty, does your face stay that way when you die at dawn, or does your mouth open for the scream of death?" I could be a bitch too. I liked it. I was stupid.

Gérard warned in my head again. *Ma chérie, I did not mean for you to provoke her. I promised you would not get hurt, but she is a dangerous creature.*

I spoke aloud. "I'll kill her ass. She provoked me first."

She unleashed a feral laugh, which cracked the blood on her face. "Kill me? The innocent believes this—precious."

"Damn, I knew your face would crack."

She lunged at me. "You whore!"

I stood my ground. I was going to let the sparks fly, and the shit hit the fan. "You talk awfully brave for someone who can't protect themselves during the day. You're dead to the world." I paused a moment for forced laughter. "Ah, I kill me, no pun intended." I crawled across the bed to face her, staying on all fours.

"You threaten me? Do you know how old I am?"

"Obviously not as old as he is." I threw a glance back toward Gérard. "Definitely not as powerful. He's the master here."

"Bitch," she hissed.

"Woof," I taunted.

Patricia stood up, and Gérard was instantly in the middle. "Enough, both of you. Patricia, retire to your chamber, now!"

"I won't. Not as long as she's here."

"See? Who's the lesser?" I couldn't help myself.

"Summer, I cannot be here at every waking moment. She is vampire. Although she will suffer greatly, I cannot guarantee she will not try to hurt you." He eyed her.

"Oh please, Gérard. I'm not human and you said it. They know it too. It's why you want me. I'm not as stupid as everyone thinks I am. I was scared when you punished her, but now I feel invigorated. Like I'm feeding off her anger—oh, my God!"

"What?" This from Doug, who was standing beside Gérard now.

"I could be a psychic vampire." My eyes were all squinty. "Maybe that's what I am. I need to go. I've got to go to the library." I slid off the foot of the bed, but Doug pressed me back.

"Slow down, love," he said. He sidled beside me on the bed and Patricia pulled her legs up on the chaise. Kitty curled up on the pillows by the headboard, and they all stared at me.

CHAPTER 35

"Why can't I go to the library? I need to know more about this. I feel—I don't know how to explain it, different."

Gérard took my hand in his and lifted my chin with his other. His lips brushed against mine. I caught a hint of the swirl in his eyes and heard his thoughts. *Ma chérie, not this night. I have brought my family here to discuss recent events. Please, I beg of you, wait until morning.*

A wash of warmth made me light-headed. I swayed; Doug caught my arm to Keep me upright.

"What did you do to me?"

Gérard grimaced. "Consider it a sedative."

"What? Why? I felt good."

He clasped my face. I tried to fight him, needless to say he was stronger and won. His gaze bore into my eyes; the cerulean blaze burned. *Remember, ma chérie.*

I gasped. He pulled me closer to his face so that our eyes were a mere inch apart. I burned from the inside out. My blood, a liquid fire. I fought; his grip tightened. Memories of Sheena, my parents, Jesse, Gale, Guillaume, and Dani's body flashed before me.

"Stop!" I begged. Doug squeezed my hand, and Kitty rubbed my back. Patricia sat on the chaise laughing.

I was no longer in the mansion, the laughter faded, and I was on the mount. I was back at the garden with my father, my red sneakers tainted with fresh soil. My fingers wrapped around a bouquet of white roses. But we weren't planting them; my memories were wrong.

"It wasn't a garden," I whispered. "It was a grave." I blinked at Gérard. "My real father's. Augusto took me from there that night." Doug pulled me into his shoulder, but I wanted to look Gérard in the eyes. "The night you took me to the mount, you knew. You always knew. But how? Why'd you do this?"

"Doug, let her go. Kitty, sit by Patricia." Gérard's voice was deep and had that echoing effect it had back at the house.

I gritted my teeth, anger seething at the surface. "Why?"

"*Ma chérie—*"

"No, don't call me that. What you just did wasn't right. You said to stand up to her, and that's what I did. Just because I felt like I was stronger or something because of it, it didn't give you the right."

"*Oui*, Patricia lives in my territory. She is under my protection; you will not be allowed to hurt her. She knows she cannot hurt you. She may try, but I will kill her, as you are under my protection as well."

"You make no sense." I hiccupped between sobs. "I feel so raw, so violated. You were there. I remember you; you weren't at rest. Who the fuck are you?"

"Summer, we knew you had a power; we need to tame it before it gets out of control. You need to know what you're capable of doing— before you kill someone," Doug said, his voice gentle.

"What are you talking about? Stop trying to spin this." The sobs stopped, but I still had tears streaming down my face. Doug had Kitty get me a box of tissues. At least no one yelled at me like Guillaume had.

"Summer, stop," Gérard's voice drifted through the room. "Look at Patricia. Look at her blood. You did that. Your power is strong. Look. You did this. This was you, not me. The power you felt was your own."

He stood back and folded his arms, glaring at me. "You know you are not human, but you know not what you are. Why have you not asked me? Did you not say that you wanted no secrets? Did you not say that you wanted truth?" His voice held an edge of anger to it, power.

"I—I didn't know." The edge of fear toyed with my stomach, almost to the point of nausea. "The piskies said I was bred for a purpose."

"*Ma chérie*, do not feel hatred for me. *Mais*, Faoltiarna and Augusto were dear friends."

"You truly knew them? Did you know what I was from the day you met me?" I couldn't decide if I was hurt or pissed. I decided to try for numb. Nope.

"*Oui*." He closed his eyes and leaned his back against the bedpost.

"We all knew," Doug added.

I swallowed a lump that formed in the middle of my throat. My trust faded before my eyes. It would have been easier if they'd punched me in the stomach. At least I knew I could live with that. Hell, I'd done that before. But this? This was worse. Much worse.

"You were afraid of me when it was your anger. Patricia fed your fears. You panicked in my Douglas's arms. We need to fix this before you go too far. The anger was not mine. It was your own. We will talk after everyone leaves. But for now, let us discuss what I had intended."

He looked sad but continued. "*Mes amis,* Summer has agreed acceptance of the first mark. The celebration at *Chez* has been cancelled, no need to explain further. The Samhain Ball will be held here for both the anniversary and Summer's inclusion to our family." He glanced at all of them.

Kitty crawled down the bed and hugged me around the shoulders. "I look forward to having you join us. Gérard is a lucky man to have won you; I look forward to you accepting the final mark." She smiled a pity smile and glanced at Gérard. "If you'll excuse me, sir, I will retreat. It would seem our Summer might like company in the library tomorrow."

"But of course. Pleasant dreams." He kissed her hand and the slightest blue flame flickered. She took a deep breath and nodded toward the rest of us. As she left the bedroom, she smiled at me.

After she closed the door, Doug rolled off the bed. "I believe I will retire early as well. The two of you need to be alone." He leaned in for a small kiss, which I granted him on the cheek, and then turned to Gérard. "Sir, I bid thee bonsoir. On the marrow, Summer." He left swiftly, leaving us alone with Patricia.

"Well now, young Summer. Do you feel big and bad because you hurt the vampire?" she taunted.

"Patricia." Gérard's voice hissed through the room. "Leave us."

"Oh, I'll leave." She got up from the chaise and bent in front of me, showing way more cleavage than I needed to see. "I think you made a mistake with your English, Master, or should I say, Executioner," she whispered harshly. Still leering at me, she continued, "It was not the first, but the third." Her laugh echoed in the chamber as she glided out of the bedroom. The door slammed behind her. Gérard's eyes sparked; Patricia screamed.

CHAPTER 36

Gérard glided to the door and took a tray from one of the servants. I wondered if she was human. Anyway, he came back to the bed and set the tray down with a bottle of blood, a goblet, some cinnamon sticks, a rose, and a bowl of dark chocolate truffles.

I didn't want to eat, and I certainly didn't know what the hell had just happened. The thought of having him angry scared me. I didn't like any part of the evening. It was easier when I thought they just wanted me for sex. That I could handle. This was a mess. The worst part was that it was my mess, and I didn't know how to feel or what to do to fix it.

But the silence wasn't something I could deal with either. I spoke absentmindedly, grasping for some semblance of explanation.

"Gérard, I've had a lot of fun the last couple of weeks with you." I stopped. People trying to kill me, my friend's murder, people dropping dead at my feet? Literally. "Ok, not so fun," I took a breath, but he interrupted.

He had the bottle of blood in his hand and took a swig without pouring it into the goblet. "*Ma chérie*. Did I not say you do not know us, our ways, our culture? You most certainly do not know yourself. This is a new obstacle for us which we must endure. We have gone too far for me to let you go." He took another swig. A line of blood trailed down from the left corner of his mouth. He wiped it with the back of his arm. His hair was disheveled around his shoulders, his robe gaped open. The raw, untamed Gérard frightened me.

He appeared on the bed behind me. I screamed.

"You are afraid; still, you do not trust me." He filled the goblet and sipped. After drinking halfway through, he took a napkin and dabbed at his lips. He cocked his head sideways, looking at me. "Are you not going to talk to me now? Are you punishing me?"

He yelled, and it echoed through the room, "Ahhh!"

"Why are you doing this?" I whispered.

"Summer," he whispered back. "You accepted the mark. I am angry with me. I cannot lie. The first mark was made the night I made your acquaintance."

"When you kissed my hand?"

He remained silent.

"So, what about when you bit me?"

He slid his leg off the bed so he could get up.

I flung myself onto his neck and laced my fingers. "Talk, damn it."

"I do not need blood for the first and second marks, but it is always stronger against someone as old and powerful as *Michel*."

"Look at me." I demanded it as hard as I could make it. "Tell me what the hell you're talking about. I've read the novels. If this is anything like them, then you'd already made me your servant." I glanced into his eyes. "Why?"

"You are too naïve. As you learn, we will discuss it, but for now, I am going to tell you how it is." I glowered at him. "Do not look at me with that face, *ma chérie*. You know naught."

"Bullshit. You gave me the third fucking mark! All I have to do is share blood with you and I'm stuck. You said you gave me the first mark and we were going to celebrate. You're a God damned liar." I was angry again. It felt good.

"*Oui*, I marked you, but *Michel* had removed them. I ask your permission because I want your relationship—for eternity. Not your servitude." He glanced around the room and drained the goblet. "Only those older than I could do that, do you not see? I marked you because I wanted you. I sought your permission for the second, but you did not understand. You still thought yourself human. Now we must do this over again. If you wish this to end, then you go your way. I will leave you without the last three marks." He pushed my arms off of him. I made a little squeak. "The night I could not hear you, I took blood—to remove *Michel's*."

I didn't want to belong to anyone, but I did love him. "What do we do? He marked me, too? You marked me without telling me. That wasn't right. What else have you guys done to me?"

"I marked you because it was better than having the visitors come with all of them knowing what you are. If I had not marked you, then you would not have had me to help you with all that has happened. We now have a relationship I do not want to lose. Before, I was the Master of all *Mount Mort* taking care of one of my people. Now, I am Master to *ma chérie*. *Michel* cannot have you. It is punishable by death, to take a servant. I have marked you by blood, the regime declares it."

"Safe from whom? You or another vamp or another? Do you even like me? Did you? I mean for me for me, not because of what I am. Truthfully, what do you gain from having me?"

"I like you. I more than like you. You excite me. I love the smell of your soaps. I love how you feel about me without my power. I love that you want me for yourself. I love to tease you. I love the way you look in your antiquated gowns. I love your everything." He threw his head back and took a deep breath. "Let me mark you again. I beg you to allow me this."

"You didn't answer me. Am I going to be like Doug?"

He sighed, unnecessarily. "*Oui et non*. If you accept the fourth, you will be bound; you already are. The only other who holds the fourth is my Douglas. It would be a lie if I said it was not for selfish reasons. But I can help you. Douglas can help you."

"How?" Was I really in a different situation than before? I had no answer, but I needed help.

He took my hand, sent that tingling through me, and kissed my index finger; it was sore. "You are my sweet; you have my heart. I want you with me forever. Without my marks, it would not be possible." Blood-tinted tears stained his chiseled cheek.

"I think Patricia just brought all the stupid shit that's been happening to a head for me. I don't ever want you to lie to me again, though. Promise me."

"I will not lie, I cannot promise." He smiled weakly.

"Whatever. I don't want to belong to the other vamp." Oh, goody. I got to pick my life of servitude. Vamp 'A' or Vamp 'B'? I didn't want to wait for a Vamp 'C'. Yippy.

"You hold my mark this night. That is why I want you to stay. Live here. Be with me."

"What—do I have to?"

"The regime does not want me to have you. You are a powerful creature, only you do not know how to use it. Summer, you could have killed Patricia this night. Patricia, herself, is powerful."

"But I thought they were after you." I slid off the bed and huddled on the chaise. "Patricia called you Executioner."

"Aldatmak wants to take over the regime. I figured she wanted my position, but you have confirmed my suspicion. It is why Guillaume holds a seat as well."

"I don't understand what you're talking about."

"The regime is a governing board that serves to protect those left of our kind and to punish those who jeopardize our existence. I serve the regime, as you have been told—I am the President and a guardian."

"And executioner?"

"At times, *oui*."

I recalled the memory at my father's grave. A man with long ebony locks stood like a statue beside Augusto. It was Gérard, I realized now. He'd knelt on the fresh dirt, lowered his face to the grave, and wept.

"Do it, mark me. At least I know where I am here, and you all seem nice enough. I don't know the other one. And the piskies sent me to you. You wept over my father; my real father." I wiped my face and tried to pull away to go wash up.

"I had no choice, Summer."

I glared at him in disdain. "No, there was a choice, but you wept, though it wasn't sadness; it was remorse."

"One day, Summer—"

"No, never speak of him. You don't get to. Now, do it." I gathered my hair into a pony and exposed my neck.

He lifted me back on the bed, caught my eyes, and his power beckoned; he caressed my neck with his lips. He hovered there, and then slowly kissed down over my gown. "Look in my eyes, *chérie*. Look close. Do not turn away."

He pressed me back and tucked his hair inside of his robe. He kept his eyes fixed on mine; a small sapphire flame grew until it took over his pupils. The flame was more intense than I'd ever seen. I had the feeling of hands caressing my body where no hands could reach; should reach. My body ached for him; I wanted him inside me.

He bit down quick and hard on the white of my right breast. I screamed in surprise.

He suckled and flicked at the wound. With each caress of his tongue, I longed to be his. I writhed beneath him; my conscience fought enslavement. His eyes went black and brought me deeper under his influence. I swooned as he withdrew. The gradual cerulean fire returned, and then just eyes.

"Summer, you did not answer about living here. Will you?"

"No." I couldn't give up all my freedom—I wouldn't.

"If Patricia comes to you again, I will take care of her. I do not want you to provoke her, nor do I want her dead." He frowned at me. "I understand your decision."

I reached for a truffle and grabbed a cinnamon stick instead. "What's this for?" I hoped he didn't expect me to eat it like that. Yuck.

"Ah, I almost forgot. Cinnamon is your spice. The Álfar were drawn to herbs and spices of many sort. Cinnamon is representative of love and sex. It is an aphrodisiac." He moved the tray to the chaise and slid in bed.

"Gérard?"

"*Oui?*"

"What's a keeper?"

"It is late, Summer. I am not the one who should explain."

"Ah, that's why you all keep avoiding the question. Tell me who, and I'll go to them."

"She will come to you."

"Who?"

"Was there something else?"

"Not going to answer?"

"*Non.*" His fingertips pressed slightly to my cheek for me to look at him. "I do not want you to go out until the Samhain has passed."

"Gérard." I looked at him and cupped his face. His eyes met mine. "Je t'aime."

"*Moi aussi, mais, vous parlez Français?*"

"Oui, un peut."

He hesitated and then asked as he pulled back enough to look at my eyes. "Do you want to discuss your father?"

"Not tonight, I've had enough."

I lay in his arms; tears dampened the pillow as I questioned what happened to the life I had only a month before. Why did Gale set me up? And where was she? My thoughts came in streams. I had to find her.

"Is this like a real ball? What'll I wear?"

"I will have your gown tailored tomorrow evening."

"I miss Gale."

"Sleep, Summer."

I slept, and for once, I could wait to learn what tomorrow would bring.

CHAPTER 37

Kitty came in with a tray for breakfast. We had steak tartar and warm bagels with butter. I left the steak tartar for her and ate two of the bagels. I was famished but raw meat mixed with raw egg was so not appealing. I guessed that's the downside of being a chef; you know what's in the food. Then again, I guessed raw food was appetizing to their kind.

"How'd it go last night?" she asked, her voice too high. Like when you try not to let someone know you want to know but are so curious, you're bursting at the seams.

"Alright. I guess I'm a little upset because he didn't ask me the first time, but I could be dead if he hadn't."

"You were afraid of him," she whispered cautiously. "That doesn't bother you?"

"I'm capable of practically killing Patricia." I shrugged. "I could do it to him."

"You mean that, don't you?" She sat next to me and patted my thigh. "I know we haven't had a chance to talk, but I figure now's good. I want to make sure Gérard doesn't get hurt. I mean, physically and emotionally. He's the best master I've ever served, and I don't want to have someone risk our way of life. We're a family."

If I understood correctly, Gérard was the reason I was orphaned. And all anyone cared about was not losing him. How bad was this other vamp? Then—epiphany!

"I'm his keeper. That's why you're here."

She laughed. "What are you talking about?"

Doug walked in as he knocked. He donned a pair of blue jeans and a jade silk shirt. He padded around in his bare feet, probably because he was a lycan. I noticed Kitty was the same way.

"Can I have the leftovers?" he asked.

"Help yourself." Kitty got up when he came in. If I didn't know better, I'd say she was nervous around him. It also made me wonder if there might have been something between them.

"I know where you were headed, and though a viable discussion, Summer's inclusion to our life was acceded by us all." He pinched off a piece of the raw dish.

"I don't mean to be rude, but I thought it was Gérard's decision."

"It is," they said in unison.

"It still affects us, and we have to pick up the pieces when it goes wrong or fall prey to a new master." Kitty wasn't giving up on that.

"I'll be here for as long as Gérard'll have me. I don't expect anything special. I want to help him any way I can. I don't plan on hurting him." I wasn't sure, but she seemed jealous. This conversation was over. "I'm going to the library to see what I can find out. I know you guys were going to come with me, but I don't feel like company right now. I'll see you at dinner, though." I got up and started for the door.

"Summer, I'll come with you. I told you I want to spend our days together. I was serious." Doug was at my side in the blink of an eye. He cinched my waist and led me toward the stairs. "Don't fret, love. She's not the only one, but . . . never mind. What is it we're doing, anyway?" He glanced at me; his left brow arched.

I stopped and backed against the wall. "Sorry, Doug, but right now, I don't want a shadow. Don't tell me that's not what you're doin'. You don't want me like he does, but I'm okay with that."

He sighed. "What are you going to do? About the house, I mean." My guess was he acted casual to hide his worry. Though I'd voiced my opinion, I hoped for a different reaction—rebuttal. Damn.

"I'm staying there," I said.

"Ah, good not to leave until everything is settled. Once all of the visitors have gone in November, we can take care of the formalities."

He wrapped his arm around my waist and whisked me up the stairs. When we were at the top, he let go to walk toward the library and stopped. "Gérard likes to have his family close."

"Why do you call yourselves a family? I thought it was called a coven or kiss or something. Then again, you guys aren't all vampires."

"We're a family because we've been together for centuries. We take care of each other and watch out for one another. Kitty is like a niece or nephew to Gérard; they're not intimate and never have been. I don't want you to get jealous or anything. The one he had a relationship with that way, died. She was nice, but not like you. I did not have a relationship with her, which is why her death didn't affect me as it had Gérard."

"Really? I thought they were in love. He took her death hard." I couldn't think of it without getting scared that Gérard would try to compare us as Doug had.

"What's bothering you? Your pulse races, but why?"

"I don't want Gérard to compare me to her. I don't want him to try to turn me into her." My heart caught in my throat at the thought.

"You are not one of the typical women of our time, and you certainly aren't the average woman of today." He laughed. "You, my dear, are a breath of fresh air."

"Gee, thanks, I guess."

He cleared his throat. "I like the way you look at Gérard. You were angry last night because you were hurt; that kind of hurt comes from devotion. I know what Gérard said to you about Patricia and you did what you thought was right. I know you took what he said to heart. He's not used to that."

"Did you know I'd already been marked?"

"Ay."

"At Brady's, when he asked me to dance."

"Actually, he marked you when you were contemplating your first kiss."

I cowered with the realization that he knew that. "Were you there the whole time?"

"Because of Guillaume's interference, you should be grateful he did. Or would you rather've been lost to us? Gérard will always be able to find you. He will know when you're in danger, and as you accept the marks, I will too."

"And the others?"

"No, only me. No one else is bound. We do not share information freely."

"Huh." Yup, platonic in practice, more in words. Did Doug even like me? Did Gérard? Had they said that? Loving things I do is not the same. Yup, I was staying in that house. "I'll see you later, Doug." I hurried off with my footsteps echoing in the great hall.

Anxious to shed the semantics and subsequent politics, I pushed the outside door open, but fear slammed into me. My breath came in shallow, tight sips. I was going to pass out, so I let myself go. Guillaume caught me.

It was only eleven in the morning.

I thought it was later than it was and wanted Gérard so bad I hurt. I was having a panic attack that didn't want to let up. The more I thought about the symptoms, the worse they felt. Guillaume held me to him and hastened down the stairs. As he followed the stone path, my breath was being sucked out of me and tears turned my hair into wet clumps of straw.

Sam came around the back of Guillaume with Officer Greene. Doug emerged in the doorway as we disappeared into the woods. He shifted to his wolf form, but Sam was faster. He shifted and threw Doug into the granite wall. Doug fell to the ground and didn't move. Sam stalked toward us while Greene watched the door.

I kicked, but Guillaume bit the bare skin of my shoulder. When he did, the fear and tension faded. Guillaume didn't say a word; he turned on his heels, his brown Aussi coat swirled like a cape. Greene trailed after us.

I was power drugged. Everything seemed surreal and dreamlike. I watched the tops of the trees and the clouds as we wound through the woods. There were several crocottas sprinkled along our path; they followed as we passed. I looked back over Guillaume's shoulder to see Sam.

"Why?" I whispered.

"Shut up." Greene snapped, and the pinch of a needle pierced my buttocks. The world grew dim. I fell limp against Guillaume's body.

CHAPTER 38

I couldn't lift my head. The pressure caused the little vein in my temple to throb; I thought it would burst. Nausea settled in. The warm scents of clary sage, dandelion, catnip, and lime, like they were all being boiled or stewed, made promise to turn the sensations into a productive event.

The odor overpowered all else. I couldn't hold on. I threw my body to the side and brought up the contents of my breakfast with Kitty. The pounding in my head worsened. I thought I'd find blood when I touched my eyes. The panic rose again. I screamed.

"She's awake, master," a dry masculine voice bellowed from the hall. The sound echoed through my being and forced another wave of sickness from the pit of my stomach. I continued with the dry heaves as a nosebleed left droplets on the red brick floor.

Voices joined the clicking footsteps in the hall. They were unfamiliar, except for one that I knew all too well.

"Well, well, the blood whore's awake." Greene stepped through the door wearing a long black robe with a hood and surgical gloves; he held a bucket with paper towels. He knelt to clean my breakfast from the gray stone floor and glared at me. His right eye was black and blue, like he'd been socked. I was glad and hoped it hurt. "Scared? You will be by the time the Michel's finished with you."

"So, why'd mommy kill herself, Greene?" I coughed out the question, doubled over from the cramps that formed from the force of heaving. My throat burned; my eyes stung.

"Don't ever speak of Mother. You killed her. You and your damned perfect family."

Guilt got the better of me. "Greene, I know your father killed your brother, Brody. You were innocent, a child yourself. That man robbed you of a childhood." I swallowed back the nausea. "He raped Dawn's mother, too."

Greene lost all the arrogance he exuded a moment before and looked me dead on, his voice a bare whisper. "Yeah, he did. She drowned herself in Sangre at eighteen. But she'd given Dawny up. My father was indentured to Michel. I became a cop, to help, like the ones at Black River who came when Sheena drowned. But Michel, he owns people. And Tiny owns him. I can't help you, Summer."

"They had help, didn't they, Greene? They weren't capable of suicide."

More footsteps and voices came down the hall and entered the room. "Master, she's ready," Greene said. He stood and left hastily.

I couldn't look around because my head pounded; the room closed in. The sounds mingled with the pain. I remained still with my eyes closed, but nothing clarified.

A cold hand, strangely euphoric, rested on my head and earned an escaped whimper. A quick jerk and a soft pillow, which smelled like lavender, was tucked under me. A little more pressure caused my body to straighten and my head to settle in the pillow's hollow. It was better than the hard flat bed.

"Bonjour, faerie défendu. Allow me to introduce myself." The magnificent hand's owner stepped back. He picked up my hand and whispered across my knuckles, "I am Michel."

Finally, Michel had a face. And wavy rose gold hair that fell around his shoulders, a small reddish goatee that attached to a pencil thin mustache, and thin eyebrows with eyes so dark they swallowed his pupils and seemed to be a sea of black among the whites of his eyes. He wore a fine pair of dress boots, black jeans, and a white button-up shirt. His accent was thicker than Gérard's.

"Why am I here?" I couldn't care less who he was. "I'm nothing to you."

"Ah, you have had my attention for some time. You are of great interest for me." He circled the room and stopped in front of a man with spiky blond hair, a pair of faded blue jeans, and a pair of dusty brown cowboy boots. "Jacques, a chair, please. Let us not have our guest strain to look upon us."

"Oui, monsieur." He left the room and came back with several folding metal chairs.

"Merci." Michel took one of the chairs and placed it carefully in the middle of the room.

Not that it put him any further away, as the room was small, like a double-sized cell of sorts—even made of stone. The cold and damp bore down with the other smells. There was no other furniture, and no decorations. Two crocottas lay on the floor, watching me from across the space.

"They will not harm you—unless I say otherwise."

"What do you want from me?" I kept my voice steady.

"Ah, what wouldn't I want?" He cocked his head to the side and peered through his bangs at me. He wasn't a bad looking man, but he wasn't my type. "Gérard was a fool to think he could keep you to himself."

"Who are you?" I know he said his name, but that told me nothing. "What are you?"

"I am Michel. I am master of the Northeastern territories. The Samhain is upon us, and I am here to take what is mine. I want to take this part, Gérard's territories, his position, and you." I tried to keep the shock from showing on my face, but he caught it anyway. "I am vampire. Gérard took the liberty of marking you after I had cleansed you the first time. Pointless." He reached into his pocket and pulled out a pack of tobacco and rolled a cigarette.

The precision in his slender, pale fingers was uncanny. His nails were manicured, yellowed, and thick. His skin opaque, brittle in appearance—he hadn't fed in a while. The ruddy lips I associated with Gérard and Patricia were instead grey.

"Such youth and strength." He peered into my eyes; a yellow light grew in their midst. "You will weaken."

"Uh, no. You kidnapped me."

"Ah, he would have you fooled."

He stood and paced over the bricks. He didn't glide but rather placed heavy footsteps, one in front of the other, heels first. I could tell he was agitated. Not all that dissimilar to Gérard when he went still, statuesque. He turned to look at me and left the room faster than I could see.

Jacques stared at me from the other chair. He licked his lips and glanced around wildly. The look on his face failed to show that sense of respect I saw in Gérard's people. Instead, I saw fear. Even on the crocotta as it stalked out the door. Perhaps untrusting was a better word than fear. The eyes you'd expect from an animal hunter, cornered. I felt sorry for them.

I thought that perhaps if I could gain Jacques's trust, he'd take me home. I smiled at him. "If you take me home, I'm sure Gérard will grant you protection." Honestly, I had no idea if he would, but I could ask.

He glanced up at me and laughed out loud. "You are home." The prior notion flew out the window. That man was nuts.

The crocotta came back, followed by Michel and Guillaume. I admired the lean lines of the creature's muscles along his back, which were accented by the bluish black of his fur. It had something in its mouth. I couldn't make the details, but I saw enough to know what it was, and sat bolt upright.

I screamed until Guillaume smacked my face. He loomed over me and grinned. If it weren't for that damn headache, I would have leapt at him. But it hurt too much, and the crocotta had my substitute mother dangling from its mouth. I had less petty things to take care of.

"Gale! Gale!" I called her name as tears flooded down my face. "Oh, God, is she dead?" I couldn't breathe.

"She lives for now." Michel's voice was arrogant, frightening. The seduction that I associated with vampires in the stories and with

Gérard was nowhere in sight. He was smug, to say the least. "Perhaps we will come to an understanding."

"Fuck you."

He turned to the crocotta. "Sam, drop her."

Sam dropped the owl and glared at me. He came over and growled softly, leaving behind the dampness of his nose. I had all I could do to keep from touching him as he went back by the door to watch over the owl.

"Isn't this where you're supposed to pretty talk me or get me to plead for her life in an effort to say you want me to help you, and you promise to let her go? You'd just kill her, anyway. Unless, of course, there's something else keepin' you from doing it." I needed to learn to keep my mouth shut because I was digging a hole. I figured if they had me here and were going to kill me, they would do it no matter what I did, so why not just get it over with?

"You should respect your true master." Jacques was such a help. "He is yours; you know. He is master of all. He's older than Gérard and stronger. He'll make you do what he wants." He seemed to be like one of those brainwashed sheep, headed straight to the slaughter with a smile on his face.

"That is talent." I sneered at Michel. The headache subsided, and my thoughts cleared. The nausea lessened and the first pangs of hunger hit. "What time is it, anyway?" It dawned on me that he's a vamp. Gérard would be looking for me, I hoped.

"Two thirty in the morning. You've slept the day away." Guillaume was all charm when he spoke. I could have taken a shovel and wiped that smug look right off his face.

The memories of the previous night with Patricia surfaced. I remembered how angry I had been. If I could get angry enough, maybe I could do it there.

Michel squatted down to my level.

"Cooperation is a two-way game. Little things like . . . oh, say kidnapping and threats to my family do not impress me. You want to be my master, but who the hell told you I'd comply? You're dead. If there's one thing I won't do, it's take orders. Especially if that someone dies daily. What's to stop me or anyone else here from staking your sorry ass at dawn?"

"You dare threaten me?" Michel flashed his fangs, his eyes glowed bright with yellow flames. The effect didn't work on me.

"The marks," he hissed.

"Guillaume told you Gérard accepted your challenge, sir. You think he'd leave yours?" Greene was back. "Do it yourself this time."

The gaunt vamp flashed sulfur eyes at him. "Non, the clever fellow took blood." He turned to Guillaume. "You failed me."

He glided out of the room; the others followed.

I was left alone in the room with Gale on the floor, Guillaume in the chair. He brushed a stray hair from my eyes. His sleek, rugged fingers were gentle, soft. I hadn't expected it. He picked up the owl, careful not to mar its feathers, and placed it on the bed next to me.

"Beautiful creatures, owls. I've always had a place for them in my heart. Vicious predators camouflaged by nature's beauty. It is something I will never know."

I bit my lip to keep from a consoling comment as he admired the bird. He was a handsome, well-meaning man when things went his way.

He retrieved a damp cloth from the small sink and wiped the rag over my forehead. He tucked my hair behind my ears, pulling the fabric of my shirt aside to see the wound he made. "I'm sure they've told you what I am."

"Yes," I whispered.

"And that I killed her?"

"Mmhm."

"I'm honored, really. She was young, credulous. I spoke to her, you know. I urged her to climb on, for only the fairest of the Sidhe could possess a true black stallion." I turned away. His voice was tender, caring. "Don't look away, Summer. It is true. But it's not fair."

"What?" Sick bastard.

"That I claimed her death but am denied yours. I'm sorry I won't be the one to do it." A tear dripped down his cheek.

Fuck. "Who then?"

"Michel."

Truth be told, I had to agree. "I'm sorry too, for I'd thought once before that if she could succumb, then so would I. I don't know that I can take whatever Michel has plans to do. If it comes to it, will you?"

"I can't." He kissed my nose and went to the door. "I wanted you, Summer, not simply the hunt, but you. It is why I put off your execution. But now, Gérard has brought an appeal to the regime. Your death will not go unpunished, at present. I doubt Michel would even risk that. Because, ironically, Gérard would be the one to kill him." He left.

I picked up Gale's lifeless body.

I cradled her to my chest. There was a spot of blood under her left wing and her right eye was partially open. Her tongue, a grey shadow inside her jagged beak, rose and fell in conjunction with each breath. As I pet her feathers, I wondered if my power would allow me to heal her.

Faeries from the world of Faerie in France were known to help humans in need, especially those who helped those faeries and held good will in their hearts. They were also in tune with nature. I knew that much, but I wasn't a French faerie.

I inhaled deep, closed my eyes, and chanted, "Make Gale heal. Better her wounds and bring her back. Her heart is good, and her fight makes her strong." I peered at her; nothing changed.

Since I had nowhere to go and wasn't hurried with time, I decided to keep trying. I concentrated on all of our times at the diner. I thought about our dinner together before she was taken, and I thought about how I felt when Sam brought her.

She lay listless on the bed. Since her condition remained unchanged, I tucked her into the blankets. I curled my aching body around her, cuddling, and wept.

I'd been happy the last few years and now my life was falling apart—again. I couldn't have a repeat of all those helpless events. I could do something about this. I just didn't know how. I had a quick flint of pain in my head; I fell asleep trying to make her well while questioning why they wanted me dead.

I heard someone open the door and rolled enough to see Sam. He sat on one of the metal chairs, slouched down, with his legs flopped open. He stared at me, then handed me a cup with something that smelled like juice, but I refused to take it. He offered me a bag of snack crackers and an apple. I still refused.

"I won't eat anything from you. I'd rather die than fall prey to any of you."

"You'll get your wish if you don't give in to Master Michel." He spoke matter-of-factly, "It would be wise for you to remember. He won't let Gérard have you." He left the room.

I heard the rattling of keys on the other side of the door; his footsteps faded down the hall.

Hunger gnawed at me; it felt like my stomach was going to eat my liver. The pangs brought waves of heartburn and nausea. I was lightheaded and dizzy. I could smell food, real food. I wanted it. I couldn't hold out. I went to the door and tried the knob. It was a heavy oak door with iron metal works. I wasn't getting out. Though I pulled and strained against it, the door resisted. The smell grew stronger, footfalls sounded from nowhere.

"I know you want it." A voice came low and soft. It seemed to seep through the crack under the door, wrapping around me. The smell was intoxicating. "Shall I enter?" The voice whispered with a French accent different from Gérard's. The whisper whirled in my head.

"I guess," I whispered back. I dug my nails into my palms to keep calm and thought to Gérard, *Michel is here, please find me.* There was no answer. No acknowledgement.

The rattling of keys brought me back to my senses. I scampered to the bed and knelt next to the owl that lay helpless under the blanket. As the door creaked open, a wave of heat and power rushed over the room. It hit me like a hot, wet blanket so that the air was heavy and limited. I gasped for air and the power retreated, barely enough to make breathing comfortable. Michel stood in the doorway with a tray.

He glided into the room. The smell of the food clouded my mind. He pulled a chair close to the bed and scooped up a bite-sized portion of meat. "Come to me, Summer, take a bite." He spoke with kindness. I knew it was probably his vampire tricks, but my hunger panged. He held the fork over the tray, just out of reach of my mouth.

I wasn't sure if I should speak, so I moved forward and took the bite he offered. I cowered back and whispered, "Thanks."

He blinked an acknowledgement and continued to feed me in the same manner until I'd finished.

His eyes filled with yellow light. "How do you do this? You meet my gaze. Gérard has not completed the marks. Two remain."

I couldn't believe he knew that but then again, he'd managed to stay undetected by Gérard. As master of Mount Mort, he was able to sense all of the beings. I figured this vamp was much more powerful and probably older. Fuck.

"Such serious thoughts cross your face. Tell me. What is going on behind those pretty eyes?"

There was no sense in telling a lie since he'd know. However, I tried for a half-truth. "Wondering how old you are." I studied the floor as I spoke, hoping not to get caught in some vampire trickery. All the books I read told tales of vampires that could read minds, hypnotize with voice or eyes, sense lies, use powers as torture, and an endless number of frightening things. So far, most were true.

"Why not ask?"

"I don't know." I wiped an unshed tear before it fell. Another took its place and spilled.

He caught one on the side of his finger and traced it back up to my eye. His skin was cool. It confirmed he hadn't fed, which increased my angst. I trembled, and he drew back, almost in slow motion. He folded his hands in his lap and crossed his legs, settling back in the chair.

"For now, consider yourself my guest. You may not wander about, but you may leave your room. Come, I will show you." He stood and reached for my hand.

I didn't feel like dying right then. I put my hand in his and let him pull me to my feet. We walked hand in hand to the door. I didn't like it.

He let go to guide me through, the way Gérard had done. I glanced back at Gale on the bed, reluctant to leave her. "Your bird will be there when you get back. You have my word." He nodded his head slightly and sent a painful surge through his hand on my back. He smiled, pleased by my shocked expression. "Hasn't Gérard shown you his strengths? Perhaps the old man has gone soft. Genevieve's line is weak." What did he mean? I'd seen Gérard; I thought I felt his powers. Michel appeared stronger, though. I thought better about all matters of Gérard and kept to small talk. "What line are you from then?"

"Clever girl, either prying for information or avoiding my question. Either way, it is quite curious."

"I'm curious. All you guys are new to me."

He studied my face, nodding. I took it as a sign he was willing to partake in a conversation. I was right. "I descend from the Aldatmak line. My mistress is Turkish."

"I've heard of her. Guillaume and Tiny mentioned her."

"You will meet her, but not now. Aren't you curious about your own past?"

I was, but he was untrustworthy, or was he? "Maybe, but I'm more interested in what all of you are and why you want me dead."

"Then let us walk while I enlighten you about us, but you are mistaken. I am the only one who wants you alive."

CHAPTER 39

Michel and I walked down an elongated hallway lit by torches. The floor was polished stone, the walls—stacked railroad ties. We passed three doors on the left and stopped at the first door on the right. "I presume you want to use the toilet. Then I shall show you the dressing room, as you may wish to change for bed."

"Bed? Yeah, shouldn't you be dying soon or something?"

"Guillaume's venom takes time to wear away. You have been with me for two days." I gasped. He raised his brown and smiled with tight lips. One that said he found pleasure in my reaction. "Enter. I will wait for you. Do not try anything rash. You cannot lock the door, and there are no windows. Killing yourself will not work as I would salvage you. I will not permit your death." He gave half a bow and directed me through.

I stepped into the stone room to face a cold, white American Standard toilet. The toilet paper wasn't on a roller, not that there was one. It was on the floor next to the toilet, between two drains. There was a roll of paper towels on the sink, which was also a plain white. A showerhead hung down from the ceiling, its knob on the wall.

All in all, it was cold and uncomfortable. There was no mirror. But there was a hand/body soap dispenser, no lotion, no conditioner. I had never used soap that was meant for both purposes; it wouldn't be a treat. Needless to say, I hurried through my deed and opened the back of the toilet. I unscrewed the float from the brass rod and unhooked the chain. I put the tank back to straights and put the rod in the front of my bra and into the waist of my panties. I opened the door a little too quickly. Michel was talking with Jacques about a wolf. They stopped abruptly when I came out.

"I'm done," I said. I realized Michel had changed his clothes and was wearing a pink button-up shirt with black slacks.

"You'll come around, they always do," Jacques said, almost in a chuckle. He reminded me of a cartoon hyena. He scared me more than Gérard and Michel combined.

"Come." Michel took my hand and started down the hall.

We stopped at the next door on the right. This time he entered before me, drifting over the white carpet. The wallpapered walls had little Oriental gold fans in neat vertical rows silkscreened on them. The tri-fold dressing screen had matching rice paper.

He pulled back a gold curtain and tucked it around a heavy brass hook before fanning through the clothes. There were all straight dresses and a few nightgowns. The fabrics ranged from cotton and nylon to silk. He removed a white cotton gown with light blue vertical stripes. It was similar to a *Little House on the Prairie* look. "I will leave this on the dressing table for when you dress for bed."

"What, no bonnet?" I was being sarcastic; he didn't get it.

"I will have one for you as soon as we return." He was serious, almost embarrassed, like he should have known.

"Don't bother, I don't need it." He'd probably expect me to wear it if he had one. "I don't see any shoes." It was true; there were no shoes, no undergarments, no robes, and no drawers.

"You do not need them. If you were going out then perhaps, but for now, it is unneeded." Funny, he was talking as if I were staying. "The mirror is acrylic and will not shatter, and there is no lock. Again, do not try to kill yourself. You will not succeed."

We headed further down the hall. The next door we passed on the right was a small kitchen. There was a freezer chest, a microwave, a bowl with napkins, a small table, a chair, and a cup of plastic silverware. There was a water fountain against the far wall; he motioned for me to go to it. I went over and took a sip. The water was cold; I wanted to drink heartily, but the rod made stooping difficult.

Out of curiosity, I peeked inside the freezer. There were frozen dinners in every combination available. One little box had ice cream cones, and another had frozen breakfast sandwiches.

"Everything's so cold. I mean that literally and figuratively. It may as well be a men's locker room."

"I see no point giving you the rewards of comfort when you despise me so. As you please me, you will enjoy more. Betray me and life can be a lot less rewarding than this."

"What do you want with me?"

"I want what is mine. I want his territories. Though ultimately, I want Gérard's removal on the P.R., and his presidency to go to someone you know rather well."

"Tiny," I stated.

He stepped into my personal space. "Take my hand. We will go for some night air. It will do you good before we return."

"Whatever." I couldn't think of anything smart to say, so I figured I would play the part until I could configure a plan.

I took his hand, and we walked to another hallway. "This is where your freedom ends. You may not pass these stairs unless I want it. The door will be locked. Now, after you." He put his arm out once again to guide me through.

We climbed probably thirty stairs before we came to an impressive stone room. The walls were decorated with rich tapestries of Roman depictions, and an iron chandelier, which hung from the room's center, held a dozen candles in skeletal claws. I shivered and sidled to a pair of French doors. Michel obliged by opening those doors. A moment that would release an unknowingly lethal beast, predestined by my ancestors—the darkness. We exited onto a balcony that overlooked a Pegasus fountain in a cobblestone driveway. Two figures were fighting below.

"Your lycan friend found you rather quickly," Michel stated, his voice smooth and calm, but his power leapt from him in stinging waves. "I would have thought you would want your master but instead, you call the wolf. How interesting, you take after your mother." He flicked his tongue over his lips. "His blood is sweet. Sam is with him, you know." He laughed. "We shall soon see. Will my beast win—or your dog?"

I trembled in his hand. I didn't want to be the cause of Doug's death. "Doug, run," I yelled, a high-pitched, girlish voice. It burned my throat. Michel grabbed my arm and whirled me around to him. "Don't kill him. Please don't," I whispered.

"Then I would suggest you refrain from future outbursts." He turned and left me at the balcony to meet Jacques, who stood in the middle of the room wringing his hands. He paced hastily in front of Michel. I didn't care. I turned back to Doug. I think he'd heard me because they were fighting directly under the balcony.

Both animals glinted crimson in the moonlight. The wolf went under the crocotta, a crushing jaw on his adversary's hind quarter. The beast jumped, but came down on the wolf's neck, teeth gnashing. The wolf contorted; guttural bellows swallowed by the growing fervor of the crocotta. My heart sank. A rush of fear like no other consumed me. I threw myself at the railing. The wind whirled the dirt below and the crocotta released the wolf.

CHAPTER 40

The writhing wolf transformed back to Doug on the stones below. The crocotta shifted back to Sam. He stumbled toward the entrance and was out of sight. Doug's hair blew in the breeze, his eyes flickered citrine in the shrouded light. Wolves howled in the distance. He answered. I knew they meant to mark their locations. Once they all knew each other's whereabouts, they'd put their strategy into play. Though I wasn't sure they could win against the power I felt in that place, or Sam's crocottas. My mouth went dry in utter fear.

Power pulsed behind me. I glanced at Michel and Jacques from over my shoulder, but my tears shrouded their images. I turned around slow, and lifted my head, focused, unblinking. I flashed back to Gale, and Doug's lame figure below, and it happened. The darkness inside me slid from wherever it had been and took over my blood, my conscience. I took controlled breaths and loathed the little laughing man and his master.

The laughing bore down on me; the wind rustled around my feet. Michel reached up to touch blood that leaked from his nostril. Jacques grew still, silent. I almost missed seeing a tiny speck of blood on his lower lip. He opened his mouth, more dribbled out. Michel lurched as I glared at him. The power inside me was thick and choking; I gasped, and blood washed from Michel's eyes before he struck.

I fell to the floor but didn't lose consciousness. Everything hurt; my tears flowed in a hot steady stream. Michel lunged straight for my neck. I didn't move but instead braced for him. His fangs penetrated; my body recognized him as death.

I felt wicked. The power caused it, but I didn't know how. I was relentless. If I had tamed my power and was trained in its use, I would have been a match. I wanted Jacques and Michel to hurt, no; I wanted to kill them. I'd never felt that way before in my life. There was a place inside of me that went still. It was a dark place that I'd never been. The place where fear, sadness, and anger dwelt. It consumed me.

I longed for the relentless flow of fear to stop, but I knew Doug could die on the stones below and it was the doings of the two closest to me. The same held true for Gale. I needed that fear to continue. I longed to go to them but fought the urge because I had a bloody vampire looming over me. I hated him, and every spike of fear, every thought of Doug's contorted body, sent a serpentine wash of power that resulted in more blood from the vampire's orifices.

I pulled the rod from my bra and pressed it to Michel's belly. But no matter how fanciful the stories; no matter how dramatic the effects on TV, it simply isn't that easy to plunge a blunt metal rod through a clothed human body. All it did was piss him off—more.

His bloodied hands tore me from the floor. I couldn't stop the rush of emotions; they were echoed in waves of black liquid within my being. I knew that Jacques had fallen into a pool of his own blood on the stone floor, but Sam had fallen next to him. I never heard him enter the room; I didn't care. Michel flung me against the far wall; something popped. A flare of pain rose through my body, causing another wave of power that made Michel's knees buckle. I tried to stand, but the vampire was on me.

His fangs sank into my neck again. I screamed. I screamed for Doug, the pain, and Gale, and everyone whose life was impacted by the vampire biting me. I screamed again, and he tore his teeth out to clasp his ears. Blood formed rivulets over the once white shirt. I was afraid of him, and my terror had become his. The more he tried to stop me, the more I was able to hurt him back.

"You will die," Michel gurgled with the blood that filled his mouth. His lips glistened with blood. I wasn't sure was his or mine.

I inadvertently reached to the bite wound on my neck. When my fingers touched the spot, it hurt. I panicked as I prodded torn flesh and wet soft tissues. The sensations at my fingertips mixed with the pain and sent another wave of darkness that collapsed Michel on his hands and knees. He crouched, became a black blur, and headed straight for me. The balcony overflowed with power. I was terrified. The blur sent me crashing through the glass French doors. Penetrating shards left me breathless.

I was pulled from the floor and airborne again. Before I could comprehend what happened, I was on the ground by Doug. Another wave of fear started, and Michel fell from the balcony, hitting the cobblestone with a crunch. He was still, but I knew he couldn't be dead because I needed his head, or heart. I searched around frantically for a stake or something sharp so that I could do the deed, but a pair of hands clasped my face and cradled me to a chest.

I eyed Michel's body and breathed in labored breaths. The darkness inside wouldn't come. It receded. I screamed into that chest. I attempted a deeper breath and prepared to scream again when it hit me. The smell of cinnamon, an earth element that was also used for protection. The comforting scent and the feel of the silk beneath my face made me look up.

My heart beat erratically; my pulse throbbed along my paining throat. I scrunched in, my nails tore at the shirt; I couldn't get close enough. He pressed my face to his chest as I sobbed on the cobblestone—the moonlight soft and ominous.

The moon was three-quarters full—the night would grow old. I had longed for him and just when I got him; he was going to die soon. Another wave of despair and fear spread from that dark place and resulted in my power rustling through the bushes around us like a breeze before a storm.

He kissed my hair and the familiar tingling sensation coursed through me. It danced on my nerves and brought the fear and despair to a controllable level. The dark place inside receded.

"*Ma chérie,* I have you now," he assured. "I should have known he was here." He nuzzled the top of my head.

"I want to go home. Take me from here." I sobbed in between sentences.

"Shhh, in time. Had I lost you—" A sharp surge almost like an electric shock went through me. It hurt, and I jumped. "I did not mean to . . ."

"Was that your power?" I whispered the last as if it were a forbidden word. Michel had seemed surprised that I hadn't felt Gérard's power, now I knew Gérard was much more powerful than I'd thought. It frightened me and that dark place crept open again.

"I should have better control, but the thought of losing you like this—It is unbearable." He let go of me and stood.

I grabbed his leg and practically begged. "Don't let go. Hold me, don't ever let go." He squatted down and scooped me up in his arms. I wrapped my arms around his neck and locked my fingers. "Please, Gérard, take me home. I want to go home, please. Take me away from here." I cried into him again. My body twitched and ached. My shoulder had such pain and my neck throbbed with every beat of my heart. My ankle hurt and my opposite leg. Every little thing hurt; I wailed.

"Shhh, I am going to give you the third mark, *ma chérie*. You will heal faster. It will ease your pain." He tried to move me so he could see my neck. "You must let go, you are stronger when frightened. Your fingers will break if I pull too hard." He smiled; I buried my face in his chest.

"Love, are you alright?" Doug's voice was hoarse and breathy.

"Doug!" I screamed. It was loud even to me, but Gérard smiled meekly and shook his head. "Sorry." I was embarrassed. Guess that meant I was going to live.

"Glad to have you back with us, love. Lycans heal fast. Don't fret," He leaned in to kiss my cheek, but eased back, glancing at Gérard.

I couldn't see Gérard's face, but I could see Doug's perfectly. "What? What is it?" I panicked and the dark place crept open again. "What?" I screeched. Hysterics won.

"Douglas is going to help you, that is all." Gérard pulled me to him and wrapped his hand around my head. "Lie still." He held me firm as Doug approached the wound at my neck.

Pain shot through my body as Doug's tongue rounded the edges. I cringed and whimpered. I tried not to scream. I tried to push Doug away but wasn't strong enough.

"*Michel* meant to take you from me, *ma chérie*. You must have made him angry to give up trying to gain a power like yours."

"Gérard?" Doug deplored. "I can't." He went to wolf form and leapt in front of the fountain.

Greene came out to the cobblestone in his pajamas. He had a flashlight and was searching the darkness. Gérard had taken me into the woods with a group of wolves, Kitty, Patricia, and more vamps. They waited motionless amidst the shadows. Patricia nodded at Gérard and disappeared. I'd forgotten about talking to him in my head, so I tried thinking about Gale in the little room and bed.

Oui, we will find her, he thought back. The memory of her brought a flicker of my power as the dark place started to tear open. Gérard quickly lowered his lips to my hair and sent a surge of calm through me. The tingling calmed me until I relaxed in his arms.

I felt safe with him. I reached up to wrap my arms around his neck and he bent into me. His lips reached the top of my blouse. Kitty was suddenly working the buttons so that my bra was exposed. He whispered in my mind, *Maintenant, look at my eyes, quickly.*

I did as told. When his eyes transformed into little blue torches, I was immediately lost. He bit down on the top of my shoulder, which made me whimper, but it didn't hurt. I felt good. There was a pleasure to it, like eating really good chocolate.

When he drew back, the flames receded, and he threw his head back. My blood trailed from the corners of his mouth. "I am sorry, *ma chérie*, but you scream too much when I do this pleasurably. You have screamed enough this night. I will make it up to you." He kissed the tip of my nose and made things low ache. Perhaps it wasn't him, perhaps it was the pain.

"She's hurt badly." A voice from behind the tree whispered.

"*Oui*, she holds the third. She will heal." Gérard sounded angry.

Doug lay still in front of the fountain when Greene shined the flashlight on him. The wolf growled and lurched on the man. Greene's screams turned to the now familiar sound of gurgling. Gérard turned my face to spare me the sight.

"Don't kill him!"

He let go of my head in time to see the wolf release the man's throat. His head lolled on the cobblestone in a pool of blood, but not separate from his body. The sight brought a sense of satisfaction over me, and a weight that I didn't know I had lifted from my chest. I looked around, but Doug was gone.

Michel moved, and Gérard handed me to the voice behind the tree.

"C'est Enrique, ma vampire."

The man held me gingerly, but I could feel his strength. Everything about the way he held me told me he wasn't letting me go. I settled into his arms and the grip relaxed, slightly.

Enrique was about six feet three inches, with short, curly black hair. His skin was a nice permanent tan, and he had a cross-shaped scar on the back of his left hand. He had a thick Spanish accent that sent shivers through my body. "Mira, chica."

Gérard was at Michel's side when the vampire rose. Patricia stood on the balcony, her mouth glimmered crimson as she glared down toward them.

Crocottas came out of the doors by the cobblestone and gathered around Gérard. I was frightened and fear tugged at that dark place. Michel rolled back on the stone and blood sprayed across Gérard, who threw a glance back. Enrique pulled me tighter. "Enrique esta aquí. You are safe, bendita."

The dark place closed, but I could tell it was waiting for another opportunity. He kissed the top of my head, which seemed to target that place.

Gérard grabbed Michel's throat before Patricia flew down from the balcony. They took him into the house where I could no longer see. The crocottas lay in wait. Doug emerged; they parted to let him through. He had Gale in his mouth; she was still in owl form. He stalked toward us; the crocottas fell in behind him. I thought they were going to attack, but as they crowded the shrubbery, they lowered themselves in submission. Sam wasn't among them.

Enrique and the others went to receive Doug and Gale. Doug placed Gale's body gingerly on the ground and turned back to human form. He took a pair of jeans from behind a tree and put them on. "Take Gale back to the mansion." He told two wolves that were hidden behind two evergreens. "Enrique, come with us. Kitty, Gérard wants you to stay and watch over the crocottas." He headed back to the house. "The rest of you stay where you are."

The look on Doug's face was grim. I had never seen him look so serious. He caught me staring and came over. His tongue grazed the wound at my neck, which didn't hurt quite as much. He pressed a little harder and pulled away when I couldn't help but whimper. He tried to heal it; the pain intensified and opened that dark place.

Whimpers escaped the mouths of the crocottas that lay in front of us. "Sorry, love. But it will help. Enrique, please calm her down before she makes us all bleed." He had blood smeared on his chin and lips. It made my brain draw mental images of what Greene's neck must have looked like and mine.

"Doug?"

"No worries, love."

I gave him a worried smile. Enrique held me tighter, and we went to the house.

Patricia stood in the doorway waiting for us. "Gérard found his coffin. He needs Summer and Doug to help." She glared at me and then said, "You are a little bitch, but I like you." She rubbed her hand under my chin and sent a wave of power through me that made my head swim.

I was calm and felt better. The pain in my neck subsided, but the pain down low grew. "Take her to Gérard, now." She barked the order and was gone.

Gérard stood with Michel helplessly dangling from his hand. As we came closer, Doug trotted up to the coffin and opened it. Gérard threw Michel inside and slammed the lid. Doug grabbed a small bag from his pocket.

Enrique gave me to Gérard, who put his hand on my abdomen with a worried look on his face. I couldn't figure out why, because I was feeling pretty good. Enrique had another bag tied to his belt. He took it off and opened it.

There was a thin silver chain inside. Both men donned a pair of surgical gloves and went to work. Michel pounded on the coffin when Doug draped the first round of chain over it. They wrapped the chain around the coffin several times, and then Doug fastened a silver cross to the top. Michel went silent.

"Bring him back with us," Gérard said. "Where's Kitty?"

"In the yard." Doug put the bag over the cross so that Enrique could help carry the filled coffin.

"Go to the mansion; put him in the southern courtyard on the altar. Wilma and the staff will prepare the guest rooms." Gérard carried me to the yard where Kitty stood in wait.

"They have shown submission, master." Kitty bowed her head and awaited her orders.

"Go with Douglas and Enrique. Assist them or the staff as needed. Patricia will do the same. When I get back, we will meet in the den. I want good food and drink for us all." Gérard turned his back to her to address the cowering crocottas.

"Your leader will be dead. His and *Michel's* deaths will signify the end of *Michel's* reign. You will serve me, and you will respect me as Master. You will come to my home where you will be prepared, as my people are. You will take part in tomorrow's ball, thenceforward, you will be oriented and oathed. Douglas Cushing is second in command. You will treat him as you treat me. Everything you do to him, say to him, or show to him is the same as doing so to me. Any attempt to harm anyone under my protection will result in your immediate death. If there are any objections, you must leave and never return to this territory. I ask now, are there objections?"

Gérard waited about five minutes, which seemed like an eternity. But then his voice interrupted the muffled cries of confused children and murmurs of frightened adults. "I ask: Do you the *Toronto* Crocotta Clan seek asylum in the *D'Aquitaine territoire?*"

The group answered as a whole. "We seek asylum and forgiveness."

"For now, take refuge at the Lake Sangre Sanctuary. My people are waiting for you and have accommodations ready. Welcome, *mes amis.*"

Gérard drifted a little way and then took flight. We went in short bursts. I could tell he hadn't fed enough. His skin was cool. I would have offered myself for feeding, but I knew that I'd lost too much blood already.

CHAPTER 41

Gérard slowed to a normal pace when he reached the mansion. He sat on a stone, beyond the main entrance, near Lake Sangre's lapping waters. He kissed the outside of the wound and pulled me to him, hugging me hard.

I pushed back, peered up into his face and saw blood-stained tears streak down his cheeks in the moonlight. I realized how much he must have cared for me, then. He felt for me. Never in my life would I have thought anyone would feel that way about me. I had felt what I thought was love but was always made to feel I was wrong. I'd been told I was too soft. Now I knew, I hadn't found the right person. Gérard was that person.

"*Ma chérie*, I am sorry, I was not there for you." He turned his head so I couldn't see his face.

"What do you mean? If it wasn't for you and Doug, I'd be dead. More than once this month." Nothing like stating the obvious. I was good at that.

"*Oui et non, ma chérie.* I was dead and could not help you. You were significantly frightened. I felt it."

"Maybe so, but I feel safe with you. I wouldn't have it any other way." I tried to make it peppy, but I ached all over. I wanted to go to bed.

"*Oui*, your chamber is ready. We shall go." He drifted to the entrance.

The front doors opened to reveal my lovely friend Patricia. She was wearing a chartreuse evening gown with matching robe. "Master, the guests are assembled." She turned and preceded us in the hall.

Gérard glided to the grand staircase in the foyer and leaped up to the balcony. He greeted the group, still holding me. *"Bonjour, mes amis.* I welcome you to my home. This night and tomorrow, you will be guests here. The ball will begin at dusk. I expect to see attendance by all, and I expect to have minimal confrontations from the visitors. If you are in need of a costume, please see Wilma. Have you met Wilma?" The group nodded lazily. They seemed exhausted.

I nuzzled against him, since he was still holding me, and tried to convey that they were tired. It must have worked. "The staff have prepared food for all and rooms to rest. Please, *bon appetite*, I look forward to the celebration this evening brings."

He stepped back and turned to go to a stairwell I'd never seen. Applause and the commotion of tired bodies maneuvering in the halls and up the stairs echoed through until he closed the door. He pushed it shut with his foot, but since his hands were full, he locked it without touching it. I assumed it was power.

He carried me down to the bedchamber's bathroom and sat me gently in the tub. It was filled with warm water, no bubbles.

He ripped my shirt, and I winced, and then my pants. He must have figured I'd suffered enough because he just tore the bra and panties in a blur. After tossing them to the floor, he proceeded to sponge me down with some sort of milky soap that smelled like cinnamon-apple oatmeal. I jerked when he touched the majority of my body, but relaxed when he washed my hair. As he knelt, pouring the water over me, I caught a glimpse of myself in the mirror.

My right eye was swollen purple, and I had scratches on my chin. My neck was missing skin and flesh from Michel's bite. I swayed. He caught me, lifted me from the tub, and cradled me in an oversized white towel. He patted my skin, leaving patches of pink and red on the fabric.

The room blurred. "I think I'm going to pass out. I can't take my own blood."

He dropped the towel and carried me to bed. While he was propping me on the pillows, someone knocked on the ajar door. A woman drifted through with a small black bag, followed by the servant Wilma, who had a silver tray with her. I remembered that he told me everything silver to me was platinum. An odd memory for the moment. I laughed.

He motioned for the odd woman to come to my side, and for Wilma to put the tray on the chaise. The woman went to work.

"I'm Doctor Kelly." She glanced at Gérard. He touched my cheek, and I slept.

The next thing I knew, I was tingling everywhere. The sensation was like licking a 9-volt battery repeatedly, at random intervals, with your whole body. It wasn't nice.

"*Ma chérie,* you must wake."

"I'm sore."

"He knocked you out so you wouldn't feel the stitches. I'm all finished—you should be good as new by tonight. Get some rest." Doctor Kelly glided out the door. Vamp, I guessed.

Gérard held the tray with ginger ale, a straw, and a mug of hot tomato soup. There was a mug of blood beside it. I checked to see if there was a lid. I hoped none sloshed into mine.

"You didn't feed?" I asked in a hoarse whisper. My throat was raw from screaming, my eyes ached from crying. "Thank you for saving me."

"Summer, do not thank me. If not for you, *Michel* would have been much harder to subdue." He looked sullen.

"From what I've read, your power gets enhanced by mine; it wouldn't have helped without the marks. You helped in all ways." I swallowed hard and winced. "How bad am I?"

"A few broken bits, a nasty gash on the neck." He sighed and then looked at my eyes. "Although you needed stitches, you will recover. You would not have recovered at all without the third."

"I know." I was melancholy. I didn't want to be alone, but I didn't want anyone other than Gérard. "I wish you didn't have to go."

"*Comment?* What do you mean, *ma chérie?* I am not leaving. Do you believe, after a night like this, I would leave you? If I had not slept, I would have been there to save you. It will not happen again." His anger swept across the room in power. The hair on the back of my neck stood on end. It hurt.

"Don't you have to die at dawn? Isn't it, like, a vampire rule or something?" I had no idea.

"It is after dawn now. It is eight thirty in the morning."

"Why didn't you—die?" I whispered the last. It was still taboo.

"I had been able to do so briefly prior to this, but now it is with minimal effort." He propped himself on his elbow, just below my waist. "Perhaps some of you has rubbed off on me."

He traced his finger over my stomach and left a trail of energy. It felt good. It was like a deep tissue massage that did a whole lot more. He slid his hand down over my hips and legs. He came back up and went over my neck. I was weak, but relaxed and without pain.

"You are healing. I feel it." He forced a smile that didn't make it to his eyes. "You will be my Summer again."

I'd forgotten about his eyes. They caught me unaware, aflame—blue. I swooned against the pillows, and it brought a true smile from him.

"You like the way you affect me, don't you?" I tried to sound like myself, but it was like my body was an empty shell and I was trying to find my way back in.

He handed me the soup. "I am not the only one who needs to feed."

We sipped our drinks in silence.

When the drinks were gone, he put the tray outside on the floor. He locked the door and went into the bathroom. I assumed to brush his teeth. I attempted to get up, but I couldn't move my lower body. Pain engulfed me and I stilled against the pillows.

He came back and slid in to wrap himself around me in the silk sheets. There was a large white down comforter this time. It felt like home. I turned toward him. I wanted to smell him, see him, and feel

him. His lips brushed mine, and I was asleep again, though it wasn't for long.

The smell of cinnamon and coffee brought me from that dozing, dream-riddled moment. There was someone next to me, but I was afraid to open my eyes. I decided to scream and get it over with, because all the times before, those smells meant I was going to have a bad day. I didn't have time to reason with myself and belted out a glass shattering, ear bleeding scream.

"*Mon Dieu, ma chérie*, why are you screaming? *Ouvrez vos yeux!* Open your eyes!" Gérard had jumped on the bed and was on all fours over me staring into my face when I opened my eyes. I looked around wildly, and saw Doug crouched on the corner of the bed, clutching his ears. Kitty was by the door, doing the same. Patricia was holding a tray with four goblets, just staring.

"Summer, you are safe." Gérard's voice wrapped around me.

"Why is there cinnamon and coffee?" I whispered, my voice demonic, "Are there cinnamon buns, too?" I closed my eyes and waited for a response.

"*Non*, I did not think of them. Do you want them?"

"No, no, no. Don't get them. I don't want them. No." I screamed, ensuring someone didn't leave before I had a chance to respond. I buried my face in the crook of my arm.

"Ok, I give up. What the hell is wrong with her?" Patricia was standing by the pillows.

"Karma," Kitty said.

"We thought you loved cinnamon coffee when you got up. We brought it from your house." Doug paused, then added, "I knew we should have made hot chocolate."

"I'm sorry. I'm so sorry." I put my arm down, their faces surrounded, staring. Not one of them knew what to do. "Every time I wake up to coffee and cinnamon, I have a really shitty day. Cinnamon buns started popping up with Guillaume. I'm tempted to give up cinnamon altogether." I pulled a pillow over my face.

"If Gérard had been human, I think he would have had a heart attack," Doug chirped. "You scared the hell out of all of us."

"And I need to be here because, why?" Patricia complained.

"Halt your querulous tongue," Gérard hissed. He forced himself to appear relaxed; his foot dangled stiffly off the bed. It was too mechanical. "How do you feel, *ma chérie?*"

"Okay." It was true. I did feel better.

"Don't move yet. I want you to have something in your stomach first." Doctor Kelly was at the foot of the bed. She was a beautiful petite woman with long black hair, straight and ragged.

Gérard's voice whispered through my head, *She is Vila, a woman betrothed and drowned before she was wed, a shifter and healer.*

Kitty handed me a cup of coffee with cream and sugar. She had a small plate with several tiny lemon poppy seed muffins that she placed on the bed beside me. She handed a goblet to each Dr. Kelly, Patricia, and Gérard. The fourth she took to a dark figure standing in the corner behind the chaise. It was Enrique.

Doug poured two more cups of coffee and made them like mine.

"I didn't know you guys liked cinnamon coffee, too." Funny, I hadn't thought of them as coffee drinkers.

"Don't know; we haven't tried it." Doug seemed to be taking in the aromas.

"If it's coffee, I'll drink it." Kitty smiled at me. Huh, I pegged her for a tea drinker.

"So why is everybody here?" I couldn't take the curiosity. "Am I going to die or something? Did you kill Michel? Did he fry?" They simply sipped their beverages. "What?"

Gérard stood and drained his goblet. "*Mes amis,* as we see, Summer is doing quite well. *Maintenant,* the ball this evening will be held in the grand ballroom. The doors to the courtyard leading to *Michel* will be guarded by the wolves, the staff will be guarded by the crocottas. I have given strict orders to prevent anyone from going into the courtyard."

"Sounds like it is settled; the war will be on if Guillaume comes. I cannot see him missing. It would be the first Samhain if he did." Dr. Kelly moved to the chaise and finished the contents of her goblet. She was wearing a red silk jumpsuit. There were sequins around the waist and neckline. It was flattering. "I must tend to the supplies before we run out. I want to be prepared. I'll see everyone tonight." She bowed her head and went to the door.

"*Merci.*" Gérard returned the bow, but not quite as low.

Once she was gone, Enrique came over and took her spot on the chaise. He was overly muscular, his black fish net shirt clung to every bit of his upper body. His jeans were snug against his thighs as he sat. The goblet seemed small in his hands.

My idea of a vampire always seemed to be a dainty, slender, fragile creature that oozed sex and lust—Gérard didn't fit my ideal. Patricia did, but most definitely not Enrique. He was more of a bouncer type. It made me wonder how many other vampires I'd met and hadn't known. I mean, the people I had seen in the diner didn't fit that ideal either.

I glanced at each of their faces and couldn't tell what they were thinking. I tried to get up from the bed, but Doug grabbed my ankle. Patricia stood by my head and placed a hand on my chest. "She is hot!"

"*Oui*, she is healing."

"I think it's her power," Kitty said.

"She smells nervous." Doug moved closer to my neck. "We should try to get her up."

"You know, I'm right here." I was a little annoyed. "I want to go to the bathroom, if you don't mind." I tried sitting up, but Patricia kept her hand on my chest. "Please, let me up."

"Not unless I am told to do so."

"Gérard, tell her to let me go." I was so not in the mood for this.

"Let her go," he said flatly. "Do you want my help?"

"Maybe." I winced. "How much time do we have before the ball?"

"Four hours." Doug said it like it was the last thing he wanted to do.

"By the way, how are you feeling?" I had forgotten he was hurt, too.

"I'm fine, love. Can't keep me down." He smiled, and it made me feel better just looking at him.

I pushed up from the pillows, my muscles stiff. My neck was cramped but didn't hurt. I swung my feet toward the floor and stood. Gérard was at my side in an instant. My knees were weak, but without any support, I was able to shuffle to the bathroom and sit on the edge of the tub. The door clicked closed behind me.

I sniffed the basket of potpourri and started the water. I dumped them in the tub. The scent of cloves, fennel, and anise smelled like a dessert. I knew there must have been magical properties to them but hadn't a clue as to what they would be. I just seemed to know, and they just seemed to be there.

I studied my face in the mirror. A purple bruise had blended with the pink of my cheek. My neck had a large area of new red skin with stitches around it. Yup, that threatened to leave a nasty scar.

I wasn't a vain woman. But I wept. The smooth skin that didn't belong and the swelling along my jaw made me feel like the hunchback. Hideous. Frightening.

"You are healing." Gérard came up behind me. I hadn't heard him enter. "The scars will take much longer, but the fractures are gone." He reached up to touch the new skin lightly. "He meant to kill you."

"It's not mine, is it?"

"*Quoi?* Oh, Summer, had I not marked you, we would not be sitting here, now. It is the reason your skin grows. That is all you." He kissed my forehead and motioned for me to get in the tub.

I eased my feet into the water and slowly lowered my body in. The spices danced along the ripples.

I was always rushing, always doing, there was always something. Now, there was a ball in four hours, but I had nowhere to go. I had nothing to do. I watched the spices for a moment longer and realized that was what Doug tried to tell me. Gérard had watched me sleep, eat, breathe, and every move I made. In fact, he had been watching me watch the spices.

I had noticed the rose decorations in the bath before, but I wondered if there was more to them than I'd thought. Roses were everywhere. "Gérard, I am asking you not to lie to me right now."

He looked concerned, but not guilty. That was a plus.

"I asked you before, but it's one hell of a coincidence that you have roses all through the mansion. Then after I met you, roses were growing outside my house. Don't you think it's a bit strange?" I couldn't help the overtones of the accusation, but really.

"Have you heard of the Medieval Rose, *ma chérie*?" He sat on the side of the tub with his hands folded in his lap. His pajama pants were getting wet. "Curious, you never accuse my Douglas. You are drawn to him. I suppose it is your nature; it is elemental. Douglas knows more than he allows."

"Do you have a book on this stuff? Maybe something about me? Something I could flip through quick?"

"But of course, I have them all. I have the full bestiary. I will have them ready for you when you are finished." He wasn't even being arrogant.

I covered modestly. I'd been sloshing around nude while he sat there and watched. I wanted him to come in and hold me.

He slid his pants off and stepped in. "All you need is ask."

I slid over so he could sit next to me. He raised each of my hands and kissed them, sending his power through me. I was drawn to him, too.

He drew back to rest against the side opposite me. "I know you want me." I started to speak, but he held up his hand. "Do not attempt a lie. I know you do, and, although you cannot tell what I am thinking," he paused and lowered his eyes, "I want you more." He sat back and smiled as the word "more" caressed around my body.

"You are such an arrogant—"

"*Non*, chivalrous." He tossed his hair back and smiled, showing full fangs. It was frighteningly flirtatious.

"If I weren't so slow right now, I'd bite you."

"Oh, such a tease. That makes twice you promised." He laughed. It slid around the room and tingled down my spine.

"Stop that."

"Why? You like it." He smiled and raised his eyebrow.

"So?"

"So, enjoy it." He settled back and closed his eyes.

"Are you mad at me?"

He opened his eyes, and I gasped. They were black with white whisps that danced. "Your eyes."

"*Oui*, your power has enhanced mine. The closer we are, the stronger it will be. Do not be afraid, after all—why would I destroy what is mine, *ma chérie*?"

"You keep saying that, but I'm not a prize to be had. I'm a person."

"You are mine because I marked you, and I am yours because you have stolen my heart."

"We don't belong to each other. You're saying that you fucking own me."

"Summer, it is not—"

"But you are, aren't you? My master, that is?" I just thought of that. I was already his servant. Shit.

He sat up again. "Look at me."

"Why?"

"Do it."

"No." Damn.

I was not having a master. Women fought long and hard to get out from under the social ideal that their husbands were their masters or keepers, and I most certainly was not going to be someone's slave.

"*Pour quoi pas*?" he gasped; frustration flashed across his face. I didn't think anyone had told him no before.

"I'll tell you why not. I'm not a freaking slave to be ordered around. You're not my master. There's no way in hell I'm going to play your mind games. I hate my ignorance of this." I waved my hands around, looking for the word.

"*Quoi?*"

Tears burned at the corners of my eyes, but it was anger. "Where are my parents, Gérard? Why'd you kill my real father?"

He lowered in the water and rested his head on the back of the tub, growing still. "You had said, but a moment ago, you do not want games." He tilted his head a little.

"I know." I looked at the bathroom door to avoid looking at him.

"But that is the way in this life, Summer. You have thought it but refuse to believe."

"If you know my thoughts, why do you make me go through all this?"

"If I wanted to sift through your thoughts, I would do so. I choose not to know all with you, though you make it almost impossible to restrain myself. What fun would it be if I knew all? It would not bode well for either of us."

"But if I didn't talk to you, would you?"

"That depends on why you were no longer talking to me."

"Am I supposed to appreciate that?" I didn't like it, but I had a taste of vamp 'B'. I'm glad I chose vamp 'A' but I'd be damned if I told him that. "Promise me you won't do what you did with Patricia here the other night, again."

"*Alors*, I will not promise what I may not be able to keep."

"But there are moments in my life I'd rather forget or never share. It hasn't all been good. Jesse is a big part of that. I'm not ready to share that much."

He smiled—a curl at the corner of his mouth. "Come; let us ready ourselves for the ball." He was up and out of the room before I could think about what had just happened.

"You didn't answer a damn question," I huffed in exasperation.

His laughter danced around me.

CHAPTER 42

A Mardi Gras princess blinked back at me, a reflection in the tri-fold mirror. My hair was piled in waves on top of my head with ringlets placed strategically around a gold and diamond tiara that complimented the white lace bodice adorned with gold sequins on the white satin ball gown. Around the skirt, layers of white created a waterfall effect over the wire hoop.

The mask was also white satin edged in gold lace and accented with white feathers that plumed above my head on the right; a diamond inlaid at the corner of each eye, like tears. The outfit was coordinated right down to the golden slippers: white feather trim along the toes, a clear strap on back, and a half-inch heel.

Gérard helped me dress for the occasion since he didn't want me to be alone. I think he liked the outfit because it made me appear more buxom than usual.

Although he saw mine, he wouldn't let me see his. He went into the bathroom to get ready. I bit my tongue to refrain from saying that the last dinner party had kinda taken away any element of surprise that he could possibly have for me.

"*Ma chérie*, please, close your eyes."

I stood directly in front of the door so I could get a good look. "Ready!" I shut my eyes tight, forcing myself not to peek.

"You may open them."

My stomach performed cartwheels while I fought the urge to run.

He wore a pair of black dress slacks with a black silk stripe down the side of each leg, a white blouse with ruffles flowing down the buttons and spilling out of a black paisley vest. There was a long black cape lined with gold silk, to match my dress, and a high collar. His hair was left loose except for where the mask, black satin outlined in diamonds and black feathers fanned around the upper half, had pulled it tight.

I focused on the floor, with quick glances at the rest of him. "You look like a chic Dracula." I loved Dracula in the old movies. Damn.

"Is that good or *non?*" He raised an eyebrow and tossed his hair over one shoulder. I had to look away. "Ah, look, *ma chérie,* for I am looking at you." His accent thick, his voice deep. "It is only better because I know you are mine. Once you accept me, it will be better for you."

"What do you mean, accept you?"

"Eh, did you have a moment to look over the books you requested?"

"I forgot about them. Do we have time now?" I thumbed through one.

"*Oui,* for what are we looking?"

"I don't know." There were books on faeries, lycanthropy, vampires, and a stack on witchcraft and alchemy and one he'd set aside titled: Álfar and Döckálfar. "Guess you guys keep up on your corner of the world. I didn't think you'd have this much. I guess it's like my obsession with cookbooks."

"I am not so far out of touch as you may believe, *ma chérie.* I practiced alchemy before my turning."

Shameful, I didn't know what alchemy was.

I took the top book on alchemy. He'd opened to a page that listed the benefits and characteristics of herbs, spices, and plants. There were several pieces of information that leapt from the page and made instantaneous goose bumps.

Cinnamon — Aphrodisiac, protection

Rose — Love, beauty, binding element for the feminine forces

Clary sage — Dream recall

Bay — Induces visions

Thyme — Courage

Dragon's blood — Cleansing, protection

"Guess you covered the aphrodisiac department," I laughed.

"*Mais, Guillaume aussi.*"

"Oh, the buns." I bit my lip.

He tapped the clary sage and bay. "Greene."

I remembered the little room with Michel and blinked it away. "At least I know where to look to possibly conjure up something." I bookmarked the page with a tissue and reached for another on witchcraft.

He pulled the tissue out.

I opened to a page that described the meaning of colors and the use of crystals and gems. It would seem that my color preferences mixed with Gérard's and were perfect complements to one another. No wonder he had the effects on me that he did.

Pink — Love, kindness — Romance
Black — Death, regeneration — Protection
Blue — Wisdom, patience — Calming
White — Innocence, purity — Purifying
Orange — Friendship, protective energy — Fire

"This section is about rocks and minerals. For instance, *ma chérie,* diamonds are for power and purity."

"Not for nothing, but this is just freaky. I wish we had time to read about everything." I flipped through the pages in awe.

"Try this one." He handed me a book on lycanthropes.

I found a page that offered what animals were symbolized in magic, and how lycanthropes can be categorized.

Owl — Wisdom, telepathy
Wolf — Loyalty, freedom
Crocotta — Prophecy, psychic power
Fox — Cunning, maternal
Dragon — Life, death

"I guess I should read the book on vampires when I'm alone." I peered at him out of the corner of my eye.

"Oh, no. I will not leave you alone to make new assumptions about me." He went still and serious. "The way you think, I want to stop any false information before it starts. Perhaps I would awaken wrapped in a fishing net. Really, *ma chérie*." He laughed again.

"Oh, shut up!" I slapped his arm.

"Such aggression. Shall I cry out in pain?"

"Well, the book you have is by Montague Summers and he was one of the experts of his time. I've heard of the book, and I bet it has a lot of useful information." I was serious.

"You could simply ask me questions. You would find it much more entertaining and most factual."

"Yeah, would you be a willing test subject if I learned some way to ward off unwanted vampires?"

He laughed. "Never in all my experience have I been asked to be willingly warded off. For you, I will try. But let us wait until after the ball. I would hate to ruin my costume." He swirled around quick enough to make the cape flare, his laughter wrapped around me, tickling as if there were hands in all the right places.

I curled, as best as I could, in that ridiculous dress. "Stop, please, stop." I gasped sips of air. "Please, I can't take it anymore." A few more sensations, and it subsided. Every nerve ending was on alert. I was ticklish, I guessed he found out. It was nice not to feel pain.

"That was most enjoyable, *ma chérie*. I should like to do this again, only closer." No sooner had he spoken, and he was on the bed next to me.

"I love it when you do that. It scares me a little, but in a good way." I threw myself back and tried to catch my breath.

He traced around the scar on my neck and drew a line to the cleavage that was exaggerated by the corset. "You are warm, and alive. I do not mean alive as in life, but you are—I am without words."

"I think I know what you mean." I did. I enjoyed being with him so much, that everything was more enjoyable. "I'm still pissed, you know."

He kissed between my breasts lightly and drew back. "Do you know why we are having a masquerade ball?" The question was more of a statement. I waited for him to answer it. "It was a celebration meant for those in power and wealth. The fun was trying to hide your identity. Every ball I have attended, I have done so. *Mais, ce soir*, I go as I am, in myth." He paused, a moment in thought.

I scooted to the edge of the bed and struggled to remain upright. How women could wear hooped dresses as a standard was beyond me. It was uncomfortable, tight, and awkward. Doing this on purpose was absurd. I rolled off the side and managed to stand.

He had gone to the wardrobe and pulled out a small garment bag.

"What's in the bag?"

"Before you see, it occurred that I am as I am, and my lady may desire to be—her creature of myth as well?"

Nervous for a vampire was absolutely ego building. My confidence level skyrocketed over that small influence I held. Those small moments were what kept me from killing myself through the embarrassment of being a complete ass. I wanted to know what was in the bag.

I guess I hadn't responded fast enough because he got even worse. "You do not have to. I did not mean anything by this. I apologize, *ma chérie*. It was simply a thought."

Well, there went my ego trip. "Will you stop? I want to know what's in the bag. How can I say yes or no until I see what's in the bag?" It sounded logical.

"Ah, well." He drifted to the chaise; the bag dangled from his hand. I stepped up to him. "Please, wait," he said.

"Why?" I tried to take the bag from him, but he held on with the force of God knows what. "Let go!"

"*Non.*"

"Will you just give me the damn bag?" I pulled as hard as I could, but the woven bag didn't give under his strength. "If you would just let me look, I'd let you know."

"*Non,* I have changed my mind." He yanked and threw me off

balance. I went forward, falling toward the floor, and braced for the impact. Right before I hit, his arm was around me. I snatched the bag from him.

He tried to get it, but I had a death grip on the handle. As I rolled to my stomach, the bag went beneath me. His body pressed against mine, and my legs were lifted off the floor by the hoop.

"*Donnez moi,* Summer."

"Let it go." Fear spilled from him, not inflicting, but rather emanating.

"*Non.*"

I tried to slip my arm under my chest so I could reach in but wound up making a pocket for him to do the same. He got ahold of the bag; I pressed down. The sound of tearing beneath me brought encouragement as I sought to prevail in our battle.

"You will mess your hair, *ma chérie.* Please let go."

"That was low. Do you think I give a damn about my hair? I should be going to this thing as the Queen of the undead, but instead I'm dressed up like some French member of high society." I pressed to the floor with all my might, and tried to shift my weight, but he was too forceful. I couldn't budge.

"Do you mock me with this?"

"Gérard, I'm lying on the floor smushed by you. Why? Because you don't want me to have what you bought for me. I am fighting you because I obviously want it, not because I'm mocking you, damn it. You really put some thought behind this. That means more than the stupid bag."

"I see." His pressure lightened.

I paused to rethink what I was going to say, because I was a little beyond happy about our situation. "I figured I'd be going as something of yours. Queen of the undead is not an insult. Jesus, haven't I told you I was a vampire fanatic before I met you? Do you think I was kidding? Ever seen the movie *Blessed be the Damned*?"

"As I said, our damnation is yet to be determined."

"I did not call you damned. The whole idea of a vampire in many books is that they are damned. Some of the books don't. So, it's not like a given. Besides," I yelled at him, "I'm talking about fiction! Now let me have the bag!"

He rolled off and stood.

I struggled like a person stuck in a barrel until he grabbed my waist and stood me up like a life-sized doll. Now, I was not going to let him get away with a win by guilt. I took the box from the bag and let the torn wrapping paper fall.

He watched, expressionless. It was like fear, worry, sorrow, and so many other emotions filled his eyes in one moment, and then nothing.

The box was no bigger than a cereal box and had mint green tissue paper inside. There was a gold ribbon that peeked out. I unwrapped the tissue paper and revealed a set of intricate wings. They were about eight inches or so long until I unfolded them. The ribbons to attach them were pale gold satin, and the material on the inside of the wire frame matched. There were gold glittering swirls decorating each. And holding the two sides together was a gold lace dragon.

"They're beautiful," I breathed.

"*Vraiment*? You like them?"

"Yes! Why did you think I wouldn't? Seriously, why?" It made no sense at all.

"I did not wish to make this more real for you." He was serious; the corners of his mouth frowned hard.

"More real? Michel almost killed me, and you were worried about a pair of fake wings?" I couldn't help it but come on.

"True."

"Can you tie them on me?"

"*Mais oui*, I would be honored." He took them gently and tied them on loops I hadn't known were on the back of the corset. "Come." We went to the mirror, and I saw for the first time what we looked like. "Queen of the undead, *non*. Mistress to the guardians, *absolument*. This night we celebrate many things."

There were two white roses on the vanity. He took one and handed it to me almost in ceremony. The other he tucked in his vest.

"You're a hopeless romantic."

"Sometimes."

Well, huh. "So, what else is this party about? Or is that a surprise too?"

"Let us go to the den. I believe the chairs will be of greater comfort for you." Gee, after all this time, he finally noticed.

"Thanks, but you're avoiding my question."

He led me out of the bathroom, through the bedroom, and paused at the door to smile. His mask was in place, which made it hard to read his eyes. It was disturbing because I was used to them giving me clues.

I took his hand, brought it to my lips, and bit him.

CHAPTER 43

I sat in the chair, staring at the fireplace. The fire roared, and the heat felt good on my bare shoulders. I couldn't sit back because of the wings, but I didn't want to say anything. My stomach growled; I refrained from looking at Gérard.

Doug stood by the stairway dressed in a long black overcoat, a white button-up ruffled blouse under a black vest, and black pants with a gold stripe. His hair was loose, though pinned by the ties of his mask. The mask itself was black satin with gold sequins around the edges. Although the costume was simple, it complemented him quite well—and me. Sigh.

Why did that bother me? My insides should have done cartwheels, but instead nauseated me.

"You must eat before tonight, love. You're one of the main attractions and won't get much of a chance to fill on hors d'oeuvres." He turned and darted up the stairs. Within the stairwell he called, "Ay."

I wondered why.

"You are hungry, *ma chérie.* Do you want something special this night?"

I shook my head, "No." But I remembered how, when I was in high school, I used to go to Brady's Tavern every time there was a school dance. I would order a bacon double cheeseburger with pickles and ketchup, and a chocolate shake. Come to think of it, I didn't know if the menu still offered the bacon double cheeseburger.

"You were smiling. Please share those thoughts with me, *ma chérie,* it is rare to see you smile."

Smiling. That word conjured images that, as of late, had less than pleasant people and circumstances to appreciate. The playful smiles I'd had with Tiny and Gale, Dani and Dawn, had given way to pity smiles and awkward grins. The way Gérard smiled with or without fangs, or the way Guillaume smiled in a cunning, dick-ish way, no longer mattered. In fact, smiling was not representative of how I felt. I was not happy. I wasn't sad, nor angry. I just was.

So why does everyone go around and say, "Smile," when clearly you can be content or happy even though your lips aren't plastered in a bow?

That one statement, "You were smiling," pissed me off. Next would be, "It's nice to see you smile." Or someone will probably say, "You're so pretty when you smile." It's inevitable.

Smiling is overrated.

"Just thinking about something my dad used to do. It was special because we didn't have a lot of money and, but he found a way to make me feel special." Sadness took over and the smile disappeared.

A tear escaped and he handed me a black handkerchief with a gold *GDA* monogram.

"Thanks."

"There are times when we must hold our memories to our hearts, and times when we share." He knelt in front of me and clasped my hands. "Love does not disappear; it becomes part of the memory. Tears are the proof it still exists."

"My mother would have flipped if she'd known I was dating you. I think my father would have taken you hunting, though." I laughed, and it felt good.

"Hunting for what? It would be dark."

"It's an expression. It means he would've threatened your life if you tried to take away his little girl." Another tear escaped, and he caught it. "I'm glad I met you, Gérard."

"*Moi aussi, ma chérie, moi aussi.* Come, welcome our guests." He stood and pulled me with him.

We trekked up the stairs hand in hand until I started to lag behind.

The hoop slowed me down and I had to hold it up in the front. I kept stepping on the dress.

Gérard moved behind me, grabbed my waist with both hands. A small squeaky scream escaped my lips, which caused him to laugh in triumph. He carried me all the way up the stairs like a child with a soiled diaper. It wasn't romantic, but he didn't have to wait around for me.

"You could have gone ahead without me. I'd have managed."

"*De rien*. Let us meet our guest." He set me down at the top of the stairs and put his arm out for me to hold. I always hated walking that way. No real reason, I simply didn't like it, but it was worse because of the dress, and I was still sore. The stitches pulled tight.

We walked at a brisk pace. I had to let go of him to stop. "You are not the one wearing this stuff, and besides, you don't even have to walk. Can you please just—" I almost said, "be human," but I caught myself.

"Just what?"

"Slow down for me."

"That was not what you were going to say, but it was a valiant effort."

I was trying to catch my breath and keep some dignity. I could run marathons and it would seem like I never exercised next to him. There were perks to not having to breathe. "I'm nervous."

I stopped and tried to sit on the floor. Sitting with the hoop did not work the way I'd hoped. I ended up on my back with my arms flailing since I hadn't expected to fall over. My skirt ended up in my face and over I went. It would be a miracle if the dress lasted to the end of the evening.

Gérard stood over me, his eyes ablaze in blue. "You certainly have an odd way of being subtle, *ma chérie*. Although you are lovely, some of your predicaments are of your own doing, *comme* ça."

"I know, but I hate this. It's awful." I struggled to get up and rolled to my stomach. After pushing back with my hands, I was able to bring myself upright. Oh, the indignity. I had to fix my dress over the hoop because it was all which ways and Doug was coming toward us with his guest.

It was a woman in a large, hooped dress as well. Her hair was adorned with cream and brown barred feathers that matched her mask, which was bronze with gold sequins. Her dress was all white. The bodice covered with bronze sequins and creamy pearls; additional feathers trimmed the bottom of her dress.

"Want some help, love?" Doug hurried over while Gérard stood and watched. I thought he was annoyed at my behavior, but I didn't give a damn. I wanted the night to either be over or, better yet not happen.

Gérard straightened my wings, took my arm, and played the leader on our way to the dining room. "And how is our guest this evening?" He glanced back over his shoulder.

She nodded and smiled politely. She was stark white next to Doug, too dramatic. I had thought it was rude that they didn't introduce us, but I had no interest in making her acquaintance.

We entered the dining room; the table had a new floral arrangement. There were blue and white roses on topiaries that towered over the silver trays. The food had been set at three place settings while a single goblet of blood waited for Gérard.

I lumbered to my chair. Gérard pushed me in. Doug did the same for our guest. I glared at her whiteness and those feathers. Then it hit me. "Gale?" I whispered.

"It took you long enough," she teased and hurried around to hug me.

I tried getting up but got stuck in the arms of the chair. It made both her and Doug laugh all the more. She squeezed me tight.

"I held your limp body at Michel's. I thought you were gone." I squeezed her back.

"You're being there helped so much. I can't tell you how good it felt to be free from them when you took me. I couldn't change 'cause they'd have done worse. Oh, Summer. Look at you." She blotted her tears and smiled down to Gérard. "You've outdone yourself once again. The costumes are wonderful."

"Sit, eat. You need your strength." I'd forgotten they brought her there in the first place, and hoped she wouldn't ever find out.

"I'm fine. Besides, they don't cook like you." She lifted her mask. "Oh, I have to look at you without this thing in my way."

"I'm still the same," I said.

"Oh, but all dolled up, you're a sight for sore eyes. And what's this I hear about you and Gérard? Is it true? You accepted the third?" She pressed her hand to my neck.

"We are making the announcement this night. It is truly a celebration." Gérard's voice flowed around us while he spoke. But in my mind, he whispered. *You understand that you are a representative of my position. The visitors will expect a certain amount of respect and hold high expectations for those whom I choose and those—who serve me.*

"Nice choice of words." I lost my appetite.

Your wit has no place this evening. I will introduce you as mine. The respect and expectations of your etiquette and poise will be all that much higher. You must not wobble around in that dress.

Then horror hit, *Does Gale know about Dani yet?*

He nodded affirmatively, although discreet. I didn't think he wanted her to think of it tonight.

Was it Sam?

He nodded again.

"It seems we have guests and visitors arriving. Feel up to it, love?" Doug gave a half-smile and arched his brow. He wasn't himself. He turned to acknowledge the dark figure approaching from the courtyard.

The figure in the shadows came to the light and was dressed in a silver tuxedo with a silver mask adorned with white and silver feathers. He was on the short side, and bald.

"Is that Tiny?" Embittered shock tore through me; that dark place inside of me started to swell. I trembled, but Gérard appeared at my side and grabbed my wrist. He calmed my nerves, and that dark place closed. I knew it was there, waiting. I hadn't known he could do that.

"What the hell happened?" Tiny was at Gale's side. I hadn't seen him come over.

"Summer's found her power." Gale told him.

"Actually, she found it with Patricia. She could have killed her." Doug informed, all the while eyeing Gérard. "She helped us get Michel."

"You have him here?" Tiny gasped. "What of Guillaume?"

"He fled." Doug looked down to me.

"What the hell are you looking at me for?" I couldn't contain myself any longer. "I didn't do anything." Gérard grabbed my arm again, but I was so angry a sharp pain went shooting through my body. He let go.

"*Ma chérie*, look at me. Look at me!" He was yelling, but his voice was hollow. I couldn't understand what he was saying.

Doug's eyes were like small, encapsulated suns. Tiny held onto Gale. Another figure emerged from the hallway; it was Patricia.

"What's the matter with her now?" I heard her, but it was like listening under water. The swishing in my ears deafened me.

I tried to speak; nothing happened. I was deaf and mute in one fell swoop. I gasped, unable to breathe, and wound up choking myself. I tried to think into Gérard but couldn't. The more I tried, the more I needed my voice. There was something wrong inside of me. I felt it in my gut.

The darkness opened and crept over my whole being. There was no love and light, and all things faerie. No, I was afraid and angry, Unseelie. I started to cry, and blood trickled from one of Tiny's nostrils.

Doug took off toward the doors of the courtyard. I couldn't let him run from me. I had to tell him it was okay; I wouldn't hurt him. It wasn't like it was with Patricia or Michel. He was mine. *Mine?* I tried to speak; instead, a wash of warmth spread across my skin and followed my eyes. Doug tripped and fell against the doors. The glass didn't break, but he landed hard.

Gérard whispered something to me and tried to kiss my forehead. I felt him like a force pushing against that feeling, but the darkness liked being free. The power was unleashed, and it felt good. I could be afraid and those who hurt me would pay. I thought about Guillaume and what he'd done. I thought about how much I hated him. The thought of him luring my sister made me angrier. And then I thought about Tiny standing right there.

"How dare he?" I growled. It sounded possessed, even to me.

Rage engulfed me; darkness melted over my skin. The calm released the anger and fear. Distant voices broke through. I heard them—all of them. But the visitors were already here. *Who were they?* It was as if my power had called to them. There were hundreds of them coming through the woods, their cries—ghostly whispers.

A hand touched one of the curled locks of my hair, and someone squatted on the other side of my chair. I tried to see them; everything was clouded and distorted. Gérard stared at me; the darkness cowered.

This time, I was afraid of him.

CHAPTER 44

"Mom?" My mother's face appeared at my side. Her placid hair and unpolished emerald eyes brought the vision from my youth to the forefront. I screamed because I wanted the vision to end. I thought it was Tiny's witchcraft. The image in front of me was blurred. I could have sworn it was Tiny. "Bastard!" I yelled.

A cool hand cupped my cheek. "My sweet, Summer. Open your mind." I did, and my vision came back to the room. My hearing focused on what was present rather than all the sounds of the visitors and guests. I realized I was still in my chair. I turned my head mechanical, slow. The most beautiful green-eyed man stood before me.

"Daddy?" I whispered.

He smiled and hugged me to him. My mother knelt beside him. She had taken Gérard's spot at my side and squeezed. They kissed and hugged me until I couldn't breathe. "Is this real?" I asked no one in particular.

"Yes, my Summer, yes!" My mother wept and squeezed my neck with the strength of ten men.

"It was too hard. We never had a chance to do it our way." My father wept.

"You've grown up." They said in unison and laughed through their tears.

"How do you know them?" I glanced back at the line of onlookers.

"We are oathed to Gérard. He and Doug are your guardians. Gale and Tiny are old friends," my father explained.

Anger peaked around the edges at the thought that everyone knew but me. I looked straight at Gale and Tiny. "You all knew where they were?"

"It wasn't like we left because we wanted to. We didn't have a choice. We could never have expected what events unfolded." My father's voice had evened out.

"Gale, you didn't tell me. Why?" I was crying. Tears burned with defeat.

"I didn't know where they were or if they were alive, hon. I tried to find them, so did Tiny." She wrung her hands. "We went to the Sidhe; none of them knew either."

"Gérard, since you know so much, why didn't you find them?" I had an instant hatred toward him.

"But he did, honey." My mother spoke and my father stood.

"When? How?" I couldn't understand why he wouldn't tell me. "What aren't you telling me?"

"*Ma chérie*, the crocottas were most helpful the other evening, at the house of *Michel*. It is where we found your parents. It was your power that enabled me to find them." He paused and small blue flames flickered in his eyes. "I told you there were many reasons to celebrate this night."

"Why not tell me then? I would have wanted to know right away. You all withheld the most important moment in my life from me."

"When you were near death?" Doug's voice was harsh. "You really have no idea how close you were. Gérard saved your life. He found your parents and ordered us to get them while he tended to you. He hasn't even slept. He's used his energy to stay awake during daylight to get you through this."

"Douglas, enough." Gérard's voice echoed through the room.

"No! I will not let her do this." Doug was angry; his eyes were consumed by citrine flames. "She is ungrateful and spoiled. You have given her everything, and she uses you. She is no different than Marie." His voice growled low.

"*Non!*" Gérard's voice caused the hairs on the back of my neck to stand.

"Boys, this is a happy time. Don't spoil it." Gale used her motherly tone, but it was rising. I'd never heard her raise her voice. It wasn't pleasant.

"No! Damn it. What happened the last time? What makes you think this is any different? I spent twenty-eight years waiting to live my life again. Gérard wanted to die. What do you think happens to me if he does? I'm his second. I'm marked, I have the fourth; I'll die. He can't go through that pain again. Damn it, Gérard. Don't you see? She's afraid; she vilifies us. We were wrong." The urgency in Doug's voice frightened me.

Gérard's face stayed blank. His eyes were consumed by the blue and his hair stirred, a soft breeze encircled him. His strawberry pink lips paled.

"Doug, I have been with her, so has Gale. You're jumping to conclusions." Tiny reassured. Not that I wasn't grateful, but I had a big ole 'fuck you' waiting for him.

"Yeah, well, if it wasn't for her, Michel wouldn't have a reason to—"

"*Non!*" Gérard's voice thundered.

Gale put her hands on Doug's shoulders. "I can't let you talk about her that way. You know bloody well she's different. You watched her and thought she was a good match. Before you brought her here, we discussed this. We all agreed to guard her, but even you cannot deny that there is more. Marie didn't have any gifts, she offered nothing," Gale hissed. "Summer made him a man again. And dare I say the same for you."

"It is true. He was angry and hurt after Marie, then Ragnvaldr. It felt like an eternity when he closed himself from the rest of us." Patricia was talking like a person. I didn't know she had it in her. "But perhaps Doug has a point. Perhaps obligation influenced many decisions. But our master is back, as is his second. They are both men again."

I wanted to disappear but had to take part of this discussion; it was me they were talking about. "Excuse me. Can I say something here?"

"Why not? But it is in vain, you speak." Doug was beyond angry. He glared at Gérard and refused to look at me.

"You're right, it was ungrateful of me to question this; I understand it was a surprise of sorts—good intentions and all. But of all the people here, you and you alone know me. Do you truly believe I'm that bad of a person?" He didn't answer. I treaded cautiously because I had no idea what was going through Gérard's head. "I'd hardly call myself spoiled. If anything, I was betrayed by each and every one of you. But you're the one that hurts most, because you were there during my darkest times. I hate that you witnessed a time of my life I'd rather forget. I hate that you know what I never wanted anyone to know, and I hate that I feel humiliated every time I face you." His shoulders lost their poise. "Right now, I hate you, Doug. I'm not happy with a single person here, but I can't stand you right now. And do you know why?"

"Why?" he whispered.

"Because I don't know how to live without you."

He said nothing.

"Why'd you do it, Doug?" He still stood there. "Why, damn you?"

"Perhaps, because I liked you."

Gérard turned to Doug and grabbed his shoulders. "*Mon ami*, you have said enough. Your concerns are valid, *mais*, I am not a fool. Do you question my judgment?"

"Ay, I do." Doug stood right up to him.

"*Pour quoi?*" Gérard leaned closer, his eyes damp with pink wetness.

I should have screamed at Doug and told him he was wrong, but I couldn't. I know what he meant. I was a big girl and had to live with my actions. "I understand." It was all I could say.

"You do?" Everyone looked so puzzled.

"Well, yeah. I had to have Gérard come to my rescue because

I couldn't save myself. It was convenient to be able to call him. He healed me with his marks; he offers me a place to live, clothes I could never afford. He gives me whatever I want, and things I don't realize I want until he gives them to me. Spoiled? Yeah, I'd agree with that, but I am not Marie." After I spoke, I realized what our relationship looked like to everyone else. "Either way, I think you need to remember what we did together. Yeah, I took your ability to heal me. I even thought about having you heal me after I'd been bitten because I hurt. Does that mean I use you too? Maybe, but I don't know what I can give either of you that would equal what you do."

Doug shifted his weight, Gérard glanced at him. I saw Gale and Tiny nod, which made my heart sink. I hoped they weren't in agreement with Doug after I painted such a lovely picture of myself. My parents stood behind me before I spoke but were now by the courtyard windows.

"What she did do, was bring him to us again." Patricia spoke softly. "He mourned, and we'll leave it at that. Perhaps at a later time we may discuss what truly sours his heart. But for now, Summer is better off with it left unsaid." She turned and walked to my parents.

"What's going on in here?" Kitty came through the entrance from the hall. She wore a hunter green evening gown with a cat mask to match. The whiskers were gold, and there were green sequins around the edges. "The visitors are trickling in." She rubbed her arms. "Keep the power levels down, please. They're gonna get suspicious." She turned and walked out.

"I want you to share my memories with Doug. Please, Gérard, just do it."

"No, I don't want to see them. And believe it or not, some things are not about you." Doug's hostility burned along my skin. He turned and left the room in a blur, which made me cry again.

"Summer, Doug had to pick up the pieces after many regretful events. He is the glue, he's always there, and would be the hand to the king, so to speak. He is more than Gérard's friend, and much more than a servant." Tiny was trying to help but made me feel worse. He kissed the back of my hand. "You look beautiful; I look forward to dancing with you." He took Gale's arm and walked after Doug. It was hard to see him as the monster I knew he was.

"Please go. We will soon make our entrance." Gérard spoke at my parents and Patricia. My parents walked away and kissed me on my cheeks as they passed to the hallway.

"Don't make Doug right, Gérard. Prove him wrong." Patricia called without looking back. Her voice had an edge of urgency to it.

"Well, it would seem that I have made a mess of things. Once again." I felt awful.

Gérard interrupted me. He spoke, but his words didn't match his eyes. "I know who you are, and that is all that matters."

"I think you need to tell the truth. I can see it in your face. You doubt me. I either have to accept Doug or this whole thing is screwed." The reality of it hit me as I spoke.

"*Je ne comprends pas.* I do not understand what you are saying." He squinted at me.

"If Doug doesn't like me for whatever reason, I won't be able to have a relationship with you. I'll hurt your power base." I stared at the floor, wishing I could take back what I said.

"I decide who and what I want." He lifted my chin. "I do not want to share what we do with him because it is private."

"But he doesn't want or trust me."

"He trusts no one. Doug wants you as badly as I, but he cannot have you in the same." Gérard looked out at the courtyard and spoke as if he were talking to someone else. "Douglas and Patricia spoke of what you know not. It is for another time, but their concerns are valid. My judgment is questioned and the reason Aldatmak seeks my removal from the regime. My position remained dormant for twenty-eight years—it is where I erred. Douglas had said it is not always about you, and on this I must agree." He let his voice trail off.

"Are you going to die?" The thought shocked me.

"He did not see the reaction you had with *Michel* after you saw

Sam attack him. He does not know how you feel about him or what you do for me. Although it may be small in comparison with my powers, it is great because there are no tricks, as you say. I give you time, *ma chérie*, because, like it or not, you are marked. Neither of you can make that go away."

I stepped up to his face, our noses touching. "Answer the fucking question, Gérard."

He turned away.

I grabbed his shoulder and turned him. Either he let me, or I was stronger somehow, because he went back against the glass.

"It's the executioner thing, isn't it?"

He smiled and his face lit up. His eyes had gone midnight blue with the faintest swirl.

He reached for my hand; I tugged on the skirt, and I kissed the back of his hand and breathed in the scent of him. Cinnamon, vetiver, and juniper made my heart leap. I let go. He took my hand back and sent that tingling power through me. He made all my fears fade and brought a hint of pleasure to those hidden places within. Not enough to do anything, but heightened my awareness of them.

"Do you have to do that? Especially when we are going into a room full of people?" I bit my lip.

"Do what?" He smiled and flashed his fangs. "That was all you. I merely took away your fears." The redness burned; I hid against his shoulder. "That is your reaction to me. Not power. Not money. Me." He smiled and pulled my hand to his lips. "This is me." He sent a quick wave of pleasure through that threatened but merely stayed at a constant level of promise.

He pulled me to him, and I knew he was happy to be there. "Oh!" My cheeks were to be red for the evening. It was that lingering effect embarrassment had when it was unexpected and prolonged.

He laughed deep and manly and lowered his face to mine, catching my eyes. "It's time." He kissed me quick and pulled me after him.

We made a pit stop at the table so he could gulp down his blood, and we were off. I'd like to say to the races, but this was no horse race.

As we rounded the corner in the hall, I could hear voices and music, a harpsichord, and strings.

"Ready?" Before I could answer, we walked arm in arm through the doors of the ballroom. I pulled him to a stop. The memories of our dinner party flashed before me, and I was nervous. My hands trembled and then he thought to me, *Smile.*

CHAPTER 45

The Grand Ballroom walls were covered with large drapes of black, gold, and white. The floor was black marble, and above us was a mural with a red dragon falling to his death from the sky. The ground was a circle of snow-capped purple mountains with hundreds of white wisps coming from a hidden lake. The chandelier hung from that same center and was constructed of Austrian Crystal bars layered over gold leaves.

"It's the Legend of Lake Sangre!" I gasped.

The room fell silent of music, laughter, and voices. There were people along the walls and seated at large, round tables. A bar at the far end was crowded, but not a sound was muttered. The faces were all masked. Hooked noses, feather plumes, and sequined eyes pointed toward us—more at me than him.

Gérard pulled me with him to stand beneath the grand chandelier. I looked at him in hopes that he would read my mind and ease my nerves. He placed his hand on my waist and used his other hand to take mine. *Dance!*

I reacted by placing my hand on his shoulder, and the music began.

We stepped side to side and turned slow, in time to the music. The entire time, he used his power to keep my eyes steady with his. If he hadn't, I would have let them drop. I had trouble looking into anyone's eyes, let alone Gérard's. Except when I was pissed.

The music stopped and so did my focus. The heat had risen up my neck and I knew I was blushing. I clasped my hands in front of me and studied the floor. Gérard started his speech. I tried not to make more of a spectacle of myself than was necessary.

"Welcome, all. It is a true blessed Samhain. We are gathered here tonight to celebrate seven hundred years on the mount, but it is also a significant occasion for our territory. I am pleased to announce the increase of our domain to include Eastern Canada." The crowd applauded with numerous cheers. "I announce the addition of the crocottas to our lycanthrope community. Their oathing to take place before the Winter Solstice." There was thunderous foot stomping, applause, and hollering. "Finally, I announce acceptance of the third by Ms. Summer Candella, daughter of Faoltiarna, Keeper of Wolves, Ragnvaldr, Elder of Ljosálfar, and Augusto Candella, our resident Bard."

He raised my left hand in his right and turned us around for all to see. The applause, whistles, hoots, catcalls, stomping—it all whirled through my head. He brought my hand to his lips and brushed it with a kiss that sent a tingling through my body. There was no pleasure, but it brought my attention back to him, and I heard him echo in my mind, *Curtsy, please.*

He did a small bow and pulled me down into a curtsy as the response increased and the cheering grew. "*Merci, tout.* Let the celebration commence!" He put his arm around my waist and escorted me to the bar.

"*Champagne.*" He told the bartender and winked at me. "You need it." I could tell he was happy with the crowd's reaction. After all, there had to be several hundred people.

"I'll be drunk," I protested.

"Drink." He handed the glass to me. I did. I was a quarter way through when it hit me and I relaxed, a little. "Better?"

I'm the daughter of the Keeper of Wolves? I thought.

He took the glass from me and set it on the bar. "I want to introduce you to an old friend."

"Gérard," I hissed.

Would you rather I had said we were engaged?

"What?"

He winked, put my hand on his arm and guided me toward a stout man in a black tux and mask with no decorations. He was about my height, with graying hair in a standard businessman's cut. "Ah, Ms. Candella. Gérard, such luck to acquire a creature so fine." He clasped my hand and bowed, low—deep.

"*C'est* Bobby. He is Master of the Pacific Coast." Bobby kissed my hand; his eyes flickered black. He seemed confused.

"She is marked by blood, old friend," Gérard said.

"Is he a bad one?" I whispered.

"Everyone can hear you, *ma chérie*. There is no need to whisper tonight." He raised his brow, nodding to the room. "Bobby is vampire, and master for a hundred twelve years?"

"A hundred and thirteen, sir," Bobby corrected and offered a small bow of submission.

It reminded me of when the English royals were greeted on TV. Everyone acted that way. It made no sense. I'd be damned if I'd bow. After all the shit I'd been through, they could bow to me.

"Bobby is vying for a vacancy at the regime's Dublin Headquarters."

"Where's your date, lady?" A welcome voice chimed up to me.

"Dawn?" I threw my arms around her and squeezed. It seemed like we hadn't spoken in ages.

"Well, look at you. Guess someone's made an impact on your wardrobe. I know you didn't pick that."

"Nope." I'd forgotten my breasts were hanging half-out. No wonder he liked the dress.

Gérard and Bobby continued on about politics and left for the bar.

"I told you to give him a chance, see?" Her eyes sparkled, delighted.

"Yeah, but you didn't tell me you're a real witch!"

"It isn't something you advertise to people who don't even know about us."

Gérard was back at my side. "Maybe I was a little closed-minded on some things."

"You think?" She smiled, and Tiny pulled her away.

Gérard directed me from couple to couple, person to person. Most of them kissed my hand and said pretty much the same thing, until we encountered a tall guest dressed in a silver gown with a deep purple corset. The piece was formfitting, keeping the sequins and black embroidered swirls from distorting the exotic façade. They had a matching feather mask. Their hair was blond and flowed below their hips in silken waves. The bangs were kept aside by the accenting purple feather. When it kissed my hand, I felt a shock. There was power there, but not like Gérard's.

Their eyes met mine, inviting, familiar; it annoyed me. I tried to think into Gérard how I felt, but he was blocking me because of all the power in the room. It was thick, like cotton stuck on my tongue. He didn't let go of my hand, which made me wonder if he was keeping mine at bay.

"Welcome, *ma chou*. This is Summer." He kissed the milk white cheeks. I didn't like it.

"And you are?" I asked.

The guest bowed their head. "A friend."

Gérard lifted her hand and peered through his bangs. I don't think he thought the same as I. He made eye contact with the masked face; it turned away, stifling a laugh. I really didn't like secrets. He held the guest's hand a tad too long. I squeezed his other one.

"Gérard, may I get a drink?" I tried to break free of him, but he didn't let go.

"*Oui, ma chérie*." He turned back to the ivory locks and bowed. "Excuse us."

He led me to one of the wait staff. "What would you have?"

"Ice water," I sneered.

"One red and *un eau*." He told the waiter while glancing around like he expected something—or someone. "*Ma chérie*, we must dance." He pulled me into him, and we started to dance as before, but his focus was elsewhere. I tried to find what he was looking for, but I didn't have time.

"May I have this dance?" My father came up behind me.

"Of course, *Monsieur* Candella." Gérard offered my hand to him, and my father whisked me off, waltzing.

"It hurts knowing what I've missed, but I'm glad to be here now." He kissed the top of my head and tears brimmed. I missed his Welsh accent.

"I missed you too, Dad." I laid my head against his shoulder, familiar but somehow changed.

My mother approached, smiling. "May I cut in?"

"I suppose you can have him." I backed away, smiling. It was good to see the two of them together. Doug was right. They were back. That's all that mattered.

"Dance with me." Tiny appeared next to me with his hand outstretched.

"I—I don't know." I did not want to dance with him. I didn't trust him because—well, obvious reasons. He wasn't the person I worked for anymore, he was someone I barely knew. I him-hawed, but figured Gérard was there.

"Come on, kid. Don't hold this stuff against me."

"You knew I was there."

"We all have secrets, even your precious new friends. I promise, by the end of tonight, you'll feel better. Come dance." He took my hand by the fingers, and tugged me in to whisper, "I never let anyone get in my way. I killed my son because no one will take my place. Sam took care of Gale's meddling daughter because a position like hers gave you a chance. Without a channel, the legend dies. Now, put on a smile and fucking dance. And if you even think about what you know, I'll kill you before Samhain's end."

I smiled as we began a box-step. I was stiff; it was awkward. We danced for a bit when someone else cut in. Before long, there was a line waiting to partner with me—all unknown faces.

I danced with each and realized I hadn't danced with Doug. *Shit.* I hadn't seen either of them at all. They were gone. Convenient.

Bobby stepped up, but I curtseyed instead of taking his hand and wormed my way to the bar. There was no use saying I had to go to the lady's room or something because he could tell if I lied. I didn't like him.

I couldn't sit well, so I leaned against the rail. I surveyed the room but couldn't spot them. Instead, I saw the exotic guest. Of course, they caught me looking and headed straight for me. I thought better of running and waited. Damn.

"Ms. Candella. What luck to find you alone."

"Yeah." The stranger's flowing hair captivated me. It calmed my heart's erratic beating, wrapping me in a nostalgic blanket of warmth.

"Why would you give up such fine gentlemen? Any girl would die to be in your shoes." They nodded at the gentlemen, still waiting.

"I don't like the attention, I guess." I contemplated asking if it was human, but it was rude—even for me. "Is it rude to ask what you are?" Oh, well.

"Can you not tell? Guess."

"Ok, a vampire?"

"No, try again." Two white pointed ears parted the furlike hair.

"A lycan?" The guest shook its head. "A faerie?"

"Oh, so close. Come, I'll show you." The guest's white slender fingers grabbed my hand. I jerked away.

"Where?"

"Away from all this noise and sedition. Don't you find it overwhelming?" The voice's tone lowered.

I figured stepping into the hallway should be okay. I nodded in agreement.

"It's beautiful tonight, let's go outside. The air is sweet; crisp." It assumed I would be okay with it, and we went.

"So, like, what do you do?" I hated small talk with people I didn't like.

"This and that. No one particular occupation, though I have my favorites."

"I see." Actually, I didn't. We entered the courtyard, void of pulsing power and inquisitive guests. We were alone. The long hair wrapped around the silver gown, flowing in the breeze. I lingered by the doors, but the guest kept walking to the dogwood. "Are you a performer?"

"Sometimes. Come. Have you seen the fountain? It's her." They glanced around before settling on the bench by the fountain.

"Huh." I hadn't realized the woman in the fountain was part of the legend. She was the one who was prophesied to lay the souls to rest. The whole mansion held scenes from the legend.

"Do you know why we are here?" The voice became full masculine. He cocked his head to the side and blinked at me with a soft smile contorting his lips.

"Not really."

"Halloween, silly." He laughed, the kind that let you know the ice was broken, and then I recognized him from too many late nights at Brady's. "It's me, Liam."

"Oh." I lifted the hooped skirt and sat next to him. "Seriously, you have ears? They go really well with you." What the hell was I saying? "Gérard said the courtyard's off limits. We really shouldn't be here."

"Mmm, it is also the Witch's New Year—the Samhain. But you know that." He looked up at the sky.

"Maybe."

"It's the moment when the barriers of time come down and the boundaries between worldly planes may be crossed—visions and celebrations—letting go of the old, welcoming the new."

"So, you're a witch?"

His face studied mine. Black eyelashes poked out of the eyeholes of the mask when he blinked. "Honestly, patience really is a virtue." The chiding demeanor was gone. He reached up, untied his mask, and the corset fell to the ground on its own. The gown was a robe that covered the majority of the ivory chest.

"I've heard that before."

"You, Summer, are the last of the Álfar bloodline." He patted my thigh. "The clan was slaughtered after the wrath of the Red Terror. They were Álfar-Sidhe, but with one specific task to their daughters' claim—keeping the dragons."

"That's actually kinda cool."

"Not as romantic as it sounds. You met with Molly; she was Sidhe. They always come in procession for the Samhain. Tomorrow they will leave. Your mother was Unseelie, but still Sidhe. Your father's blood was stronger."

"So, what can I do?"

"Summer, you are complex, as were all keepers. They were sired by an Álfar Elder of the Norse and borne from a Sidhe Elder of the Celts. The daughters were bred to protect the dragons of Midgard, and ease death's passage."

I looked into the amethyst eyes with natural black outlines and lengthy lashes. He was gorgeous. Surreal. "But my father's Druid."

He cocked a dark grey eyebrow. "Not your real father."

I couldn't take it. "What the hell are you saying?"

"Your father was a monarch who organized political relationships and over saw the Alfar's mission—to keep honor and justice no matter the sacrifice."

"And my mom?"

"It truly is Faoltiarna. She is Sidhe of the fey, a noble of faerie. Many of your relatives inhabit the waters, some the forests, some the burrows of the dead. You, see?" He seemed to make perfect sense to himself. I shook my head no, and he continued. "Well, have you noticed anything about yourself? Are you drawn to certain earthly elements? Need I point out that Gérard is, in fact, dead?"

"What?"

"You have, haven't you?" He blinked several times. "Gérard awakened your memories. In doing so, you will understand all on your own. But know that Aldatmak, Tiny, Guillaume, and the rest of them believe that part of you sleeps."

"Wait, they don't want me to remember? Why?"

"Because you have a prophesy to fill."

I recalled Tiny's little conversation on the dance floor and shivered. "Liam, I don't think I'll ever awaken them. Tiny had Dani killed. He said she was the only one who could do it."

He shook his head and pulled his hair into the collar of the robe. "Those called wildmen and wildwomen have been able to bring the different realms together. We roam the forests, oft referred to as dark spirits. Some are mistaken for vampires and simple witches. Some are called yokai. It depends on the country—no, the culture." He faced me straight on and gave a terrific smile in the whole sense of the word. "I'm your key."

"Do you mean to tell me; this is a sort of New Year's party for you and that you bring us all together?" Yay, I was getting it.

"No, Summer." He looked up at the sky again. The moonlight lit the silvery slivers of hair and the amethyst irises that stared, unjudging. "The fantastic part? Ragnvaldr had done this with you, Gérard, and Douglas. The three of you have brought a convergence of the realms. Once you perform as foretold, the convergence will be done. It is unheard of with a hybrid."

"Because Gérard marked Doug and will mark me, the three of us complete like what? What is the significance of this?"

"As dreaded by the regime, your powers will bind the living, the dead, and that which resides between. Only the Sidhe possess the ability to cross realms, the others cannot. Not even the Ljosálfar. They already reside in the land of the dead. Do you not see the magic you possess? You will do what has not been done, at least not documented. Of course, the traditionalists will try to prevent this from happening." Turning his body to the fountain, he stood and raised his face to the moon. "They already have," he laughed, a bitter cackle of sorts. "It's why you are the last of Ragnvaldr's daughters."

"Because they were afraid of what they didn't understand. But Tiny doesn't know that you have the same ability as Dani. That means you need to go. He'll kill you too."

He laughed. "He can try. But I'm more than a shifter, Summer. I'll be there when you need, no need to call. Besides, we're family."

He shifted into a white fox and scampered off to the other end of the courtyard, his robe and mask strewn along the stones. I headed back to the ballroom, trying to register what just happened. When I neared the entrance, I noticed a golden mask on the ground. I bent to pick it up. A white rose was attached to it.

"Summer," someone called from the shadows.

"Whose there?" I knew better, but I had to look closer. There was a dark figure in the corner off from the doors.

"Do you not know me?"

I couldn't think. The dark place inside of me opened; I trembled. "What are you?" The figure was neither man nor anything I recognized.

"Ah, it would be wise to settle your power. You do not need it with me." Its words rushed over the courtyard. "Lake Sangre beckons, the Dragoness."

CHAPTER 46

I clenched the gold face mask and rose in my hand, intrigued by the shadow, and grateful to the fox who was back to being human, and dressed just as he'd been prior to our little conversation. The information he gave me was what I wanted to know for weeks, but I guess timing is everything.

Going inside didn't feel right. I wanted to check out Lake Sangre, but I wanted Gérard to go with me. I would've taken Doug, but his words still stung.

I followed the path through the courtyard to a trellis that hid the crumbed mortar of the retaining wall. I hooked my shoes on my wing straps and slipped off the hoop—leaving it there so I could climb the trellis and get up on the wall. I used my toes to dig in and up I went.

I hated heights, so I toddled along to where the ground rose up outside the grounds. I dropped down from the ledge and landed fairly well. I was glad there was still some fluff under the dress. I put the shoes back on and crept along the wall.

The music inside had turned to background noise; my pulse pounded in my head. I was getting a panic attack because I was alone. I needed company. I hated that I wanted Gérard because it made me think Doug might be right.

Why did I want Gérard so much? Was I really that needy? I'd have settled for Doug right then.

The figure from the courtyard emerged from the stone strewn shore.

"Dragoness, you have come."

"What are you?" I crept toward the voice. I stepped carefully but hadn't known I was so close; the edge of my dress was wet. "What do you want with me?"

The voice whispered and rustled through the surrounding conifer limbs. "You beckoned."

Amber eyes flashed from the overgrown brush. I stepped further into the lake. "Doug?" I called. The eyes faded into the darkened mass of limbs.

The gruff voice returned, tarrying on the waves. "You have the rose. But where is the mask?"

I was mesmerized by the figure though not yet manifested. It wasn't solid, more like a black shadow that had melted over the burgundy water. "I have it."

"*Ma chérie*, this is old magic," Gérard's voice came from behind me, and I slipped into the water. He offered me his hand, but I didn't take it. The water was warm, welcoming. The dark mingled with the mist and flowed toward me.

"Old indeed." Tiny appeared behind Gérard. The guests trailed behind them in a line.

"Traitor!" The voice rumbled as if there were thunder overhead but there were no clouds, no storm.

"What does it mean?" I asked Gérard, but he'd gone still.

"The traitor comes forth." The figure hissed and swirled above the water.

"We're going to the church for Dani's funeral. You should come," Tiny urged.

All the guests traversed up the path. A green light flickered in the windows of the church and smoke escaped from the chimney. Someone had already been up there. Doug's wolf form appeared next to Gérard and scampered off through the woods ahead of the line. Lycanthropes shifted; others chanted. The languages used were foreign to me. I didn't understand what was happening, but I knew Gérard was my safety.

"We must go, *ma chérie*," Gérard agreed.

"Not yet, I want to stay." I was calm and felt good. I didn't know why, nor did I care.

"Here? It is unwise." Gérard peered; blue flames overtook his eyes. "Please, come with us, Summer."

"I'll be up later; I want to stay. I need to." I couldn't explain it, but I belonged there. "Tell me who ordered my death."

"It was the regime, Summer."

"But who hired Guillaume?" I had a moment of terrifying realization. The sinking feeling engulfed me. My power sparked. Pain shot through my chest.

"I must go. Be mindful tonight. The powers that come are immense and you have not yet embraced your own. I will help you as best I am able." Gérard stepped away, hesitated, and flew off. He had to choose between guarding the guests or staying with me. I guess I would've made the same choice. I wasn't scared anymore. I was strong, confident, and balanced.

White lights danced across the water like fireflies, but it was too late in the season for them. I thought they might be the piskies or something. It was nice because I could imagine these things and knew I could be right.

I made my way to a boulder on the shore and leaned against it. My silk hose clung like a second skin. I figured they'd have runs in them from hiking through the woods anyway; I slipped them off. I dipped my toes in the water and splashed to make retreating ripples. I scootched to a smaller partially submerged rock so I could dangle my feet.

The moon was in full view, large and white, as it reflected off of the burgundy water. The reflection danced as if to music I couldn't hear. The waves barely broke when the figure reappeared.

"The powers are strong this night, as Master Gérard has told," the shadowy figure said.

"Apparently."

"Tonight, you cross realms and reach to both the living and the dead."

"And you need me for that?"

"No, I am neither." The voice trailed off.

A faint blue light emerged within the remnant pussy-willows and weeds. "Who's there?"

"I pose no threat. I've come to help."

"Kitty?"

She stepped closer and stopped. She had a white candle and placed it on a flat rock. "Decide where they stand and place them wisely. For what you hold will prove true in life."

"I don't understand."

"Remember, the offerings." She shifted to her fox form and disappeared into the woods. Wait, she was a fox too.

"Where will you place them?" the voice urged.

I put the rose on the right side of the candle and the mask on the left. The flame wavered. I sat back on my rock. What the hell was that supposed to do? "So, which one's the traitor?" I hoped it was Tiny.

"Long ago, I was free." The figure spoke soft and sullen. "I escaped him. The air, the water, the land, it was all free. But it did not last. It never did. That ship arrived, bringing with it those from whom I fled."

"And who was that?" I was interested, but skeptical of everything, both with this figure, and everyone. My own parents were untrustworthy. Doug still had some trust to gain, but was higher on the list than anyone else, even Gale.

"My master—the hunters. Once I had been free in the lands far-off. It was after the grand-seer foretold of death and destruction that forced the Álfar Elders to submit to the regime; defeat led to execution."

"You mean to tell me, that the regime authorized the genocide of the Álfar? Who the fuck are these people?"

"Our keepers were slaughtered. I sought refuge and roamed through England, France, and finally Spain. I met a man. The son of the martyred seer who prophesied the death of the Álfar. He promised eternal freedom and friendship."

"Sounds too good to be true." A lot like my situation.

"He simply wanted my blood in return. The blood was to be given without question, and only to him. At the time, I saw no harm. I unknowingly pledged my allegiance to him. For, what could the blood of a dragon do?" The voice fell silent.

"Dragon?" I almost fell off the rock as I whispered the word back to the figured vapor.

"I am the dragon of Lake Sangre." The voice trailed off into the woods, then silence loomed overhead.

"You're the Red Terror!" I gasped.

"No." That one word moved the smaller unmanaged hairs on my neck. "The traitor gave me that name."

I frowned at him. "You have a flare for the dramatic, don't you? Do you have a name?"

"Yes," he whispered.

"Well, what is it?" I had to go through that with all of them and wondered if it was because they were supernatural or just old.

"Peyron."

"Nice to meet you, Peyron. Please go on. What happened next? I need to know—everything."

"He was friend, as I was his liege. He called and I let him partake of my blood. He had a sword. It was forged for him from the Döckálfar, a small sword, as he was a small man. We went to different lands within different countries. Everywhere we went, death and plague followed." The voice held the sting of deep-rooted sadness.

"The Black Plague?"

"No." The figure rose as the lights from the line of visitors heading to the church neared an end. The church windows reflected an internal firelight, orange, yellow and red. The mount seemed to be aglow.

"I'll have to go soon." I tried to impress the urgency in my voice.

"My master and I would leave each place until we came to a small town off the Nordic Sea. A land he thought promised of riches, for as he brought death, he stole of gold, and currency. The townsfolk were healthy, happy, and prosperous. As he ordered my wrath, I met a powerful man who offered to give me salvation if I fled. He called to his daughters, and they released my binds. I did not know then who or what they were. My master ordered me to give blood once more, but I refused. I was free. I took to the sky and flew over land and sea until I found this place." His voice hushed to a whisper among the rustle of leaves. "I settled upon this land and lived unbound. No master. Only the people of the land who knew not of me and the daughters of Ragnvaldr. We stayed here where I thought I would not be found."

"But you were, I mean. You're here." I felt bad for the shadow, but I knew the story differently. "You killed innocent people, villages, and settlements. Tiny slew you to set their souls free."

"No!" The dragon's voice thundered and echoed through the mount.

"Then tell me. Don't try to scare me, just tell me. Getting angry doesn't fix anything." I was getting an attitude with a dragon spirit. I needed to question my sanity.

"My apologies, Dragoness. I remain humbled in your presence. Tonight, you cross the realm and I am here. For 700 years, I waited for this time to come." The figure whirled around. "As the seer told, the Legend was made. Tonight, I reclaim my honor."

"I really have to get up there." I was impatient now. The lights at the church had turned to a steady white light in the distance; it illuminated the gravestones and mausoleum.

"He killed them, all of the daughters and wives, with the magic of my blood. He brought the masters to see. That man you call Tiny bound me with your kin and the will of the Döckálfar sword to make this lake. The water forever red with our blood." The spirit expatiated. I saw lights that resembled those in the church, in the mausoleum. He must have, too. "Evil reigns within that man. He is not what he seems. He has great magic—evil, dark magic." The figure dove into the water without making a splash.

I pulled my feet out of the water and found them stained crimson.

"My blood," I whispered. The figure was no more. Drums beat on the mount, so I put my shoes on anyway, and ran toward the graveyard.

CHAPTER 47

"Something's wrong, I can feel it." I called back to the dragon spirit. "What do I do?"

"Release me, I will help you. Use your power before death comes once more, for only the elders' daughter may possess a dragon."

"How?"

"Darkness befalls this place, as innocent lives will be lost." The dragon spoke and was no more.

I ran straight up the mountain. I had no problems, even in those ridiculous shoes. As I neared the top, the visitors encircled the mausoleum. There were lights inside and movement. I tried to break the circle, to get through, but the power kept me outside.

I couldn't see Gérard anywhere. Tiny, Gale, Gérard, and Doug were all out of sight. My father and mother were in the middle. They stood back-to-back; their chins bobbed to their chests.

Guillaume carried Dawn toward an altar set up on the steps to the mausoleum. She was bound and gagged. Her screams muffled from a makeshift gag. Her costume had been stripped from her body. She lay pregnant and nude against the hard wooden board. The ropes that held her body tightened as she struggled against them. Her hands and feet were shackled. It was then that I realized she wouldn't have the baby. She was due any day.

Richard was nude as well, bound but not gagged. As he fought, the ropes cut through his skin, his pain rushed over the air. The crowd of visitors cheered. They paraded toward the altar. I knew, but not with my eyes—someone else's. Gérard's maybe?

"Mes amis, we have a visitor on this momentous occasion." A

familiar voice rang above the crowd. Michel stood in full splendor with his white puffy sleeved shirt gaping open. His hair and costume resembled that of Bela Lugosi. He spread his arms. "Summer, come join us." He laughed; the crowd cheered.

"When hell freezes over," I hollered back. I'd never known true hatred until that moment.

"The whore wants to be with her lovers." Guillaume stood at the entrance of the church. "Would our friends keep her from them?"

"No!" The crowd screamed and howled.

"Dragon, how?" I whispered as softly as I could.

Tiny emerged from the mausoleum with a smile as wide as his face. Now I knew where Gérard was, and I remembered that Doug was in wolf form.

"I spoke with an old friend tonight. He wanted me to say 'hi', next time I saw you." I was stalling.

"Ah, the sassy Álfar air flows across your tongue like the sweetest nectar. Oh, how I've missed it," Michel said, his voice carried down the mount like a cool breeze.

The vampire Bobby stepped out from behind him. "Isn't anyone going to tell her that she doesn't belong? That he's not supposed to have her. Doesn't she question who killed her kin?"

Michel laughed. "You naughty, boy. Perhaps she will have more reservations about where she makes her bed. But that is for another day." He whispered over the cool grass, "If he lives."

"Summer, your naiveté has turned to ignorance. You dare believe he is the one to protect you. Did Guillaume not warn you? And now, you belong to him. Now you are marked and lost to us all," Tiny called.

"Fuck you," I yelled up to him.

He laughed. "Such petty words. I commanded the massacres of Europe, Asia, and the eastern mountains of North America. I alone caught the Red Terror, and I alone brought reason to the regime to rid the Álfar of their ill-begotten daughters. I bound the last beast; if freed, his allegiance is pledged to me."

"You're a murderer," I hissed.

Michel chuckled. "No, my dear, Gérard is the murderer. He executed all the Álfar and their children. That is, except one. Guess who?"

"What?" I dropped to my knees.

"As Guillaume and Aldatmak serve on the regime, Bobby and countless others have come to understand our President's assailable ways. I clearly stand before each and every denizen and proclaim that I will undoubtedly preserve our kind, monsters and men akin, free to embrace our terror, heedless of shadows. Our people will live among the regulars. And if that brings collapse to the regime, our existence will flourish. For centuries regulars hunted us, still the regime dictated our fate. I say it is time for change."

Tiny stepped up, his hand clasped Michel's and raised it skyward. "Raise your hands to the rightful Master of the Northeastern Territories, Michel D'Aldatmak."

The circle clapped, slow and rhythmic. One by one, they began to whistle and cheer.

How the hell was I supposed to take that? I figured it was a threat to kill Gérard, and let it be the focus for my fear, but that darkness wouldn't come. The pit wouldn't fucking open.

Liam appeared at my side; his long white hair brushed over me. His almond-shaped eyes filled with amethyst light and the darkness within me came to life. The power burst forth like a rush of water and poured like a river overflowing its banks. It poured until it broke the circle and it poured until it knocked Tiny from the entrance of the Mausoleum. I felt the power warm within me. It flowed within my blood, through my hair, and over my skin. I welcomed it. Every scent, every touch, every sensory was alive unlike I'd ever known it could be.

"Grab her," Guillaume called to someone.

I didn't care who was there. I called that power. I made it mine. I welcomed my anger and turned it into a liquid mass. Tiny stood in the middle of the large circle near the mausoleum's steps. I pushed my darkness through the encircled visitors.

Tiny met my eyes and raised a golden dagger for all to see. He was chanting something. I didn't know what it meant, but it called that darkness I'd only learned I had. He was speaking a different language, nothing I'd ever heard. I fought to get to the altar. The people wouldn't part. I had to push through them and meander through the headstones.

All of a sudden, Tiny's voice rose, and the crowd went silent. He grabbed hold of Richard's hair, pulled his head back, and drew the knife across his throat. I screamed and lunged through even more people. The crocottas that had shifted formed a barrier in front of me.

Dawn lay weeping. No doubt, from the blood that trickled from across his throat, and the weakening pulses from the carotid arteries. Though he wasn't dead yet, I knew he would be.

"I'm coming, Dawn," I shrieked.

Tiny handed the dagger to Michel, who licked the blood from the blade and stood over Dawn. I tried to push through the crocottas, but one bit me. My ankle was still within its jaws when Michel sliced down Dawn's pregnant belly. Her agony tore from her throat. Blood leaked down her sides. The sound of the repeated gasping screams brought on nausea. I struggled against the mouth attached to me. But I was too late. Michel pulled forth the baby. Greene's baby.

"You bastard!" Greene and I screamed in chorus. He tried to run to the altar, but the crocottas stopped him. Dawn lay bleeding, succumbing to death. Pain and delirium rendered her unconscious. I dropped to my knees. Tears scalded my cheeks. I searched within for that warm dark liquid to fill me, but I couldn't get it to come like it had at Michel's. I grabbed a fist full of dead leaves and grass, clawing at the dirt to make the pain go away. To make what I'd witnessed go away. But it didn't.

Instead, the ground shifted beneath me, and I realized it was a grave. I looked back to Michel. He had given Guillaume the baby. The cheval mallet bit the newborn's abdomen and pulled something dark from within. I remembered, in lore, a kelpie would eat all but a child's liver. Guillaume's kind didn't practice that restraint. He licked over the bloodied organ. Greene collapsed on himself. I realized then, he loved her, and I pitied him.

He rocked, a useless attempt to wipe away the evil baring down. My heart ached for him, Richard, and Dawn. It was that ache that commanded my power to listen, but not as I expected. The original residents of Mount Mort emerged from their graves—decayed flesh and bone dragged themselves from the fresh earth. They made their way to Guillaume and Michel. I commanded my power to kill them. Guillaume fell. Blood leaked from his eyes. He dropped the baby, Little Richard, and I knew he had joined his parents in eternal repose.

I glared at Michel. I could call death, and he was, in essence, dead. Tonight, I crossed the realm. Michel looked at me in horror. Blood trickled from his eyes and his mouth fell agape. A scream tried to escape, but there were no sounds. I squeezed his heart with my anger. I squeezed until I could squeeze no more. I felt it. But my power wasn't good enough.

There was a new power fighting back. It was Tiny. He stood by my parents and called to me. "The Álfar may have power over the dead, but it has little to do with the living."

I stood my ground; my eyes focused on him. The power proved its presence as the leaves swirled at my feet. He was right, but the almond-eyed man said the Sidhe blood meant I could cross the realms. And from what she'd said, Midgard was the same as the real world to me. And Tiny was in the real world. He wasn't like them. He had practiced the dark arts and depended on the power of other things.

With my back to Lake Sangre, I called the dragon spirit.

"I am the last of the Álfar-Sidhe. I call upon the *Wardens of the North* to protect this land. I call upon the *Wardens of the East* to bring peace. And I call upon the *elder spirits* so that I may cross the realms of death, life. I call to the waters of Lake Sangre, release the imprisoned spirit."

Tiny chanted. Gale's owled form screeched, but all was interrupted by a thunderous gurgle. The mount grew silent, and I knew. "Dragon, as the last *Álfar Dragoness*, I summon thee. Do you answer my call?"

"I answer and I am here." A thunderous voice roared from behind me, raspy, deep, and familiar.

I turned to see a striking red dragon with large talons and spiked tail. His wings seemed as large as the courtyard and his body as long as the mansion itself. He took flight, and his voice echoed. "My power is yours. I serve the Álfar Dragoness."

The dragon launched skyward, his silhouette dark against the moonlit sky. His massive body moved with stealth and grace. The guests looked on, entranced. "Of spirits wicked, and cruel, let sacrifice provide renewal, and with peace we offer grace, for repentance hath no face." The dragon lunged toward the mausoleum.

Tiny turned to run inside.

"Revenge upon the traitor, this Samhain be." The dragon swooped and bit Tiny in half; his head and torso were gone while his waist and legs remained. Blood, and things black against the dark, streamed down them until they collapsed. The dragon roared and soared high above the mountain. Michel and Guillaume ran toward the church, but the dragon circled back. He plunged his spiked tail into the stone building. The roof and walls crumbled. Tiny's lower half tumbled down the steps.

I refocused my power to hold Michel. The power wrapped around him, a feat that bought time until I was able to force myself to walk toward him. The power sought grounding. My legs grew heavy as I advanced toward the ancient vamp. He was unable to move, still and helpless. A wolf appeared at my side. "See to Gérard, now." I commanded it and it went.

Guillaume stood over my sister's grave. "I do not make mistakes. But I see now, it was you who had to die. And now you will." He had magic that I did not understand; it frightened me. He hissed her name, "Sheena."

Her petite, decayed corpse clawed its way to freedom. The white satin, yellowed by time, was dotted with black dirt and mold. Her yellow hair, a mass of pale straw. I never wanted to see her like that.

"Guillaume!" I yelled. "Put her back, damn you."

I backed away from her. She ambled toward me, mouth gaping. I had to see her for what she was, not who she was. I ran toward the altar, sifted my way through the waning corpses as they herded the guests, and grabbed the bloodied dagger from Dawn's lifeless corpse.

"Guillaume, stop," I pled.

My sister came within a foot of me, and I swung the dagger around my body and felt it connect with decayed flesh, and whispered, "In death, find your peace." I followed through and looked back to see I'd decapitated my sister. "I'm sorry, Sheena. I'm sorry." I cried, but I knew it wasn't Sheena. It was a reanimated corpse brought forth by dark magic—Guillaume's magic.

The fear released my hold on the power inside, and it consumed me. Blood poured from Guillaume's nose and mouth. He clawed at his face until it was raw. He collapsed to his knees—screams billowed. His eyes had gone black. He'd lost control of his power on land. He tried to stand, but instead turned. Before me stood the red-eyed black stallion, the cheval that took her life.

Doug emerged from the mausoleum with a silver cross dangling on a chain. He ran with it in his bloodied mouth and took one solid leap at Michel. My power had bound him, as he was mine in life. Guillaume watched in horror as he dropped the cross on Michel's chest. We all watched as it melted into him. "Take him to the altar," I said, turning my power on the crowd. The dead were entranced, their remains dry and splintered. Still, they obeyed with grayed skin and hollowed eyes. The sound of bodies dragging through the leaves as they clawed their way to where I stood, mingled with visitors weeping and lycans shifting.

"Guillaume, call off this spell."

"Not mine." He spat blood toward me, and I sent a wave of power into him that forced blood to spray from his nostrils.

The dragon came back and picked Guillaume off the ground with his talons. As he drew him into the air over the lake, he flew higher and higher. Reaching as high as the clouds, he completed the deed.

The horseman's body, dismembered, hung lifeless in the bloodied talons.

The crowd was stunned by the mount as it lay in ruin—the remnants of Tiny, the rubble of the church. Several ran to help Gérard and Gale. My father helped Doug tie Michel to the altar. My mother blinked at me in surprise, and possibly horror.

I ran to the mausoleum but was headed off by a wolf. Brady was there beside Mrs. Finch, both hunched toward me. "Dark Elves!" I exclaimed. I thought they were going to take Gérard. Brady had a sword. I assumed he must have made the one the dragon told me about. I couldn't let it happen. No one was going to harm Gérard, not until I had answers.

A crocotta crept out of the darkness behind me. Brady slammed into him with the small sword. Mrs. Finch ripped out the animal's bowels with her bare, arthritic hands. "Not elves—dwarves, and preferably, dvergr, dear." Okay, they were on Gérard's side. Goody.

I hastened to the altar and the bastard responsible.

My best friend and her family lay dead at my feet; I didn't weep. Instead, anger filled me. Rage against the wicked and evil.

"I win," I said to Michel.

He laughed, and his laughter burned over my skin. Sam had worked the chains loose. Guess silver didn't matter to a crocotta. Michel flew off. But vamp Bobby was there. He lunged at me. I still held the dagger and swung it like I had to Sheena. It hit his wet resilient flesh.

The wolf appeared at my side and eyed me. I nodded and Doug lunged at the Californian vamp. He finished the job. With one quick shake, he tore the vamp's head from the remaining sinew. The dragon circled overhead. I glanced back to the mausoleum. Mrs. Finch and Greene carried Brady's limp body. Doug came up to me buck-naked. He'd torn his shoulder, blood glistened around his calf. Though he limped, he managed to sit by me.

I resisted the urge to break the silence because of an intense fear that being heard would somehow lead to more deaths. I took a moment to study the mount as the original residents lost their animation and as the visitors snapped from whatever influence Tiny and Guillaume held over them. I watched the guests' procession drift toward the courtyard—bloodied nudes and tattered finery. I realized then I was truly unique, but not alone. I did belong; I had to accept it. I didn't want to.

CHAPTER 48

Doug changed to human, as two of his wolves approached, still in animal form. They looked different from folklore and real wolves. It was like seeing a human-sized wolf with amber eyes. The fur was the same as the real ones, but there was something different in the tails and paws. The proportions were out of whack, but I couldn't quite figure exactly how.

All the shifters seemed to become exact replicas of the animal they were linked with; however, these were creatures all their own, lycanthropes. But Doug was different. He was perfect.

Not that long ago, I'd seen a documentary on the belief in werewolves; people believed themselves to be werewolves because of hallucinations from eating tainted rye.

Of course, back then, people believed that the changes in form occurred because of witchcraft or magic. Today, they believe that these creatures are simply mythological. Those with extreme body hair are considered to have a disorder, and those who believe themselves to be a werewolf are simply deranged.

I hated them. All of them, for either their being or believing, but most of all, I hated Gérard. Why? Because he wasn't there.

Doug stared at me for a moment and then at the ruined church. "Hell of a funeral, huh?"

"Where's Gérard?"

"Our guests are heading back. We should join them."

"Answer the fucking question!" I was about to get hysterical.

"Calm down, love. We'll need to join the party and mingle. You and I." He attempted to stand. "Sam's around, somewhere."

"How'd he get away?"

"One of the crocottas attacked you, and well, we all went to your safety. He set Michel free." He licked his wound again. "I went after them, but they got away." He wasn't as remorseful as I'd expected. "It's what I do. I keep you safe." He smiled; it didn't meet his eyes.

"Doug, where is Gérard?" I hadn't seen Gérard but when I saw the Mausoleum, I knew it was bad because there was a crowd gathered in and around the entrance.

He paused again. "He awaits."

I didn't believe him. I straightened my dress. I was a mess. "I need to change, and you need clothes."

He gave me a wicked grin.

I left him there.

I wandered down the mount, stopped by the water's edge, and screamed. Doug limped over as fast as he could. "What? What?" He searched around, expecting to see something.

"Can't I be allowed to vent?" I started to cry. "God damn it, I will not cry." I cried harder.

"Aw, love. Come 'ere." He stepped closer and wrapped his arms around me, and a burst of power rushed toward us. Doug turned to guard me and knocked me back. I lost my balance and fell over the rocks in the lake.

I landed with a splash. Tears blurred my vision, but I recognized the approaching voice.

"*Ma chérie, mon dieu.*"

"All right, love?"

"No, no, I'm not okay. I hate this." I took a deep, sobbing breath. "I'm in a wet dress, my hose were bloodied, I have crap in my hair and the two of you are lookin' at me like it's the greatest thing."

"All the same, love, but you are cute."

"Why is it the two of you are always around when I'm at my worst? Were you there when I had my hair done? Did I get to wear my carefully chosen clothes, or my costume? Did I get to do anything nice?" I sobbed again and brought my fists down in the water.

They stepped back; amused. "Stop smiling at me, damn it. I felt like a fool the first time I met you." I pointed to Gérard and then focused on Doug. "And you, you hate me. You think I'm like some vengeful twit. Let me tell you, I haven't had it so nice, and if you think I'm spoiled, then so be it. It's been less than a month for me to be pampered by your standards and let me tell you . . . they SUCK! Besides, have you ever seen me not in a life-threatening situation or something? What is it with you people?" I sat back in the water, dress, and all.

My hair hung around me in loose curls.

Gérard stepped in, costume and all, and pulled me to him.

"True, it hasn't been a fairytale for you. Now, I hate to interrupt this little chat, love, but I must take leave," Doug said.

"Let me go." I pushed Gérard aside and leaped up grabbing Doug's arm. I pulled. Gérard helped me.

Doug fell in, the burgundy water mingled with the drying blood. We laughed, and I cried a little more. "Never a dull moment, love." He stepped out, and I noticed his leg was almost healed.

"Gérard, are you okay?" I'd forgotten to ask.

"*Oui*, it will take more than silver to kill me, *ma chérie*. The question is, are you? It takes a lot of power to do what you did." He took both of my hands and kissed them. There was no power, no tingling. We were just a man and a woman at that moment, and it felt strange. "It is an addiction, *non*?"

"What?" I asked.

"My power," he sighed and was gone.

"Yeah," I whispered toward the mansion. "But I don't need it."

I realized my wings were gone. I felt around for them to no avail but found the dagger. I grabbed it and headed toward the mansion, alone hastening as the entrance drew closer.

When I reached the courtyard garden, Doug and Gérard had stopped by the windows. A faint light flickered in the reflection. I stepped back to peer around the stone wall. There was a growing glow near the church.

A young child, I recognized from the diner as Tavin's son, ran toward us. "Master Gérard," he panted.

Gérard knelt on one knee, steadying the boy with a hand on his shoulders. "I understand, Brody. Go inside. Wilma will take care of you."

Within a matter of minutes, Wilma opened the door and led the boy into the safety of the mansion walls. He didn't seem to be much older than seven or eight years old. I didn't remember seeing any children in the ballroom.

"What is it?" I asked.

"You know Tavin?" Doug asked.

I nodded. He was the one who helped me escape the media crew outside Chez Fenris. How could I forget?

Doug nodded toward the mount. "That is his son. It appears that someone wants their servant back. Three of my wolves are down."

"I thought he flew off," I said, in ignorance.

"The thing about Michel is, he'll never relent." The disgust was thick in Doug's voice. "I'll go."

"Do not make haste, *mon ami*. We will go, but not yet." Gérard put his hand on my arm. "Perhaps Summer's new friend may be of assistance."

"What do you mean?" I trembled at the thought of facing Michel and Sam again. Damn.

"*Ma chérie*, it is *Michel* who is the problem. He is determined." His face was blank as he studied the distant glow. "*Et,* Sam is *Michel's* servant."

"Where's my, uh, new friend?" I had a plan but wasn't sure it would work.

"In the back," Doug said.

We walked along the wall to the where there was a clearing between the courtyard and the lake.

Déjà vu! A large hill-ish figure grew out of the grass. As we approached, a fox scampered by. I knew it was Kitty.

"Are you asleep?" I whispered to the dragon. I crept up to it on tiptoe and reached for its nose. He had been curled up in the clearing. The moment I neared his nostrils, his ambergris eyes opened. He lifted his enormous head, and I gasped. "I'm sorry, I—"

"All is well, mistress. You beckoned, and I answered. We are bound." He raised his muzzle higher and blinked, slow. "It has been a long time since I have felt the cool earth beneath me, the autumn air crisp and sweet, and the feel of human touch." He nestled his head back down and blinked again.

"May I touch you?"

"Please." He snorted; I jumped.

"Forgive me, mistress," he yielded.

"It's okay." I reached up again, and this time I felt the soft, cool wetness of his nose. It was leathery, like petting a cow's nose. I stepped closer to muscular forearms and shoulders. His skin was red, no, more oxblood in the moonlight. It was taught and had the look and feel of a good side of leather. "Your skin is soft! I thought it would be rough."

"It feels good to be touched again." The dragon spoke, a whisper in the air.

"Welcome back, old friend." Gérard walked up behind me.

"Aye, it has been far too long." The dragon shifted his eye toward Gérard. "It is a blessing for us all, for the Dragoness lives." He looked back toward me and then back to Gérard. "You will do well by her."

"*Oui.*" Gérard patted the dragon's side and kept his hand on him as he spoke. "We had not known Tiny was responsible. For that, I beg your forgiveness. Gale would not have thought that of him either. Not such horrors."

"It was long ago. Now is a different time." The dragon was sweet and soft-spoken. I'd forgotten for an instant that he'd killed at least two people.

"I hope you'll find me to be what you expect," I said.

"Nay, I shall hope you will be more than I expect. Luck has not been at my side, Mistress." He closed his eyes and drew in a deep breath.

"I will. You can call me Summer; it's my name, you know."

"Ay, but Mistress, holds my respect."

"If it's what you like, then."

"The lights." The dragon motioned toward the mountain behind us with his tail. "Are they not what you came to discuss?"

"A clever creature; curious, and cleaver; to be so forward when you were all shadows and games just hours ago." I tried to point out the irony and patted his leg.

"Aye. How may I be of assistance?"

I stared at the mount and watched the light dance in the distance. It was fire. "I'd wanted to plan a murder, but Guillaume's dead now. I could try to harness my power to slow Michel if he's still up there. He couldn't fly or run when I had him before. Then you and Gérard could fly up. Since Sam is Michel's, he'd be with him. So, Gérard could rip Sam's throat out, and you could bite off Michel's head, but I want to stake him." I turned back to them. "Doug could come with me, and he can take care of Sam's heart. And since I ruined dinner, Gérard could feed off of Sam and bleed him dry then Doug could eat the heart." My eyes lit as I spoke, and a thought occurred to me. "There's no way they could survive that kind of maliciousness." I was proud of my idea. I could play the part like the best of them.

Doug smirked at me. "No offense, but I don't eat people. I kill them."

"Oh, sorry." Whoever said ignorance is bliss was an idiot.

"No worries, but I'll take a lick of Summer, anytime."

I pressed my face to the dragon's cheek.

"I would love a tasty meal, but I cannot bleed him dry if he belongs to *Michel*. He has more power than a victim, as you depict." Gérard looked through raised eyebrows and spoke cautiously. "You have come up with this horrific scene and expected us to play the parts? If you were to bear witness to us all performing such deeds, would you not be disturbed?"

"I figured that's what you did before bottled blood. Hunt down lone humans, maybe forage for rodents." I stared at the ground, hoping they would forget I even spoke.

"I, for one, like the plan. I will do it. But I want to eat them both." I swear the dragon smiled.

"Please don't tell me a dragon is making fun of me now." I put my hands over my eyes, wishing I could hide.

"Ay, but I will take care of them. Tell me to do it and it is done." The dragon shifted to its feet and lifted his head high. "Well?"

"*Un moment, s'il vous plait*, do you believe I sucked on rats?" I thought Gérard was going to piss himself. He kept laughing, the breathy, voiceless kind that strains your muscles and makes your eyes water. Doug joined him. The dragon blinked at me, and Liam's form took off in the woods. "Where do you get this from, *ma chérie*?" He smiled wide and showed full fangs.

"Sorry. I'll remember not to plan anymore murders." I bit my lip.

"Kiss me." His lips were in front of mine before I knew he was there. "Peyron, watch her." I felt his power and tried to pull away, but he'd wrapped his arms around me.

As he drew back, he smiled and kissed the tip of my nose. "I will return. Do not leave this spot." He was gone.

"Doug, he's going to get killed."

"No worries, we'll return. If Gérard gives you a sign, send Peyron, but you stay here." He pecked my cheek and whispered, "I bought the bear."

"What? Don't go!"

I was talking for no reason; he was already gone. And the crowd of visitors had gathered on the lawn. I stayed next to Peyron and watched them approach with caution. My parents and Gale were by my side within minutes. The crowd stopped in front of me; their identities all concealed. Their sequined masks reflected the courtyard torches and moon light. Fear ran cold through my veins—what the hell did they want?

Greene stood at the edge of the yard; his gun drawn. Tears glistened on his cheeks. "I can't do it anymore. He destroyed my family—my life." His lower lip trembled as he fought to control it. "My son is dead!"

"Greene don't." I urged.

"You were right, Summer. I killed them—my mother, Dawn's mother. I hate that I made love to my sister. But love is love. They threatened to kill her, my Dawny. Richard couldn't keep our bloodline going. Tiny demanded I covet her and father a child. He said the sacrifice would repay my father's debt. He swore I'd be freed. And now, I'm to be this creature." He put his fur covered arm in front of him. "Bound as a lycan? I can't live with it, Summer." He raised the gun. "The bastard killed my son!"

"Greene," I yelled.

I lunged for him but was too late. He'd placed the barrel of his gun in his mouth and pulled the trigger. His body collapsed, and with it, the air left me in soundless screams.

Darkness flowed through me and left in waves of power. I didn't know how to control it. I knew it hit something, but I wasn't sure what or who. I steadied myself on Peyron and fought to put that power back. It was rebellious.

CHAPTER 49

The crowd focused on the mount behind the dragon. I soon understood why. Two figures were headed toward us; one broad, the other was undeniably Gérard. The hair bounced and tousled as he strode through the high grasses and decayed leaves. I glanced at Peyron and Gale. They weren't excited but I couldn't relax. Where the hell was Doug?

Ma chérie, I return; with Sam. Remain calm. Gérard's voice whispered through my mind.

Gérard appeared before the mass; his face sunken; crimson lines trickled from his ear. He had a mouthful of blood that he spat on the ground before he spoke. "*Mes amis*, our anniversary has come to an end. I thank you for celebrating my return and the most eventful Samhain in centuries. Tomorrow begins the new count for the next hundred years; we look forward to seeing everyone once again." Short and formal; it wasn't like him. He shoved Sam to the ground.

Then I remembered. I crossed the realms. I was holding the dead. Gérard was dead. My power had hit something—Gérard. I knew he'd read my thoughts; he nodded affirmatively.

My father always said, "Think before you act, Summer, for happiness always has a cost. Nature keeps her balance."

I breathed at him. "Where's Doug?"

He didn't answer. The darkness washed through me, and I ran. I tossed the shoes behind me and ran up the path to the mount. I focused on the flickering light that seemed to grow and ran harder. The ground was cool beneath my feet. There were no obstacles. I would make it. I would find him. Of all the people I'd lost that night, Doug would not be one of them.

The darkness kept the tears at bay—until I made it to the edge of the cemetery. There was no fence on the mountainside. The ground was littered with broken headstones. Gérard's mausoleum was still intact, though it didn't look as majestic as it had just weeks before. The church lay in ruin, a fire burned beside it in the garden. The garden I'd remembered. Lliam, Brady, and a few other townsfolk worked in tattered costumes to carry bodies of victims I hadn't known to the growing blaze.

I watched in despair as one tossed Dawn's baby in the inferno; I dropped to my knees. Another tossed my sister's remains atop. I went numb. All that power, all that raw disgusting gallantry brought on by three dark men: Tiny, Michel, and Guillaume. All that death and destruction; a needless war. And still I knelt there, wondering why.

I crawled toward the altar, afraid.

Nothing.

I crawled through the ivy-covered graves and spotted a dark figure behind a broken pink granite heart. It didn't move. Sickness went through me in waves.

The figure wasn't dark, but rather black slacks and wingtips, the blouse—blood-soaked.

That's when the tears stung. They burned with acid as they filed in well-formed streaks down my face.

"Doug?" I whispered.

No answer.

I crawled the rest of the way to him and saw my father in his arms. I pulled his lifeless body into my lap. There was so much blood. But not a scratch.

I breathed into him, "Daddy, no. I'm so sorry. I never meant to hurt you. I love you. I won't let you go. Daddy, please come back."

Gérard squatted beside me, his hand on my shoulder.

"I did this?" I whispered.

He didn't answer, but instead kissed my hair and bit his wrist. He whispered something in French before putting it to Doug's mouth and turned away from me.

I kissed my father's cooling hand and slid away from them. I couldn't fix what I'd broken, but there was another part of the legend. The Samhain was drawing to a close; there was still time. I would fulfill the prophecy, but never would I hurt someone I loved again. I would never use my power again.

I turned to look over the lake as Liam approached, his amethyst eyes aglow. He shifted to the white fox before he wove around my legs.

Patricia appeared from the blaze by the church and drifted toward the courtyard. Liam dropped the rose and mask and scampered after her.

I took them and recalled the offerings my father made to the Lord of the Hunt. I stepped up on the protruding rock in front of Gérard's mausoleum on top of the mount, my arms raised to the gods, goddesses, spirits, and whatever else was up there. One final time, I offered the rose and mask to the elders of the South and West. I thought to open the realms. "Put an end to new deaths and guide the fallen. And through the power born unto me, release the souls trapped beneath the burgundy waters, for tonight I reign over Lake Sangre and plead for peace and protection for the inhabitants of the mount."

A breeze rustled the leaves through the headstones and down the smoldering terrain. It made its way to the calm waters and formed ripples and waves that crested white. A milk white mist formed over the surface.

Soft weeping voices whispered, "Sumar, hefndu okkar. Summer, avenge us." Women, young and old, emerged from the waters; veils with rose and ivy crowns adorned placid hair. Over a hundred tear-streaked faces surfaced. Darkened skin encircled their longing eyes. Some huddled unto themselves while others embraced in love and joy. Then it happened; they left in wisps as the wind carried them away with their whispers, "Þakka þér, systir. Thank you, sister."

After seven hundred years, the souls of Tiny's victims, my Nordic sisters, were free.

My father, Augusto, and Sheena appeared before me. Sheena hugged my legs, and they, too, were gone.

I called the dead and the living. Nature and a power I recognized as that which I used to call Peyron. The realms opened and Gérard and Doug took their places—Gérard on my right, Doug on the left. As they drew near, I realized the seer was right; I am the last Álfar-Sidhe, Dragon Mistress of the Norse, by birth. But by legend, I am the Guardian of Lake Sangre.

CHAPTER 50

Needless to say, we held a mass memorial for the victims who included Dani, Dawn, Greene, Richard, Little Richard, Lil, and Madame Molly. I learned Dani compromised our ways, in Tiny's eyes at least. Michel saw Dawn's sacrifice as a means to Gérard's seat, by way of weakening me. Doug said a regular may never know our ways; but my friends attempted to reveal it all to me. It cost them their lives, but only in the dark and poisoned mind of a man seeking an excuse. Their deaths were needless. I'm far from regular, and he knew.

I also learned that Liam was really a double agent working for the Preternatural Internal Affairs (P.I.A.) that was appointed by someone named Marjolaina, who promised a visit in the spring. At the same time, I learned that the garden in my memories was actually my real father's grave, though no one offered anymore on it. I didn't press.

Over the course of the week, the guests had all retreated back to their homes, and Gale threw herself into her work at the diner. She asked me to be her partner since Tiny was gone. I accepted, honored by the opportunity, saddened by why.

I refused to speak of my father, Augusto. The guilt covets you, eats you alive. Even though Gale said he grieved for Sheena, and I was able to put that grief to rest. Still, no one could tell me I wasn't capable because I killed him.

My mother decided to stay at the mansion under Gérard's protection until Michel was caught—and I was tamed. She also told me that she would let me know my ancestry, and Gérard's involvement, after I had time to absorb everything. I wasn't happy about it.

As for the crocottas, well, they were to be oathed to Gérard upon returning to their homes. Gérard contacted the regime regarding his takeover of the additional Northeastern territory, warranting a visit from a councilman named Bernard in the near future. And Peyron took up residence in Lake Sangre.

See, autumn was the final turning point where harvesting nature's bounty brought a false sense of satisfaction before the onset of winter. The long, dark days of winter reminded me of the cold darkness I held within myself. After all, winter is the season for reflection in preparation of new beginnings, of spring.

Though only weeks away, I looked forward to this time, learning about myself. Fear of the unknown held consequences; I decided it was best to keep renting the house across the lake. This way, I was forced to take a step back and examine the relationships I had built. Closure and acceptance still lay ahead, while the darkness continued to haunt me. I knew that if I couldn't harness my power, then I would continue to kill the people I loved. I also knew they could kill me, so I decided not to move in yet, just in case.

Gérard wasn't pleased with my decision, and Doug played the go between, but I stood my ground. And maybe, just maybe, I was afraid to admit Patricia was right. I was afraid of playing with the monsters.

ABOUT J.C. PLAZA

As a young child, J.C. Plaza told tales of creatures living beneath the floorboards to her pet mice, while teaching her Chihuahua Spanish. Later, she earned a BS in Clarinet Performance, and an MBA. She also married her high school sweetheart, birthed two enchanting children, and moved to the Pocono Mountains of Pennsylvania where she started her doctoral adventures, leading to an early retirement from her music career.

After hanging up her clarinet, she kept her black velvet dresses and turned them into the inspiration for her rekindled passion, fantasy storytelling.

Now, she spends her time giving life to dreams because fantasies are meant to be shared.

DARK FANTASY MERCHANDISE

I have always been a big fan of fantasy mugs and other items. Here are some of my favorites that are aligned with the Lake Sangre fantasy stories

Beautiful faux suede pillows, coffee mugs and other items.

https://jcplaza.com/shop/

Clothing, pennants, pillows, mugs, etc all with dark fantasy designs.

https://jc-plaza-author-llc.printify.me/products

Sample of some of the products.

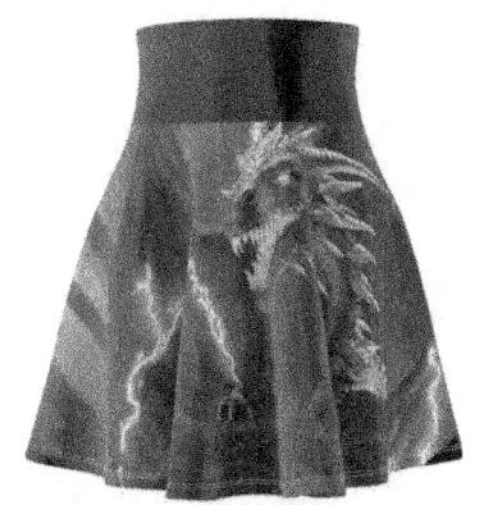

Dragon Skater Skirt

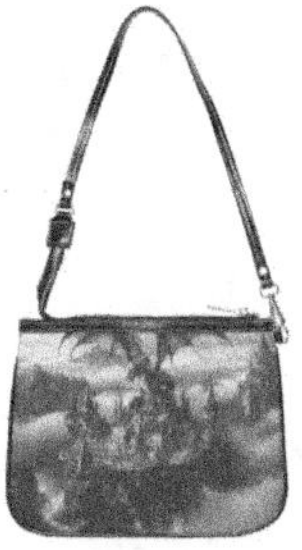

Dragon Handbag

Kitsune Male Mug

Witch Queen Mug

Scarecrow Puzzle

Lake Sangre Faux Suede Pillow